ALPHA HEAT

(Heat of Love, Book 2)

LETA BLAKE

An Original Publication from Leta Blake Books

Alpha Heat (Heat of Love #2)
Written and published by Leta Blake
Cover by Dar Albert
Formatted by BB eBooks

First Edition, 2018
Print Edition

ISBN: 979-8-88841-003-5

Other Books by Leta Blake

Contemporary

Will & Patrick Wake Up Married
Will & Patrick's Endless Honeymoon
Cowboy Seeks Husband
The Difference Between
Bring on Forever
Stay Lucky

Sports

The River Leith

The Training Season Series
Training Season
Training Complex

Musicians

Smoky Mountain Dreams
Vespertine

New Adult

Punching the V-Card

Winter Holidays

The Home for the Holidays Series
Mr. Frosty Pants
Mr. Naughty List
Mr. Jingle Bells

Fantasy

Any Given Lifetime

Gay Romance Newsletter

Leta's newsletter will keep you up to date on her latest releases and news from the world of M/M romance. Join the mailing list today. letablake.com

Leta Blake on Patreon

Become part of Leta Blake's Patreon community in order to access exclusive content, deleted scenes, extras, bonus stories, rewards, prizes, interviews, and more. www.patreon.com/letablake

Acknowledgements

Thank you to the following people:

Mom & Dad, without whom I couldn't be following this dream. B & C, my lights to travel home to after visiting made up worlds. My patron John McDonald, and all the wonderful members of my Patreon who inspire, support, and advise me. Keira Andrews for the amazing editing work. Anna for the help and insight into the aro/ace representation. Mia, Jessica, and Sadie for beta reading. Leigh Barduga who wrote *Six of Crows* and inspired me in ways she never intended. A.M. Arthur for loving *Slow Heat* so much that she made up her own Omegaverse books (look for *Breaking Free*)!

And thank you to my readers who make all the blood, sweat, and tears worthwhile.

A desperate young alpha. An older alpha with a hero complex. A forbidden love that can't be denied.

Young Xan Heelies knows he can never have what he truly wants: a passionate romance and happy-ever-after with another alpha. It's not only forbidden by the prevailing faith of the land, but such acts are illegal. Resigned to his miserable future, Xan contracts with Caleb, an asexual, aromantic omega with special requirements of his own. Their friendship is a comfort, but Xan craves the love and sexual dominance of another alpha.

Urho Chase is a middle-aged alpha with a heartbreaking past. Careful, controlled, and steadfast, his friends dub him old-fashioned and staid. When Urho discovers a dangerous side to Xan's life that he never imagined, his world is rocked and he's consumed by desire. The carefully sewn seams that held him together after the loss of his omega and son come apart—and so does he.

But to love each other and make a life together, Xan and Urho risk utter ruin. With Caleb's acceptance and support, they must find the strength to embrace danger and build the family they deserve.

This gay romance novel by Leta Blake is the second in the Slow Heat universe. It's 130,000 words, with **a strong happy ending** and a well-crafted, **non-shifter Omegaverse**. It features alphas, betas, omegas, male pregnancy, **heat**, and **knotting**. **No cheating.** Content warning for brief sexual violence.

For Keira Andrews, for being a true friend

CONTENT WARNING: Brief sexual violence depicted.

PART ONE

CHAPTER ONE

HIS STOMACH TWISTING in a giant knot, Xan climbed out of his car in front of Jason and Vale's blue clapboard house on Oak Avenue. He gazed at the home, noting the fresh coat of paint, the impeccable front lawn and gardens, and the little rocking chairs on the front porch, complete with cheerful cushions. Jason and Vale had nested hard since they'd collided with each other as *Érosgápe* in the library of Mont Nessadare University four years ago.

Xan forced away the dull, familiar pang that was part jealousy and part longing for a love like that. He'd been about to leave his symbolic corner office within the largest division of his father's business on High Street to head home for the day, but after hearing Jason's shaking voice and urgent plea, he'd driven over to his best friend's house directly.

All three of their lives were so different now from those pre-imprint halcyon days. Sometimes Xan barely recognized himself in the mirror. But one thing never changed: he was Jason's best friend, and he would be there for him through thick and thin.

Frighteningly, things seemed to have gone thin again, because Jason had sounded panicked when Xan picked up the phone an hour earlier. He'd requested Xan come by as soon as possible, refusing to give further details.

Approaching the front door, he stepped back in surprise as it swung open before he'd even had a chance to knock. Jason ushered him inside. His blond hair was messy, and his face very pale. Worse, his long, lanky frame trembled beneath his wrinkled suit. He obviously hadn't changed since returning from his new job at his father's shipping business, having set aside his passion for science to fulfill family duty, the same way Xan had when the time came for him to step up.

Xan straightened his own bow tie anxiously as he followed Jason down the hall toward Vale's study with a sinking feeling in his gut. He hadn't seen Jason this distraught in years, not since he'd settled things with his older *Érosgápe* omega, Vale Aman, and settled into domestic bliss. The knot in his gut tightened.

The sun shone through the wide back windows of Vale's dusty, brick-floored study, but the profusion of colorful, autumnal leaves in the well-tended garden didn't soften the tense atmosphere at all.

"Glad you could join us," Vale said softly. His green eyes were red-rimmed and his lips, set in his handsomely trimmed dark beard, appeared dry.

Xan's throat closed up as he took in Jason and Vale's other assembled guests—Rosen, Yosef, and—*shit*—Urho. All held places of high esteem in the couple's life, and all looked as shaky as Xan felt.

"Sorry if I kept everyone waiting," Xan said, swallowing thickly. "But I came as soon as I got Jason's call."

"And how's Caleb?" Vale asked, like the entire room wasn't about to explode with anxiety around them.

"Caleb's good." Nervously, he babbled on, "Well, he wasn't feeling well this morning, so I had to run to the drug store for a tonic for him, which made me late to work, and so it was harder to escape this afternoon."

"It's all right," Vale said with eerie calm from his perch on the leather wingback chair he preferred. "Tell Caleb we hope he gets well soon." His face was even paler than usual, and his lips drew into a tight, false smile.

Jason took his place rigidly behind Vale, his blond hair flopping onto his forehead and his blue eyes bright with some wild emotion.

Vale nodded toward the sofa. "Rosen just arrived, too."

Xan cast a glance toward Rosen, the ridiculously dark and handsome half of Vale's best friends, a beta couple sitting closely together on the leather sofa. Rosen's lover, Yosef, sat at his side with their hands intertwined, a miserable expression on his face. Yosef's impeccably sculpted white hair and beard gave away that he was quite a few years older than Rosen, but they were still an unfailingly attractive couple. Vale had been close with them for years.

Xan ran a sweaty palm over his own limp hair. If they were in attendance looking so worried, the news he'd been summoned to hear must be that Vale or Jason was very sick.

"So what's going on?" Xan asked, unable to keep quiet a moment longer. "What the hell's happening?"

Urho stepped out of the shadows. Xan gulped. Urho was tall, muscled, and full of that strong, alpha energy that Xan craved like a kind of air he was denied the right to breathe. The flames in the fireplace played on Urho's dark skin and highlighted his salt-and-pepper hair, making Xan's squirmy gut twist with highly inappropriate lust.

"I've been asked to impart the news," Urho said, solemnly. "It's both an honor and a burden, but one Jason and Vale have asked me to bear—"

"Just tell us," Xan interrupted, a bolt of surprise going through him. He normally danced around Urho, tongue-tied and anxious, saying all the wrong things, but tonight he wasn't going to even try keeping his mouth shut. He had to know why his best friend looked like he'd just been handed a death sentence.

Urho's chin came up, and he gazed at Xan for a long, calm moment before nodding. "All right. As it turns out, Vale, against all odds, and despite Jason's best efforts, is pregnant."

The silence in the room echoed off the windows and buzzed in

Xan's ear like a fly. Jason's shoulders collapsed, and he ducked his head to hide his face, even as he reached to squeeze Vale's shoulders, giving support as Vale's alpha.

"Excuse me?" Xan said, blinking between Vale and Jason. "Did you say that Vale is pregnant?"

"I did." Urho's strong mouth drew into a straight line and he regarded Xan seriously. "This is obviously a problem, one that is both private and communal, in that we all love and admire Jason and Vale, and will—"

"What in wolf's own hell, Jason?" Xan snapped, interrupting Urho without a thought. "You know he can't have children. Why would you knock him up?"

Jason didn't lift his head, and Xan almost didn't make out his muffled response. "It was an accident."

"An accident?" Xan scoffed.

Vale raised his palm. "What's done is done. Now all that's left is to deal with what's happened."

"You'll have an abortion, obviously," Xan said, nodding firmly and casting an approving glance toward Urho.

He'd been there when Urho had performed the surgery on Jason's pater that had saved the man's life four years earlier. He also knew that Urho was the doctor responsible for performing an abortion on Vale when he was a young, unmatched omega.

There was no doubt what should happen now. Given Vale's physical scars from that first abortion, he couldn't sustain a pregnancy, nor survive one himself. Everyone knew that. It was part of what had nearly cost Jason and Vale their contract despite their *Érosgápe* bond. Jason's parents had wanted him to take on a surrogate omega instead so that he might have a child, since Vale had no hope of giving him one.

"No," Vale whispered. "That's not going to happen this time."

"Excuse me?" Yosef asked, his white eyebrows shooting to his hairline. "What are you saying, Vale?"

Rosen straightened where he sat, gripping Yosef's hand until his knuckles went white. Xan wished he'd taken a seat when he first entered. He felt a little woozy where he stood with Vale's denial echoing in his ears.

"Please," Jason whispered. "Please reconsider."

Vale shook his head. "Urho's examined me, and he thinks—"

"I don't care what he thinks!" Jason exclaimed, coming around to kneel at Vale's feet. "I only want you. I don't need this from you. I don't even want a ch—"

Vale put a hand over his mouth. "Shush, before you say something you'll regret."

Jason's blue eyes went wet, and he ducked his head, resting his forehead on Vale's knee. He shuddered as Vale ran his fingers through his blond hair soothingly, and Xan felt the echo of Jason's trembling in his own knees.

"I don't understand," Yosef said again. "Vale can't survive pregnancy. We all know that."

"Historically, that was true," Urho said. "Before Jason."

"So you're saying things have changed?" Rosen murmured, lifting his chin, dark with late afternoon stubble flecked with some blue paint he hadn't entirely scrubbed free. In all likelihood, he'd been pulled away from his oil painting by a phone call similar to the one Xan received.

Urho said, "For reasons that are best kept private, it does seem that there is a new elasticity to Vale's scar tissue and passage that wasn't there before. I have several theories as to why that is, but the fact remains that it is, unexpectedly, true."

"I can't carry to full term, most likely," Vale said so calmly that Xan wanted to punch him. Jason scooted closer, burying his face further in Vale's lap, his body shaking as Vale went on. "So Urho will induce the labor early and we'll hope the child survives."

"That's sick," Xan spat. "You can't do that. Not to Jason." He nodded at Jason where he was curled by his omega's feet. "Look at him. Think of what losing you would do to him."

Vale's green eyes softened. "I think of almost nothing else."

"Could have fooled me."

Vale seemed to barely restrain a flare of temper, but he held it back. "It hasn't been an easy decision, but I trust Urho. He wouldn't put the odds on me surviving if he didn't believe it with his whole heart."

Jason lifted his head then, his face blotchy with tears and his mouth wobbly. "He doesn't put odds on you surviving, he puts odds on you *probably* not dying, and that's not at all the same thing."

"Darling, you can't ask me to give this up. Unplanned as it was, as terrified as we both are, this is our only hope. This one, beautiful mistake that we'd never, ever make again."

"Don't get poetic on me," Jason whispered fiercely. "You're willing to risk destroying yourself—us, *me*—for something that, according to Urho, is just a bundle of cells with a tiny little heartbeat."

"But he's ours," Vale said dreamily. "Our bodies knitted together to make a new life. How can we choose to end it?"

"You sound like Pater."

"No, your pater admitted he had no hope of living through the birth. I plan to follow all of Urho's prescriptions to the letter. I intend to live to see our child born, to hold him, and raise him into a fine young man. To see you reflected in him, and myself, too. I won't be giving up so easily."

"So why are we here?" Yosef asked gently, his hands still twined with Rosen's and his expression grave.

"Because we'll need your support," Vale said. "Jason, especially."

"No, you, especially," Jason whispered. "You must be cared for every moment of every day."

"Ridiculous. I'm not an invalid." He shrugged. "Later, as the months pass, yes, I will need to be careful, but right now I'm as fit as a fiddle. I can continue my work—"

"No!" Jason snarled. "I won't have those idiot alphas at Mont Nessadare scenting you and knowing you're pregnant. That you're fragile." He shook his head. "You'll take another leave of absence."

Xan sucked in a deep breath, and, yes, there beneath Vale's usual scent was a new one, something that was a bit like damp earth, seaweed, and the iron scent of blood. The scent of Jason's baby growing inside, tucked away, cells multiplying by the second, feeding on Vale's life force to grow his own.

An urge to throttle Vale rushed through Xan, an irrational desire to hold him down and force him to concede that this pregnancy, this self-proclaimed mistake, *needed* to be terminated. But another part of him scented Jason's genes in the child, and a tender protectiveness rose up in him, an urge to take care of his best friend's omega and their tiny new babe.

"We'll need your help," Vale said, meeting everyone's eye one by one as he brought Jason's head down into his lap again, gently tracing his ear to calm him. "I can't say when or exactly how, but you're the friends we know we can count on for anything."

"We're always here for you," Rosen agreed.

"For you and Jason both," Yosef said grimly.

"You can count on me," Xan added, lifting his chin, loathe to be left out. "For anything at all. If I can provide comfort or support, I'm happy to do it. And Caleb will want to help, too."

"Thank you," Vale said as he rubbed Jason's shoulders. "We're struggling with this, but we'll be all right."

Jason rose then, wiping a hand over his face, rubbing away tears. "We wanted you to find out from us directly, face-to-face."

"And your parents?" Yosef asked.

"Already know," Jason replied, but the curt tone and the way he mashed his full lips together made it clear he didn't intend to say more on that subject right now.

Rosen and Yosef were the first to depart. Yosef hugged Jason and whispered something to Vale about pulling legal paperwork together regarding his health care in the event that Jason wasn't able to make decisions. Vale nodded and then accepted a hug from Rosen, too.

Urho hung back from the goodbyes, clearly preparing to stay a while longer. His broad shoulders and chest stretched out his suit jacket nicely. Xan licked his lips, letting his gaze linger. He'd admired Urho physically and as a man since he'd witnessed the way he handled Jason's pater's miscarriage and the aftermath four years ago.

Physically strong and mentally sharp, Urho was a bit old fashioned perhaps, but something about the way he moved in the world—with confidence and certainty—left Xan's throat dry with lust.

Shameful, illegal, and unholy lust.

Two alphas together were an abomination, and Urho was conservative enough to never entertain the idea and kind enough to have no desire to exert power over another in a flare of sexual alpha expression. That sadistic power play Xan lived to find in another alpha, the sexual thrill he couldn't get enough of, no matter how dangerous, was the sort of thing Urho would never offer.

Rosen and Yosef crowded near Jason and Vale, giving comfort and reassurances, and extending promises. Xan didn't plan to linger, but he didn't want to leave without talking to Urho alone. Catching Urho's eye, he nodded toward the bank of wide windows across the room.

Xan reached the windows first and opened the sash to let in

some fresh air. He frowned when Urho came behind him and closed it.

"It's damp out. It won't do for Vale to get a chill right now."

"Is he under house arrest then?"

"No, of course not." Urho let out a frustrated sigh. "I only want to keep him safe."

"That's Jason's job," Xan said, narrowing his eyes.

Urho's devotion to Vale pricked. It was inappropriate at best and demonstrated designs on another alpha's omega at worst. But the reason it nettled him so much had more to do with his own thwarted desire for another alpha to treat *him* with half as much regard and protection. And if that alpha were a man like Urho? It'd be a dream come true.

But that was what made it all so infuriating. He'd never have the parts to inspire an alpha's devotion. He'd never go into heat. Never experience the multiple orgasm potentials of an omega. Never bear a child. No, instead he was an alpha himself. Never mind that he didn't want to be and could barely stand to fulfill his role as such.

"What's your true feeling on this?" Xan asked, shoving aside all the uncomfortable, illicit feelings and thoughts that swamped him whenever he was around Urho. "Will he make it?"

"I can't promise anything, but he has a decent chance."

"Decent isn't good enough."

"A strong chance," Urho corrected, his brow lowering and his calm, dark eyes growing troubled. "Believe me, if I could swear to his safety to relieve everyone's mind, I would in a heartbeat. But I'm a cautiously optimistic doctor, not a fortuneteller."

"Perhaps we should consult one of those from the Calitan district," Xan hissed. "Their word is probably as solid as yours."

Urho's shoulders snapped back. "Your mouth will get you in trouble one day, pup. You're talking to an alpha almost twenty years your senior with military history and a license to practice medicine. I'd say I have a good deal more authority than a fringe spiritualist living on the ill-gotten profits of spit-gummed hope and lies."

Xan rolled his eyes.

"If you were an omega, I'd take you over my knee," Urho whispered, glancing toward Jason and Vale. "I'd do it even now, alpha or not, if I weren't concerned about upsetting Vale."

Xan's cock stirred, and his heartbeat quickened. An urge to get in Urho's face gripped him. Perhaps Urho wasn't beyond alpha aggression after all. But now wasn't the time for Xan to indulge in his fantasies or push an older, more powerful alpha's buttons. Urho was right about that much, at least.

"You called me over to insult me?" Urho raised a brow, dark eyes sharpening.

Xan shook his head. "I wanted your unguarded opinion."

"You already have it." Urho's mouth drew into a flat line. The air between them grew heavy and thick. Xan held Urho's gaze until Urho jerked it away. Urho's cheeks darkened, and his Adam's apple bobbed as he swallowed before stalking off to rejoin the others.

Xan's shoulders slumped. He didn't know why he sabotaged every conversation he had with Urho, and yet he did. Unbidden, the memory of similar exchanges over the last four years—Urho intoning an opinion and Xan stupidly challenging it—came to mind, going all the way back to the vacation by the sea their small group of friends had taken the summer after Vale and Jason had imprinted, and long before Xan had chosen to contract with Caleb.

Dissatisfied and itching for something he'd never have, Xan frowned as Urho offered to walk Rosen and Yosef out to catch their taxi. Xan waved his goodbyes to the betas and caught another one of Urho's scowls before the little group left the study to head out into the damp autumn afternoon.

Alone with Jason and Vale now, Xan approached them. Jason

stood by Vale's leather wingback chair, a young, stormy sentinel guarding his beloved. Xan summoned a sympathetic smile and knew the moment it slid away from him, revealing his discombobulated confusion.

Vale gripped Xan's hand. "Don't look like that. Jason will need your strength."

Xan huffed. "Not half as much as he needs you, period. But I'll do what I can."

Vale's smile was wry, but he turned to Jason and said sweetly, "Why don't you walk Xan out? If it's all the same to you, I'll stay here and get comfy by the fire."

"Are you cold?" Jason asked. He grabbed a throw blanket from the leather sofa and carefully draped it over Vale. Vale didn't look cold to Xan, but Jason took his time wrapping him up and tucking the blanket in carefully.

Xan knew his own omega, Caleb, enjoyed being taken care of in these small ways—truly any human did, no matter their gender. But between *Érosgápe*, the caretaking dance was instinctual, uncontrollable, and a testament to their bond. It was touching to see Jason and Vale engaging in it. Xan wished, not for the first time, that he was an omega and had a loving alpha to take care of him.

Zephyr, the gray cat that Vale had owned long before Jason had come along, slipped into the room. Her silvery fur was clean and fluffy, and she meowed conversationally as she trotted toward them.

When she leapt onto Vale's lap, his fingers slipped into her fur, and Xan wondered how soft she must be. He'd never had the honor of petting her. Like with Urho, she tended to hiss at him and lunge as though to bite whenever he drew close. She adored Jason, though.

Jason leaned down to whisper something to Vale and then turned his attention to Xan, a wrecked, pitiful smile on his lips. "Thanks for coming. I'll walk you out."

"I'm parked just out front," Xan said, stepping through into the hall.

Urho passed them on his way back from seeing off Rosen and Yosef. Xan's gut tightened, but Urho just nodded to him, offering no true goodbye or good wishes.

"What were you talking to Urho about?" Jason asked as they exited into the cool, damp, fall afternoon. The trees were starting to lose their green and turn lovely shades of orange, yellow, red, and rust.

"Just an honesty check. I wanted to see if he changed his story about Vale's chances when it was only the two of us."

"And?" Jason's body tensed, his gaze raking over Xan's face, looking for the truth.

For once, Xan wasn't even sure what answer Jason hoped for more. "Urho would never put Vale in jeopardy. He's half in love with him still."

It stung to even say it. What had Vale done to earn both Jason and Urho's affections? Aside from being born an omega with all the right scents and lures, all the appeal and seduction of his pheromones, and the promise of a delicious heat mating? His personality was so-so, his face handsome enough, but old. Why did he get everything Xan had ever wanted?

He clamped down on his jealousy and forced himself to admit the truth: *Vale's a good man. Charming, funny, talented, devoted, and worthy in many ways. Any alpha would want him.*

Why didn't that admission make him feel any better?

As they approached his new lime-green car, Xan changed the topic. "What did your parents say about all this when you told them?"

"My parents agree with Vale," Jason whispered bitterly. His eyes flashed, and he shook his head. "I couldn't believe it when Father said he thought Vale was making the right choice. After all he's been through with Pater in the past! But somehow, he agrees that Vale is different. I think he feels it's worth the risk this time because it's not his omega. And because this is their only hope of a grandchild." Jason's eyes grew wet again. "This awful, horrible mistake."

Xan knew Jason's parents, especially his father, longed for a grandchild, but he couldn't imagine Miner Hoff encouraging Vale to risk his life for one. He didn't say that, though, and instead asked what he'd wanted to know from the moment he heard of Vale's pregnancy. "How did it happen?"

"It's a long story."

Xan punched Jason's shoulder lightly. "Sum it up."

A long sigh rushed out of Jason, and his shoulders collapsed even more. His eyes closed as if he could block out whatever he was about to say the way he could block out sunlight. "We were at his parents' old cabin in the mountains, the one I finally had refurbished to sell."

"I remember. That was earlier this month."

"Right. And there was that early mountain snow storm."

"Knocked out the roads leading up to the cabin," Xan said, recalling how subdued Jason had been since returning from that trip. Pieces started to come together. "You guys were stuck."

"For five days while the crews worked to dig out the roads. The phones were down. It was just us. All alone. It was wonderful at first. Romantic and fun. But then…" Jason shook his head, anguish peeking through again. "It's been happening more and more as he gets older."

"An unexpected heat?"

"Out of the blue. No warning. I—" Jason's Adam's apple bobbed convulsively, his eyes going distant and dark. "I tried to hold back. There were no condoms. I hadn't packed any. I didn't expect—" His voice broke. "The roads were blocked. He was screaming in pain. I didn't have a choice."

15

"Of course, you didn't." Xan touched his arm gently, but Jason pulled away. Xan tried not to let that hurt.

"I've spent the last few weeks praying for a miracle. Not every omega gets pregnant with every heat. I told myself there was every chance he'd be safe."

Given that not every heat produced a viable pregnancy, Jason certainly had good reason to hope. Xan himself was now all too familiar with fruitless heats. He shuddered, remembering the only one he'd endured with Caleb so far. Horror streaked through him again along with traumatic memories of his kind, loving omega on his back, screaming in agony while Xan had tried his best—and failed—to satisfy him.

Thankfully they had a few more months before another heat was due. Though Xan still didn't know how he was going to handle it alone. He'd failed so miserably last time.

And wolf-god help them if Caleb started having unexpected heats, too. Though Caleb was only five years older than Xan, so hopefully that unpredictable period of his life was still some time into the future. With any luck, by then Xan would have solved his problem. Because it was *his* problem, not Caleb's, and he needed to come up with a solid plan—for them both.

"I let him down," Jason whispered.

"I'm so sorry."

He didn't have an *Érosgápe* connection with Caleb, and he wasn't even in love with his contracted omega like many alphas tended to be, but he *cared* about Caleb like a family member or a dear friend. He couldn't imagine the burden of guilt Jason carried now, much less how terrified he must have been at the idea of possibly losing Vale. Pregnancy and birth were dangerous for omegas in the best of health and the prime of life.

What an idiot Vale was! He should allow Urho to abort the baby! But Xan couldn't be too surprised by Vale's selfishness. He'd

16

always known Vale wasn't good enough for Jason. He'd said so the day Jason imprinted on him, hadn't he?

And he'd only just started to think maybe he'd been wrong about his initial assessment, what with Jason being so blissfully happy, and Vale being so damned good to Jason. But maybe this situation just proved he'd been right from the beginning.

"I tried my best," Jason went on, his voice rough with emotion. "But I failed him. He should hate me, but he says he doesn't. He insists he loves me more than life, but he still wants to have our child."

"Of course, he loves you." Xan's irritation prickled again. Who wouldn't love Jason? Sweet and strong, dedicated and devoted, he was one of the dreamiest alphas Xan had ever known.

He'd been in love with Jason himself back before Vale came into their lives, and he'd only gotten over it by taking up a bad habit so consuming that it drowned out everything else...

Xan's cheeks warmed, and his knees went weak with yearning. Temptation snuck in, hot and sharp, clouding his senses with the urge to satisfy needs too long unmet.

He could make a detour on the way home. Get a hit of the darkness he craved. A hit that would rattle his teeth and bruise his body to be sure, yet Xan could never seem to get enough of it.

He shook his head free of the fog and focused on Jason again. His heart ached at the terror he saw in his best friend's eyes. Reaching out, he cupped Jason's cheek. "Vale loves you just as much as you love him. You're *Érosgápe*. And if things get dangerous for him, I'm sure he'll make the right choice."

"Get dangerous? They already *are* dangerous, Xan." Jason blew out a frustrated breath. "Vale's got scar tissue inside, a lot of scar tissue. I feel it every time I fuck him. Urho says it's grown more flexible since I came into Vale's life. Something about me knotting him so long during heats and fisting him regularly between..." His cheeks flushed scarlet, and he ducked his head. "Urho says the scar tissue has been stretched out, that it's not so tight as it used to be. The anti-inflammatory properties of alpha semen have also contributed, he claims. But I don't know if I can trust him."

Urho's dark eyes, somber and serious, flashed in Xan's mind. "Of course, you can trust him. He would never hurt Vale."

"You said he's still half in love with him," Jason said, nodding thoughtfully. "I've told you, right? Before I came along, they were lovers?"

"Yes." *Because Vale gets to have everything.*

"I don't think Vale ever truly returned his feelings," Jason said, relief lacing his words. "If he had, then I don't know that I could see Urho as a friend, especially since he still cares for Vale."

Xan's stomach soured with the familiar, churning jealousy he'd been struggling to fight off. If that was true, then Vale was an even bigger fool than Xan had realized. And luckier than any worn out, old omega deserved to be.

He swallowed the nastiness down again. It was poison in his gut. He didn't *want* to have these feelings and unkind thoughts anymore. He wanted to let go of envy and regret, because he liked Vale, and Vale was good for Jason. He truly was.

But Vale had everything he'd ever wanted and didn't deserve it any more than Xan did. Less even, maybe, for all Xan knew. And now...

He bit down on his cheek, punishment for his black-hearted thoughts. He knew Vale had endured his share of suffering in the past, but Xan allowed envy to cloud his empathy too much and too often. He didn't like that side of himself and vowed to improve it. "If you need me, just call. I'll be here for you."

Jason slung his arms around Xan's shoulders, collapsing against him in a hug that went on a long time. Xan breathed in the once-familiar scent of Jason's skin and hair. He still longed for what they'd had together, but he'd learned to live without it. For better or for worse. Still, he lingered in Jason's arms, hoping to give as much comfort as he got from their embrace.

Once Jason released him, Xan promised once again to help in whatever way he could. He smoothed Jason's hair and sent him on his way back into the house. "Go be with him. You need each other now."

As Jason mounted the steps to the front porch, Xan climbed into his car and, after a very short debate with himself, pointed it toward the darkness he'd come to depend on. It would blot out all longing and envy, all loneliness and want. It would replace those miseries with sensation and fear, with humiliation and pain.

One more fix wouldn't kill him. Unless it did.

And even that idea didn't scare him the way it should.

CHAPTER TWO

URHO WATCHED JASON stir the fire with the poker. His shoulders were still slumped, and the misery that had radiated from him ever since he and Vale had returned from being snowed in at the Amans' old cabin continued to seep from him like a poison.

He'd have to pull Jason aside later and tell him how important it was that he find a way to be happy, support Vale, and keep Vale's confidence and attitude buoyed despite his own fears.

"My biggest concern right now, in the early stages, is keeping Vale calm," Urho said. "Later, say, in a few weeks, my concern will change to the upcoming flu season. It's already begun, which is a bad sign, and there have already been several flu-related deaths in the poorer districts. They say the strain doesn't respond to the usual tonics and medicines. A move out of the city proper might be worth considering then."

"As I said earlier, Vale will take another leave of absence from his work," Jason said firmly. "There'll be no argument about that, do you understand?"

Vale shrugged. "It hasn't been as enjoyable teaching there this year without you on campus. It's no skin off my nose to let you pamper me here at home." Though Urho knew Vale well enough to see that he was trying to appease Jason more than truly looking forward to months of putting his feet up.

"Good. Should I hire beta servants to care for him while I'm at the office?" Jason asked.

"I'm pregnant, not infirm. For wolf-god's sake, don't go over-board here."

"He's right. No need to make him a pallet on the first floor of the house quite yet," Urho teased. "He can get up and down the stairs by himself. So long as that demon beast doesn't try to trip him."

Jason's eyes zeroed in on Zephyr where she sat on Vale's wide desk, cleaning her asshole with her scratchy tongue, oblivious to all their attention being focused on her. "Maybe we *should* move the bed down to this room. If I keep the fire going, it'll stay plenty warm for us."

"You're being ridiculous," Vale murmured, and then yawned.

"You need to nap," Jason said, leaving his poking at the fire to come and pull Vale up to standing, as though he were already heavy with child. He led him toward the leather sofa and urged him to stretch out.

Vale met Urho's gaze and rolled his eyes, but did as Jason demanded.

"I could use some chamomile tea," Vale said once he was settled. "Would you bring me some?"

Jason kissed Vale's face half a dozen times and tasked Urho with making sure Vale rested until he returned.

"I have a few more notes I'd like to take," Urho said, waving him off. "As well as some measurements."

Jason hesitated. He always insisted on being in the room when Urho examined Vale's asshole, passage, and womb. Like most alphas it was hard for him to allow his *Érosgápe* to be touched by another alpha in those intimate areas, but unlike most he preferred to be present rather than heading to a bar in order to get drunk and pretend it wasn't happening.

In that way, he was like his father. Urho remembered well how Yule Sabel had cared so personally and intimately for Miner after his brutal miscarriage and the subsequent removal of Miner's womb.

"I'm just going to listen to his heart, take his pulse, measure his stomach, and make note of his pallor. I might palpitate his abdomen externally. Nothing that will require fully disrobing."

Jason nodded stiffly and then left to fetch the tea as Vale had asked.

"He's such a sweet baby alpha, isn't he?" Vale mooned, unbuttoning his shirt to give Urho access to his chest and stomach.

"I suppose." Urho thought of his *Érosgápe*, Riki, who'd often said such things about him in their early life together. The ache for his lost love remained to this day.

"I was surprised when Xan was one of the last to leave," Vale commented, tilting his head to catch Urho's eye when he knelt down to press the cold stethoscope to Vale's skin.

Urho smiled to hear his friend's heart booming steadily, and then he dropped the device lower, listening hard for the tiny fetus's heartbeat. Sighing with emotion when he heard it, he sat back on his heels.

Vale added, "He normally leaves earlier than anyone else."

"He's usually eager to get back to his new omega, I imagine." Urho made note of the rates of both Vale and the baby's hearts in the leather-bound casebook he carried in his bag. "Today was an obvious shock to him. He probably lingered only to make sure Jason was going to be all right."

Vale was quiet as Urho pressed the measuring tape over his stomach. The growth was barely visible now. Within a few weeks, the child would start to expand against Vale's middle and force his muscled, trim abdomen to begin to protrude.

Vale asked, "Do you still think he's handsome?"

Urho wished he'd never drunkenly admitted to Vale that he found Xan's eyes pretty and wished even more that he'd never once mentioned the roundness of the boy's ass. He always drank too much at their little soirées; it was a problem that used to irritate Vale when Jason first came along and Urho, inebriated, couldn't resist the temptation to poke at him. But now it was a problem only to himself, for he found himself confessing things to Vale that he shouldn't.

Ignoring Vale's query, he said, "Your heart and the child's sound fine."

"Jason will be glad." Vale nudged Urho with his foot and raised a brow. "You didn't answer my question about Xan."

A vision of Xan's plump mouth sneering about fortunetellers popped into Urho's mind, and he gritted his teeth. There was no way he was going to admit to the arousal Xan sometimes sparked in him—not while he was sober, at any rate. Vale should know him better than that. "How do you stand that boy's insolence?" He held Vale's wrist gently to take his pulse one more time.

"Xan isn't insolent," Vale said, though his left brow rose, making it clear he knew Xan was exactly that. "Nor is he a boy."

Urho shook his head irritably.

"He might be young, like Jason, but they're twenty-four now. He's contracted to an omega. That's a large responsibility, and he's been placed in charge of a very profitable division within his father's company."

"As a figurehead. Everyone knows his beta brother truly oversees the work."

"Perhaps. But he's well on his way to being a man. He's the same age I was when I first met you."

"A lifetime ago."

Vale's lips tilted up with a smile. "Why are you so hard on him? You don't mind when other alphas behave as their nature commands."

Urho sat back on his heels. "And how, exactly, is that?"

"Demanding, assertive, and with little respect for the fact that some other alpha might hold the floor or know more than they do." Vale buttoned his shirt again and sat back on the sofa with a knowing glimmer in his eyes.

Urho packed away his measuring tape, stethoscope, and notebook. He rose to standing, his knees aching slightly after kneeling on the polished brick floor, reminding him that he wasn't quite as young as he used to be. But his heart was, as always, tender toward Vale. "You think so little of alphas, do you?"

"I think alphas are accustomed to having their own way and to being heard."

"Jason does plenty of listening."

"Because he's young and respects me as a person."

Urho snorted. "No doubt. But you've just admitted that his youth plays a role."

"He's not a pushover, you realize."

"Of course not." He gazed out the study's wide windows to the garden Jason had planted to court Vale and saw the evidence of Jason's determination in the way it thrived even as the cold of autumn descended.

Yes, he'd seen how Jason went after things. A dog with a bone, even if he was softer than many alphas tended to be. He also knew Vale had no complaints about Jason's prowess in bed. Urho had heard Vale's pleasured wailing often enough on their vacations together by the seaside. It was one reason he'd rented his own house this past summer, just to escape the reminder of what he'd lost.

Vale gazed up at him wickedly. "And, if I'm being completely frank, my dear, you like it when Xan reveals how little unconditional respect he grants you. It stirs you."

Urho grimaced. "Not in any way that's admirable."

"And that's what's so intriguing about it." Vale leaned forward. "Little alpha Xan rousing staid, admirable Urho. It's remarkable really."

"He doesn't 'rouse' me." Irritation burned beneath his skin.

Vale clucked his tongue and dropped back against the sofa as though disappointed.

Urho remembered well the first time he'd met Xan, wide-eyed and red-cheeked. There'd been something even then that thrilled in him at the boy's presence, and it hadn't been proper. It'd been primal and raw, a surge of alpha expression like he'd never felt before. The urge to show the boy just who was in charge, to command him, and force him down to his—

He inhaled deeply and busied himself repacking his equipment.

It was disturbing.

Alpha expression was something he rarely experienced. Yes, he'd faced it when Jason turned up on the scene, but he'd squelched it quickly, lest the boy's overwrought hormones set them on a destructive path from which they'd never return. But any urges toward alpha expression in others generally unsettled him, and they left him ashamed when, inexplicably, they cropped up.

Which they did again and again in Xan's presence.

He'd never been able to make sense of it. Even today, when Xan had spouted off in his usual way, Urho had wanted to push the boy to his knees, grip his dark curls in one hand, force his mouth open with the other, and shut him the wolf-hell up with his dick.

He shook his head hard, hoping to dislodge those titillating thoughts for good. "The boy is annoying."

Vale's chin tilted up, and he held Urho's gaze. "The 'boy' is braver than you know."

"He's got a strong stomach, I'll give him that." He remembered how Xan hadn't even flinched when he'd walked into the room where Miner was bleeding out after a brutal miscarriage, and how he'd rolled up the sleeve of his shirt and offered his Wolf 3 blood to help like it was nothing to him. He'd even watched the blood transfer from his own body into Miner's without turning green.

"I said braver than you *know*."

"It's almost like you want me to take your word on his personal heroism without providing the details of it."

"You should. Have I ever lied to you?"

Urho rolled his eyes at that. Vale wasn't a liar, but he'd been known to withhold information if it worked to his advantage. "Have you ever been completely honest with anyone?"

"I don't keep anything from Jason now."

"Anyone who isn't Jason?"

"You. Almost entirely."

"I'm honored."

"You should be." Vale smiled tiredly. "And you should give Xan more latitude. I do."

Urho sat next to him on the sofa, leaning in close to say softly, "Speaking of the latitude you give him, I fear it's too much. He doesn't treat you with the respect you deserve."

Vale waved his hand, shooing off his words. "Xan deals with a lot."

"I'm surprised Jason allows it."

"There's nothing Xan could say or do that would bother me. Jason knows that's how I feel and, besides, he doesn't let Xan go too far."

"By whose definition?"

"I assure you, there's no tone or snotty comment from Xan that could ever get under my skin. He's been burdened unfairly in this life."

"Oh, yes, being the son and heir of a ridiculously wealthy alpha of impeccable name and long-standing heritage sounds incredibly trying."

"If you knew what I know…" Vale's eyes flashed. "Let's put it this way: Riki would be ashamed of you for saying something as unkind as that."

Vale almost never brought up Urho's dearly departed *Érosgápe* omega, knowing the wound of Riki's loss still ran deep. If he was willing to shame him with Riki's blessed memory, Urho must truly owe Xan an apology.

Urho sighed. "I shouldn't talk about things I don't understand."

"You shouldn't, and yet you so often do."

"I'm sorry."

Vale's smile was a wonderful reward. Urho missed the days when it was aimed at him alone, usually before they spent a rowdy and raunchy evening wearing nothing *but* their smiles. Jason imprinting on Vale in the library four years earlier had put an end to that side of their relationship, and Urho still missed it.

Not that he'd been celibate in the intervening years. Far from it.

He was often enlisted to help in the heat of uncontracted omegas or the occasional nymphomaniac—an omega suffering from insatiable lust. Interminable heat was the new name for the disorder, but Urho preferred the old-fashioned term since it allowed for a broader interpretation. The distinction was something he and Vale had vehemently disagreed on in the past, and probably would again in the future.

Regardless, he had ways of getting his physical needs met, but it didn't mean he didn't miss their old camaraderie and sexual connection. He smoothed a hand through his hair and said, "You're in good health. Jason's cooking has done you well."

"He spoils me."

Urho had to agree with that. It wasn't common for an alpha to cook or clean, the home being the purview of omegas since the time after the Great Death. But Jason's alpha father had been more egalitarian with his omega than most. Jason had adopted his father's ways and taken them to the extreme—doing most of the cooking or cleaning himself and letting Vale idle in spoiled splendor.

Jason's footsteps entered the room and the woody, comforting scent of chamomile filled the air. He balanced a teapot and three mugs on a tray, the epitome of a doting alpha waiting on his ailing omega.

A prick of envy was followed quickly by a well of bittersweet longing. Urho remembered the days he'd nursed Riki through seasonal colds and the occasional stomach virus. Holding his sweet, young love's body close—heedless of contagion or fear and only desiring to impart comfort—had been a gift he hadn't known to cherish at the time.

The loss of Riki burned him deeply, a pain he couldn't always ignore. His nerve endings endlessly sought the man who'd been their completion, the man who'd died trying to birth Urho's only son—the same son who'd died with his pater during that horrible, late-term miscarriage. Even loving Vale had only dampened the pain so much.

Urho's throat clogged with emotion, watching as Jason smoothed fingers over Vale's cheek before he turned to offer Urho a mug of tea.

"Thank you, but I should be on my way," he said gruffly.

"But what about Vale?"

"Would you like me to stand over him and watch him night and day for any signs of trouble?" Urho chuckled.

Jason's eyes flared dangerously. "No, but I thought you'd be here if we need you."

"I'm just a quick car ride away. There's no reason to expect any problems at this juncture."

"When *should* we expect problems?" Jason asked, sitting down at Vale's side, his own mug of tea steaming, un-sipped, in his hand.

"I'd say things might grow more difficult for Vale in the mid months, as his body struggles to cope with the child's growth. It's a large stressor on every omega, no matter their health. Despite our ancestors' best efforts to design omega bodies to bear children, there is a limit to the changes they were able to bring about. Omega hips are narrower and their womb less robust than those of the human females in the days before the Great Death."

As Jason grew pale again, Urho left off the reiteration of dangers facing even healthy omegas and decided to discuss the potential discomfort ahead instead. "Vale's scar tissue might prove painful during the high-growth months. Jason, you'll need to continue to stretch him internally. Regular, daily massage with your fingers and even your fist, if he can bear it, will be key to making this pregnancy and birth as easy as possible."

"And you'll induce him when?"

"When the time is right." Urho was going to have to wing that aspect of it. He wanted to allow the child as much time as possible to grow strong in hopes of sparing Jason and Vale the pain of a stillbirth, but he wasn't going to allow it to grow large enough that Vale wouldn't survive. His scar tissue was more flexible now, but it only had so much give, and if he were to tear...

"I promise not to let it go too long."

Jason's jaw tightened, and he darted a glance at Vale before whispering, "We could still abort."

Vale huffed.

"Yes, but I think your omega has made his wishes known," Urho said.

"What about my wishes? As his alpha? As his *Érosgápe?*"

"You've made those wishes known as well. Your priority is Vale. So is mine. We're all on the same page." Urho infused his voice with warning.

Jason put the mug aside and stood. "I'll walk you out."

Urho pushed aside the urge to kiss Vale's temple as he might have done if they were alone, knowing Jason wouldn't take kindly to the friendly gesture. Vale's "baby alpha" had long ago made peace with the fact that Urho and Vale had been lovers, but he still didn't like them to be openly physically affectionate.

Instead, Urho smiled warmly down at Vale, cozy and coddled on the sofa, and said, "I'll be back next week. If you need me before that, just ring."

As he and Jason stepped outside, the orange leaves of the great oak in front of the house sifting down around them, Urho spoke sternly. "If you allow your doubts to infect him, his outcome could be compromised."

"Maybe if he understands my fear, he'll change his mind."

"He does understand, and he won't," Urho said, gripping Jason's arm and forcing the young man to face him. "But even if he did, do you really want him to abort the child because you made him? Wouldn't he hold that against you?"

Jason's jaw tightened and released, but he nodded sharply once. "You know him too well."

"And so do you."

"Yes." Jason's resignation was clear. "How do I shake this, though? How do I move on like I don't think that every second that child grows inside of him is one more second closer to me losing him?"

"First, you must stop calling it 'that child' and think of it as your son. As the son you made together in love."

Jason wiped a hand over his face.

"Second, do you have so little trust in me? If I didn't believe he could make it through this, I'd advise an abortion immediately, illegal as it may be, and at considerable risk to all of us. And you know if I gave that advice, he'd go through with it."

Jason's cheeks flushed. "And how should I feel about *that*? I'm his alpha but he trusts your opinion over mine."

"My medical opinion, yes. He doesn't trust my love over yours. He doesn't share himself with anyone else the way he does with you. Surely you know that."

Jason crossed his arms over his chest, a stubborn flash in his eyes, but he said nothing.

"Consider what I'm saying, Jason. You *must* find a way to get past this, to find joy with him in this miracle. Make him believe that *you* believe." Urho sighed, trying to find the right words. "If you don't have faith in him, should there come a bad turn, he won't have faith in himself to pull through it."

Jason chewed on his bottom lip, brow lowered in thought.

"Omegas always believe in their alphas more than anyone else, especially during the trials of birth. How many times have I seen an omega turn to his alpha for encouragement in the delivery process and gain strength from his faith? Give Vale every reason to believe he *will* live, and that you want him and this child as much as he does."

Jason took a deep breath and nodded. "You're right."

Urho almost laughed. He knew what it cost Jason to admit that, but he only put his hand on Jason's shoulder and squeezed, trying to impart all the paternal affection he rather surprisingly felt for the young alpha who'd stolen his lover.

"Wolf-god be with you both," Urho said solemnly before turning to walk down the sidewalk to where he'd parked his car away from the falling leaves of Vale's old oak tree.

It wasn't a long drive home, but he was eager to get there. He planned to listen to some music on the radio and sip a nice glass of wine. Perhaps he'd read a book, one of Riki's old favorite fairy tales. Something fantastical that would sweep him away from his worry for Jason and Vale.

And, more importantly, stamp out all thoughts of that annoying alpha pup Xan Heelies and his beautiful, impertinent mouth.

CHAPTER THREE

"**D**ID YOU COME?"

Wilbet Monhundy's voice was rough in Xan's ear—and his hands around his throat even rougher. Xan squeezed his asshole around Monhundy's throbbing cock, hoping to distract him from the evidence of his climax cooling on the floor between his carpet-burned knees.

"I said *did you come?*" Monhundy growled, squeezing Xan's throat hard enough that his vision swam. The roughness of Monhundy's pants against Xan's buttocks and the rasp of his still-buttoned shirt over Xan's naked back was a visceral reminder of how vulnerable Xan was—exposed, penetrated, and at Monhundy's mercy.

"Yes," he confessed, choking out the word. He broke into a cold sweat as his body shook under the violent onslaught of Monhundy's cruel thrusts. "I came."

Monhundy growled, fucked into him harder, and shoved Xan's face down against the colorful carpet as he emptied his load into Xan's spasming ass. As soon as he'd caught his breath, he hissed, "You know what that means." Monhundy jerked his cock free, leaving Xan gaping open—used, worthless, and dissatisfied.

Worse, *dissatisfying*.

Xan wiped the tears from his face with the back of his hand, his legs shaking as Monhundy rose up behind him and jerked him to his feet. Unsteadily, he stared around at the richly decorated receiving room, the choices undoubtedly those of Monhundy's contracted omega.

The wood floor was covered in beautiful carpets, and the crushed velvet sofa was of the most cutting-edge design. The handsome table next to the leather armchair held a beautiful tea service with roses on the side of the cups. Xan took a shuddery breath.

This was the room where he was going to die.

Monhundy yanked him around, his square-jawed face creased with revulsion and cruelty. Towering over Xan, he looked every inch an ideal alpha. Bulky muscles, wide shoulders, and strong thighs evident even under his clothes, and a massive cock that put Xan's own to shame. As Monhundy stared down at him, Xan's heart pounded, and his pulse rushed wildly in his ears.

The smash of Monhundy's fist against his cheekbone took his breath away, and his vision exploded into stars. He fought for balance, like riding out ocean waves. Then his breath vanished again as Monhundy's hands gripped his neck and squeezed.

Hard.

Xan's eyes rolled back. He clawed helplessly at Monhundy's strong hands around his throat as Monhundy lifted and shook him like a rag doll. His still half-hard cock slapped against his stomach, and Monhundy knocked his legs apart.

"Filthy unmanned slut," Monhundy hissed.

Xan tried to scream, his stomach heaving as Monhundy kneed him in the balls. Vomit lurched up his throat and into his air-hungry mouth, nearly choking him. He forced it back down. Another drive into his balls left him convulsing as Monhundy held him aloft by his throat. Then Monhundy dropped him to the carpet.

Xan panted there, sucking in a desperate breath, only to wretch and choke on the pain ripping up through his gut.

"Sick, twisted, unmanned, piece of shit," Monhundy said, spitting in Xan's face and kicking him hard in the thigh. "You *know* what happens when you come. Don't you?"

"Yes," Xan rasped.

"That's right. I get to teach you another lesson." He dropped down to grip Xan's hair and jerk him up from the carpet. Saliva and vomit rattled in Xan's throat as he pulled in tortured breaths and peered up at Monhundy's face, still stupidly handsome, even twisted with rage as it was.

"Get on your knees," Monhundy spit out, rising and standing tall.

Xan hastened to obey. "I'm sorry. Please…"

"Please what? Fuck your ass again? You're a nasty bit of trash, coming here begging for me to plug you up with my cock. Then you go and ruin it by coming." His nostrils flared. "You sick, disgusting piece of filth." He spit in Xan's face again. It ran down his cheek and dropped to his heaving, naked chest. "Who comes?"

"The alpha."

"And what are you?"

"Scum."

"Not even scum, and not an omega. That's for sure." He nudged Xan's legs apart again and insinuated his boot against his throbbing balls. Xan held himself motionless except for his wretched sobs. Sweat ran down his naked back. "Unmanned whores don't get to come. Say it."

"Unmanned whores don't get to come."

"Do you know why I fuck you?"

Power. The pleasure of seeing him on his knees begging. The sick joy of hurting another alpha.

Xan clamped his lips closed.

"I fuck you because it entertains me to sit across from your father at business meetings and know that I've had his only alpha son and heir crying on my cock."

"Please don't tell—"

Monhundy smacked his face hard and Xan's head rocked back. "The rule is I fuck you until I come, and you, unmanned whore, don't."

"I'm sorry." Xan hadn't meant to come. The fuck hadn't even felt good. Monhundy sawing into him without any preparation or even spit for lube had left him screeching in pain, but somehow his sick, twisted mind had responded to it. When he'd come hard and uncontrollably, spraying jizz onto Monhundy's receiving room carpet, he'd been as shocked as he was scared.

Monhundy dragged Xan by the hair and pushed him face down to the carpet. "My omega won't be made to clean your foul emission. Lick it up."

Xan sniffed, tears and snot clogging his throat, but he did as he was told, licking the sticky pool of his semen. He gagged and choked, trying to swallow it down.

"Look at you. You love it."

Xan moaned, his asshole still aching and his balls throbbing. Monhundy pushed thick, rough fingers into him and jabbed at his sensitive prostate. Xan squirmed and whimpered, licking up the last of the come.

"I bet you'd take another of my loads and love it," Monhundy said, disgust lacing his voice. "I bet you'd let any alpha have you. More than one, even. The most depraved of the depraved."

Xan didn't point out that Monhundy was the one who'd originally started this sexual game between them. Throughout school, he'd bullied Xan relentlessly. Even then, Xan had recognized the sizzle of violent attraction on Monhundy's part, the burn of alpha expression. And then, after Xan had left school and Monhundy had graduated, the dark fascination between them had only escalated.

Every time they ran into each other—at parties, at bars, at clubs—fists came out on both sides, and threats, too. Until one day,

Monhundy, drunk and enraged from a late-night confrontation between them in a pub on the wrong side of town, had waited for Xan to leave alone. When Xan finally departed, Monhundy had used his great height and enormous strength to drag Xan into a dark, stinking alley behind the pub.

"Do you want me to fuck you?" he'd gritted out.

"Yes," Xan had said.

Then Monhundy had punched him repeatedly until he couldn't see straight.

"Do you still want me to fuck you?" he'd growled in Xan's ear.

Tears running down his face, Xan had nodded. "Yes."

Without another word, Monhundy had ripped down his pants and dry fucked him up against the alley's brick wall.

Xan still clearly remembered the rough slide of the bricks against his cheek and the shockingly painful penetration of Monhundy's alpha-sized cock. He'd screamed his head off but Monhundy had silenced him by cutting off his breath that night, too. Xan had struggled, but Monhundy was twice his size and strong as a horse. Eventually, Xan had surrendered, certain he'd be fucked to death there in that filthy alley.

Shockingly, he'd come that horrible night, too, painting those alleyway bricks with his semen. It'd been too dark for Monhundy to see the evidence of Xan's demented brokenness. But Xan had stared at the streaks of white from his crumpled position on the pavement where Monhundy had dropped him and left him for dead.

In that moment, he'd known the depths of his own depravity. He'd lived, yes, but he'd been ruined in more ways than anyone knew. He'd never forget what it felt like to lay there in that alley— pants down around his ankles and his body dripping with Monhundy's come and his own blood. The shame stayed forever on his heart.

That had been Xan's first taste of the darkness. And after he'd discovered it—the pain, the pleasure, the horror—he couldn't stay away. Seeking Monhundy out became his addiction. He made a game of getting Monhundy alone and taunting him until he cracked and brutally fucked Xan again and again. He pushed his former bully—now his abuser—harder each time until the incidents between them became so violent and dangerous that Caleb feared for Xan's life, and, wolf-god, Xan couldn't blame him.

Now he'd taken things farther than he ever had. He'd dared to drop by Monhundy's own house to beg for it. If Kerry, Monhundy's omega, had been home, nothing would have come of it. Xan would have found another excuse to explain why he'd come by, some sort of business discussion that Monhundy would have seen through, but his omega would have bought. But Kerry was away, visiting his ailing pater, and so Xan had dropped to his knees as soon as the beta servant who'd escorted him into the receiving room was dismissed.

And Monhundy hadn't failed to give Xan a fix of his favorite drug.

Monhundy raked a hand through his dark hair and stared down at Xan, eyes glittering with loathing. Xan swallowed down the last of the come he'd licked up and opened his mouth, offering his throat for use by Monhundy's refreshed and ragingly hard dick.

He half expected Monhundy to plunge into him and choke him to death, proving his dominance through the ultimate in alpha expression. Xan closed his eyes and shuddered, submitting to the inevitable, both terrified and titillated by the thought.

Just like that, all of his pain and guilt could all be over. All of it.

"Go home," Monhundy said, standing up and kicking him in the ass with the toe of his boot. He closed his pants and tucked in his shirt. He sneered down at Xan with his perfectly cut jawline and fashionable flop of dark hair. He tossed his strong shoulders back proudly. "You disgust me."

Xan stood slowly, his knees protesting and his stomach lurching again. He got dressed as quickly as possible. He buttoned up his shirt, knotted his bow tie messily, and hitched his pants up over his bruised hips. He'd just managed to get them closed before Monhundy gripped him by the back of the neck and steered him toward the front door where he tossed him and his shoes onto the front sidewalk. Xan, still weak and beyond shaken, sprawled onto his ass, the concrete cutting into his palms.

"Don't come back," Monhundy commanded, spitting on Xan once more for good measure. "I'll call you if I ever want to use your filthy ass again. But don't hold your breath." He tossed Xan's coat out and then slammed the door and locked it.

Xan shuddered where he sprawled on the cold concrete. The sky above twinkled with stars and the moon rode the clouds—white and pure—the all-seeing eye of wolf. His scraped palms burned, and his knee was twisted up beneath him. Tears slipped down his face helplessly.

Slowly, he rose, whimpering as he tugged on his coat and shoes before stepping onto the main sidewalk that ran by houses glowing with warm lights that weren't meant for him. He felt like an outcast, cold and alone.

His body was a bruise and his injured balls screamed with each step he took. His asshole burned hotly, and he wondered if the wetness below was blood seeping through his pants or, if possibly, he'd pissed himself while being strangled. He'd done that once before—when they'd fucked in Monhundy's office one night.

Monhundy had choked him out and then hadn't been pleased at Xan's urine wetting his office sofa. Xan had thought he might truly meet his end that night, too. His left eyebrow still held the scar from the damage Monhundy's fist had done afterward. He ran his tongue over another scar on the inside of his lower lip.

As he limped away from the Monhundy mansion, he tightened

his coat around himself protectively. Trying to keep steady on his feet, he soldiered on despite the pain. He'd parked around the corner and down two blocks to avoid having his too-obvious green car sighted by anyone who knew of his and Monhundy's enmity, and thus might ask questions.

Those two blocks seemed an impossible distance to travel now, beaten and bruised as he was. He carefully put one foot in front of another, grateful for the empty sidewalk and quiet streets. At least there were no witnesses to his walk of shame. He hoped he wouldn't pass out, though, as colored dots swam in his eyes and his breath came in short, sharp pants.

A long, golden-toned car passed him and then slowed, stopping not far away. Xan pulled his collar up, hiding his face, and quickened his steps, praying the person would just move on and leave him alone.

"Xan?"

The deep, sturdy voice was familiar and safe, but it also lit up a warning deep in Xan. He put on a burst of speed, but the man he was trying to avoid didn't give up so easily. He heard a car door slam and then the thud of footsteps, the distinctive tread of a strong alpha heading his way. Xan's eyes filled with helpless tears. What could he say? How could he explain? Panic gripped him. Of all the people in the world to see him like this!

Urho's hand gripped Xan's arm and whirled him around. His baffled expression was almost comical, and Xan nearly laughed, but when his mouth opened only a peculiar sob escaped. Xan clapped his palm over his lips, holding in the rest.

Urho's handsome face darkened. "Wolf-god, what's happened?"

Xan jerked his arm away. "I'm fine. Leave me alone."

He limped on, his asshole spasming painfully and his balls aching. He tried to swallow down a betraying whimper, but it wouldn't be held back. It burst free as he tripped over an uneven bit of sidewalk.

"For wolf-god's sake, man, let me help you," Urho said, wrapping an arm around Xan's lower back to hold him up. "Were you mugged? Was there more than one of them?" He gazed around, hunting for the attackers who'd left Xan in this state. Then he sniffed the air before leaning in and scenting Xan from chest to neck. A strangled noise exited his throat. "You've been…" He gasped, as though he struggled to even say the words. "One of them forced themselves on you?"

"No," Xan denied, his voice rasping. "Just let me go. I need to get home."

Urho frowned, his alpha nose clearly picking up the scent of semen. "Let me help you. You're bleeding and—"

"This isn't your business," Xan said, drawing himself up as haughtily as he could manage given the pain he was in. "Thank you for your help, Dr. Chase, but my omega is waiting for me at home. He'll be worried."

Urho choked, frustration plain in his dark eyes. "Let me drive you."

"My car isn't far." Xan pointed ahead. "Around the corner."

Urho gripped his elbow to steady him and said, "Then I'll walk you to it."

Xan nearly protested again, but his twisted knee throbbed, and his entire body shook as he tried to walk. He ignored Urho's eyes all over him, no doubt cataloguing his wounds. His suspicion was confirmed with Urho's next words.

"Whose handprints are around your neck? Your attacker's? We should call the police. Immediately. And we should get you to a hospital."

"No! No hospital."

"At least allow me to examine you at my home. It's just a street over. Come with me."

"No. My omega is waiting for me. I need to get home to him."

"Xan—"

"Look, I wasn't mugged. Or attacked."

"Of course, you're embarrassed to admit what happened," Urho spoke gently, like Xan was a wild thing that was going to bite. If he tried to muscle him into going to the hospital, Xan just might prove him right. "What alpha wouldn't be? But this is a crime. Xan, you must see that you can't leave it unreported."

Xan didn't reply, concentrating on getting one foot in front of the other. Even with Urho's steadying hand, it was hard to stay upright. Finally, he said, "It's a crime, but it wasn't rape."

"So you know your attacker," Urho said darkly. "You don't want to name him."

"I just want to go home."

"I demand to know who did this." Urho spoke with authority that rattled Xan deeply and made him want to obey. But he couldn't. There was too much at stake. For Xan, especially, and for Caleb, too. Urho's idea of help would only make things infinitely worse for everyone.

Xan kept walking.

Urho followed on his heels. "I demand to know what alpha has put his hands on you in this abominable manner? Who forced you into a vile act of submission?"

"I'm unmanned," Xan whispered furiously, spinning to face Urho in the street. He had to put a stop to this before Urho attempted to use his greater physical power and size to manhandle Xan into compliance.

"I can see—and smell—that you've been forced to submit," Urho said, lowering his voice to a tender calmness meant to soothe. "But that doesn't make you unmanned. This is a violation, not a lasting condemnation of your character."

"You don't get it!" Xan cried. "It's how I am. Ask Jason. Or

Caleb." His throat hurt from having been squeezed. He could barely force out the words. "As an unmanned alpha, I get what's coming to me. Understand?"

Urho shook his head, eyes narrowing in confusion. The silver in his dark hair shimmered in the rising moonlight. "This is nonsense. You have an omega…"

Xan groaned, turning his back on Urho again. He needed to get to his car and make it home before he passed out from pain and before the horror he'd no doubt feel keenly in the morning caught up with him in the present.

"I get what's coming to me," he said again, darkness surging up inside. The ink-black of his soul, fed so thoroughly by his encounters with Monhundy, past and present, confirmed that he was broken and twisted. Unmanned, unlovable, and utterly unworthy. "I get what I deserve."

Urho's hold on him loosened, shock working its way over his face, his eyes widening as he finally seemed to understand that Xan was no victim.

"That's my car," Xan said, nodding to the lime-green spectacle he'd bought on an optimistic day—a day when he'd felt more like his real self, the one who didn't give in to temptation and come to Wilbet Monhundy's house begging for a beating.

Urho's voice was ghostly as he asked, "Are you capable of driving home?"

"Yes," Xan lied. He wasn't sure, actually. "Caleb will take care of me. Don't worry."

Urho stared at him, his lips drawn tight and closed.

"And, please, don't mention this to Jason. He's got enough on his mind." Xan stepped away from Urho's strong grip and climbed into his car, fumbling the keys before he was able to start the engine and pull away from the curb.

In the rearview mirror, Urho stood on the sidewalk, hands in pockets, staring after him with a dark expression. Vomit pushed up into Xan's mouth, and he swallowed it down, groaning miserably. He'd never had Urho's good opinion, but he sure as wolf-hell wouldn't *ever* have it now. He'd be lucky if the man didn't turn him in to the police.

Given how close he'd come to death tonight, Urho's opinion of him was the last thing that should matter. And yet, for the whole, surreal drive home, Urho's dark, bewildered eyes and tightly drawn lips, the evidence of his disgust and disapproval, were all Xan could think about.

It hurt almost as much as his physical injuries.

"OH, DARLING, WHY do you do this to yourself?" Caleb asked. His cool, long fingers trailed gently over the marks on Xan's throat, and his kind, blue eyes shone sadly. The moonlight and cold night air spilled into Caleb's sumptuous bedroom through the open sash, washing over Xan's feverish, red, bruised, and broken skin. He wore only pajama bottoms, his robe discarded on the floor by the bed. Sounds of the city drifted in the windows.

"I don't know. I can't stop myself when the need hits me."

Caleb sighed. "One day, he could kill you." He helped Xan into the bed, facedown, so that he could treat Xan's worst injuries from Monhundy's kicks to his back.

"I know. And then what would happen to you?" Xan conceded, his eyes drooping with exhaustion. The cool sheets and blankets felt good on his hot skin.

Caleb tucked his blond, chin-length hair behind his ears as he peered at Xan's wounds. He treated them as gently and lovingly as any pater with his precious child. It made Xan feel loved and safe in a way he knew, deep down, he wholly didn't deserve.

The hot poultices that Caleb laid across Xan's bruised back and hips soothed him. The soft bed Caleb nested in nightly with fluffy pillows and soft blankets beckoned Xan to sleep. But he'd need to return to his own room before long, where he'd ache with loneliness the way he deserved, and dream of an alpha that could love him as though he were a true omega.

"As if that's what worries me most," Caleb murmured. Though Xan wouldn't blame him at all if that were his biggest fear. Caleb had his own secrets to keep and needs to meet. There was a reason the so-called "unmatchable omega" had contracted with an unmanned alpha, after all. Of course, those reasons were a secret between the two of them and not known to the world at large. So long as Xan didn't spoil things with his recklessness, they didn't ever need to be.

"We might not be lovers in the truest sense, but I do care for you, Xan," Caleb said, smearing arnica lotion over the smaller bruises. Xan hissed and hid his face in the crook of his arm. "More than as a cover for my own defects. We are friends, aren't we?"

"Family," Xan said firmly, his alpha-given proprietary urge rising up hard. Caleb wasn't his true love, but he was his omega. They'd made promises and contracted after all. Caleb was most definitely *his*, and while they might not share the things other contracted couples shared, no matter what, they were family now.

"Then as your family, but, more importantly in my opinion, as your true friend, I'm begging you to stop seeing this monster."

Xan held back the cutting, accusatory remarks that leapt to his tongue, knowing they reflected his own fears about his worth as an alpha and not Caleb's actual opinions. The nasty blame echoed in his mind all the same.

If you don't stop now, someone will find out, Xan. How long can this remain a secret? And what then? If you're discovered, you won't be the only one to pay a price. Caleb will suffer, too. And your brother,

Ray. The family will be humiliated. Your parents. And your friends. Association with you will be damnation for everyone who cares for you. Why are you so craven and selfish? Why are you so disgusting?

"Xan, stop beating yourself up," Caleb said, knowing him too well. "You've done enough of that tonight by letting that alpha abuse you again. Does he always have to hurt you so much?"

"He likes it."

"Do *you*?"

Xan squeezed his eyes shut, tightness in his throat making it hard to speak. "I don't know what I like anymore."

Caleb sighed forlornly. "And I'm of no help at all."

"You're all kinds of help. You're patching me up, aren't you?" Xan tried to sound devil-may-care, but the pain in his voice ruined the effect. "You're a wonderful omega."

"What were you even doing on that side of town?" Caleb asked gently, as always trying not to sound nearly as critical as Xan knew he had every right to be.

"Visiting Jason and Vale. I was going to come right home, but…" He shuddered as Caleb rubbed arnica into his back. The sick ache of pressure on the boot-shaped bruise made him nauseous. He should tell Caleb about Vale and Jason's news, but he just didn't have the energy.

"He's your cocaine," Caleb murmured, mentioning the drug that had flayed open and destabilized Caleb's childhood when his father became addicted to it and lost the family fortune.

There'd been so many reasons Xan's parents had opposed their match, including Caleb being older, at twenty-nine, and carrying a dubious reputation. The history of addiction and scandal had been another black mark. They'd only given in when they'd realized Xan was determined beyond reason to contract with the beautiful Caleb and that he wouldn't even entertain the idea of any other omega. Now his parents liked Caleb better than they liked him, but that was another story altogether.

Xan bit down on the inside of his cheek, remembering how he'd once thought Caleb was the savior he'd been looking for. How terribly wrong he'd been. And now he'd dragged poor Caleb down with him, making the handsome, patient man subject once again to the poorly managed addiction of the alpha in his life. Shame rose hotly to his cheeks.

"I'll quit him," Xan promised. He no longer knew how many times Caleb had implored him to stop submitting to Monhundy's violence and how many times he'd agreed, only to decide a few weeks later to endure it "one last time."

"You must, before he murders you."

"Or the truth gets out."

Caleb sat back on his heels, his brow arched as he gazed imperiously down at Xan. It was an expression he excelled at. "Your priorities remain skewed. Your life is more important than your reputation."

"My father wouldn't agree. Or Ray."

"You don't give your brother enough credit. As for your father… Well…" Caleb trailed off, both of them no doubt remembering the family dinner when Xan's father had declared that he'd rather have a dead son than an unmanned one after a rumor about the nature of Xan's proclivities had come to his attention. "The state you're in, I'm surprised you were able to make it home."

"I had help," Xan admitted.

"Someone drove you?" Caleb asked carefully.

"No, Urho Chase saw me trying to get to my car, and he assisted me."

Though Xan *shouldn't* have driven himself. He'd nearly passed out twice as he'd tried to navigate the streets, blinking in and out of consciousness as the world dissolved around him. Luckily, the roads had been mostly deserted, but still, the trip had been harrowing.

When he'd arrived at their upscale house in Center Square, just a half mile from his parents' palatial home, he'd been grateful to see Lenser, one of his most discreet beta servants at the front door. He'd handed over the keys to the car, asked Lenser to put it in the garage, and headed inside, glad to be home in one piece, and aware that while Lenser would ask no questions and spread no rumors, he'd still seen his employer in a state no man could call respectable.

Thank wolf-god that betas didn't have the scenting ability of omegas or alphas, or Lenser would have known the truth instantly. As Urho had.

"Dr. Chase is an alpha," Caleb said, sitting back with wide eyes. "You arrived here reeking of the monster's semen. There's no way he didn't smell him on you."

Xan's gut tangled up and hot humiliation and cold fear rushed over him at once. "He did."

"And you told him what? That you'd been attacked? Set upon by some alpha who…?" Caleb's uncertainty drove into Xan with a ferocious need to protect him, to promise his omega that everything would be okay. He was an alpha after all, no matter what sick things he got up to sexually. He still felt the urge to protect his omega from harm.

"I told him the truth."

Caleb gasped. "You… Why?"

"As you said, he scented it on me. He demanded we call the police. You know how Urho is, so upright and correct. And I wasn't thinking clearly enough to come up with another plan. The truth seemed the only way out."

"And what truth was that?" Caleb's blond brows rose. "The one you tell me or the real, honest to wolf-god truth?"

"The least amount of it I could afford to tell while still stopping him from doing the so-called 'right' thing and calling the police."

"And did you tell him about Jason?"

Xan flinched. "No. That's not something Jason would want." Though he'd hinted to Urho that Jason knew *something*, hadn't he? He slowly met Caleb's eyes. "I didn't realize you knew about Jason."

"Not from you, that's for certain. And, no, not from Jason either. But I'm not a fool. I know you well enough now and I've seen how you look at him sometimes, the way you still long for him. And I've seen how he looks at you with affection and, well, for lack of a better word, guilt. He knows you far too well and treats you too generously to just be an old friend."

"We were lovers, yes."

"What ended it?"

Xan sighed. "He found Vale."

"I see." Caleb knew the story of Vale and Jason's imprinting. They told it now like it was a sweet tale, waxing lyrical over the moment like it hadn't been violent, terrifying, and basically assault. The rose-colored glasses of *Érosgápe* love had taken the sting from it for them. Not so much for Xan.

"And now Dr. Chase knows about you."

Xan buried his face in his hands. "I was delirious and in pain. I don't know how much he understood or believed. It's not too late to handle it, control the story."

"Mmm," Caleb hummed. "And what did Dr. Chase say?"

"He was confused. I'm surprised he let me drive home. I think his shock is all that allowed him to release me."

"As if that's a good thing! You'd have been better off under a doctor's care. Who knows what that monster has done to you?" Caleb adjusted a poultice that had slipped with Xan's squirming. "I wish you'd let me look."

"No." Xan enjoyed Caleb's care on his external wounds, but he had limits as to what he'd let his omega see of the aftermath of indulging in his addiction.

"Dr. Chase…" Caleb sighed again. "He'll have questions."

"I'm sure."

"He'll call Jason."

"I don't think he will. Not right now."

Caleb looked doubtful, and on another day, he'd be right. But Urho wasn't going to bother Jason, not if it would add stress to Vale. The pregnancy, terrifying as it was, would at least shield Jason and Xan from dealing with that awkward conversation.

"Dr. Chase is old-fashioned," Caleb said quietly. "I know you admire him, and I've seen how you look at him."

"What's that mean?"

"You know what it means, Xan." Caleb didn't sound angry, just sad and tired. For both of them. "I know you admire him," he said again. "But is he trustworthy?"

"I think so. Yes." Especially now when Vale was delicate. Urho would never put Vale at risk; his loyalty and investment there was too strong, and that meant he'd keep Xan's secret. At least until Jason and Vale's baby was born…or not born, as the case may be. His gut twisted up.

"I suppose I'll have to trust your assessment."

"I know I made a mistake tonight."

"Darling, you make this mistake far too often. It breaks my heart." Caleb nuzzled the back of Xan's neck. There was nothing sensual in the action, only a needy seeking of reassurance. An omega gesture, and Xan responded as he should, with an alpha's comfort.

"We're all right, Caleb. I promise I'll always take care of you."

Caleb huffed softly and then pulled back. "I'd rather you took care of yourself."

"I'm tired," Xan said, carefully rolling onto his back, dislodging the poultices, and sitting up. He broke out into a sweat from the effort, and as he gingerly stood, Caleb helped him up.

"You need to rest. What excuse will you use tomorrow?"

"I'll go to work," Xan said.

"But your face…"

Xan touched his swollen cheekbone and grimaced. "I take it there's no hiding it?"

"Not even with the stage makeup we have left over from that costume party we attended."

"I'll have to claim flu, then."

"Yes," Caleb agreed. "I'll make the call in the morning."

"Thank you." His knotted gut relaxed.

If Caleb called, his father wouldn't scream and yell, and he'd likely leave Xan alone for at least a few days. Caleb, like so many omegas, knew just how to speak to an alpha to reduce the threat of aggression, and Xan was grateful for that.

How many family dinners had been salvaged by Caleb's smooth interference when Father began his usual vicious picking on Xan? It was hard being the family's only alpha offspring, with all the hopes of the future pinned on him, especially when he was so very, deeply flawed, and everyone suspected the truth, even if they didn't quite know it for sure.

"I can make it on my own," Xan said, bending to pick up his robe and hissing in pain as he did.

"Let me help." Caleb slipped the soft robe over Xan's shoulders.

The cold breeze from the windows prickled his skin, and he was wracked with a painful shudder. In his own room, the beta servants would have stoked his fire for the night, and he'd be able to snuggle into bed toasty and warm. It was only Caleb who preferred to sleep in an ice-cold room.

Caleb's pale skin glowed in the moonlight, perfect and unblemished. His hairless chest and abdomen were revealed by the V of his white silk robe, and Xan wished, as always, that he felt moved at all by the sight. It was, by all rights, a beautiful one. Caleb was the epitome of an omega—delicate and sweet, handsome and fit, with sensual quirks, like sleepy eyes and a pouty mouth.

Most alphas ached to defend and possess him. He'd been coveted for many years at the Philia Committee soirées for unmatched omegas, but he'd refused to entertain anyone's offer until Xan had come along. And even then, he'd rejected Xan until he'd finally understood their needs were perfectly matched…

At least most of the time.

Xan took the tub of liniment Caleb had been using on him and kissed him gently on the cheek. Caleb walked him to the door of his room and, just before Xan left, took him into a gentle hug. "Sleep well, alpha mine," he murmured.

Xan's throat tightened, and he bit out, "And you, my omega."

The hallway was long, and his room was on the opposite end of it. The house was, aside for a few rooms Caleb had claimed as his own, decorated to Xan's ornate taste. And the hallway was no exception. Mirrors lined the walls, giving his usually vain appetite a constant view of himself. But tonight, he kept his eyes on the soft, red carpet that rolled out down the wooden floor. He didn't need to see himself all black and blue and red. The consequences of indulging in his dark addiction were never something Xan reveled in.

He passed the wide stairwell down to the first floor and continued past the closed doors of other bedrooms, unclaimed, and, as of now, mostly undecorated, save for two rooms designated for guests.

The house itself was larger than they needed, but Xan still had some futile hope of filling the many rooms between his and Caleb's with children—somehow, some way. If he could solve his problem with performance during heat…and if his sperm would behave and knock up Caleb sooner rather than later, he'd like to begin with that dream immediately.

It was his duty, after all, to carry on the Heelies name and to provide a family for Caleb to love. Caleb desperately wanted to be a pater and Xan had promised him he would be.

Wolf-god, he'd promised Caleb so many things.

Xan sighed, opening the door to his warm room before closing it carefully behind him. The wide bed stood between four wooden posters and beneath a red canopy. The fire burned in the grate, just as he'd known it would, and the sheets had been turned back welcomingly.

He slipped off his robe and pajama pants and threw them over the velvet chair in the corner. He dug his toes into the long, pearl gray shag of the rug he'd purchased in Rapersten during a business trip a year ago. He'd been only the figurehead, of course, there to smile, shake hands, and sign the contracts his brother Ray had negotiated with the rug dealers there. But he'd selected this rug himself from the piles and piles in the warehouse he'd visited.

Carefully, he lowered himself to his bed and stared up at the flat, red expanse of cloth over him. His thoughts raced hard against the lingering pain, like wild horses storming through his mind. He'd brought all of this on himself, he knew that, and didn't deserve forgiveness for it. But what had he done to deserve this craving? Was he born evil? Had he done something so horrible in a past life that wolf-god saw fit to punish him even now in this one?

A little over a year ago, he'd been hopeful that his abnormal lusts were something he could put behind him. He'd contracted with Caleb and they'd agreed to live a celibate life, except when heats came on. This fit Caleb's needs perfectly and his own better than any other omega match could have done.

He'd thought their partnership was going to be his salvation. They'd make the family his father and pater required, and he'd continue as the figurehead while his brilliant beta brother ran the family business. He'd find peace with what he was allowed.

Xan had been entirely confident the plan would work. He'd learned in school that during heat, an omega's pheromones drove an alpha to instinctive arousal and lust. He'd been sure there could be no problem on his end when exposed to the scents of Caleb in heat. He was an alpha after all. He'd been so certain that he'd outright promised Caleb that he'd never suffer even a moment of pain when the time came.

Oh, how hilariously presumptuous that all seemed now.

It was right that his body was hurt so badly that the helpless, hateful laugh these thoughts brought up left him gasping in pain with hot tears burning his eyes. The only thing that'd gone right in that pitiful plan was choosing Caleb, who was more understanding than Xan had any right to expect.

Xan didn't plan to ever forgive himself for all the ways his plan had fallen apart. Caleb, though, was always ready to forgive and forget, to move ahead and forge a new strategy together, tugging Xan along with him when he balked from shame. Caleb had gone all in with him, ready to ride the storms of their life until the bitter end. He was a ridiculously good man, and Xan didn't deserve him. Not even a little.

Of course, Caleb didn't agree with him. Instead, Caleb called himself equally flawed, and always said they were a perfect match. Even after a night like this.

An owl screeched outside his window, piercing his veil of wretched self-pity. He reached for the tub of liniment and discarded his underwear. Leaning back on the bed, he spread his sore legs wide and reached down to test his swollen, bleeding entrance.

He was always too ashamed to let Caleb tend to this wound.

With tears standing in his eyes, he scooped out two fingerfuls of liniment and pressed them into himself, whimpering as the pain flared. Then, fingers still inside, he rolled onto his side, sobs wracking his body. The arnica soothed even as his fingers opened up the wounds.

He loathed that he was incapable of turning his back on the darkness for long. Why couldn't he just stay away and stay celibate, like Caleb? When they'd made their solemn contract together, he hadn't thought it would be so hard, or that he could possibly be so very depraved.

In the dry heat of his bedroom, curled up in his soft bed, his asshole throbbing with his heartbeat, Xan cried himself to sleep.

CHAPTER FOUR

URHO SAT STUBBORNLY in the well-appointed drawing room to the right of the fashionable entryway. It wasn't a room he'd been in before during the few parties Xan and Caleb had thrown over the last year since they contracted together. The furniture didn't seem to Xan's taste. It was simple and classic, lacking in the elegant yet quirky self-awareness that Xan's clothing and furnishings always revealed. Perhaps this room was Caleb's doing? If so, the omega had timeless sensibilities.

Mid-morning sunlight filtered in through the soft, white curtains, lending a further sense of calm to the room. On another day, Urho would have enjoyed having tea and relaxing here, but his nerves made the lack of fussy details on which to focus his attention nearly unbearable. He crossed and re-crossed his legs restlessly.

The door to the hallway opened behind him, and Urho rose, still facing the window. He crossed his hands in front of him and lifted his chin, prepared to meet Xan in whatever state he found him this morning. Despite having thought of little else all night, he was suddenly speechless without any idea of where to start. So he closed his eyes, waiting to hear how Xan greeted him first.

"Dr. Chase," a smooth, soft voice murmured. It was pleasant, a quiet tenor laced with an iron undertone Urho recognized. He'd heard omegas wield that attitude on alphas his whole life.

"Mr. Riggs," Urho replied politely, opening his eyes and turning to take in Caleb. He wore loose, casual clothing: white pants and a soft-looking white, short-sleeved shirt that opened in a small

V to expose his delicate collarbones. His pale arms hung loosely at his sides, an attempt at appearing calm and collected, but Urho didn't miss the way Caleb's breath came quickly or how his pulse pounded at the base of his long throat. Urho said, "I'm here to speak with your alpha this morning."

"Xan is resting." Caleb called over his shoulder for tea to be brought before stepping farther into the room. His longer-than-entirely-fashionable blond hair hung to chin-length, but the front was combed back from his face and held in place with a sparkling blue-jeweled barrette. His similarly colored eyes cut through Urho like blades. "He isn't well."

Urho's stomach dropped. "I saw him last night. Does he need medical assistance? I'd like to help."

Caleb's right brow went up, but he didn't say anything for a moment as a beta servant, a mere slip of a boy, brought in the tea service and put it on the table before Urho. It wasn't what Urho would have expected in Xan's house either. Instead of a quirky, elaborate, and cutting-edge design, the pot was smooth and white. The cups didn't have handles and were made of the same fragile but plain ceramic white clay.

After the boy left again, Caleb took a seat opposite Urho in a simple cream-colored, tall-backed chair with no arm rests. He crossed his legs carefully, and Urho noticed for the first time that Caleb was barefoot and each of his toenails was painted with some shiny, glittery substance that caught the morning light.

"Let's cut out the formalities, what do you say?" Caleb looked up at Urho through his lashes in a way that could only be called coy. A very omega thing to do when feeling cornered. "We've met often enough to use first names."

"Of course." He smiled, trying to grasp onto the familiar back and forth of social graces to dispel the discomfort he'd wallowed in since the night before. He settled back onto his chair. "Call me

Urho."

"And you may call me Caleb." He relaxed back in his seat, but with the same air as Vale's cat when she watched birds out the study windows: relaxed but focused, poised for attack. "So, how can I help you, Urho?"

Urho attempted to soften his own body into a more soothing position. He didn't want Caleb to think of him as the enemy here. "As I said, I saw Xan last night. He was injured."

Caleb's cheeks flushed, but his eyes didn't sway from Urho's gaze. "Yes."

"If he requires a doctor's care, I'm discreet and ready to be of service."

Caleb carefully poured tea for both of them, his long fingers deft and strong, though they trembled slightly. "I'd like that. However, I doubt he'd hold the same opinion."

"He's a stubborn ass."

Caleb's smile was swift and surprising. Urho hadn't been granted it many times in their prior meetings. Xan's omega had always seemed, if not shy, perhaps cautious. Now his smile signaled a potential opening between them. "He is, yes," Caleb agreed. "Many people don't understand that about him. But I'm not surprised you do."

Urho wasn't sure who in the world could ever be surprised by a stubborn alpha, but Xan typically turned in a convincing performance of a superficial fop with no substance to back up his mouthy opinions. Between that act, Xan's bow-ties and the tight pants that hugged his ass in ways that made Urho's eyes linger too long—not to mention his bright, somehow guileless blue eyes—Urho could imagine many serious men might fail to register Xan's true nature.

In the morning light streaming through the windows, Urho noticed not for the first time that Caleb was slightly older than Xan. Fine lines started at the corners of his handsome eyes. If Urho had to guess, he'd say Caleb was older by at least five years.

It was unusual for an omega to contract with an alpha that much younger without an *Érosgápe* bond to tie them. Not unheard of, but all the same, it was of interest. Why would he choose Xan over other alphas his own age, men who were perhaps a bit older and more established? Surely there had been offers. Especially for an omega of Caleb's beauty and obvious intelligence.

"Xan admires you, you know," Caleb said carefully, like he was dipping a toe into the ocean to see how cold the waves might be.

Urho's heart thumped hard, and he frowned, confused by the abrupt heat blooming in him, making him sweat. "It's not unusual for a younger alpha to look up to an older alpha," he said, but his voice sounded tight, and he didn't know why.

Caleb hummed softly, his gaze shrewd as he took Urho in. Shifting on the soft chair, Urho loosened his tie. The room was suddenly stuffy, and he wished Caleb would open a window.

Silence clicked between them for a few stilted moments, but eventually Caleb asked, "What do you plan to do with the information you discovered last night?"

Urho's pulse seemed to grow very slow and yet very loud before bursting into a gallop. He studied Caleb's calm expression, searching for some sign that Urho might betray Xan's trust by discussing this matter honestly with his omega, but he found no innocence there.

Caleb's challenging gaze told him that whatever happened to Xan last night, whatever the truth of it—rape or alpha expression gone wrong—Caleb was in the know about it all. Urho let out a sigh of relief. "I plan to do nothing other than offer my assistance as a physician."

Caleb nodded, sipping at his tea, and so Urho did the same. The flavor of orange rinds spiced it nicely, and he took another, longer sip. The sound of a door opening and closing somewhere above them caused Caleb's eyes to flick speculatively toward the ceiling, but then he met Urho's gaze again, holding his silence.

"So what happened last night?" Urho asked after a long moment where they simply drank tea and studied each other, with the occasional break to stare at the patterns the sun made on the floor. "What he told me makes no sense."

"He was out of his mind," Caleb said softly. "I'm not sure what caused him to seek out—" His lips twisted, and he bit off the rest of that sentence. "His reasons are his own."

"He claimed he wasn't assaulted."

Caleb's laugh was bitter. "I suppose it depends on what one calls assault, wouldn't you agree, doctor?"

"He appeared to have been attacked in the most grievous of ways."

And Urho had let him drive away alone. He had no excuse for his behavior. He'd been so overwhelmed by the scent of another alpha on Xan's body, the pheromones of sex and pain layered together. It had roused him deeply and disturbingly. And the iron trace of blood on the air had horrified him in a way that it had no right to horrify a doctor.

He flashed back to Xan's eyes, normally so lustrous and blue, dark with fear, shadowed with desperation, and wild with pain. Urho shuddered, remembering Xan's words. *"I'm unmanned."*

And the way he'd stated it!

Permanent. Final. Not the temporary ego loss of a man who's been forced into the submissive position in an unfortunate and disgusting episode of alpha expression. No, there was more to it. A guilty confession. A history.

But there couldn't be.

Urho wouldn't believe it. He refused. No alpha would accept being permanently unmanned as a way of life for himself. Especially not an alpha with so much to lose. And Xan, as the heir to a very large fortune, had everything to lose.

"He said he's…" Urho hated to use the slur.

Being labeled "unmanned" was not only a perversion of nature but it was dangerous. Imprisonment wasn't even the worst thing that could happen to a man who'd turned his back on the Holy Book of Wolf's commandments in this damnable way.

Urho squirmed in his chair. "He said he's…"

"Yes."

"But he can't be."

Caleb's voice was cool. "And if he is?"

Urho rubbed a hand over his face. "How? He's an alpha. No alpha would allow such a weakness in themselves." He stirred restlessly in his chair and lifted his chin, searching for the words that must be true. The words he'd told himself since he'd watched Xan's taillights disappear the night before. "He fought back. He's wrong about what happened last night."

Caleb's blond lashes blinked rapidly.

"He was assaulted," Urho went on. "By a man overcome by uncontrollable alpha expression. Perhaps drugs or drink played a role, or some slight to the man's omega. I don't know. It was a power play of the most vicious sort, and he fought back. Of course, he did."

Xan was a small alpha; there was no way he could win against a bigger man, and nearly all alphas were bigger than him.

"There was no fight," Caleb said softly.

"Of course, there was a fight. He was injured." Urho's stomach churned uneasily.

"He was beaten," Caleb corrected, his fingers trembling harder as he put his teacup down on the small table between them. "There is a difference."

Urho stared at Caleb, his stomach roiling. He tried to get a grip on why, exactly, he cared so very much. He'd been a medic in the army and seen terrible things. And he'd recently left his post-military research work at the university behind to pursue a life of service in helping the poor in the Calitan and Delta districts.

He'd seen all sorts of people in his lifetime, depravity of all kinds, and yet somehow what Caleb was implying about Xan seemed more unacceptable than anything he'd witnessed out in the world. The idea that irritating, mouthy, handsome Xan Heelies would truly seek out this kind of treatment was unthinkable.

"He wants this?" Urho whispered, his tongue thick.

"Not *this*," Caleb said, shaking his head. "Who would want to be so abused? But..." he trailed off, his gaze going toward the door, and Urho knew who stood there when Caleb's eyes took on a gentle expression. "Darling, you should be in bed."

"I have a visitor, apparently," Xan said stiffly. He stood with one hand on the doorknob and the other in his pocket. He wore fashionable but loose trousers, and a soft gray sweater with a high collar that brought out the white flecks in his blue irises. His left cheek was distorted with a bruise and his eyes were lifeless shadows, nothing like the dancing, laughing pools Urho had first admired when they'd met.

"A stubborn visitor, according to Ren," Xan went on, mentioning the name of his housekeeper and the beta servant who'd greeted Urho at the door. "Someone who won't leave until they see me, or so he was told to tell me. And now that someone is upsetting my omega." He raised his chin, the small dent in the middle looking deeper in the light from the window.

"I'm not upset," Caleb said, smiling at Xan warmly. "But I do enjoy your protectiveness, dear."

"You *look* upset," Xan reiterated, his eyes hard on Urho.

"I apologize if I've overstepped with your omega," Urho said quickly. Heat prickled him all over as he gazed at Xan. His heart pumped faster, as though he was in the wrong to be here, trying to help this man who was, supposedly, a friend. "He was only being hospitable in your absence."

Xan raised a brow and said nothing.

Caleb cut the vibrating silence. "If you won't go back to bed, then I suppose you should come in and take a seat. Have some manners."

Xan crossed the room slowly. He kept challenging eyes on Urho, only sparing a glance for Caleb when he sat down on another soft chair next to him, wincing as he did.

Clearly, the damage to his anus was sufficient to still bring him pain the next day. Urho opened his mouth to scold Xan for not asking him here as a doctor and a friend to deal with it, but then he shut it again.

Xan had said the night before that he deserved this, and, by the Holy Book of Wolf, if he did go seeking out this kind of thing, then perhaps he did. Urho shuddered in disgust, but he didn't know if it was at himself, the Holy Book, or Xan. He was in over his head and he didn't know where to begin.

Caleb seemed to have no such reservations. "You must have Urho examine you."

Xan snorted, but his gaze darted away from Urho's finally, dropping to the floor. He reached for Caleb's hand and when it was granted, he held onto it. Urho stared at the two of them, trying to understand. Why did he feel as though he'd walked into an upside-down world, one he both wanted to comprehend and to run very far away from?

"You're injured, and I'm scared," Caleb said. "As your omega, I demand you allow it."

Xan squeezed his eyes shut, his cheeks flaming, but he nodded. "Dr. Chase—"

"We've been friends too long for that." The repressed emotion under all this civility was making Urho itch.

"Urho, then," Xan said, his eyes landing on him with anger burning down deep inside. "My omega would appreciate it if you'd examine me. He's concerned for my health."

"As he should be. You look terrible." Urho took a deep breath, taking in the scent of Xan's skin, the other layers of odor over and around him. He frowned. "There could be a hint of infection already."

Caleb's eyes went wide, and he clutched at Xan's hand, knuckles going white.

"Now you *are* upsetting my omega," Xan said darkly. "But let's get on with it."

Urho's head swam. He felt as though the tea had been drugged. He stood when Xan did and watched through a fishbowl of confusion as Xan kissed the top of Caleb's blond head and then motioned for Urho to follow him to "somewhere more private." Since when did an alpha need to keep anything private from his omega?

Xan led the way toward the staircase, but when he glanced up at it, his shoulders rounded in defeat. "I'd rather do this on the ground floor."

"We could return to the drawing room. Surely Caleb would want to be present for…"

"You need to stay away from him," Xan muttered.

Urho frowned. "I have no designs on Caleb. What do you take me for?"

Xan laughed, though it held little mirth. "I'm not concerned about that. Caleb is special."

"All alphas think their omegas are special."

"Perhaps, but I want to keep him safe."

"From me?"

"From things that upset him."

Urho huffed. "I imagine the bruises on your face at this moment must upset him much more than anything I could say or do."

"We both know that's not true," Xan said ominously, beckoning him down a narrow hallway. "One remark to imply that you intend to go to the authorities over what you know about me would undo him."

Urho let out a breath laced with hurt. Is that what Xan thought of him?

Xan finally opened a door to a small, un-renovated but well-lit room with a very dated daybed tucked against the front wall beside a table and chairs. It looked like an old nursery. Perhaps it had been for the previous owners. He knew Xan had purchased the house in an estate sale after the death of a widowed omega.

"Will this do?"

Urho put his bag down on the table and forced his voice to steadiness. "Undress. I'll need to see your injuries from head to toe. Use the blanket on the bed for privacy, if you must, but I'll need to examine your anus."

Xan stood motionless, staring at Urho. His pupils grew so dilated that the blue was nearly obliterated. "Why are you doing this?" he finally hissed. "Why are you here at all?"

"You're injured." Urho floundered. "What kind of doctor would I be if I didn't check on you this morning?"

"What kind of doctor were you last night that you let me go home alone in this shape?"

"A shocked one. A human one." He scrubbed a hand over his face, feeling the stubble he'd missed in his haste that morning. "I handled it all badly."

And he didn't understand why. Had it been any other man on the street, any other alpha confessing to being unmanned, he'd have known how to behave. And any other *friend*, especially, he'd have insisted on taking home and caring for him immediately. What was it about Xan that always threw him off? And why did this revelation that the beating behind these injuries hadn't been entirely unwelcome terrify Urho so much?

No, it was all nonsense. Never mind if Xan claimed to be unmanned. The boy had been delirious last night. He couldn't have meant what he said. Just as Caleb couldn't have meant what he was implying this morning either. Urho refused to believe it.

His stomach was full of snakes, rolling and slithering into living knots as he wiped a trembling hand over his face again. "Forgive me."

"I nearly passed out at the wheel."

Urho cleared his throat, trying to regain his footing in their conversation. He was in the right. He needed to remember that and hold the upper hand. "I'm sorry. Should we begin the exam?"

"Fine."

"Take off your clothes."

"No."

"Your omega requested that I examine you."

Xan crossed his arms over his chest and lifted his chin. "Leave him out of this. What are you doing here, Urho? What do you really want from me?"

Urho motioned at the bed as he took a seat in a tiny chair at the small table. His knees came up too high, and he felt ridiculous and stupid. "I couldn't sleep last night. I regretted the way I let you leave. As a doctor it was incorrect. As a friend it was unforgivable."

Xan remained standing. "But you ask my forgiveness, anyway?"

"I wouldn't blame you for withholding it."

"You're an asshole," Xan snapped.

"So are you."

"True." His lips quirked with an almost smile. "But let's be frank, we're barely friends. You don't owe me anything. If you want to be of help, then go home, forget you saw anything, and leave me alone."

Urho frowned and sat up straighter. He wanted to dispute this description of their acquaintance, but the fact of the matter was, he didn't spend time alone with Xan. Not ever.

And there was a reason for that. Xan always made his skin feel too small, and his world too dull, and his heart too shriveled. Xan made him itch all over with irritation, and brought on a desire to grab him by the neck, shove him to the floor, and...

And what?

Do whatever that alpha had done to him last night?

No, he wanted to fuck Xan and make him *love* it, not beat him to a pulp and make him suffer. No part of him wanted that.

Urho's face heated. He hoped his dark complexion kept Xan from seeing it. But, even if it did, he supposed there wasn't much he could do to hide his bewilderment. The inside of his mind was a circus of desires and fears he didn't understand. He couldn't imagine he was any good at hiding that fact.

Xan stared steadily at him.

"You confuse me," Urho said, finally. "I'm here to help, but you're treating me like the enemy."

Xan's shoulders slumped. He frowned, casting a hard look at the wall just over Urho's shoulder. His knees seemed to tremble, and he finally sat on the day bed, away from Urho. He plucked nervously at the blue quilt beneath him.

"Talk to me," Urho commanded. "Enough of this strangeness and just tell me what happened last night. Use your words. I know you have lots of them. I hear you spout off with impertinence all the time."

Xan's plump lips twitched like he might smile, and Urho sat up straighter, relaxing into this familiar role. He was an older alpha with experience and good advice to offer. Like with Jason, he could be an uncle figure, perhaps. Xan wasn't any different.

Never mind that Xan's bruised cheek pulled at something inside

Urho, like a fishing hook to some part of his soul, tug, tug, tugging until he wanted to rip it free or…do something else. He yearned to act—to be tender or violent, he wasn't sure. But he definitely wanted to behave in a way that was forbidden.

He swallowed hard and took up the uncle role again, leaning into it for strength and steadiness. "Tell me," Urho commanded.

Xan shot him a glare, as though he might argue or refuse, but then he simply calmly stated, "I'm unmanned. I explained to you last night."

"You were attacked. You fought back," Urho said, returning to the story he had mostly convinced himself had to be the truth. Except for the part where he knew it wasn't—because he'd smelled Xan's semen last night, too. And he was only now willing to admit it.

Still, he lumbered on with the easier lies, willing Xan to take them up and own them, too. "You have nothing to be ashamed of. You were overpowered and—"

"I went to him, Urho. I go to him regularly." Xan's eyes burned hot. "To get fucked."

Urho's mouth clamped shut, and he squeezed his fists tight. Revulsion swept over him. The image of Xan beneath another man, taking his cock, being owned by him, forced acid to rise in his throat. "No."

"Do you understand now? We aren't lovers. It's nothing like that." Xan shuddered, as if the thought of the man who'd abused him being his lover disgusted even him. "I had a lover once and I know the difference. But that's over. So I make do with what I can find. What I deserve."

"You had a lover?" Urho's hair stood on end, and he ground his teeth together. His heart rate ticked up, a flood of unacceptable feelings roaring within him. In their wake, cold swept through, chilling him head to toe.

Xan didn't take up that topic though; his eyes went distant as though he was somewhere else, not there at all anymore. Urho swallowed so hard that the noise echoed in the small room.

Finally, Xan's eyes met his again, and he asked, his voice raw with defeat, "What else do you want to know?"

"Who is he?"

"Does it matter?"

"What he's doing is unlawful. He should be arrested."

Xan snorted. "According to the law, it's *me* who should be arrested."

"You don't...you can't want..." Urho's head spun, and the room was too warm. He worked open his tie and unbuttoned the collar of his shirt.

"I do!" Xan said, his cheeks flushing. A redness spread up his pale throat. "He never seeks me out. I go to him. Always. I find him, and I beg him. I taunt him and *push* him until he fucks me. It's a game to him. Nothing more."

"What is it to you? Also a game?"

"I wish."

"What does that mean?"

"It means it's a wretched darkness in me that I can't contain or control."

Urho shook his head, still disbelieving. "You don't beg him to leave you injured like this."

"No," Xan agreed. "But I know what I risk when I'm with him. I've known his animosity toward me for a very long time. I know how to provoke him. And I do."

Urho wiped a drop of sweat from his forehead. His insides tumbled wildly. "Help me understand."

Xan huffed. "How?"

"Explain it."

"I just did."

"Again."

"I'm unmanned. I've told you twice. What more is there to say? Get it through your head."

Urho closed his eyes. Had Xan been raped in the past? Is that what had led him to believe this kind of treatment was what he wanted? "When did this start?"

"The association with the man who did this to me? Or my being unmanned?"

"The latter."

Xan picked at the bedspread and shot Urho a wary glance before he finally replied, "It started in school."

"With whom?"

"My lover."

"And this so-called 'lover' forced you?"

"No! Never. He was my friend, and we played together sexually. It was different than what I do now." His voice went very small, and he couldn't meet Urho's eyes. "It was nice."

Urho's temples throbbed. "Who was he?"

Xan laughed, still plucking at the bedspread. "Like I'd tell you. It's not your business. Besides, that's over."

Urho stared at Xan. Suddenly little cues and glances between Jason and Xan took on a new meaning, and Vale's words from the night before came back to him again. A rage he didn't understand gripped his heart. "*Jason* was your 'lover'?"

Xan's mouth crumpled, and tears sprang in his eyes. "No."

"You're lying."

Xan swallowed audibly and then pressed his trembling lips together. "Jason is… He's my best friend. He understands me. That's all you need to know."

"He's aware of this brutal connection of yours?" Urho motioned toward Xan's bruised face, knowing damn well that Jason couldn't possibly know. He'd never let it go on, and besides, Xan had pleaded with him just the night before not to mention it to him.

"No. And if you tell him, it'll only upset him, which won't be good for Vale."

Urho's jaw clenched again. The snotty tone Xan took when he'd mentioned Vale told him all too well that he knew about Urho's former relationship with Vale and feelings for him. In a friend group so small, there was apparently no hiding things like that.

Though, until last night, Xan had done a damn good job of hiding his secrets. His and Jason's. Long-banked anger flared deep inside Urho. Jason had taken Vale away *and* damaged Xan.

"For that and so many reasons, I hope it's clear to you that what I do is my business, and no authorities need to be dragged into this," Xan added imperiously. "The person who would be hurt the most if I were arrested is Caleb, and he's innocent in all this."

"I wouldn't see anything bad happen to you," Urho said, leaning forward to rest his elbows on his knees. The thought of Xan hurt again tore at him, but he tried to remain composed. "That's why I can't let you say these things anymore—to yourself, or to anyone. You must promise me that this—whatever this brutality is—is something you will never seek out again."

Xan's jaw jumped, and he glared sullenly at Urho, but he jerked a nod.

"I have your word?"

"I've already told Caleb I'm done," Xan snapped. "He's the only one who has any right to demand anything of me, anyway."

Urho sighed, relief and irritation coursing through him in equal measures.

"Speaking of Caleb, he'll be wondering what's taking so long," Xan said. "I don't suppose you'd be willing to tell him that you examined me and I'm fine."

"I would not."

Xan grunted, pulling the sweater up over his head. "Then let's get started. The sooner this is over, the better."

The red and purple bruising beneath Xan's sweater was frighteningly impressive. Looming over him, reminded of how small Xan was, Urho listened to his lungs and heart, his own racing pulse making it hard to hear through his stethoscope. Closing his eyes to block out the damage done to Xan's body, he steadied himself against the rage and helpless hurt buffeting about inside him.

When he was calmer, he opened his eyes again and with trembling fingers tested Xan's ribs for breaks. The dips and planes of Xan's muscled stomach and chest were mostly hairless, and his pale skin contrasted against Urho's fingers sharply. Xan hissed in pain as Urho applied some pressure, testing the damage he found. He felt his ribcage carefully, relieved to find that despite the horrific colors blooming all over Xan's torso, his ribs didn't appear broken.

Then he carefully touched the fingerprint bruises around Xan's neck. His heart ached as he asked Xan to turn his head this way and that and then felt carefully for damage. He didn't like to think of what could have gone wrong had a little more force been applied.

Turning to his bag, Urho removed a liniment that promoted healing. Opening the lid of the small glass tub, the scent of arnica and licorice root filled the air. He scooped a dollop onto his fingers and smeared it over the worst of Xan's bruises, finding the skin hot and fragile beneath his hands.

Xan stared up at him, breath coming in shallow pants, and his nipples rose into peaks. Urho's heart thumped, but he cleared his throat, wiped his fingers on a handkerchief from his bag, and then murmured, "I'll need to see below as well. I can smell the onset of some infection there."

Xan's cheeks flushed even brighter, his pulse pounding visibly in his throat. But he unbuttoned his pants and pushed them down to his ankles, revealing a nicely shaped and half-hard alpha cock, as well as a thick bush of black pubic hair.

Urho's balls tingled, and his own cock thickened. He turned away to his bag, pretending to search for something as he ruthlessly tried to squash the rising arousal flooding him. "I'll need you on all fours," he said, but his voice was rough and strange even to his own ears.

When he turned back around, Xan had complied. His ass was up in the air, and his knees and forearms dug into the thin daybed mattress. Urho's breath caught in his throat. He blinked hard. Xan's back was bruised as well, several boot-shaped welts were perilously close to his spine, and even his ass cheek sported a red, round bruise.

But his pale skin glowed in the morning sun, his dark hair was glossy and beautiful, and his ass was gorgeous—juicy and plump, the sort of ass an omega would be proud to possess.

But he's not an omega. He's an alpha, and it's absolutely forbidden.

Urho swallowed hard, adjusting his cock in his pants. Then he knelt to get a better view, pulling the pale globes of Xan's ass cheeks open to examine his anus. He found it like a seashell, hidden at first by a whorl of dark pubic hair. As he brushed the soft hair aside, heat flashed through him like a lightning strike. He gulped, and saliva flooded his mouth.

Xan twisted to gaze back over his shoulder. Urho's cock rose to full hardness as he caught Xan's worried, blue gaze. "Is it all right?" Xan's voice trembled slightly, and Urho wanted to grip him by the hips, tug him close, and kiss the puffy, red flesh in front of him. He wanted to keep that tender hole safe forever.

Urho shook his head hard, trying to gain sanity again.

Xan's eyes went wide with fear. "How bad is it?"

Urho cleared his throat. Blood roared in his ears, dots swirled in his vision, and his cock pulsed pre-come in his pants. He shuddered, gripped by a crazy urge to lean forward and not only kiss, but lick the puffy, damaged flesh. He shook it off with great effort, forcing his focus back on the task at hand. "You're swollen there. There are small tears."

"But it's not ruined?"

"Ruined?" Urho repeated, his brain sending up fireworks, his cock straining. "It's going to be fine." He took a deep breath, still scenting the underlying hint of infection. He should check inside for fissures. After picking up the lube he'd set aside, he slipped on a thin plastic medical glove made from the same material as alpha condoms. "Spread your legs a little wider for me. I need to feel you internally."

Xan moaned pitifully, and his cock twitched and swelled to rise against his stomach. His balls shifted up tight to the base of his shaft, and his thighs trembled.

Urho's own dick throbbed so hard he felt the echo of it behind his eyes. "Wolf-god," he whispered.

"I'm sorry," Xan murmured, redness running up his back and flushing his face. "I can't help it. But I promise, I won't come."

Urho growled, trying to block out the visual that popped into his mind: Xan, back arched, asshole wrapped around Urho's dick as he streaked the daybed beneath him with copious wads of alpha semen.

"He hates it when I come," Xan whispered, and Urho nearly blacked out as rage rocked him. He sat back on his heels, breathing hard, cock jerking within his pants. He sucked in a jagged breath.

Xan spread his legs wider and hid his face on his forearms. His cock hung there before Urho's eyes, long and thick, bigger than any omega's, and growing harder by the second. Urho poured lube onto one gloved finger, closing his eyes and trying to get a hold of himself.

He must be getting sick, spiking a fever, or perhaps going insane, because as he swiped over Xan's abused asshole, he wanted nothing more than to rise up and plunge his own cock into it. He bit down on his lower lip and shivered.

Xan arched his back into the lordosis position, presenting himself like an omega would. Urho's balls drew up hard. His breath pushed through him greedily, a rough susurration he could hear echoing around the room. He pushed his finger in and tried to clear his mind of the screaming, possessive lust that swamped him, but it was no good.

It didn't matter that it was wrong, or that the Holy Book of Wolf condemned these feelings, or that as a doctor he should not be touching a patient when he was aroused in this manner—this confusing and wrong manner. It didn't alter anything.

He closed his eyes, taking slow breaths, and focused on his duties as a doctor. He felt inside, pretending Xan was a patient in the Calitan district, an older beta who'd been taken anally by an alpha, perhaps. It didn't matter, so long as whoever he was touching was not, and never could be Xan Heelies.

But the pungent scent of Xan's arousal filtered into his lungs, uniquely his and beyond delicious, until Urho couldn't pretend any longer. He wanted to press his face closer to Xan's skin, to breathe it in more fully, to wallow in it, and then fuck it.

What the wolf-hell is wrong with you?

When he was sure he could control himself, he pulled his finger free, removed the glove, and sat back on his heels. "You're going to be fine." His voice broke, and he cleared his throat, trying again. "There are no fissures and the small tears will heal. The infection I scented earlier has barely started. I'll leave medicine for you."

He stood slowly, his cock not easing, and turned around to hide the evidence from Xan as best he could. He counted out tablets into a small pillbox for Xan's medication and tried to think around the wild panic ransacking his mind. He'd never wanted to fuck another alpha before. No matter how handsome or pretty, no matter how small or tight-bodied. Not until Xan.

"Can I get dressed now?" Xan asked, his voice small. "Please."

Urho kept his back turned as the rustling behind him indicated Xan's eagerness to cover himself. He tried to think of something—anything—that would make his own arousal dissipate before the moment came when he must turn around to face the boy.

Instead, an image of Xan the day they met, four years younger and pretty as the day was long, bloomed in his mind. Xan had stood in the summer sun in nothing but his swim trunks, his compact body shimmering with sweat and the drying water from a romp in the waves. Urho's breath had caught, and he'd stopped dead in his tracks, pinned in place by the sight of the boy.

Something similar had only ever happened once before in his life, on that beautiful day he'd first seen Riki. Right after seeing his mate and stopping mid-sentence, silenced by Riki's beauty, he'd scented Riki's perfection and imprinted on him in a wild and violent way. They'd been *Érosgápe* from that moment on, forever, and even now.

Obviously, imprinting had not followed that awestruck moment of seeing Xan on the beach; it couldn't have physiologically. But now with the musky, strong scent of Xan's arousal still flooding his nose, Urho's brain and body itched with lust and a demented sense of proprietary ownership—*mine*—that he couldn't explain or begin to understand.

Xan was an alpha. Urho was an alpha. The Holy Book of Wolf and the law of the land made it plain—never could two alphas share a bond of that nature, not without paying a terrible price. Until that very moment, Urho had always believed in the rightness of the strictures.

But now...

"I smell you," Xan whispered, the air between them crackling with energy. "Your arousal is heaven to me."

Urho could barely restrain himself from pulling Xan into his arms and making him submit to the protective, insistent urges rising up inside him. He didn't recognize himself with all these feelings. He didn't know where to put them.

"Stop," Urho gritted out, instead. "That's disgusting."

The air sucked out of the room and Urho struggled to breathe through his shame.

"I'll give Caleb your regards," Xan said from behind him, his voice cold now and threaded with hurt. "And I'll pass on your opinion that I'll be fine. You can leave the pills and your instructions with my doorman. Then I trust you to find your own way out and spare us both any further humiliation and discomfort."

Urho opened his mouth, turning to issue orders for care, to demand another promise that Xan would never again seek out whatever monster had done this to him—or possibly to drag him into a violent kiss—but Xan was gone, the door left barely open and the sound of his footsteps dissolving down the hallway.

Urho's knees gave way, and he dropped to the too-small chair, his heart lurching. He struggled to hold himself back from charging after Xan as shame and bewilderment made him their bitch. He sat there long enough to hear the echo of Xan and Caleb's voices moving through the house toward the upper levels. And then even longer until a beta servant came and suggested that he'd be happy to show Urho out.

Confused, the world a popping, fizzing, spinning, insane place now, Urho handed over the pills, gave instructions for Xan to take them, and then allowed the servant to show him out into this new and nightmarish unknown.

THE SUN WAS setting when Urho parked his car on the curb outside of his home. His stomach still ached, and his hands shook from the ordeal at Xan's house that morning. Because that is what it had been, he told himself firmly—an ordeal and nothing more.

It seemed callous and wrong to be more distraught by the events of the morning than he was over a stillbirth in the Calitan district that afternoon. And yet he couldn't shake the sensation that his very bones still rattled from the minutes he and Xan had shared in the old nursery together.

He'd tried to put it behind him, driving out to the clinic with determination to lose himself in his work. He'd found the staff buzzing with worry over an omega who'd come in well ahead of his expected laboring time. Things had gone downhill from there for both omega and babe.

Urho had been lucky to save the man, and he'd had the sad job of holding the man's hand as he'd sobbed over his lost child. Where the alpha was who'd impregnated him, there was no one to say. Not all omegas were lucky enough to be *Érosgápe*, or even contracted, and not all were contracted to a man who cared for their well-being.

But after the pitiless stillbirth, Urho had tried to unwind by sorting through files in his office. It hadn't worked. Then he'd dealt with a few drop-in patients. They'd gotten his mind off Xan, but only temporarily. He'd finally given up when he realized he was replaying his conversation with Xan over and over, rather than listening attentively to a young omega presenting with continued bleeding following a tough birth the prior week. He'd managed to focus long enough to put the man's mind at ease, prescribe some herbal tablets to help with clotting and healing, and schedule another consult in a few days' time.

After that, he'd driven past Xan's house again, peering up at the windows and ransacking his mind for a reason to ring the bell. He'd eventually forced himself to drive on home, confused by the urgent, restless sensation beneath his skin.

He couldn't sit still. He couldn't think straight. He kept returning to Xan as he'd last seen him, ass up on the daybed, and the swirl
of pubic hair around his swollen asshole—used and yet beautiful.
Somehow beckoning to Urho with his red pucker.

And now, still dazed, he sat squirming in his car, staring up at
his own three-story, faded red brick house. The home he'd shared
with Riki before he'd died.

A bolt of need rocked him hard, and he slid from his car with
his jaw set and a fresh certainty in his step. Riki always brought him
clarity, in death just as he had in life. Just being in his presence
would soothe Urho and bring him to his senses.

He rushed through the front and side gardens, past the rose
bushes his *Érosgápe* had once cherished, and into his house through
the library entrance. He took the back stairs up to the hallway
leading to a suite of rooms he claimed as his own. He let out a long
breath when he successfully avoided any beta servants, especially the
nosy—though incredibly talented—cook, Mako, who would
undoubtedly be worried about the state of dinner if Urho didn't
make his appearance soon.

He passed through into the bedroom. It was cool and dark
there. The space held only a large bed with a light blue canopy that
matched the drapes and a chest of medications that he kept for
emergencies.

Riki had chosen the décor the year before he died, and Urho
still remembered the sweet smile on his beloved's face when he'd
stood in the room, surveying his choices. Urho had agreed with him
when Riki had proclaimed it perfection.

One wall was dominated by a large painting of the ocean—
crashing waves, blue skies, and soft-looking white sand—another of
Riki's choices. The other wall was entirely mirrored, making the
dark room look even bigger and affording them both a beautiful
view of their lovemaking. Riki had been quiet and unassuming for

the most part, but he'd loved to watch himself as Urho had fucked him silly. He'd said it helped him believe that his life was true, that the beautiful happiness they shared was real, and that Urho was sincerely his in every single way.

Urho sat on the bed, undoing his tie and shuffling off his jacket. He stared at the blue curtains floating over the wide windows and then turned to gaze at himself in the mirror. Haggard was the only description for his face at the moment. He'd shaved that morning, but already his afternoon shadow was creeping up, making the dark circles under his eyes look even deeper. He kicked off his shoes and raked his hands through his hair.

"Riki," he whispered, standing up and heading into the small, interior room that used to be Riki's study.

The décor still consisted of wallpaper showing soft, blooming roses that Riki had chosen, and his light, maple desk. But the walls were now lined with the old photos Urho hadn't been able to bear leaving out and about in the house.

Everything from a picture of them on the courthouse steps on the day they signed their contract, to their first trip to the seaside together—Riki's blond hair tousled in the ocean breeze, a pipe clenched in his white teeth, and his green eyes glinting with joy. Next to him, a younger version of Urho gazed at the camera, too, with pure pleasure, not a glimmer of sorrow yet in his dark eyes or in the creases of his smile.

Those had been the days when he'd believed he and Riki would grow old together and raise a passel of young, brown babies who'd look like him in skin tone but be like their pater in temperament— gentle, good, thoughtful, and kind. All the things Urho now aspired to be, when, back then he'd simply allowed Riki to be all those things for him.

Above the mantel of the fireplace where no fire had burned since the day of Riki's death, there was a large, painted portrait of

Riki, standing proud and wearing a shy grin. His hand rested on the bulge where their baby grew.

Urho had insisted on the portrait, one of the few things he ever made Riki do against his will, because he'd wanted to always remember the way Riki's cheeks had glowed and his own heart had stuttered at the sheer beauty of his *Érosgápe* carrying his child.

He stared up at it now, old roaring, conflicted emotions battering inside him. He knelt on the floor across from the desk where a lock of Riki's hair sat beneath a glass dome. It was the only bit of him that resided here in the house now. His young body had been retired to the Chase lot in the Zimmermon graveyard on the edge of town. Six feet down he rested, along with their child.

Yes, Urho had buried them together. The small, tiny babe lay folded into Riki's loving arms eternally. Just the way Riki would have wanted it, had he lived to hear their child's pitiful first and only wail.

He gulped against the salty tears that started now. He hadn't cried in this room in years, and yet for some reason, today he needed Riki more than he had in a long time. *Needed* him, bone deep. Wanted his soothing fingers in his hair, and his soft voice telling him that everything was all right. He craved his calm acceptance of whatever life brought.

And he desperately wanted to hear him say, "I love you, just as you are, even if you want to fuck Xan Heelies, even if you want to love him, and even if you want him as your own. Because you're perfect, Urho. Wolf-god's gift to me, and there's nothing you could want that I wouldn't want you to have."

He wiped the heel of his hand over his eyes and shook his head. "Really, Riki?" he asked the air. "Could you forgive me this strange lust? These wolf-damned desires?"

He stared up at the portrait of his omega, his beautiful, shyly smiling man, and lowered his head. Exhaustion swamped him, and he sat on his ass, burying his face in his forearms and riding out the waves of revulsion and self-loathing, the weird jittery want, and the anxiety he just couldn't shake for Xan's well-being. And Caleb's, too, as an extension of Xan.

Eventually, he rose on shaky legs and lit several sticks of incense, chanting the prayer for lost *Érosgápe* with a trembling voice, and then turned back to his bedroom. He rang down to let Mako know that he wouldn't be taking dinner, helped himself to a calming tablet, and fell into restless tossing and turning beneath his blue covers.

The sun rose, and he hadn't slept a wink.

CHAPTER FIVE

"SO YOU'RE SURE he'll keep our secret?" Caleb asked out of the blue, as though they'd been talking about Urho yet again, when, in fact, Xan had been trying to retire that subject once and for all since the mortifying examination two mornings prior.

"Like I've said, he'll keep my secret. He still knows nothing about yours." Xan gazed into the mirror over the ornate vanity in his bedroom, dabbing the stage makeup against his cheek. "Let's forget it ever happened."

Caleb made a noncommittal sound and opened the windows to the cold, foggy morning outside. The air smelled like wet pavement and the sounds of the morning commute drifted in. "Do you truly have to go?"

"You know I do."

Xan would have preferred to stay home, but his father had summoned him to the office. "Flu or no flu," Doxan Heelies had barked over the phone, and that, unfortunately, was that.

And it would *definitely* be unfortunate when he arrived obviously beaten and not at all sick. He hoped the bruises underneath the makeup would give him a pallor that might be mistaken for illness, and perhaps he could fake a convincing cough. Though just breathing hurt his bruised ribs.

In the mirror, Caleb watched him carefully, his eyes knowing in a way that Xan usually found calming. But this week, with so many humiliating incidents stacking on top of each other, that gaze crawled beneath his skin.

"What?" he demanded, patting more makeup over the lumpy bruise on his cheekbone. There was no way to hide the distortion even if he managed to cover up the livid colors.

"Dr. Chase has handled heats for widowed and uncontracted omegas, hasn't he?"

"Yes. And he used to handle Vale's before Jason."

"Right, I recall you telling me about that." Caleb pushed his soft, chin-length hair behind his ear. "But he handles others too, doesn't he? Men he doesn't know quite so well? I believe I've heard Vale and Jason talking to him about the intense heats of his gardener's brother? The young man he helps regularly?"

Xan put the makeup down, his cheek half-covered, so that the still exposed purple-red glared even more brightly against the cover-up. He turned to face Caleb, watching him closely. Envy burned in him over the gardener's brother who had the privilege of having Urho service his needs.

Caleb lifted a brow. "Well?"

"He has, yes."

Caleb's voice leapt. "He's discreet. He knows about you. Perhaps we could tell him that I have interminable heat and—"

"No." There were any number of reasons he didn't want to go down that path, but the biggest was his concern for Caleb's social standing and reputation. A diagnosis of interminable heat would be a death knell in society. It didn't matter what name was used—nymphomania, interminable heat—everyone knew it meant your omega was a slut who couldn't get enough, and the diagnosis was tantamount to social ridicule and ruin for everyone involved.

Besides, what would his father say if he found out? Never mind that it wasn't even *true*!

Caleb tapped his lower lip thoughtfully. "We have a few months to come up with another solution but let the record show that I wouldn't be opposed to this one."

Xan frowned, a spark of frustration threatening to burst into flames. "I have a connection, someone with access to medication that might provide me with the necessary stamina to make it through this time." That this connection was again Urho was a thorn in his side he didn't share.

Caleb's expression softened, and he approached Xan, taking the makeup from him and applying it to Xan's cheek with the most tender of touches. "You can't be something you aren't, darling. And, truth be told, I wouldn't want you to be."

"I *am* an alpha," Xan said, closing his eyes as Caleb worked on his face, finishing with the gooey paste makeup and then adding some powder on top that tickled his nose.

"Physically, perhaps, but in your heart, you're an omega, and that's part of what makes us such a beautiful match." Xan opened his eyes to Caleb's sharp smile and gentle eyes. "We're a good family, darling, never doubt that. But heats are a problem and neither of us wants a repeat of last time."

Xan shuddered. "No." He rose and pulled Caleb close, tucking his face against Caleb's long neck, holding him tightly. "I'm sorry."

Caleb stroked his back. "It was our first together. We didn't know how it would go. We both expected my heat pheromones to produce a stronger response in you, the way the hormones produce such a strong need in me. Now we understand the way it will be and can plan ahead. But it's time to start planning, alpha mine. We can't leave it for the last minute."

Xan kissed Caleb's cheek. "You're right of course. I'll find out more about the stamina medication today."

Caleb's forehead creased into a frown, but he didn't say more while Xan finished dressing. He even helped with his green and gold plaid bowtie and then kissed his mouth with a smack. "You can do this. Whatever he throws at you, whatever words your father says, know that you have me here at home and I believe in you."

"You're too good to me."

"No better than you are to me."

Xan huffed. That was a lie, but he appreciated that Caleb seemed to believe it, anyway.

His family's corporate offices on the uppermost side of Blue Vein took up the top four floors of the newest tower built there. The amenities were marvelous, with a full kitchen, executive washrooms, and an elevator to take instead of steps, but Xan loathed the place all the same. It was, again and again, the site of some of his most humiliating moments outside of Wilbet Monhundy's grasp.

The hush that fell over the main office floor as he marched toward his father's conference room proved that the makeup hadn't done a sufficient job of hiding the latest evidence of his dark addiction. His stomach burned anxiously as whispers reached his ears, far too blurred by the rustle of papers and clack of typewriters to decipher, but the tone was undeniable: Xan was in trouble again.

Just as he was about to turn the corner toward the door of the conference room, he was grabbed and yanked into his older, beta brother Ray's office instead.

"There you are," Ray said, his sand-colored hair flopping over his broad forehead and his wide, hazel eyes peering anxiously into Xan's own. "I've been waiting for you."

"Father said—"

"Father's left you to me this time," Ray interrupted gently, his thick, golden eyebrows winnowing down in concern. His suit was pressed, but he went without a tie, preferring a more casual, open-throated look. "And thank wolf-god for that. He was ready to..." Ray closed his eyes and took a slow breath.

"Ready to what?"

Ray's expression gentled as he looked down into Xan's face. "It doesn't matter. I convinced him to let me deal with you. He's in with the Monhundys discussing their latest demands. Which, no thanks to you, from what I gather anyway, aren't exactly allowing for much in our favor."

Xan swallowed dryly. "The Monhundys are here?"

"Yes, the florid father and the prickly pater." He rolled his eyes. "At least the brutish brat has stayed home to deal with his omega. The poor thing came home sick after visiting his pater with the flu apparently, which is rough going this year." Ray's eyes turned thoughtful. "My doctor friend, Lils, says it will be an epidemic this season, and a deadly one at that."

"Oh." Xan's stomach churned.

"Regardless, Wilbet Monhundy's omega is down with it."

"That's…terrible." Yet sweet relief flowed through him. He couldn't have borne the humiliation of seeing Monhundy's handsome, knowing face in the office while he still wore the bruises from their last encounter. He wished Kerry good health, of course, but he couldn't help but be glad that the young man was too ill for Monhundy to leave him alone. Just more evidence of Xan's own depravity as a human being, he supposed.

Ray tugged him deeper into the office, closer to the broad windows that reflected the sun's rays as they bounced off the windows of the other tall buildings going up all around them. He touched Xan's chin. "Wolf-god, your face," he murmured, shaking his head. "Baby brother, what are we going to do with you?"

"It's nothing. A bar brawl."

Ray's expression showed how little he believed him, though he only said, "You and these bar brawls. They have to stop." He looked so like their pater in that moment, so affectionate and loving that Xan's heart ached.

But his pater's presence had been missing from Xan's life for the last few months, ever since Father declared Pater had spoiled Xan and made him soft. Supposedly, being denied Pater's support now was meant to toughen him up. Though Xan was pretty sure it was simply a punishment to them both, really.

Even if Ray wasn't Pater, he *was* safe, and Xan relaxed as Ray touched Xan's chin again. His brotherly concern dampened the sting of his demands. "This stops. Do you understand? It has to end. Now."

"I've already promised Caleb—"

"As you have a half dozen times before. And, as you've promised me, too, in the past. Don't you remember? Last year, before you contracted with Caleb, when the rumors were swirling about you and some alpha getting up to—"

"Those rumors were completely untrue!"

And they had been.

Xan had already been getting his dark fix from Monhundy for several months when the rumors began about him and one incredibly handsome alpha actor named Gil Regelly. Mr. Regelly starred in many plays at the city theater, and it was well known that he went without an omega by choice. Cross rumors swirled regularly about his preference for betas as sexual partners—and even, it was whispered with the eagerness of scandal, sometimes other alphas.

Xan had been intrigued by the rumors, and when the opportunity arose to meet him, he hadn't hesitated. Certainly if Mr. Regelly had wanted more than the few words they'd exchanged under the supervision of Jason's pater, Miner Hoff, then Xan would have let him take it in a heartbeat. But Mr. Regelly hadn't seemed interested.

Xan went on. "I met Mr. Regelly one time, and one time only, at the Sabel-Hoff house. I was never alone with him for even a minute. Jason's pater was with us the entire evening."

Because Mr. Regelly was Miner's friend, and he'd arranged the meeting. Xan had sensed the whole thing was a set up. Jason's pater knew more than he should about a lot of things, but he was very good at keepings secrets, so Xan didn't worry overly much about that.

"I know. So you explained at the time," Ray's brows lowered again. "But there's something going on, and it's not barroom brawls. The Monhundys even alluded to the rumors about you yesterday when setting up this appointment, and, of course, that set Father off."

Xan's pulse galloped. "He thinks everything that goes wrong for the company is my fault."

"No, just the things that go wrong because people are whispering about your sexual proclivities and whether or not you truly are unmanned."

Xan coughed, trying to school his face to something akin to offense, but his heart jump-kicked and he felt faint. Ray had never actually said the words out loud before. He'd hinted at it in the past—everyone in the family had. But no one had just said it all bold and bald like that. Xan didn't know where to look.

"Not that I give one damn about what sort of cock you like, baby brother, because, believe it or not, I really don't." Ray's voice gentled, but Xan couldn't look at him. He stared out the window at the building next to them, at the way the blue sky reflected in the windows.

Ray went on, "As a beta, these Holy Book of Wolf protocols and strictures about sex and reproduction seem all too clearly about keeping control of the breeding stock, so to speak. Frankly, if you were any other man, I'd say love who you love and enjoy what you like, and we'd put this aside." He placed his hands on Xan's shoulders, their weight warm and firm. "But you're Xan Heelies, and that means you're the alpha son of our father, the heir to his business, and the man people need to believe is capable of being more than a pretty figurehead here."

Xan opened his mouth, but only a strangled noise came out. He closed it again.

"Our clients and the company's employees need to see you as mature enough to take over when Father eventually leaves the helm. But parading around looking like you've been worked over with a meat tenderizer is no way to do that. Neither is allowing rumors to bloom about whether or not you bend over for alpha dick. Or any dick for that matter."

Xan jerked his gaze back to Ray and croaked out, "I didn't want to come in! I wanted to stay home. But Father—"

"No, Xan. This isn't about Father." Ray squeezed Xan's shoulders. "This is about what we need to do now. The gossip mill is working overtime and we have to get this under control. Bringing you in today was clearly a bad idea, but it's too late to do anything about that now. You've been seen, and we'll have to contain this damage as well."

He turned away, heading over to his paper-stacked desk. The place on Xan's shoulders where Ray's warm hands had been went cold, and he shivered as he forced himself to turn away from the window.

Ray motioned toward the chair opposite, and they both sat. Xan's heart clacked hard like a steam engine on the line, making him both nauseous and sweaty. He wanted to undo his bow tie to give himself more room to breathe, but he didn't want to appear so undone in front of Ray. He hadn't denied anything, but he hadn't admitted to anything either. Maybe there was still a way to salvage this.

"So what's the plan?" he finally managed to ask. "How do we spin this?"

"You're being sent to Virona," Ray said with a sigh. He leaned across his desk, steepling his fingers, slightly knocking askew a framed photo of their lost brother, Jordan, who'd died as a child. Despite the kindness in Ray's eyes, his voice brooked no argument.

"Your house there is being prepared. The one pater left to you in a trust. It was his family home, if you remember? The Lofton Estate. It's large. Too big for just you and Caleb. I suggest filling it with children as quickly as possible, and, in the meantime, host influential guests."

"Virona," Xan said, his pulse rushing in his ears so that he wasn't sure he'd heard properly.

"By the sea, yes. Three hours from here by rail. Not exiled, but definitely distanced. Perhaps it'll give you time to think about your association with whoever did that to your face." Ray winced. "As well as reconsidering your relationship with whoever it is that you're screwing. I can only pray they aren't one and the same." He wiped a hand over his mouth, heaviness and sorrow evident in the drag of his features.

Xan cast around for the right words to say to fix this, but he came up empty. "What will I do in Virona?"

"Direct the opening of a satellite office," Ray said. He tapped a file folder on his desk. "I'll send weekly instructions. You'll carry them out. Handle problems that come up on your own to the best of your ability. Most of all, Xan, you will prove yourself." Ray leaned back in his chair. "This is a good opportunity for a fresh start. The rumors won't have made it to Virona yet, and, so long as you don't find a new associate there with which to stir things up, you can clear the air, gain some traction in the business, and redeem yourself in Father's eyes."

"And what about your eyes?"

Ray leaned forward across his desk, his brows rising earnestly. "I love you always, baby brother. Don't you know that? I've spoiled you as much as Pater has, perhaps more. So it hurts to send you away, especially when I can see in these bruises how very much you might need me right now. But Father believes this is the best compromise. He was in favor of a much more drastic step. But

Pater and I made him see reason."

A more drastic step than sending him away? Xan's mind ran wild with possibilities of what that could be and kept coming back to the same one again and again. "But I'm the only alpha. The only one of us who can inherit. By law."

Ray nodded. "True. In this branch of the family. If you're proven to be unfit to inherit, though, Father can legally name another alpha relative as heir."

Xan squeezed his fists. The flash of a smarmy smile and floppy brown hair over gray eyes came to mind.

"Our cousin Janus? Seriously?" Xan snarled. "Father would entrust that smug, obsequious, yes man with the company?"

"Better a yes man, brother, than a bomb about to explode."

Xan swallowed hard. "Tell me what Father said, what you're trying to save me from hearing."

Ray sighed. "All right. I suppose you should know. Maybe it will get through to you when nothing else has. Father said he'd rather leave the company and fortune to Janus, with me in charge of operations, per the law of succession by declaring you unmanned publicly, than to allow his legacy to be tarnished."

"By me?"

"By your actions."

Xan's chin wobbled, and tears stung his eyes. He hated the disappointment in Ray's voice, and all because Xan was born wrong. Why couldn't their situations have been reversed? Xan could have been a beta happily—well, more happily than he was an alpha—and Ray, as an alpha, would have done their father proud.

"Don't look so sad," Ray said, his hazel eyes going soft. "The house in Virona is beautiful. You probably don't remember it, since we haven't been there since you were a baby, but you and your omega won't be disappointed. You can decorate it as you see fit, too. I'll make sure you have a large expense account for the purpose.

I know you'll love that."

"Caleb has his opinions about furnishings now."

"Of course, he does," Ray said fondly. He and Caleb got along famously at family dinners. "Then divide up the rooms. Make a game of it." Ray smiled and leaned forward across his desk again. "We'll miss you at the Autumn Nights feasts, but—"

"But Father wouldn't have let me attend, anyway. He's keeping Pater from me."

"*But* this can be a fresh start for you. Have your own feasts, invite your friends, and entertain clients. Show Father that you're your own man in ways that don't humiliate him."

Xan's throat constricted, but he nodded. "Caleb enjoys throwing parties."

"Yes, once the house is aired out, you can entertain. Father will like that. Especially if you can include that Sabel boy. Father's still hoping Yule Sabel will cut him a good deal on new delivery trucks. We plan to provide three-day delivery to our clients across the country by year end."

Xan's mind whirled at all the change that had just been thrown at him, but he managed to murmur, "That's good news."

"Buck up. You're not being sent to the wilderness. Virona is a lovely town with many fashionable restaurants and stores. You'll enjoy it there. Caleb will as well. He likes to make art of some kind, doesn't he? There are a couple of rooms in the detached wing that would work perfectly for a studio. If I recall, Pater enjoyed the morning light there, reading with his tea. And, of course, the shore is beautiful, even in winter. I'm certain you'll find the atmosphere bracing. And healing, I hope."

"I don't think what's wrong with me is something that can ever heal."

Ray's sympathy hurt almost as much as his disappointment. "I know, baby brother. Believe me, I understand you inside out and I have since you were quite small. If I could change the world around us so that you wouldn't suffer, I would. But all I can do is help protect you. Even if it's from yourself."

Ray rose from the desk and came around, pulling Xan up to hold him in a loose hug. "Now go home and tell your omega what's happening. There'll be a lot to plan in the next few days. You're expected in Virona by week's end."

CHAPTER SIX

URHO WAITED IN his small, two-door car by the curb, watching the house on Oak Avenue until Jason stepped through the gate. Jason straightened his coat as he headed toward where his own four-door was parked out front.

Urho knew enough of Jason's schedule. He had only a few seconds to catch him before Jason would drive to the research labs on Phinea Street where he spent his mornings doing work on a pet project there before he was forced to head into the offices of his father's automobile manufacturing business for his day job.

Urho waited until Jason was opening his car door, then he pulled alongside him, and slammed the gearshift into park. He jumped from his car and grabbed Jason's lapels, barely registering Jason's shocked expression before shoving him up against the side of the car.

Crying out, Jason's fists came up, ready to defend himself. Their eyes locked and Jason's swam with questions. Urho held him hard against the side of the car until Jason jerked free, resettled his coat, and shouted, "Wolf-god, Urho! What's wrong with you?"

Urho gripped Jason's lapels again and got up into his face. Two sleepless nights had left him feeling wild, and if the reflection in the car window was anything to go by, he looked even wilder. "You fucked him!"

Jason's expression crashed through pissed to confused and back again. "Who? Vale? What are you talking about?"

"You fucked Xan."

Jason's face blanched, and he pushed Urho away hard, darting glances around the empty sidewalk. He peeked at the neighbor's house whose gate they now stood in front of and lifted his hand, offering a smile and a reassuring, "Good morning, Mr. Ragnak. Everything's fine here. A friendly tussle, but we're all right."

Urho didn't turn around to see what the neighbor made of Jason's niceties and his own explosive words and instead got up in Jason's face again. "You fucked him." He shook him hard with each word out of his mouth. "And you *fucked him up*."

"Will you keep your voice down?" Jason pushed Urho back, surprisingly strong for his sapling build. He smoothed his hands over his new, fashionable coat—no doubt picked out by Vale—and took a slow breath. "If you give me a chance, we can talk about this. Reasonably. But you have to calm down, Urho. You look like a maniac."

"You ruined him."

Jason's eyes sparked. "Xan isn't ruined. But if you don't shut up, he might be." Jason reached out reassuringly, but Urho ducked his touch. His stomach lurched and his eyes felt gritty with lack of sleep.

"You shouldn't be driving," Jason said. "You're a disaster right now. I don't know what's going on with you, but if you'll calm down, you can come back to the house with me and talk this over…" He trailed off, his gaze swerving back toward the cozy home he shared with Vale. "No, Vale doesn't need to see you like this. He'll get upset and it won't be good for him or the baby."

Urho clenched his jaw, holding back from taking a swing at Jason, furious that he could be so calm, so smooth. Not at all the gangly baby alpha he'd been four years ago—back when he'd apparently been fucking *Xan*, as his *lover*, and then gone on to ruin Vale's life, too, by imprinting on him. Who gave a good wolf-god damn how happy they were together now? It was clear Jason was a curse.

"Urho," Jason said softly. "You're exhausted. Let me drive you home."

"No."

"Fine. We can look for a quiet place to talk. This is so unlike you. You're worrying me."

Urho swallowed hard.

It was true he wasn't acting right. Something had happened to him when he'd touched Xan's body, when he'd slipped his fingers past Xan's puffy, swollen anus and held his hips steady so he wouldn't flinch. Something had come unhinged. He didn't understand, and he didn't think talking to Jason about it was going to fix it at all, but as he rubbed his tired eyes he had to concede that punching him probably wouldn't help either. What had he been thinking coming here?

"C'mon," Jason said kindly, urging him into the passenger side of Urho's own car. "Where are your keys? I'll drive."

Urho indicated they were still in the ignition and let Jason take over. Then he leaned back, hand over his face, trying to gain some measure of sanity as Jason buckled in behind the wheel and guided them out onto the road.

After a few minutes of stressful quiet, Jason said, "Here. Vale likes this park. He brings me here to watch the ducks with their ducklings in the spring."

"Entreo Park," Urho said, removing his hand from his face to confirm. "He used to bring me here, too."

Jason huffed softly but made no other remark about Urho daring to bring up his former entanglement with Jason's *Érosgápe*, despite the obvious provocation of it. "The ducks have probably gone south for the winter, but we can still have a walk around the pond."

Urho's footsteps felt wobbly and strange, as though he'd

downed a bottle and a half of liquor. His mouth was dry, and his hands shook. What devil from wolf's own hell had come to possess him? Or was Riki punishing him now for the sins of his unwanted thoughts and feelings? Had that moment in the study been only wishful thinking, putting words in his omega's mouth? And now his beloved's ghost haunted him from the grave?

"Talk to me," Jason said finally, guiding Urho to a low wooden bench by the side of the muddy, winter-brown pond. The trees around them released colorful leaves and etched dark lines into the expansive gray sky. Birds going south cried out every few seconds. "What's going on with you?"

"I don't know." Urho's voice was gruff, like he'd gargled glass. "I don't recognize myself."

"I barely recognize you either, so I understand that." Jason cleared his throat. "I hate to ask given your line of questioning, but is Xan all right?"

"He's fucked up." Urho bit the words out. "He's demented."

"Is he?" Jason asked with a sympathy that Urho wanted to wrap around himself and hide in, like a soft blanket. "I don't think he is. I think he's wonderful."

Urho swallowed hard but said nothing.

"Did he…try something with you?"

"No!" Urho's insides roared to life, cool rage and hot lust colliding. Xan hadn't tried anything with him at all! And what was wrong with him that he'd wanted Xan to? If Xan had made a move toward him that morning after his examination, if he'd acted instead of remarking on Urho's lust, what could have happened between them?

Anything. Anything at all!

"All right," Jason said. "So what's going on?"

He choked on his reply. Xan was his patient, wasn't he? He'd treated him and prescribed him medication, touched him as a doctor—though his resulting arousal hadn't been doctorly *at all*—and, even if Xan wasn't his patient, guaranteeing him privacy, he'd asked Urho outright not to tell Jason anything. "I can't say."

"I see," Jason said again, oozing calm concern that no longer seemed comforting and instead made Urho want to clock him. "But Xan's safe?"

Urho gritted his teeth. "How the fuck would I know? I'm not his keeper. Though he needs one."

Jason held up his hands in surrender. "Got it. Well, it doesn't seem like you plan to tell me much, even though you're the one who came to my house and roughed me up."

Urho grunted. He shook his head, not knowing where to even begin. "You fucked him."

"Right. So, I guess you have questions for me about that?" Jason asked, bracing his forearms on his knees and letting his blond hair cascade over his forehead and nearly into his eyes. His next words held that fond softness again, and Urho's heart ached. This must be why Vale loved this pup of an alpha so dearly. "Let me help you, all right? Talk with me."

"He's courting a world of trouble." And the next bit was delicate to address, but he said it anyway. "He'll drag Caleb down with him."

Jason frowned. "So, he's begun something with another alpha? And I don't suppose you're going to tell me how you know about it?"

Urho stood, raking his hands through his hair. He paced by the side of the pond, his legs aching with the need to move. "You admit that you know what he's done, what he still does?" He whirled on Jason, pointing a finger at his face. "You admit that you fucked him, and that you were lovers?"

Jason nodded. "I do."

"Did you abuse him too?"

"What in wolf's own hell, Urho? Abuse him? What we did was—look, I love Xan."

"You love him?" Urho spit out, disgusted.

"Not like that. I love him like how Vale loves you."

Urho wiped his hands over his face, pacing back and forth again. His legs trembled. "Why did you do it?" Facing Jason again, Urho made a lewd motion with his hand.

"Have sex with him?"

"Yes! Was it alpha expression? Did he provoke you and you couldn't control yourself?"

"No." Jason shifted uncomfortably, his cheeks going a darker pink. "I found him attractive. He's handsome and has a good body. What we did was fun. We played sexual games together for several years and pretended it was practice for when we had our omegas." Jason smiled slightly. "We were friends, and it grew naturally from there. I never felt violent toward him and I never forced him. I wouldn't have wanted to."

Urho snorted, his heart racing. Was that possible? Sex between alphas was condemned, but Jason spoke of it like it was the same as playing with betas for pleasure, or two omegas finding tenderness at Mont Juror before they discover the true joy of being with their intended alpha. He made it sound natural.

"That's all it was for me," Jason said gently. The cool winter breeze brightened his eyes and ruffled his hair. "But, eventually, for Xan it became more. I recognized that too late to keep from hurting him." He sighed. "I love him as a friend, as my dearest friend, and it killed me to hurt him. Luckily, Vale has grown to love him, too. And, yes, Vale knows everything. So you don't need to worry about surprising or wounding him with this information. He took it in stride, much more than I ever imagined possible. But then Vale's perfect, so I shouldn't have been surprised."

"Perfect? The man barely stirs himself to dust the house more than once a year and lazes about writing poetry while you do all the hard work."

Jason smiled fondly. "He's perfect to me."

Urho rolled his eyes. His armpits were sweaty, and he scented his own rankness rising up. Had he even showered that morning? Or the morning before? "He loved you? Romantically? Xan, I mean."

"Yes." Jason winced. "I hoped once he found an omega that…" He shook his head. "But I don't think that's what's happened. Though I know he cares deeply for Caleb."

"He's unmanned," Urho whispered.

"He is," Jason agreed. "I think he always will be."

"He'll destroy himself and his omega, too, if he doesn't stop what he's doing."

"And what, exactly, is he doing? And with whom?" Jason sat straighter, pushing the hair off his forehead, and pinning Urho with hard eyes. "Did you see him with someone? Is that what this is about?"

Urho wiped a hand over his mouth, words wanting to vomit up out of him. But could he tell Jason the truth, or any measure of it, without violating his oaths as a doctor? "I saw him after. I smelled it on him."

"Oh."

Then, unable to hold back, he burst out with, "He isn't safe."

Jason rose to his feet, his normally pink cheeks paling. "Is he hurt? Do I need to go to him?"

Urho shook his head. "He asked me not to tell you. Because of Vale. And the baby."

"No. Of course not. He wouldn't want Vale to worry." Jason bit his lower lip, staring at the gray-brown water of the pond in front of them. "I need to go to him, anyway. Make him confess to me what he's doing and whom he's seeing. It's dangerous, you say?

This relationship?"

"Of course, it's dangerous!" Urho glared at Jason. "He could go to prison!"

Jason swallowed hard. "He's not foolish enough to get caught."

"Isn't he?" Urho motioned at his own chest. "Hasn't he already been caught? By me?"

Jason sucked in a breath, blue eyes flashing. "You're going to turn him in?"

"Don't be an asshole."

Jason huffed. "I'm not the one who grabbed you off the street, roughed you up against the car, and then proceeded to be the most dramatic asshole ever in the entire history of assholes, all right?"

Urho nodded once. He couldn't argue with that, as much as he wanted to, so he just slumped back down on the bench. "He's fine right now. You don't need to rush to his side." He hoped.

Jason sat again and turned to him, a thoughtful crease between his brows. "I understand that acting on his desire for other alphas is a potential problem for Xan, and for Caleb, of course. But you're distraught. You've never particularly liked Xan, as far as I can tell. So why do you care so much? I mean, aside from common human decency and all that."

Urho didn't know how to answer. Why did he care? He'd been torturing himself with that very question for the last two days. He barely knew Xan. They were nothing more than acquaintances, fellows of the same cohort. They'd never shared an intimate minute in their lives. Not until the moment on the sidewalk when Xan, all broken eggshells and messy insides, had spilled out his confession, and not until Urho had slipped his finger inside the man and felt his trembling desire all around him, in the very air he breathed.

"I don't know," he repeated.

Jason stared at him solemnly. "I see."

Urho leaned forward, elbows on knees, and covered his face.

His coat stretched tightly across his back, squeezing him. As the immensity of what he didn't want to admit grew, he felt like he might burst the seams.

"Let me take you home. You need a good breakfast," Jason said, rising and putting his hand out to help Urho stand on his still-quivering legs. "And a long restful nap."

Urho followed Jason from the park like a duckling trailing his mother back to their nest. He didn't know the last time he'd let himself be led, or allowed another alpha, especially, to treat him so gently, but he didn't have the energy to fight it.

Jason drove them to Urho's house, walked him in and asked Mako, the cook, to bring him some lunch, and then saw him onto the library sofa. He waited until the food was delivered, talking about pleasant, light things, like the books in the library he'd like to borrow. As Urho ate, he sipped a mug of tea and avoided any further mention of the events of the morning or the man Urho was losing his mind over.

Then Jason called for a cab, gathered his coat again, and stood over Urho on the sofa. Urho's belly full of soup and his exhaustion gave over to sleepiness.

Jason said, "You should rest now. And, if you can manage it, don't worry any more about Xan. I'll talk with him and Caleb tomorrow. Together, Caleb and I will make sure he stays safe."

Urho doubted that greatly, but he didn't argue.

"As for your feelings, Urho?" Jason added with a knowing sigh. "If you can't accept them, they'll eat you alive."

He turned away and let himself out, leaving Urho examining the library ceiling until he finally slipped into a fretful sleep.

CHAPTER SEVEN

XAN STOOD OUTSIDE the door to Urho's impressive home, his knees trembling and a sick temptation swelling inside him to leave without knocking and instead head several streets over to Monhundy's house for another taste of just how monstrous he could truly be.

Swallowing hard, he stiffened his resolve and lifted the brass knocker twice. As the boom echoed in the large house, he wondered why a man as well-to-do as Urho didn't have a doorbell. Probably Urho considered them too new-fangled, as old-fashioned and strict as he was.

A tall, middle-aged beta servant asked his name and led him to a room near the end of the entry hall, adjacent to a set of stairs rising to the second floor. "Make yourself comfortable. I'll let Dr. Chase know you're here," the beta said, a small smile on his lips.

Xan nodded and turned to the room at large, surprised to see that he'd been taken to the library. Larger than his reception room at home, all four walls were lined with books, spines in every color from ruby red to grass green facing out in ridges that rose to the ceiling.

In the middle of the room, across from a banked fire, sat a sofa and two leather chairs with a long, low table between them. Xan stood behind one of the chairs, his hands on the high back for stability, and waited for the sound of Urho's footsteps.

There was no warning, though, before the door opened and Urho stepped inside on socked feet. His pants were wrinkled, and his shirt was, too. His hair stuck up in some places as though he'd slept on it and hadn't tidied the coarse salt-and-pepper curls yet. Xan had never seen the usually dapper, uptight Urho looking so disheveled.

"You're here," Urho said, and his voice sounded like he had taken up smoking in the time since they'd last seen each other. "Are you all right? Have your injuries worsened?"

Xan swallowed again, his throat tight. "I'm feeling better, actually. Thank you for the medicine and your help the other day. I know it must have seemed as though I didn't want it."

Urho stared, like he couldn't believe Xan stood in his library. Finally, shaking himself, he gestured toward the furniture. "Have a seat. Wherever you like."

Xan walked around to sit in the leather chair, leaning back and trying to still the jumpiness of his hands and legs.

Urho sat on the sofa across from him and ran fingers through his hair. His red-rimmed eyes scanned around the room. "Jennor will bring some tea."

Xan nodded, and the door opened on the same beta servant carrying a ceramic tea set and a plate of cookies on a big tray. He put it down in front of Xan and Urho and then, when Urho nodded, left the room without a word.

"Help yourself," Urho said, gesturing to the cookies before pouring the tea into small, red teacups. "Take as many you want. You look as though you've lost weight since I saw you."

Xan wondered at that. It was true he hadn't been eating well; between physical pain and his shame, he'd been pushing his food around for the last few days. Still, he couldn't have lost enough weight for someone to really notice. His brother Ray hadn't said anything, and neither had Caleb. Did Urho see him so very clearly?

"I'm fine," he said, putting several of the buttery cookies on a plate and accepting the tea Urho passed to him. "You look..." He gestured at Urho and left the words unsaid.

Urho glanced down at his clothes and huffed a strange laugh. "Forgive my slovenly appearance. I was napping earlier and—well, let's just say it's been an odd couple of days."

"Rough times at the clinic?" Xan asked.

"There was a stillbirth, yes."

"I'm sorry. That must be difficult."

"Moreso for the omega than for me, but, yes, it does always bring back hard memories." He glanced toward the only painting in the room, a portrait of a beautiful, blond, smiling man, wearing a red shirt and black pants. The man held up a scroll emblazoned with a combined family crest—presumably the Chase family and whatever Urho's omega's family name had been.

"He was handsome," Xan offered. A burning sensation started in his gut, but he didn't want to examine it too closely. Being jealous did no one any good. And besides, the man was *dead*. And had died quite young from what Xan understood. He hadn't lived long enough to have a life to be envied even if he'd been in Urho's bed.

"He was perfect," Urho said in a hushed tone, as though even the memory of his beloved was too holy to speak of aloud.

"This is a big library," Xan said, changing the subject, but not daring to broach the one he actually came to address. "Mostly science books, I guess?"

"Quite a few. But I have some literature in my collection, too."

"I'm more of a comics and nickel-novel type, myself."

Urho's lips quirked in the first evidence of a smile he'd shown since he'd first come in. "I have some of those as well." He rose and walked over to a bookcase near the door, ran his finger along the spines, and then came away with a blue book as thick as two finger-widths. "Here, this one is from before your time, I'd bet. But you might enjoy it."

Xan took the book as Urho returned to his seat on the sofa. He flipped it open and colorful images leapt forth, along with the usual comic cells and speech bubbles. He glanced back at the cover: *Cervantes and Snail, a complete collection.* "I've heard of this, but you're right, I've never read it."

"Take it with you. It was a favorite of Riki's, but it'll just molder here. You should enjoy it."

Xan licked his lips, a breathless, strange feeling descending. He'd never heard Urho mention his omega's name, but there was no doubt that Riki was the blond man in the portrait. He cleared his throat. "I wouldn't want to take something special of his."

"It shouldn't go to waste. Take it."

Xan nodded and tucked the book into the pocket of his jacket. It fit perfectly. "So," he said, an unusual shyness creeping over him. He glanced up at Urho through his lashes, surprised to find his friend's dark complexion had gone vaguely pink.

Was Urho also remembering how Xan had grown hard as he'd pressed his finger inside and moved it around? Xan's own face flushed hot and his cock thickened against his thigh. "You must be wondering why I'm here."

Urho attempted a real smile, white teeth against dark skin, and then sighed. "I'm just glad that you are. I've wanted to see you again. Needed to, really."

Xan's throat went dry. "Why's that?"

"I've been thinking about your situation. Truth be told, I've thought of little else."

Xan shifted miserably in his seat. His stomach churned.

Urho held up a hand. "I'm not going to lecture again. I want to understand your predicament."

"No one can."

"I want to try. You need this?"

"Most humans need sexual release," Xan said defensively. "Not *all*, but most."

"And your omega—"

"Doesn't interest me."

Urho cocked his head. "But what of his needs?"

Xan glanced away. "We have an agreement." He wasn't about to mention the truth about Caleb. That was Caleb's secret to share if and when he wanted to.

"I see."

But Xan could tell that Urho didn't truly see.

"He has a lover?" Urho asked. "A beta, perhaps? Someone you find unthreatening to your relationship?"

Xan pushed out a breath. "I didn't come here to talk about him." Though he had, hadn't he? In a way? The pills he wanted to ask Urho for were only necessary because of his obligation to Caleb. "I wondered if you'd prescribe something for me. Something for stamina."

Urho frowned, leaning forward to rest his elbows on his knees. "Stamina? Sexual stamina?"

"Yes. I have a hard time keeping up with Caleb during his heats. There isn't another one coming for a few months, but I want to be prepared. I heard there were new pills that allow alphas to last a long time and rebound more quickly."

"He suffers from nympho—I mean, interminable heat?"

"No. The problem is me."

Urho's dark eyes narrowed. "Because what you want isn't what Caleb offers," he said quietly. "His pheromones don't arouse you?"

"They do." But the smell of Caleb in heat only made him crave being penetrated all the more. He'd been a mess during their first heat together. Horny and full of longing, unable to take care of Caleb's suffering and unable to fulfill his own needs either. He dreaded it coming round again. He had nearly gone mad listening to Caleb's cries of pain. "But not in the...right way."

He shook off the veil of sickening guilt that dropped over him, focused on Urho again, and said, "I need help. It's hard for me to admit—even harder to ask—but you know our situation better than most, and so I'm asking you. Please, help me."

Urho's body tensed, and he closed his eyes, taking a ragged breath. When his lids popped open again, Xan didn't recognize staid, old-fashioned Urho in the wildness he saw in the depths there. "I can give you the pills."

"Thank you!"

"But I can offer more than that."

Xan swallowed thickly. Was he going to suggest himself as an alpha surrogate for Caleb's heat? He let out a shuddery breath, not sure what he hoped for, but signaling for Urho to continue.

"You can't continue to see the man who hurt you."

Xan groaned. "We've already—"

"Listen to me!" Urho commanded and Xan's mouth snapped shut. "If you need this so badly, come to me for it."

Xan gaped, taking in Urho's pounding pulse, visible in the dark hollow at the base of his neck. He ran his gaze over Urho's messy hair and his earnest—so intensely earnest—eyes. He sucked in a harsh breath. "What are you saying?"

"If you need—" Urho wiped a trembling hand over his mouth and then started again. "If you need help with your cravings, come to me instead of that man who abuses you."

"Come to you for what?" Xan asked, blinking rapidly. "For a lecture? Tea? Medicine of some kind? What exactly do you plan to give me?"

"Sex. I'll give you sex."

Xan stared at him, his mind whirring and his heart sprinting madly. "You'll *what?*"

Urho's voice shook. "I'm offering to help you. I help omegas in heat—widowers, those without mates, those with nymphomania.

This would be no different. And it'll keep you safe."

Xan scoffed. "No different? Are you kidding me right now? It's completely different."

"Why?" Urho choked.

"The Holy Book of Wolf says so, for one. The laws of our country say it is, too. If you followed through on this offer, you'd find the actuality of the act plenty different. I'm not like an omega on the inside. I'm more like a beta in texture and feel."

Urho licked his lips, his eyes growing glossy. "Those things may be true, but it doesn't change my mind. It wouldn't be the first time I've broken the law or defied the Holy Book to protect someone."

Of course, Vale and his illegal abortion. And maybe other omegas, too. Who knew exactly what Urho had been complicit in, despite his uptight ways?

Xan lifted his chin. "I'm not a charity case."

"No, you're..." Urho trailed off, shivered, and stopped speaking.

"I'm what?" His heart thumped.

"You deserve help with this problem."

"Are you sick?" He gestured at Urho's sweaty skin. "You look feverish and this offer is clearly the product of a clouded mind."

Urho growled. "I'm not sick."

Xan stood up. "Look, I just wanted pills to deal with Caleb's heat. I don't need a pity fuck from you or anyone else."

"You want a violent, almost-rape, then? You'd rather him nearly murder you than accept me?" Urho leapt up, his fists clenched and his voice shaking.

Xan licked his lips. What was he doing? What was he turning down? This was his chance. He should take it. He should fall to his knees and beg Urho to make good on this generous offer right now, right now, *right now*.

But he couldn't. He'd give anything for Urho to truly want him that way. But that's not what this was about. It was about helping him, being some kind of hero. Doing something disgusting for the sake of Xan's welfare, and not out of desire or need for Xan in return.

And if Urho was another alpha, any other alpha, maybe that would be enough.

But he was *Urho*. The man Xan had admired for four long years now, and this charity and pity wasn't what he wanted.

"I came for help with Caleb. That's all."

Urho swallowed hard and stepped forward.

Xan's knees went weak. "What are you doing?" he whispered.

"Get on your knees," Urho commanded, eyes glinting dangerously.

Xan swallowed audibly, and his breath came in dizzying gasps.

"I *said*, get on your knees." Urho's fists clenched, his voice dropping into a deeper, terrifying register.

Xan quivered all over, his throat going dry. His body obeyed the words without any input from his spinning mind. The carpet beneath his knees was soft, and Xan's cells seemed to roar with shocked arousal as Urho stopped in front of him.

"What are you going to do?" Xan asked, pulse pounding.

"I'm going to fuck your rude, ungrateful mouth," Urho muttered, eyes shining and hot with lust as he motioned at the front of his trousers.

Xan licked his lips.

"Get to it."

Xan's fingers trembled as he loosened Urho's pants and shoved them down his thighs. His breath caught in his throat as Urho's dick sprang up and almost slapped him on the chin. He stared at the thick, dark length and licked his lips. The tip of Urho's cock peeked through the sheath of foreskin, and pre-come glistened there, a small shimmery promise of the delicious feast to come.

Xan's asshole quivered, and he bit his lower lip, wishing that he wasn't still so sore. If Urho wanted to fuck him, it was going to hurt. His fears about whether or not Urho really wanted him retreated. With a fat, slick cock dripping in front of his face and the scent of Urho's arousal rising thickly around him, it was hard to deny the truth.

"Open your mouth," Urho ordered, desperation and a hint of rage slipping into his voice, making the hair on the back of Xan's neck rise. He hurried to obey.

Urho's head tipped back as Xan traced his pointed tongue against Urho's slick cock head, gathering his pungent alpha pre-come and wallowing it around his mouth. The bitter tang made his nipples pebble and his cock flex hard, dribbling his own pre-come against his thigh.

The scent of their desire twined in the room, and Urho groaned as he threaded his fingers into Xan's hair. The sharp tug forward took Xan's breath away, but he was ready. Spreading his lips and jaw wide, he kept his eyes tilted up on Urho's face as he swallowed most of his cock down, and then relaxed his throat to allow Urho to push in even further.

Tears pricked his eyes, and his dick pounded against the fabric of his tight pants. He gagged slightly when Urho pushed in to his balls, gasping for breath as Urho slipped out of his throat with a moan. Then, hands gripping Xan's hair, he thrust right back in.

Xan whimpered and gagged again as Urho set up a rocking pace. His hips twitched forward and back, allowing Xan a drag of breath between thrusts, and then depriving him of it again, and again, and again. Xan floated away on the rhythm, lost to all but the need to breathe on time and the way the fabric of his pants rubbed against his cock head when he shifted his hips in tandem.

He reached up to grip Urho's forearms, clinging onto him as Urho gripped Xan's hair. Tears slipped down Xan's face and thick saliva dripped down his chin, coating his neck and Urho's balls, but the face fucking didn't slow.

Urho's eyes remained on Xan's face, and every twist of his features transmitted his pleasure and spoke of the bliss he took from each push into Xan's throat. "Touch yourself," he finally gritted out, shaking Xan's hand free of his forearm. "Make yourself come. I want to smell it."

Xan's eyes rolled up, gratitude at being allowed what Monhundy always denied swelling in him. He gripped his dick through his pants. He squeezed in rhythm to Urho's thrusts. His balls buzzed with rushing jizz, and his thighs and stomach jumped and strained as the urge to come grew. He gripped Urho's forearm harder with his other hand and surrendered, opening his throat and relaxing his mouth.

Urho cried out, sensing the submission, and crushed Xan's face to his dark pubes as he crammed his cock deep into Xan's throat. Xan's yell was muffled, his orgasm yanking him into explosive bliss. Come pumped wildly from his cock, massive loads of it streaming down his leg, hot as piss.

He gagged and choked around Urho's fat cock, pleasure gripping him in a seizure of sensation as his orgasm raged on. Urho yanked out of his mouth, aimed, and yelled as the splatter of his hot come marked Xan's cheeks, lips, tongue, and throat.

Urho's cry echoed in the room. Xan panted hard, sucking in hot, sweet air, tasting Urho's pleasure in it like a musky perfume that coated him from head to toe. He licked his lips and used his fingers to shove Urho's come from all over his cheeks and chin into his hungry mouth.

Urho stared down at him, eyes glassy and sated. A smirk of satisfaction twisted his mouth and a hint of proprietary pride gleamed in his eyes. He sat on the chair and pulled Xan to kneel between his thighs. He studied his face carefully and then slid his fingers through the lingering mess of come on Xan's neck. He brought a fingerful up to Xan's mouth and pressed it inside.

Xan sucked Urho's salty finger and tongued the end of it gently. Urho grunted before leaning in to take Xan's mouth in a hot kiss. Urho's tongue slipped over his, and Xan kissed him back. He drew in closer, almost crawling into Urho's lap, hearing small urgent sounds and knowing dimly that they came from his own throat.

Xan gasped when Urho drew back for a breath, his heart racing and cock thumping with renewed need that ached in his balls like a bruise.

"There," Urho murmured, slumping back into the chair, his pants still around his thighs and his bare ass on the leather. His cock was still mostly hard but was now going soft.

Xan bent close to lick it adoringly, a kittenish contentment flooding him in the aftermath of what they'd just done. He took hold of the root, fattening it up, and pressed the sensitive head into his mouth to gently rest against his tongue. It dribbled another spurt of come, and he swallowed it eagerly.

He closed his eyes, breathing deeply of the filthy scent that rose around them. This was the lust the Holy Book of Wolf condemned, this tender moment with Urho's cock in his mouth. A warm reverence welled in him, alongside a new, shaky fear.

Urho stroked his hair, his fingers quivering against Xan's scalp, but the sensation was soothing. Reassuring. Xan could relax. He wasn't about to be beaten for coming, or for enjoying this, least of all for wanting it.

Minutes passed, and Urho's cock grew fully hard again. It forced Xan's lips wide as he suckled the head gently. Urho did nothing about it though. Simply ran his hands over Xan's hair, making contented sounds. Finally, he said, "I know you enjoy being fucked but your hole can't take it until it's healed."

Xan squeezed his eyes closed. He wanted to beg. Instead he

sucked Urho's cock more enthusiastically, bringing him up to a state of arousal that couldn't be denied again. He reached his hand into his own messy pants and squeezed himself as he sucked and licked, bobbed his head, and groaned, as once again he brought Urho to climax. This time he swallowed the copious seed down.

Moaning, Urho slipped his cock from Xan's mouth. He pressed Xan's face to rest against his trembling thigh. His tight, dark balls twitched not far from Xan's lips, so he scooted forward to lick and kiss them eagerly, hoping for one more round before whatever this madness was came to an end. One more orgasm before Urho woke to the reality of his offense to wolf-god and Xan had to face his exile to Virona.

Urho allowed him to lick his balls for a few minutes. Then he pushed Xan back by the shoulders and pulled his pants up from where they'd been around his ankles. He removed his gorgeous cock from Xan's sight.

"Are you still in need?" Urho asked.

Xan pressed his palm against his hard cock, jammed between the fabric of his pants and his thigh. He gazed up at Urho dumbly.

"Show me," Urho said, sounding surprisingly calm. "Stand up, take it out, and show me."

Xan swallowed hard, but he rose, his hands working to get his pants open. The wads of come inside were overwhelming with pheromones and the scent flooded both their noses as he dropped his pants to his ankles. Urho licked his lips, leaned forward, and nuzzled Xan's hip briefly before opening his mouth and sucking Xan's come-slick cock in to the root.

Xan's knees almost buckled as his dick pressed against and then passed Urho's slick, hot soft palate. Heart skipping wildly, he dared to thread his hands into Urho's course hair, holding on so that he didn't fall. Urho groaned.

Instantly, Xan shuddered, pumping his load into Urho's throat.

He cried out, shocked by the suddenness. He tossed his head back to the ceiling, pleasure blinding him until he couldn't breathe—shaking, jerking, coming so hard that his bruised muscles ached.

And then Urho released him, Xan's cock slick with saliva, sliding from between Urho's hot lips reluctantly.

"Turn around. Bend over. Put your hands on the coffee table."

Xan barely managed it without falling over, ankles twisted in his pants bunched at his feet. But he moved aside the tea set and positioned himself on quaking arms, ass up in the air. He nearly hyperventilated as Urho's hot hands landed on the globes of his ass and opened him for the second time in a week.

And then what he'd wished for—what he'd dreamed of the first time Urho had done this—*actually* happened. Urho's hot breath glided over his ass cheeks, and then his slippery, hot tongue slid down Xan's crack and tickled against his still sore asshole.

Urho muttered something unintelligible. Xan gripped the edge of the coffee table and cried out as Urho ate out his ass like he'd been dreaming of it as long as Xan had. The tea service rattled as Xan twisted and jerked in response to the sweet invasion of Urho's tongue.

Xan's cock twitched and jumped, pleasure rocketing over his rattled nerve endings, sending him into a state of madness. He rocked his hips, groaning, fevered, needing more than just Urho's tongue—and then Urho pulled away.

He pressed a soft kiss to Xan's aching, needy, hungry pucker. "This is mine now. Do you understand? This hole belongs to me."

Xan cried out and came again, his body arching, come shooting onto the coffee table, the carpet, and his own face as he hunched and bucked, shocked by the wild and erotic shattering of his former understanding of sex and gratification. This, this declaration of ownership from Urho, was everything he'd ever wanted. Everything he'd known he'd never truly have.

He collapsed to the table, the cold wood a shock on his hot belly. The soft carpet beneath his knees again. Urho stroked down his back, slipped his fingers over Xan's saliva-wet hole, and tapped it with his thumb. "Say it. I want you to say the words."

Xan whimpered, shame and want fighting inside him. "My hole is yours."

"Who does it belong to?"

"You."

"For how long?"

Xan swallowed, trembling all over, uncertain of the answer. "Forever?"

"Mine. Forever." Urho kissed his hip and then his hole.

He tugged Xan back from the table and into his arms. He held him, kissing the top of his head, and the side of his neck above his collar. They moved to the sofa, collapsing there together. Their clothes were still disheveled, the scents of sweat and come dominating the room.

In shock, Xan rested with his head on Urho's shoulder. His pants weren't even fully closed, but they were both covered now. He watched avidly as Urho's muscled chest rose and fell as he drifted off to sleep.

Time passed, and Xan slowly came to his senses. Light faded outside, showing golden through the windows, and the clock on the mantel ticked. Carefully, he disengaged himself from Urho's arms and reworked his clothes into a semblance of respectability, but only just.

He attempted to clean what he could of the mess they'd made on the floor and coffee table, using napkins from the tea service. Urho slept through it all, handsome and careless in sleep, his mouth slack and the edges of his eyes relaxed.

Finished with his attempts to obliterate evidence of what they'd done, Xan stared down at the man. He had no idea what any of this meant. Or what the promise he'd made entailed. But he knew he needed to go before Urho woke and they had to have some sort of awkward conversation that ruined everything that'd come before.

Slipping from the library, he let himself out the front door without alerting any beta servants and hustled down the street to his car. His body still sang with the pleasure he'd experienced, but his heart and mind were trepidatious.

He didn't know what had come over Urho, how long he'd planned to make his offer, or even why he'd done it. But there was no way the promise he'd elicited at the end meant anything real. A promise extracted during a sexual high was no promise at all, and why he'd want to lay claim to Xan's asshole was a mystery, too.

But Xan couldn't stop remembering the way Urho had demanded he repeat the words. He'd sounded sincere and resolute, as though Xan's ass was something he'd been coveting for far too long and was determined to keep for himself.

Shaking the thoughts away, Xan focused instead on just getting home.

It wasn't hard at all to drive past Monhundy's house for once, and when he reached his house, he handed the car off to Lenser with a sigh of relief.

He climbed the stairs to his room. He needed to shower before seeing Caleb and reassuring him that he had the solution to the heat problem well in hand, and also some rather big news to impart. He hoped Caleb would take it well because they had no choice but to leave in just a few days for a new life in Virona.

Removing his jacket, he took out the book Urho had given him. He opened it and stared at the inscription in the front:

For Riki with my love—Urho

He quivered, jealousy and wonder challenging each other in his heart. He flipped through the pages and then placed the book on the table beside his bed. Stripping off the rest of his clothes, he strolled into his bathroom, checking the mirror for evidence of what had happened.

Streaks of dried come on his neck and cheek, his tousled hair, and the still-glimmering shock in his eyes greeted him. He closed his eyes, breathing in the scent, letting it into his lungs, imagining it passing from particle to particle, until his whole self was touched by the remnants of what had taken place.

Then he turned on the shower.

As the hot water poured down on him, washing away the intoxicating scent of him and Urho together, clarity descended, and another realization hit. He sank to the floor of the shower, his heart twisting hard. "I'm wolf's own evil," he whispered.

Because of his wicked nature and inability to resist temptation, he'd let Caleb down yet again. He'd left Urho's house without the needed pills for Caleb's next heat. He truly was the worst alpha in the entire world. Caleb didn't deserve to be stuck with him.

And he'd lured good, upstanding Urho into temptation as well. He scrubbed himself ruthlessly. He didn't deserve Urho's scent.

CHAPTER EIGHT

URHO WOKE COLD and alone in his library, the air still swirling with the scent of his and Xan's come. He hadn't meant to pass out like that, but three nights of no sleep and riled up emotions—followed by exquisite and filthy sex with the man he couldn't shake from his head—had wiped him out.

Rolling onto his side and into a sitting position, he pulled his hands through his hair and peered around the room, hoping to find Xan in some corner, or standing by the window. But no. There was no evidence of him aside from the remaining dried semen on the carpet and table, and the vivid scent of sex on the air.

Urho exhaled a shaky breath, filled with uneasiness. Where had Xan gone and why? A sick sensation slipped into his veins. Had Xan felt coerced into the sex they'd engaged in? Had he really *not* wanted it despite his trembling lust and relentless orgasms? Had Urho taken advantage of the boy?

He wasn't used to negotiating sexual encounters outside of acting as a surrogate during heats. And wolf-god knew Urho hadn't planned to have sex with Xan today. Not like that, anyway. When he'd made his offer, he'd imagined it as a future thing. A situation where Xan, unable to withstand temptation, would come to him and drop to his knees, look up at him with those big blue eyes, and ask for…

Wolf-god, he was getting hard again.

Apparently, he truly was a pervert. There was no getting around it. He'd had sex with another alpha and now yearned to do it again.

Obviously, he'd also lost his mind somewhere in the last few days. There was that to consider as well.

He tilted his head to gaze at the portrait of Riki, endlessly smiling. No change there. And he'd committed this sin right under his beloved's watchful eyes. Why didn't he feel more ashamed? He wiped a hand over his face and set about cleaning up the remainder of the mess his collision with Xan had left behind. It looked as though Xan had already tried his level best with the napkins.

As he scrubbed the carpet, his ears peeled for the footsteps of beta servants, all of whom seemed to have thankfully found something terribly important to occupy them after Xan's arrival in the house, he tried to process the events of the day.

He'd been overwrought. He knew that much. But as for what had led him to order Xan to his knees? That had been lust and something more—a refusal to watch Xan walk away and into the arms of a man who didn't value the beauty of his form, the vibrancy of his mind, or his passionate need to be handled with the same command and respect as an omega.

Urho gasped, sitting on his heels and gazing back up at the portrait of Riki.

How had he come to that conclusion? He'd sensed it from the beginning, perhaps. So, when Xan had turned on his heel to walk away from his offer, some part of him had simply known what to do: treat him like an omega, command him to his knees, and own him.

And he'd done it.

His balls filled, and his cock rose. He closed his eyes and saw Xan's arched back, his small hole presented to Urho complete with quivering haunches and flushed need. He'd licked it, kissed it, and demanded ownership of it, and Xan had given him all of that without hesitation. He'd given his seed, and his pleasure, and Urho wanted more. Needed more.

And he needed to know Xan was safe.

Rising from his cleaning, he wiped a hand over his sweaty forehead and peered up at Riki again. "Forgive me, beloved."

But he knew, somewhere deep inside, that Riki didn't mind. He'd only ever wanted Urho's joy, and if he found happiness again in this madness with Xan, then Riki—far away in wolf's cozy den of death—would support it. Even if the world called it sin and he might be imprisoned? If his soul might burn for this and be separated from Riki and their child forever?

Urho shook his head.

He didn't believe in a wolf-god who punished, though he knew many did. Perhaps because he was a military man and a doctor, and he'd witnessed so much suffering that he truly believed the only thing wolf-god might offer is peace to all but the worst of humanity. Life was otherwise too full of misery to believe in anything else.

He took the stairs up to his rooms, avoiding the servants and glad for the betas' relative lack of scenting abilities. He locked the door to his bathroom, flicked the shower on, and then hesitated once he was fully nude. He stared at himself in the mirror, taking in his wiry chest hair and dark skin leading down to his thick, alpha cock.

His pubic hair was pitch black, unlike the salt-and-pepper of his head. He was still muscled and strong, and he imagined lifting Xan into his arms, holding the boy like a treasure, and impaling him thoroughly.

Shuddering, he shut his eyes, took his cock in hand, and simply held it. The heat of his palm and clench of his fist kept him at the peak of arousal. He slipped it up and down his shaft, watching his cock grow harder, amused and amazed.

He hadn't been so easily aroused since the last heat he'd acted surrogate. Omega pheromones were a guarantee for excitement though. Odd that just thinking of Xan had a similar effect.

Wolf-god, what had he done?

As he reluctantly showered off the mixture of his and Xan's come, he replayed Xan's arrival and the brief conversation that had led so suddenly to what the people of the Old World had called fellatio. He recalled Xan asking him for pills for sexual stamina. The boy hadn't needed help in that regard today.

But if he was truly unmanned, obviously, he wouldn't.

Urho released a long breath. The slur unnerved him, playing at the edges of his mind. He'd accepted it and now he took responsibility for it. If Xan were truly unmanned, then Urho would keep him safe. And if Caleb needed help with heats, if Xan needed pills to make it through, then he'd provide those, too.

Drying off and dressing, he made up his mind. After going into his bedroom pharmacy, pulling out a tub of pills, and dividing them out into a pillbox, he called to Mako to hold his dinner. Then he left the house with a hammering heart and a whisper of worry in his mind, along with a hint of warning throbbing in his pants.

He needed to see Xan.

Face-to-face and man-to-man. And if he was jittery inside and feeling high on emotions he hadn't experienced in years that was all the more reason to go to him.

Now. Before he lost his nerve.

"Do you think he ever gets lonely?" Caleb asked, lolling on his bed in a loose pair of pants and a V-necked white shirt.

His blond hair was tousled, and his fingertips were stained red from new ink he'd been trying out in his print studio. In a small room in the back of the house, he created bits of art on sheets of thick paper. He was never quite satisfied with any of them, though, and showed the outcomes to no one, not even Xan.

But he never threw away his so-called failures either. He hoarded his ink and paper creations in stacks that Xan was convinced were a fire hazard, but he kept that opinion to himself.

"Who?" Xan's mind had gone immediately to Urho, though he'd hoped they were done discussing the man. He'd told Caleb that he'd stopped by Urho's house and that he'd agreed to prescribe the medications.

Assuming Urho simply hadn't had the pills on hand, Caleb had hugged Xan hard. "Thank you," he'd said. "You truly believe this medication will help?"

"I hope so."

But hope didn't seem to cut it for Caleb, because he'd pressed on, asking, "And if it doesn't?"

"We'll make a backup plan, but unfortunately any plan we settle on will have to be made in Virona," he'd said, and then he'd explained all about his meeting with Ray.

It was a relief to talk to Caleb about his father's displeasure, his cousin Janus's favor in his father's eyes, Ray's intervention, and their upcoming displacement, but it was strange to be so open about those issues, all the while keeping the true events during his visit to Urho's house a secret.

Even as they'd discussed the motivations for the move and the necessary preparations for it, he'd remembered the hoarse cry of Urho's pleasure and the hot splatter of his come against his skin.

Xan wished he hadn't needed to wash so thoroughly. He still craved the scent of it. He wanted to taste it again. Most of all, he wanted to feel the way he had in Urho's arms—at his command, quite nearly beloved.

He'd almost believed Urho *cared*.

But that was ridiculous and just the product of an overactive imagination. Xan was moving to a new city very soon, and Urho's offer, generous as it was, and pleasurable as the sample had been, wouldn't be of any help when he was three hours away by the seaside.

Also, maybe he was still in shock. He didn't know what to think, what to believe, and a large part of him wanted to run away from Urho as quickly as possible before he let himself do something stupid like hope. Even if the move to Virona did feel like punishment for something he couldn't entirely control, between Monhundy and now this, it couldn't have come at a better time.

"I'm speaking of Ray, of course," Caleb said, referring back to his question of loneliness. "He works so hard for your father, day and night. Does he even have a lover? Do you know?"

Xan shrugged. Their interactions had always been quite one-sided: older Ray trying to keep younger Xan out of bigger trouble. It'd never occurred to Xan to ask his brother about his feelings, romantic or otherwise.

"I think he must be lonely," Caleb said, rolling onto his stomach and propping himself up on his elbows to smile at Xan.

Xan stared out the window, watching the beta servants below working on the layout of their spring gardens—the fruits of the servants' labor now something he and Caleb would have to miss.

"Perhaps he is," Xan conceded. "But that's his problem. Ours is preparing to move. By the weekend. It's not much time to get everything ready."

Caleb nodded, rising gracefully from the bed, his long legs and arms moving like a dancer. "I'm glad. This is exactly what I've prayed for." His eyes shone. "I've asked wolf-god for this every night, lighting the incense, and kneeling by my bed like a good omega should."

Xan blinked. "What do you mean?"

Caleb crossed to him, folding into Xan's arms. "I love you dearly, my friend. To get you away from that monster, I'd go anywhere, do anything."

Xan hugged him close and fought down the lump in his throat. "What if I find another monster in Virona?"

"You won't," Caleb said fiercely. "We'll build a new life there without any monsters in it. You'll see."

Xan kissed Caleb's temple and sighed. The monster was inside him. He didn't think there was any true way to escape that fact.

"And what about your family?"

Caleb shrugged, moving out of Xan's arms and across the room to the vanity, where he sat down and began to brush out his blond hair. "You know how I feel about them. Leaving them behind is a bonus."

Xan nodded, remembering the long, thin people who'd birthed Caleb and then treated him as nothing more than a pawn to marry off to the highest bidder.

The fact that Xan had chosen him, and Caleb had at last consented to be contracted had been met with great rejoicing in the Riggs-Holo household. But that had died out when Caleb insisted their contract contain language forbidding his parents from access to the Heelies' funds outside of an annual gift consisting of a sum that was nothing to sneeze at. But that annual gift wasn't even a drop in the massive bucket of money the Heelies, and now Caleb, had access to.

"And what about my own family?" Xan asked quietly.

Caleb's gaze caught his in the mirror. "Darling, you're more likely to be allowed access to your pater again if you do as your father asks. Unfair as that sounds and no matter how it hurts. Surely Virona is far enough away to put a damper on your urges, but not so far that your pater couldn't come visit if your father lifts this ridiculous ban?"

"Pater must agree with it," Xan said, voicing the fear he hadn't ever allowed past his lips. "We all know how it is with omegas, with *Érosgápe*, especially. If he didn't agree with Father, he could make him concede. All he'd have to do is express his disappointment in Father and he'd go on his knees to make it right again."

Caleb put the brush aside, turning around to seek out Xan's eyes. "Your pater loves your father and takes his side in all things. From what I've witnessed in my short time with the family, he always has, and I suspect he always will. No matter his own thoughts and feelings on certain subjects, namely you, he will side with your father. It's the way of their relationship. Thank wolf-god it's not the way of ours."

A knock came at the door then, and Caleb moved to answer it, finding their head housekeeper, Ren, at the door. "Yes?"

"Dr. Chase is here to see Mr. Heelies, sir," Ren murmured, glancing over Caleb's shoulder toward Xan. His steel-blue eyes glinted in the low light in the hallway and his salt-and-pepper hair was combed back neatly. "He *insists* on seeing him. He's made himself at home in your library this time, Mr. Heelies."

"I see," Caleb turned to lift a brow at Xan. "What's this about?"

Xan's tongue wet his suddenly dry lips. His library was a mockery of Urho's beautiful space, with few books and hastily chosen furniture. He'd planned to expand it over the next year, but now he'd have to focus on the library in Virona instead. "I'm not sure. I'd better go see."

"I'll come with you."

"Don't," Xan said breathlessly, putting out his hand to stop Caleb from following.

Caleb's eyes took on a suspicious gleam, but he shrugged and fell back. "Whatever you say, darling."

Xan could smell Urho's skin from the upstairs landing. He'd never been so aware of another human being before in his life. He briefly wondered if this was what it was like for *Érosgápe* and then quickly dismissed the question. He'd known many alphas claimed to be able to smell their omegas from rooms away, but he'd never believed it.

He enjoyed Caleb's clean scent as a comfort, but he'd never hunted for it the way his nose seemed to automatically seek out Urho now. He scented sweat and skin with a waft of excitement and arousal underneath it. Xan's knees weakened as he started down the stairs, and he had to grip the banister tightly to prevent a tumble.

Urho stood by the fire, which roared under the new beta boy's ministrations. Spotting Xan out of the corner of his eye, the boy rose and nodded, scurrying from the room like he knew something was amiss. Xan's heart beat against his breastbone and his throat tightened anxiously. He stepped into the room, holding his head high and rubbing his sweaty palms on his clean trousers.

Urho turned to him, setting his strong shoulders back and proud. His eyes were penetrating and almost angry as he peered at Xan from across the room.

"Why are you here?" Xan asked, with a foolishly trembling voice. It wasn't polite, and Caleb would bemoan his lack of manners, but nothing else really mattered.

"You forgot this," Urho said, pulling a hand from his jacket pocket and producing a pillbox. "For the upcoming heat."

Xan swallowed hard. "Yes. Thank you." He stepped forward to take the small, brown box, but Urho grabbed his forearm and pulled him in close.

"And you forgot to tell me goodbye. Omegas always say goodbye to their alphas."

Xan's asshole spasmed, his cock fattening up against his thigh. His throat clicked as he swallowed again, soundless, wordless astonishment gripping him.

"That's what you are, isn't it?" Urho whispered. "An omega."

Xan whimpered, his body trembling. Urho yanked him closer, supporting Xan's weight with his strength. "It's what I wish I could be," Xan murmured, his heart in his throat and a sting in his eyes.

Urho nodded. "I've read case studies in medical school," he started but then he clomped his mouth shut, as though regretting the words. "You're beautiful," he said instead, and Xan closed his eyes, ducked his head, and tried not to fall to his knees in abject submission as Urho said, "I want you."

Xan groaned. "This is…" He fought for the words, his knees already bending and his weight shifting down. Urho held his arm tightly. "This is highly irregular, you know." What a prissy way to put it! He wanted to snatch the words back.

"It's a sin," Urho said roughly. "Against the law. Against wolf-god. I've heard it all. I've thought it all, too. Once upon a time."

"When was that? A few days ago?" Xan bit out, but it lost its anger in the breathiness of his voice.

"Perhaps. But today when I had you, I knew it for the lie it's always been."

The room slipped sideways around him, and Xan struggled to stand even with Urho's help. "You don't know what you're saying."

"Have I ever struck you as the kind of man who doesn't understand himself?"

"Yes."

Urho chuckled and touched the bruise on Xan's cheek. "There's my smart-mouthed boy."

Xan leaned into Urho, letting his head rest against his chest. He felt the rapid beat of Urho's heart against his brow. "What does this mean?"

"You promised me something today. Do you remember?"

Xan shivered despite the fire burning at his back. "Yes."

"What did you promise?"

"That my asshole belonged to you." Shame and desperate longing rose hot up his throat and into his cheeks, and he burned as he stood with his face buried against Urho's shirt.

"Look at me," Urho rasped.

Xan forced his head up and met Urho's gaze.

"Do you intend to break that promise?"

Xan shook his head.

"Good. Because I'm going to make a promise to you now: I won't let anything bad happen to you. I'll protect you. You'll never suffer under that man, whoever he is, again. And if I ever discover his name I'll put paid his crimes."

Xan's head ached, and his cock throbbed. He was dreaming. This was a dream. No alpha would ever want him, not this way. Not in a way that elicited promises and offered up some sort of vague future. Especially not an alpha like Urho who had all the qualities to make it easy to find an omega to contract with: wealth, looks, kindness, and reputation. The works. What could he want with Xan?

Urho went on, "I promise to fulfill your needs, Xan, so that you won't have to seek out hurt and humiliation. Not anymore."

Xan couldn't breathe. Dots swirled in his vision, and Urho's head lowered to his, slick lips opening and taking his in a hungry kiss. Urho groaned into Xan's mouth, releasing his hold on Xan's arm to grip his hips and tug their groins together.

Their kiss turned into a grapple as Urho began to strip Xan of his clothes. Xan, bewildered and willing to take what he could get, tried to help, but his hands mainly just got in the way. The rug before the fire became their landing place, and once they were both naked, they rocked together urgently. Pleasure grew, and grew, and grew, until Xan sobbed in need and Urho met him with an intensity that shook the quiet room. Urho's fist around his cock, and his fingers caressing Xan's still swollen asshole, were like fireworks of sensation; his lips on Xan's mouth were a constant caress and his tongue an invasion. His passion promised more than Xan had ever expected.

The culmination of their hunching, gasping, sweat-slick collision came with a shuddering cry from Xan and a loud groan from Urho, as come pumped between them, filling the air with the scent of spunk. Urho clutched Xan close, kissing his hair, his cheeks, his neck, and muttering strange endearments that Xan had never heard from anyone before.

"Sweet man, sweet joy," Urho whispered, gripping Xan's hips and rubbing their come-covered cocks together again. "That's my good omega."

Xan shivered in shock, his heart still racing, as the heat from the fire warmed their bare skin. Twice in one day they'd collided this way, and he didn't understand why, or believe it was real, or know what came next.

"I'm moving to Virona in a few days' time," Xan said finally, as the lust cooled and the silence grew unbearable.

Urho's hand stilled where it rubbed Xan's lower back. "Moving to Virona? Why?"

"Banished, by my father, for… Well, for this." Xan laughed helplessly, a pearl of sadness growing in the shell of his wonder. "For not being a proper alpha. For doing things that make people talk. For the unexplainable bruises, past and present."

At the mention of bruises, Urho lifted up and in the light of the fire perused Xan's body, checking for additional damage done. "Did I hurt you?"

Xan shook his head. "No." Then he took a deep breath and confessed shyly, "It was complete and utter bliss."

Urho nuzzled him, kissed his chest, and then settled down on the carpet, tugging Xan to rest in his arms. "You can't leave for Virona. I can't protect you from there."

Xan smiled bitterly. It wasn't a declaration, but it was better than nothing. Plus, he had incontrovertible evidence that Urho did want him sexually, but he supposed it would be nice to be wanted emotionally, too. As a true lover, not just as a cause.

But he'd take what he could get. "You won't need to protect me there." *Hopefully.* "The man who hurts me lives here and I'll be three long hours away from him."

Urho growled low. "I'll kill him if he touches you again."

"He won't. Like I told you. I always went to him. He doesn't really want me. Not that way."

Urho seemed to struggle with how to respond, and he eventually settled on pulling Xan even tighter to him, placing his fingertips against Xan's asshole and stroking lightly there. Xan licked his lips, his cock rising hot against Urho's thigh. He said nothing else for a long time as Urho played with his sensitive anus and brought him to a state of desperate neediness until he rubbed violently against Urho's leg and orgasmed with a shout.

"You're as randy as any omega," Urho muttered, scooping Xan's come up in his fingers and taking it into his mouth. He hummed softly at the flavor and Xan's cock jerked again at the sight. "Taste as good as one, too."

Xan whimpered. "Stop. I can't take much more. I'm going to die right here, and Caleb will find me in the morning, drowned in a puddle of my own come and still sporting a hard-on."

"That mouth," Urho growled. "Always with that mouth."

Xan whimpered as Urho pressed fingers against his hole again.

"I want to fuck this sweetness so badly," Urho groaned. His cock, unbelievably, had also returned to life.

"You can ride the train for three hours anytime you want and do just that," Xan offered. He wanted it now, but he also knew Urho would never penetrate him when he was still injured from another alpha's cock. For so many reasons.

"You're truly going to Virona?" Urho asked.

"I am."

"And Caleb?"

"Going with me, of course. He's my omega. My family."

Urho nodded and sat up. Xan followed suit. "What will Caleb think of this?" Urho asked, motioning between them, worry lining his tone.

"Caleb would be happy to answer that question for you," came a soft voice from the vicinity of the door.

Urho grunted, tugging Xan close and throwing a blanket from the nearby leather sofa over them both.

"Apologies," Caleb said, stepping into the room fully and shutting the door behind him. His white loose pants and V-neck shirt against his pale flesh made him look like an angel from wolf-god's own heaven. "I came in search of my alpha and found more than I bargained for. I thought you must be at each other's throats, and maybe you have been, but in a completely different way than I imagined."

Xan flushed, his heart pounding. "We were talking and then—"

"Nature took its course," Caleb supplied, smiling. "I'm glad. You've been dancing around each other for a long time."

"Glad?" Urho said, frowning. "Dancing?"

Caleb smiled warmly at him. "Xan and I aren't lovers except during heats when it's absolutely necessary, so I'm delighted to see him with someone far less monstrous than that, well, monster. Someone wonderful, in fact." Caleb sat down on the sofa and crossed his legs, revealing his painted toes. "You can get dressed now. I think we should all talk, don't you? Though, wolf-god, this room reeks of come."

"We could go to your drawing room?" Xan offered, moving around under the blanket as he tugged on his clothes.

Caleb rose again. "Excellent idea. I'll leave you to it. Get dressed and maybe use the washroom across the hall. Meet me in no more than five minutes, please. That means keep your hands to yourself in the meantime, alpha mine."

"Yes, omega," Xan murmured, his cheeks so hot that he felt like he might burst into a bigger flame than the fire roaring on the hearth.

URHO WASN'T SURE what to expect, but Caleb was beyond easy with what he'd walked in on and smiled kindly as he poured bourbon into a glass and passed it over to him. Then he passed Xan a glass as well before mixing up a beautiful whisky cocktail for himself.

"Relax," Caleb said, taking the seat on the cream-colored sofa next to Xan and leaving Urho one of the upright chairs he'd sat in on his last visit. "I'm not angry. I'm relieved."

Urho wiped at his face. He could still smell spunk and lust rising from both Xan and his own flesh, despite having washed as best they could in the sink. He sipped his bourbon, feeling the burn in the back of his throat, and waited for sanity to hit.

The events of the day were wild, out of control, off the rails in every way. Surely, he'd wake from this soon? It reminded him all too clearly of when he'd first met Riki—the compulsion, the impulsivity. Was it even possible to imprint again? And on an alpha, no less?

Wolf-god, what had even brought him here tonight? The pills, yes, but he could have sent them over with a messenger. Or arranged for Xan to pick them up at his office the next day. The truth was he'd wanted to be near Xan again. He'd needed it. Almost like the way he'd needed Riki in the past.

What did it all mean?

"I'm assuming Xan told you about our exile?" Caleb asked.

Urho jerked back from his reverie. His stomach soured slightly, but the knowledge that Xan would be far away from the man who hurt him allowed him to nod with approval. "Yes. That's for the best. Until the monster, as you call him, loses interest."

Xan huffed. "He's never been interested!" he exclaimed with annoyance. "I don't know why you think he would be. Just because he fucks me when I—"

"I don't want to hear what he's done to you," Urho gritted out, clenching the glass in his hand. He took another fast sip, trying to calm the flash of possessive rage.

Caleb's brow arched, and he looked between Xan and Urho with interest. "Let's not discuss that since it's so upsetting to all of us and Xan's vowed to be done with the man, anyway. The reason I thought we should talk now is in regard to something else altogether."

"We owe you an explanation and apology," Urho began, shamefacedly. "I don't know how to offer one, though. This is quite unexpected, and no doubt violates your contract and offends your sensibilities as—"

"No," Caleb interrupted. "You don't have to explain anything. Nor do I wish to give you permission." He raised a hand, staying any comments from Xan or Urho. "Not because it isn't granted, but because Xan doesn't need it. It has always been part of our contract that fidelity isn't required or even desired. Instead, what I want to address is the subject of my upcoming heat. It's several months off still, but we can't have a repeat of last time."

Xan's lower lip went into his mouth and he squeezed his eyes shut in obvious shame before whispering, "I promise to handle it. Urho brought the pills for me tonight."

Urho's head swam. He tried to move on from Caleb's comment that fidelity was not in his contract with Xan and instead focus on this new topic. He gulped his bourbon down and Caleb rose to refill his glass.

Xan pulled the pill case out of his pocket and showed it to Caleb. "These will surely solve the problem."

Caleb frowned, carefully setting the bourbon bottle on the low table between them and taking a seat again. "You're not the first alpha I've gone through a heat with," he said, obviously taking care with Xan's feelings. "You love me, I know, but you aren't made for this, darling. Please let someone help you."

Xan stared at him wide-eyed, the bruise on his cheekbone gleaming in the low light. "They took better care of you? The men your family hired?"

He sounded gut-punched, as any alpha would. Xan's contradictions—omega-like one minute, and traditionally alpha-like the next—rattled Urho's sense of reality. His scientific mind clamored for more information, more pieces of Xan's confusing puzzle. He wanted desperately to understand.

"Of course not," Caleb said. "But they fucked me hard and long, and I didn't suffer for a minute." Caleb took Xan's chin in his hand, preventing him from disappearing into his collar. "Look at me. I'd rather be your omega than theirs on any other day of my life, but when I'm in heat, I need an alpha who can take me for as long as possible. Until even the most intense wave passes."

"I can take the pills! I can—"

"You can. And you *will* take the pills. But I want to ask Urho to help us. You're lovers now."

Were they lovers?

Urho's mind spun even faster and the drink in his hand trembled. Xan wasn't denying it and Urho wasn't sure that he should, or even could, but when he'd made his initial offer to help Xan, becoming his "lover" wasn't what he'd planned on. He'd just meant to help out—like with being a surrogate to an omega.

And yet he'd essentially demanded it himself, hadn't he? He'd asked for a pledge of fidelity after the first orgasm, for wolf-god's sake! Who was he kidding? They must be lovers. He'd made it so.

Fuck. He squirmed and cleared his throat.

"There are no secrets for you to hide from him," Caleb went on, oblivious to Urho's churning thoughts. "He's a safe choice. A strong choice. And it would please me to be, even for a little while, part of what you share with him. Only during heats, of course," Caleb said, shuddering and sneering with a hint of disgust. "Only when I want it."

"Oh," Xan murmured. "Of course."

"You only want sexual touch during heats?" Urho asked to clarify his understanding. Perhaps Caleb simply didn't want *Xan*, but why would he have contracted with him then? "You feel no desire any other time? You're frigid?"

"Frigid is a rude word," Xan said.

"I feel aroused at times, but I prefer to satisfy it with my own hand. In general, I don't feel sexually attracted to other people." Caleb sat up straight and brittle, almost daring Urho to challenge or insult him. "Also, for what it's worth, I prefer the term asexual to the more colloquial and insulting 'frigid.'"

Urho nodded solemnly and said nothing. He'd heard of such men—usually betas, though he'd read case studies involving omegas and alphas. He'd never met an asexual person, though, as far as he knew. He wondered what it must be like to scent as an omega, to smell the delectable odors of an alpha, and not be attracted by it.

Was Caleb disgusted even? He'd appeared disgusted by Xan and Urho's scents before. Maybe, one day, he'd be a close enough friend with Caleb to ask. For now, he simply inclined his head again and said, "If your alpha agrees, I'd be honored to help service you during your heat."

Xan let out a soft, wounded sound. He slumped on the couch, his eyes on the carpet and his lower lip in his mouth again.

"Darling, it's not an insult to you. It's a gift. You can share this now with your lover—both the pleasure and the burden." Caleb reached out to touch Xan, but he shrank away. "What's bothering you? I'd hoped you'd be happy."

"I can handle the heat on my own. I'm strong enough."

"You're very strong. And a wonderful alpha," Caleb said, using the voice omegas always employed when trying to soothe an alpha's ruffled feathers: fond, quiet, sweet. "I'm proud to call you mine."

"But…" Xan rubbed his fingers over his eyes.

"No 'but' at all. More of an 'and,' darling. *And* your lover is trustworthy, strong, handsome, and used to surrogate duties. He's a perfect choice. Swallow your pride and accept this help."

Xan shook his head. "But what about your reputation? Everyone will think you suffer from interminable heat."

"Oh no!" Caleb gasped and clutched his chest. "People will talk!" He rolled his eyes and then smiled indulgently. "Alpha mine, people have talked about me for years. They speculated about what damage—mental or physical—might cause me to refuse so many offers to contract, what kinky sexual activities I must indulge in to be so hard to match, and then there's you! And all the rumors that fly around about your barroom brawls and proclivities. Let them talk! They already do! I'm beyond caring. And your money makes us rather bulletproof."

Xan rose to his feet and Urho watched as his boy (*his boy? he was losing his mind here!*) paced the floor. "My father will be appalled. Last time, he made sure I understood that servicing you, getting you pregnant, was my sole responsibility and that I needed to step up to the plate and be a man."

"You have stepped up to the plate by getting access to the pills for stamina and by providing a wonderful surrogate option in your lover. I don't think Urho will be gossiping about his duties toward me at parties!"

"Of course not," Urho said, stung. He sometimes discussed his surrogate work with Vale, Jason, Yosef, and Rosen, but if Caleb and Xan wanted to keep this between the three of them, of course he could be trusted to do that.

"Good," Caleb said, turning back to Xan. "As for your father, he'll be fine with it. Leave him to me."

Xan's lips twisted. "He does like you."

"Because I flatter him."

"True. But I'm not sure that me arranging for a surrogate will impress him *or* make him think I should be allowed to see Pater."

"Your father is keeping you from your pater?" Urho asked.

"It's nothing," Xan said, flapping a hand, but he still chewed on his lip, so it was clearly very much something.

"I think he'll be more impressed that you've arranged a discreet way to prevent my suffering than if you allowed the next heat to be another failure."

"I want to be able to do this myself," Xan said with longing. "I want to be the alpha you deserve."

Caleb rose and pulled Xan up into his arms. "You accept me the way I am. This is me accepting you the way you are, darling. And I'm encouraging you to accept yourself."

"Limitations and all?"

"No, Xan. *No.* You and me? We're without limits. This is even further proof of that. Boundless love and friendship and boundless acceptance—that's what we give each other."

Xan nodded against Caleb's neck, and Urho stood slowly.

It was a risk, and he didn't know if he was overstepping, but they'd had a very intimate discussion in front of him, *about* him, even. Despite all sense and reason, he'd laid some sort of claim to both these men now. So he wrapped his arms around them both, joining in their embrace.

Caleb stiffened for a moment and then relaxed. When the embrace ended, Caleb said, "Now that's all settled, I'm going to leave you two alone." Caleb kissed Xan's cheek. "I'll be in my room. Come to me before bed?"

Xan nodded, and his eyes followed Caleb out the door before he collapsed on the sofa again, covering his face. Urho stood by helplessly, confused about what he should do next: return to his chair, sit beside Xan, or maybe take his leave? It'd been a confusing day for them both, surely. Maybe Xan would prefer to be alone?

"What happens now?" Xan said, his voice muffled through his hands over his face.

Urho chose to sit next to him on the sofa, close, but not quite touching. "I admit I don't know. I've never done this kind of thing before."

The honesty seemed to prod Xan from where he was hiding, and he dropped his hands, a self-deprecating smirk on his lips. "Believe it or not, I have. Not exactly this, I suppose, but I've had a lover before."

"Jason."

Xan swallowed hard and nodded, darting his eyes toward the fire. His bruised cheek shone in the dancing light. "We don't talk about it. The two of us. We never mention it. It just exists there. A memory that we both feel, but we ignore."

Urho knew exactly what that was like. He and Vale were the same. "It must be difficult to see him so happy."

"It has been, yeah. At times. But I love him—as a friend—so I'm glad for him, too."

Another point of feeling they had in common. "And sad for yourself."

Xan shrugged. "I've been very sad for a long time, but I wasn't sad with you today in your library. Or tonight in mine. Shocked, maybe. Surprised, for sure. But not sad."

The glow in Xan's eyes was probably hope. Urho wanted to coax that small flame to life, but he had to be sensible about it. No matter what he felt, or what they'd done, they couldn't flaunt this in society and not pay a price. "I've been sad for a long time, too."

"Because of losing Riki?"

Urho nodded. His beloved's name on Xan's lips should have rankled, or at least brought with it a stab of guilt given what he'd done with Xan right beneath Riki's portrait earlier in the day, but it didn't. Instead a warm pleasure filled him as though maybe Xan might hear Urho's stories of Riki and help keep him alive by listening. To his surprise, what *he* felt was hope, too. "I still grieve him."

"Of course, you do. And then you lost Vale," Xan said cautiously, as though Vale was the more prickly topic when it came to Urho's prior loves.

Urho smiled. "That was hard, but nothing like losing Riki. My relationship with Vale was always doomed to end even if Jason hadn't come along that night in the university library."

Xan sucked in a breath. "I can't believe I didn't notice you then. I was too busy holding Jason back from just *taking* Vale right there in front of wolf-god and the whole wide world to notice anyone else. That and dealing with the realization that my own puny plans for my future with Jason had just gone up in flames." Xan snorted, but then went on wonderingly, "Until just now, I'd nearly forgotten that you were there that day."

"Both of us supporting characters in other men's love stories."

"Yes."

Urho smiled. The fire crackled. "This room is very modern."

"Caleb likes things to look clean. He wears white except for his baubles and paints, and his room is a nest of white fluffy everything. He says it's calming to him, and he keeps his areas as sparse as possible. Everywhere except in his print studio. *That* is a bird's nest and a fire hazard, if you ask me. But it makes him happy, so I don't forbid it."

Cool relief flooded Urho to have left behind discussion of love and past lovers. He grabbed on to this new information about

Caleb. "He's an artist?"

"Supposedly," Xan said, laughing gently. "I haven't seen any of his work, but he spends a lot of time in there and then comes out covered in ink. It's cute." Xan's eyes sparkled fondly. "He's cute."

A strange, fragile jealousy grew in Urho—unbidden and imperfect. "And you don't want him between heats at all?" Clarification on that seemed incredibly important. "You're truly all right with his frigidity?"

Xan frowned. "I am. I don't find him physically or sexually exciting. He smells like an omega, and the alpha in me does respond to that in some ways. Like, I want to protect him and care for him. But fucking him is not something I want to do. Which is lucky since Caleb would hate it if I did. And we already told you the word 'frigid' is very rude, and it makes Caleb angry. He prefers asexual."

Urho inclined his head. "I tend to fall back on the old-fashioned terms. Vale is always arguing with me about that. Out of respect for Caleb, I'll try to remember to use this new term."

"It's not new. It existed in the Old World, too. It means someone who doesn't feel sexual attraction."

"And he doesn't?"

"No."

"Not even during heats?"

"Not really. He says being in heat is like having a really, unbelievably intense itch that he can't reach. It feels amazing when someone finally scratches it for him, but that doesn't mean he's attracted to the person doing the scratching. He says he prefers it be with someone he cares about. Would most like it to be someone he loves as a friend." Xan chewed on his lower lip again.

"But his heats are like any other omega's?"

"I guess? I don't know for sure. I don't have any experience other than the one heat we've shared together, so I can't say." He closed his eyes and shook his head. "It was a disaster. A complete wreck. I couldn't stay hard for very long and he was in so much pain. I tried fisting him, and using the alpha dildo, but it wasn't enough. He needed a knot, and it was…" Xan's mouth wobbled. "I hate myself for that entire situation. I let him hurt."

"You didn't call for assistance?"

"I asked my father to arrange for something once I realized that I truly wasn't going to be able to satisfy him, but by the time a suitably discreet man arrived, the heat had passed. I managed to knot him once a day for the duration—"

Urho held back a gasp. That wasn't nearly often enough. Poor Caleb! He must have been in agony.

"I think with the pills…?" Xan rubbed at his eyes, pinching between his brows and sighing in frustration.

"They'll help," Urho agreed. "But I'll help, too. Caleb won't suffer again."

"But we'll be in Virona by then." Xan looked up worriedly. "Won't you need to stay here with Vale for his pregnancy?"

Urho frowned. "When is Caleb's heat due?"

Xan counted on his fingers. "Two months and two weeks, give or take."

"Vale isn't due for another three months. If things are going well at that point, it's possible I could leave him for a week." But it was doubtful. That was a slim window and Vale would be in the most dangerous stage of the pregnancy. Urho would need to be here for him.

Xan must have read the truth on Urho's face because he shook his head. "I don't want to risk Vale or the baby's life for this. You need to be close by in case anything goes wrong."

"There are other options. You and Caleb could return here for the duration of his heat. You could say he wanted to be comfortable in the home he's most familiar with. Surely your father wouldn't argue with that?"

"No," Xan agreed. "He probably wouldn't. Father is generous with Caleb. I think he pities him being contracted to me." He nodded slowly, blue eyes distant and thoughtful.

"That way you would be close and if I needed to leave the heat to deal with Vale, I could."

"It's a lot to put on you," Xan fretted.

"I'm strong. I can handle it."

"Heats are tough and tiring. You'll be worn out when Vale needs you most."

"It'll be fine. With two of us, the heat won't be a problem to manage at all. Especially if Caleb is not a nymph—suffering from interminable heat."

Xan huffed a soft laugh. "Old-fashioned asshole words are hard to let go of, huh?"

"I'm learning."

Coming back to his main worry, Xan asked, "But the pills will help?"

"The pills will provide you with a great deal of stamina, but if your interest isn't there..." Urho lifted his hands helplessly. "There's no forcing that. Still, I believe if I'm with you then you might find the situation more exciting." Urho cast a hot glance up and down Xan's body, imagining him naked again.

Xan's cheeks flushed beneath his bruise and his eyes brightened. "Definitely. I have other ideas, too. I was thinking during Caleb's heat, I'd ride a dildo myself and pretend it's..." He trailed off, licked his lips, and smiled hotly. "I could pretend it's you. That might help keep me hard. Of course, if you're actually there..."

Urho flushed hot all over. "You're going to arouse me again. The image of you with a dildo pressed inside and thinking of me. Filthy."

Xan's cheeks glowed pink in the firelight. "How many days until I'm healed enough that you can take me?" he asked, licking his lips. His eyes shone hungrily again.

Urho's cock ached as it thickened against his thigh. "Remind me, when do you leave?"

"Sunday."

Urho groaned. "I don't think you'll be healed enough to take me for a good deal longer than that."

Xan squirmed, scooting closer to Urho on the sofa. "I can handle it. I can take a lot of punishment."

Urho touched his cheek where the bruise still distorted his handsome face. "Punishment is the last thing I want to give you."

"But what if I need it? For something bad that I've done?" Xan blinked long and slow.

"Like…like a spanking?"

"Yes," he hissed, shifting on the couch, his arousal on display distorting his pants.

"I'll tell you what," Urho said, leaning closer. "If I hear of you doing anything worthy of punishment, I'll dole it out. But only if you truly need it."

Xan licked his lips. "I'll need it. Definitely. Really soon."

Urho's heart skipped a beat. "Then I'll have to come up to visit you and dispense a spanking or two. I couldn't stay more than one night, in case something goes wrong with Vale, but I could steal away once I've checked in on him. If all stays well."

"You'd do that?" Xan asked, eyes wide and happy shock in his voice. "You'd visit me even before Caleb's heat?"

Urho took Xan's chin in his hands and rubbed the cleft there with his thumb. His insides trembled, confusion and certainty warring. His voice shook as he said, "How else will I tend to the beautiful, sweet hole you've promised to me?"

Xan's lashes fluttered, and he groaned. "I'm going to come in my pants if you say things like that."

"You smell so good," Urho whispered, leaning close and nuzzling the sweaty place behind Xan's ear, overcome with the urge to cover Xan and protect him. To make him smell like Urho's own come and saliva and skin. To mark him as his own for all to scent and know. "I want to suck you and taste your juices again."

Xan turned to Urho, kissing him quickly.

The night dissolved once more into lust and madness. Any attempts at holding a reasonable conversation were lost in a lush raft of scents, skin, and desire. Urho sucked Xan's cock, and allowed Xan to drain his dick again, too. His balls ached like when he was a newly imprinted youngster and he'd fucked Riki for days upon days. He stroked Xan's hair as the boy swallowed his come again, gazing up at him with wide, hopeful eyes, begging for Urho's approval.

"Good boy," he whispered, his voice slurring with satisfied lust and exhaustion. "Such a good boy."

Xan buried his head in Urho's lap and kissed his softening cock. "Are we lovers, Urho?" he asked tremulously.

"We're lovers," Urho agreed, the weight of the words shaking him to the core. "My beautiful one. My alpha-shaped omega. My lover."

Xan quivered, and a sob burst free. Urho hushed him and fed him cock again, petting his head as Xan suckled him gently and cried.

Somehow it felt holy.

CHAPTER NINE

THE SUN ROSE on Urho wrapped around Xan in a soft bed covered by a canopy and warm, wooden furniture. He blinked into the sunlight, lazy satisfaction shifting into confusion and then dismay that he'd somehow spent the night in Xan's home, lost in pleasure and flesh, feeding on Xan's small noises and salty tears. The lingering scent of their combined pleasure smothered him, and he threw back the covers, eyes sharp and throat dry, searching for the bathroom.

Xan groaned and slept on, his dark lashes pressed against his sleep-pale cheeks, and his red mouth open and wet with drool. The formerly livid bruises on his face, back, and ribs were now shaded green and yellow. Urho remembered how heedless he'd been of them last night, and the way Xan hadn't complained in the least. Either the boy enjoyed pain or was willing to endure it in exchange for pleasure. Urho cleared his throat, but Xan only whimpered in his sleep and drowsed on.

After pissing in the attached bathroom, Urho pulled on his clothes from the day before, buttoning up his shirt slowly, staring at the young man in the bed, trying to make his life fit back into shapes he understood. Unable to make that happen, he finally stepped up to the bed, smoothed Xan's hair off his forehead and kissed him there.

A warmth he'd almost forgotten, a kind of joy and peace combined, creeped through him. He might not know the future, but this moment of staring at this beautiful man was his forever. He didn't regret it.

Leaving the room and shutting the door carefully behind him, he set out toward the front of the house, uncertain if he was on his way out or simply looking for some kind of breakfast. He only knew he was too restless, rushing with anticipation and dosed with a liberal amount of shock, to sit still.

The stairs led to the front hall and two beta servants stood whispering by the door. When they saw him, their faces shuttered neutrally, and the one called Ren stepped forward asking, politely, "Sir, would you like your coat and hat? Or are you going to be joining Mr. Riggs for breakfast?"

Urho opened his mouth to ask for his things, but then his stomach rumbled. The last food he'd eaten had been the soup Jason had forced into him, and he'd been pretty physically active since then. Besides, he supposed that facing Caleb bravely and alone, rather than running off like he was ashamed, was the least he could do after the generosity Caleb had shown last night in discovering him naked with Xan.

His neck felt hot as he said, "Perhaps some breakfast."

"This way, sir." Ren motioned him toward a room beside the kitchen Urho remembered from parties. It wasn't the large dining room, or the ballroom used for dancing, but a small morning room with a table that, during parties, was laden with appetizers and sweets.

Now it held only Caleb, sitting in a white robe with messy blond hair and a hint of what looked like silver glitter on his eyelashes. Urho hadn't noticed it the night before, but it sparkled in the morning sun when Caleb lifted his eyes and broke into a pleasant, if somewhat reserved, smile. He put aside the newspaper he'd been reading and gestured at the table.

"I apologize if—"

"Of course not," Caleb interrupted, as he was wont to do.

"Please join me. Have a seat. Xan sleeps late typically, something that will have to change in Virona." He picked up a piece of toast and slathered it with marmalade, closing his eyes as he took a bite and hummed. "The perfect flavor. Do you like marmalade?" He motioned toward the half-empty jar on the white tablecloth.

"Occasionally."

"It's my favorite," Caleb said, smiling as he chewed. He nodded at the beta servants, and a steaming plate of bacon, eggs, and potatoes was placed in front of Urho.

"Usually Xan just has some hair of the dog if he's been drinking the night before, or a bowl of oatmeal, but I thought you might want something that would stick to your strong bones." Caleb pushed a strand of chin-length blond hair away from his mouth and took another bite of his marmalade toast.

Urho smiled at the beta servant who disappeared shortly after verifying that Urho had everything he needed. "You have a lot of servants here," he commented, more accustomed to the three servants at his home and none at Vale and Jason's. Yosef and Rosen, both betas, didn't hire servants, either.

Caleb nodded. "I admit I like being spoiled. When I was quite young, my family had a fairly decent fortune, but you may have heard from rumors past that my father lost it all."

"Cocaine. And the resulting poor choices."

Caleb raised a brow at Urho's boldness in saying the words out loud, but said only, "Exactly," before stuffing his mouth with more toast.

"I have a few servants, but my Riki was a private type, and he liked to take care of me himself."

Caleb swallowed and smiled gently. "You loved him dearly, I can tell. You were *Érosgápe*, I take it?"

"Yes."

"You're a strong man to have gone on without him. Many

can't."

"He made me promise." Of course, the promise had come close to the end, when Riki knew he wouldn't survive. Urho had assumed the promise was elicited for the sake of the child who also died but he didn't want to meet Riki in the afterlife and discover he'd been wrong. So he'd soldiered on despite every desire, especially at first, to put an end to himself.

"Ah." Caleb's voice dropped into a compassionate tone.

Urho ate in the resulting silence for a while before saying, "You must wonder what my intentions are with Xan."

"Do you even know?" Caleb asked, his blue eyes catching Urho's and holding his gaze. "I suspect you don't have a clue what you're doing or why. Acting on instinct and rationalizing after the fact."

Urho took a sip of water and then cleared his throat. Caleb saw too much and too clearly. "I planned only to offer to satisfy his needs so he wouldn't be tempted to go to *him* again. I didn't expect…"

"To like it? To want him for your own reasons?"

"I should have anticipated both of those things, shouldn't I?" A wry, tight smile twisted the corner of Urho's mouth. "But you're right. I didn't. Until it was happening and everything flashed clear, like when I imprinted on Riki all those years ago. And again, when it was over, and in the aftermath, I realized…"

"You realized?"

Urho looked around, trying to see if any servants were lingering.

"We're alone. They won't disturb us again without making a ruckus as they enter. They're used to us."

"Ah." Urho wiped his mouth and took another bite of his food, stalling for time, but Caleb wasn't having it.

"Go on. I'm interested to hear what stolid, sensible Urho is feeling when he's thrown all of that to the wind." He grinned crookedly.

Urho sighed, wanting to argue the description, but he knew he'd polished that reputation over the years, in part to obscure the things he did as a doctor that were not so very sensible. "Everything's more confusing when I'm not near him. Right now, I wonder if it was a mistake to make my offer, to have discovered this part of me; to want him, all of it. What good can come of this? We could be arrested, imprisoned." He gestured with his fork in frustration. "We can never be a proper couple. He's contracted to you as your alpha, for wolf-god's sake. Pretending to be my omega is pointless." Urho's voice rose slightly as the fears he forgot about completely while in Xan's presence frothed to the surface.

"Do you plan to run away then?"

Urho stammered, but Caleb went on before he could answer.

"Are you going to run from the first taste of joy you've had in years? The future that we could all three forge?" His voice grew harder. "The *promises* you made to him and me last night?"

"No," Urho replied gruffly. "That's not what I want either."

"I didn't think so." Caleb sat back in his chair again, his body losing the sharp aggressive lines that had accompanied his questions. "As for whether or not Xan is an omega, when he's in your arms, he's whatever you both want him to be. Will he ever go into heat or bear your children? No. But he'll do anything in his power to please you if you just give him the chance."

"I'm not running," Urho said flatly. "Even though it would be the smart thing to do. Not to mention the safe thing. But, no." He rubbed between his eyes and sighed. "You don't have to convince me. I'm going to keep my promises and, in exchange, I expect him to do the same."

Caleb smirked, his eyes glinting mischievously. "So you've already exacted promises from him too? You move quickly, Dr. Chase."

"I thought we were on a first-name basis now."

"We are, but sometimes a man has to tease another man when they're so very transparent to everyone but themselves." Caleb laughed and crammed more marmalade toast into his mouth, his eyes crinkling at the edges as he chuckled and chewed.

"I'm sorry to disturb breakfast, Mr. Riggs," Ren said after knocking loudly and being called into the room. "But Jason Sabel is here for Mr. Heelies. How do you recommend I proceed?"

"Send Jason in here," Caleb said, wiping his mouth with a napkin. After the servant exited, he turned to Urho. "This should be awkward. But I'm sure we'll all survive."

Jason entered the room dressed in his usual suit, with a tie obviously chosen by Vale, and his hat in his hand. His eyes went wide seeing Urho at the table, but after only a moment he smiled good-naturedly and said, "Caleb, Vale sends his love."

"Of course, and mine goes to him."

"He would have sent some to you, too, Urho, if he'd known I'd see you."

"I'll be by this afternoon. He can tell me then."

"Good. Thank you." He turned his attention back to Caleb. "Anyway, I stopped by to see Xan?" He darted another glance to Urho. "I have reason to believe he might need my help with something in particular. And I wanted to talk with him, one-on-one. But Ren says he's not up yet?"

"He had a very strenuous and late night," Caleb said, his tone rife with implications and his eyes twinkling merrily. "He's exhausted this morning. Poor lamb."

"Oh, I..." Jason trailed off, turning inquisitive eyes to Urho. "Why are you here, exactly?"

"Urho came over last night to bring some medication to help me with a private health issue. And then he stayed for breakfast," Caleb said as though that was perfectly natural. "Why don't you join us?"

"Oh, well..." Jason licked his lips. His eyes nearly gobbled up Urho's plate of food. "All right." As the beta servants provided Jason with a heaping plate of eggs, bacon, and toast, he added, "Vale's not much of a cook—"

"You can say that again," Urho muttered.

"And normally that's fine. I fend for myself. But he hates it when I eat breakfast at home now that he's pregnant. He says the cooking smells so early in the morning turn his stomach." He spun to Urho with a raised hand. "But don't worry! I always leave him a homemade oatmeal bar on the counter and a full glass of milk in the fridge as well as those vitamins and powders you prescribed for him. He swears to me upside down and backwards that he eats and drinks it *all* when he gets up."

"I'm sure he does," Urho reassured.

"I am, too. I think. I mean, he's so fussy right now," Jason said. Worry crackled over him like electricity over a wire.

"I only just heard about Vale's pregnancy," Caleb said, with a respectfully subdued quality to his voice. It was a tone omegas often took when discussing a state of being always fraught with discomfort and the threat of death for them. "I haven't had time to send a congratulatory note or flowers. But I will try to do so once we get set up in Virona."

"Virona?" Jason asked, distracted from his own worries at this comment. "You're going to the sea now? The cool weather will be coming in soon. What sort of holiday is that?"

"It's not a vacation. We've been sent up by Xan's father to open a new satellite office there."

"Permanently?" Jason's brows shot up.

"For a long time, if not forever." Caleb pushed his hair behind his ears. "You and Vale are welcome anytime. You can pop up for a short visit or feel free to stay at length. The house is huge, from what I've heard—much bigger than this one—and it's right on the ocean. The sea air is good for health any time of year. Isn't that right, Urho?"

Urho nodded, his gut tying up at the thought of Xan so far away from him.

Caleb went on, "I know Xan would love it if you and Vale could make the trip."

"Not until the baby comes," Jason said, chewing his breakfast slowly. His mixed feelings about Xan's move were written clearly on his face. "But we'll come up directly after, if everything goes well."

"Everything will go perfectly," Caleb insisted, with a superstitious zeal Urho recognized from years of dealing with omega health. To behave as though a pregnancy wouldn't go to term, or that the omega wouldn't come out of labor in perfect health, was bad luck amongst omegas. "Vale will be strong, and the baby will healthy. And vice versa."

Jason nodded. "Thank you. From your mouth to wolf-god's ears. But back to the subject of this move. It's so far. Virona is a three-hour train ride away."

"It's quite far," Caleb agreed, nodding pleasantly.

"Can't someone else handle the satellite office? Ray or that annoying Janus?"

"Apparently not."

"Is this because of…" Jason trailed off, clearly uncertain how to proceed, but he looked to Urho for guidance.

"Because of?" Caleb prompted.

"Urho?" Jason implored, clearly wanting Urho to take up the slack or answer his question through some sort of telepathy.

"Because of Urho?" Caleb laughed before Urho could speak. "Wolf-god, no. News of *that* hasn't spread to Xan's father quite yet. It's because of other rumors, mostly. Probably the same rumors you heard about the trouble Xan's been having lately? Yes? And, I suppose, they really do need someone to head up opening the satellite office."

"Wait. The news of Urho and…" Jason glanced at Urho again, and then his brows shot up. "Oh. I see. Ah, well, um. Good. That's…good. That's great even." He took a big gulp from his water glass before digging into his food. He didn't say much for several minutes and they all ate in silence. Or, rather, Caleb watched the two of them eat, having apparently put away as much marmalade toast as he could hold.

"I thought we were keeping that bit of information just between the three of us," Urho finally said, when his throat came unstuck and his own hot cheeks had cooled. "The fewer people who know, the better."

"I assumed Jason already knew." Caleb's smooth, pale brow furrowed. "The way he was looking at you, the comment about Xan being in trouble. Did you not know, Jason?"

Jason shook his head and wiped his mouth with his napkin. "I suspected something could happen, but I didn't realize it had begun. Or that it could begin. I don't know. Obviously, I'll keep my mouth shut."

Caleb's face paled. "I'm sorry," he whispered to Urho.

"Mistakes happen," Urho said. But that was exactly the problem, wasn't it? They couldn't afford mistakes, even casual ones.

Caleb had lost a bit of his usual composure. "When it comes to Xan, Jason has his own secrets to keep. Right, Jason?"

Jason cleared his throat. "I do. And I wouldn't endanger Xan for anything the world. Or you, Caleb. Or, frankly, Urho for that matter."

"While I'm glad our little group is so liberal minded," Urho said, his stomach fluttering, "I'd rather this news traveled no further than this table. Not even to Rosen and Yosef's ears. For our safety and everyone else's."

"I have to tell Vale about it," Jason said. "We don't have secrets from each other."

"It's not your secret," Caleb pointed out. "It's Xan's and Urho's. And mine. And if Urho wants to tell Vale, then that's his business, but I do think you should keep this news to yourself."

Jason scoffed.

Caleb flushed, his eyes glinting dangerously. "I know, I'm a hypocrite, and this situation is all my fault, anyway. But my mistake won't make telling Vale the right thing to do."

"I'll tell him," Urho said. "He'll figure it out at some point on his own. He's brilliant and observant and he probably somehow already knows."

Jason laughed, his eyes bright as always when thinking of his omega. "That's true." He went dreamy. "He's probably written a poem about it."

"Wolf-god, I hope not. That'll get us arrested for sure. Likely for violating the Wolf Reform Party's creative laws of moral decency."

"His poems are beautiful," Jason defended. "Especially the ones about me."

Urho groaned. "You're *Érosgápe* and thus totally besotted. He could fart on a sheet of paper and you'd love it."

Jason laughed again and didn't dispute the accusation.

"Well, look who rose from the bed before ten," Caleb said, his eyes going to the door.

Urho's throat went dry as he met Xan's gaze across the small room. His heart flipped in his chest, and his hands began to tremble. "Good morning," he said, and even his voice sounded frayed by the sight of Xan in his pajamas and bare feet.

"Morning," Xan said, his gaze sliding to Jason. The lingering bruise on his cheek glowed in the morning light. "Is Vale all right?"

"We were actually just discussing how perfect he is," Caleb said, chuckling and plucking up his flute of orange juice and sipping it.

Xan rolled his eyes. "I've heard it all before. Twenty times. At least. In some cases, upwards of a hundred."

Jason chuckled, but his eyes hung on Xan's bruises worriedly. "You tease, but you have nothing but praise for Caleb as well."

"True. Because Caleb's perfect," Xan said, smirking and taking a seat by Caleb's side.

"Amazing how every alpha says the same of their omega," Caleb said. "Did you think your Riki was perfect?"

Urho ripped his eyes from Xan's exposed collarbone, where a red love bite bloomed. "Riki? Yes, he was absolutely perfect." He glanced back to Xan, whose eyes softened in sympathy.

"He was handsome too," Xan said. "I saw his portrait yesterday when I was in Urho's library."

Jason nodded. "It's a good portrait. He has a nice smile in it."

Caleb rested his elbow on the table and his chin in his hand. "And that's the way it goes, isn't it? Alphas adore their omegas, and omegas adore their alphas. The beginning and the end. The natural order of things."

Urho caught Xan's gaze as the beta servants brought in his bowl of oatmeal and a small, decorative plate featuring a single fried egg. He left unspoken his question of whether the natural order of things could ever be turned upside down. Was it possible for an alpha to adore another alpha? If it was, did he truly want to find out? Despite the risk and against all odds?

Urho knew he was risking rather a lot here, but Caleb was right: he hadn't felt so alive in years.

"What happened to your face?" Jason asked Xan casually, but with a sideways glance at Urho.

"Bar fight. The usual," Xan said dismissively, waving it away.

Caleb hummed under his breath and took another swallow of his orange juice, sending challenging looks Jason's way.

"You get in a lot of bar fights for someone who doesn't go to bars that often."

"True." Xan took a bite of oatmeal and closed his eyes tiredly.

Jason flicked a glance at Urho, who tried to appear reassuring. Caleb smiled and finished up his orange juice.

The topic was dropped.

Breakfast proceeded as it normally would at that point with jokes, discussion of the move to Virona, and no further heavy conversation between them. As they broke up, beta servants came in to escort Jason and Urho out. Xan's only concession to what had passed between them being a tersely stated reminder addressed to Urho that he left for Virona on Sunday, and a significant gaze. Urho had nodded in return.

It was only as they reached the sidewalk in front of Xan's home that Jason returned to the topic of his original reason for visiting.

"Urho, do I have your word that whatever madness you brought to me yesterday is finished? That Xan is safe, and I don't need to worry about him being hurt?"

"I can't promise that," Urho said, opening the front gate for Jason and glancing back at the house behind him. "I made him an offer to act as his surrogate—" *his lover*, his heart hissed, "—and he accepted it. I'll obviously hold up my end of the bargain, but I can only say that he's promised to hold up his. Time will tell if he actually does."

"So whatever man he was seeing, the man that you believed was unsafe? That's in the past now? It's over?"

"He gave his word."

Jason groaned. "I guess that'll have to be good enough. It helps that he's going to Virona. I take it the man lives here?"

"Yes."

"And his father found out about him?"

"I'm not sure about that, but there seem to be rumors that his father can't deny or ignore. Rumors that imply something not entirely according to protocol is happening."

"And you still aren't going to tell me who he is?"

Urho snorted. "If I knew myself, the animal wouldn't still be breathing."

Jason nodded, slowly trailing his gaze up and down Urho's body. "Just remember what I said about your feelings, Urho. You can say words like 'surrogate' all you want, but you sound more like an alpha protecting his omega to me."

Urho swallowed thickly.

"Hey, that's all right. In fact, that's what Xan *needs*." Jason put his hand on Urho's shoulder and squeezed. "Don't let your hang-ups and fears prevent you from giving him that."

"You're a mouthy pup."

"Not half as mouthy as Xan can be," Jason said. "But you like that about him, so you probably like it in me, too."

Urho cuffed Jason's shoulder, and they parted ways, hustling toward their respective cars. "I'll be by later to check on Vale," he said. "I'll phone if there's a problem, but there won't be."

"Thank you," Jason called out from across the street. "For taking care of Vale, for helping with Xan, and for everything."

Urho hoped Jason's gratitude wasn't unfounded. After all, Xan was leaving town on Sunday, they hadn't made firm plans to see each other in the interim, and promises made in the heat of the moment always felt less solid in the light of day.

He supposed it was the same as any aspect of life. There were no guarantees. He'd learned that early on with Riki.

He turned to his car and opened the door, climbing inside and starting away from Xan and Caleb's house.

Only time would tell.

CHAPTER TEN

XAN PACED BY the train, his heart in his throat. He hadn't seen Urho in person since the morning after their night together. They'd spoken on the phone twice briefly, but neither of their schedules had permitted them to meet.

Urho had been called out to Sullen District to deal with an omega seemingly pregnant with twins—a dangerous aberration that would need to be handled carefully. And Xan had been taxed with upending his household, and the lives of his beta servants who'd chosen to come along, to make it to Virona by his father's deadline.

Still, Urho had promised to be at the train station to see him off. Even if they couldn't do more than hug manfully, it was important to Xan to see his new lover's face one last time before they were separated for who knew how long. He needed to be sure he hadn't hallucinated the promises between them, or Urho's commitment to them.

"He'll be here," Caleb said, fixing the emerald circle pin on his collar, a fashion that declared him a bonded omega. They were only bonded in friendship, but in public Caleb always wore a showy pin anyway to deter attention. His beauty tended to attract more of that than he desired, and Xan, being a small alpha, didn't always run off other men by his presence alone.

"What if he changed his mind?"

"He hasn't."

"How do you know? He's risking a lot! And for what?"

"For you."

Xan rolled his eyes. "Oh, what a prize!"

Caleb pulled up his silvery cowl scarf over his hair in the nippy autumn wind. "Indeed," he said earnestly, as though Xan hadn't spoken with cutting sarcasm.

Then Xan spotted him. Broad shoulders in a well-fitted trench coat, a grey fedora on his head, and a serious set to his face. Xan's insides turned to mush. His heart quickened, and he sucked in a hard breath full of hope.

"Hi," he mumbled nervously when Urho was close enough to hear. "I didn't know if you'd make it."

Urho's smile was white against his dark skin. "Seeing you off safely is my first priority today."

Xan swallowed hard, examining Urho's eyes for some sense of what the man was feeling. "Do you think you'll be able to visit? Like we discussed?"

Urho reached for his shoulder and clasped it warmly, gazing down into his face. "Nothing would give me greater pleasure, but I'm afraid I can't promise to come by any particular date. Between the twins in Sullen and Vale's delicate state, I might not be able to get free for a full day and night."

"Three hours on the train to Virona and back is far," Xan agreed, his heart sinking. "If there was a problem with Vale or the omega pregnant with twins, you wouldn't be able to get home in time." He said it aloud so Urho wouldn't have to, and so Xan wouldn't feel like Urho was just making excuses.

"Is there a chance we could meet halfway?" Urho asked.

Xan's clenched stomach loosened. "I need to see what my father has planned for me in setting up the satellite office, but surely the weekends will be free?"

"Caleb wouldn't miss you if you came to meet me?"

Caleb smiled and answered, "I'll be far too busy setting up my new print studio and planning the upcoming Autumn Nights feasts

160

to miss Xan for part of a day—or more. In fact, I'd be happy to spare him so the two of you can renew your *commitments*."

Urho licked his lips, a flash of embarrassment in his eyes. "There's a wonderful little apartment I sometimes rent by the canal in Montrew. No one would be the wiser if we spent some happy hours there together."

Xan grinned, his stomach flipping with excitement and his throat tight with longing. He wanted to be with Urho now, to throw his arms around him and kiss him goodbye like so many bonded and beta couples were doing all around him on the platform.

A whistle blew, and a conductor shouted, "All aboard for Virona!" Xan smiled sadly at Urho and took his hand in a firm handshake. Urho jerked him in close and wrapped him up in a strong hug. He patted his back in a fatherly way, likely to remove any suspicions from onlookers' minds. "Remember your promise to me," he whispered fiercely in Xan's ear.

"I haven't forgotten."

"Promise again," Urho said, pulling back enough to not draw attention, but lingering close enough so that he could whisper.

"Are you serious?"

"Yes. I want to hear it. What's mine?"

"Me?"

"And specifically?"

Xan swallowed hard. "My ass."

"Promise it."

"On wolf-god's own salvation, I promise my ass belongs to you," Xan murmured, his neck flushing.

"And your mouth too," Urho said sharply.

Caleb laughed quietly next to them, but Xan ignored him, and so did Urho. They stared intently at each other, the rest of the platform fading away.

"My mouth is yours too," Xan murmured breathlessly.

Urho nodded and ducked his head as though about to capture Xan's trembling mouth with his own. But Caleb slipped between them, embracing Urho hard and laughing. "Wolf-god, you'll get us all arrested if you don't control yourself."

Urho hugged Caleb back before stuffing his hands in his pockets. He cleared his throat and nodded as Caleb and Xan gathered up their small bags for the private compartment. Xan held his gaze as long as he could before turning to climb onto the train. By the time he'd settled his belongings, gotten comfortable in his seat, and turned to look out the window, Urho had left the platform.

"He didn't stay to watch us go," he said to Caleb, who was sorting through a large bag, apparently looking for the stick of gloss he used on his lips, which he pulled out.

"He probably had to go to the bathroom to deal with the pressing problem of his hard dick," Caleb said nonchalantly, smoothing a balm over his mouth. He handed it to Xan. "Put some on, darling. The train compartment is always so dehydrating."

Xan complied, his own dick not entirely soft either after the exchange of promises. "We didn't make plans to talk while we're apart."

"The house will have a phone, surely. You know how to use it."

"But what if he doesn't expect to hear from me? What if he doesn't want me harassing him?"

Caleb tossed the lip balm back into his bag and stared at Xan with a raised brow and impatience creasing his face.

"What?"

"He made you promise absolutely filthy things just now and you think he doesn't want to hear from you? Xan, my love, you are ridiculous."

Xan laughed nervously, his stomach fluttering and his skin prickling all over. "I just wish I didn't have to leave. Things had only just started with us. What if he forgets about me?"

"Don't let him." Caleb pulled a small book from his bag.

"Maybe I should send him flowers."

Caleb snickered softly. "Oh, yes, please do."

"What's funny?"

"You. Trying to court him like an alpha courts omegas." Caleb opened the book and thumbed through the first pages as though looking for his place.

"Should I not? How do omegas court alphas?" He tried to think of what he'd seen Vale do, or Caleb, when they wanted to show their affection. He drew a blank. "Should I court him like an omega instead?"

"Court him like you, Xan." Caleb sighed fondly. "You got him where you wanted him by being yourself. Don't stop now."

Xan slumped in the seat as the train lurched forward. "Where I want him is next to me."

Caleb sighed. "Alas, you have me instead."

"That's not what I meant."

"I know. I'm teasing." Caleb rested his head on Xan's shoulder and kissed his jaw. "Darling, you're exhausted and exhausting. Let's rest on this train ride, all right? Because we'll have so much work to do setting up house as soon as we get to Virona. Try to calm your mind."

"I'm sorry."

"It's new. Of course, you're concerned. But, never fear. Your alpha is still committed to you." Caleb straightened, cracking open his book again. "Now's the moment to allow time and distance to do the work of making him frantic to see you."

"So I shouldn't court him then?"

"Oh, definitely court him. That would be too fun to miss."

Xan rolled his eyes, but in the back of his mind made note to call a florist when he could. He'd have a beautiful bouquet delivered to Urho at his home. He wanted to make sure Urho didn't forget him, and most of all he needed to make sure Urho understood that Xan's intentions toward him weren't purely sexual.

His gut tensed.

What if sex was all Urho wanted from him though? He squirmed. *Everything* was so tentative. The offer Urho had made was for one thing only, but his behavior implied another. It would be foolish to trust in it, surely.

"Here," Caleb said, passing over another book from his bag. "Read. It'll get your mind off things."

Xan sighed when he looked at the title. It was a book of Vale's poetry. "What else do you have in your bag? A puppy?"

Caleb laughed and flipped the page of his book. Over his shoulder, Xan saw that it was also poetry.

With a groan, Xan stared unseeingly at the opening stanza of the first poem for a few minutes. Then he snapped the book shut, flopped back in his seat, and stared out the window. He wished he had the book Urho had given him, but he'd packed it up in a box he'd sent ahead with Ren and the servants.

The fields outside flashed by in grays, browns, greens, and the occasional splash of red or purple from early turning leaves or late blooming wildflowers.

Caleb patted his knee gently but continued to peruse his book of poetry.

"How do you know about relationships and courting?" Xan asked, sitting up straight again. "It's not like I've ever been very good at that stuff with you." Or vice versa, for that matter, but he wasn't about to say that.

"You forget I was highly sought after for several years." Caleb smiled gently. "Until I turned down so many offers to contract that rumors began. *And* you forget that I do have omega friends. We talk, you realize. Trade stories. I have little to offer of my own, of course, so I mainly listen. When I was younger, courting was all anyone ever talked about."

Xan took his hand and stroked the palm lovingly, tracing the lines. "You're not exactly old."

"Of course not, but *now* all my omega friends want to talk about is babies." His voice went wistful. "My dear friend Tad from school is due any day now. Did I tell you?"

Xan shook his head. Caleb rarely talked about his days at Mount Juror and even more rarely of his friends from school.

"Yes, Tad is excited. His third child." Caleb frowned, removed his hand from Xan's, and went back to his book.

"We'll have a child," Xan said softly. "I promise."

"Of course."

Xan studied the side of Caleb's face, admiring his strong, high cheekbones, fluttery gold lashes, and soft lips. "We should invite some of your friends to stay with us in Virona. Probably not Tad until he's delivered, but any of your other friends you miss. It's a big house, and the sea is beautiful any time of the year."

Caleb dropped his head to Xan's shoulder again. "I do love you, dear. You try so hard to make me happy and I couldn't ask for more."

Xan dropped a kiss to Caleb's hair before closing his eyes and letting the rocking of the train send him off into a dream. In it, Urho held a fat baby by the sea, water splashing around his legs, and Caleb stood by him cooing, both of them lit by the light of a pale, wintery sun.

Xan woke several hours later with anxious hope thriving in his heart.

THE HOUSE ROSE up high above the town of Virona. Its size and aging grandeur promised more space than either Caleb or Xan could hope to fill with children in their lifetime.

They stood beside the rather ordinary car they had rented at the railway station and stared up at the pale marble facade of the house which appeared blue-ish beneath the overcast sky.

Wide, tall columns reached up to a flat, red, barrel-tiled roof that had faded out to orange. Expansive arched windows mirrored even more gray sky, broken only by reflected glint of the colorful town below. The front entrance consisted of broad, imposing marble steps leading up two large, dull bronze doors. Both were currently shut and without doormen to open them.

The house was beautiful, but in its neglected state, it felt cold. Nothing about it reached out to welcome them. It was a hard, barren womb.

"It looks haunted," Caleb said, tilting his head and studying their new residence gravely.

"It's just the gray day," Xan murmured reassuringly, tucking his arm around Caleb's back. "The oppressive clouds and the storm blowing in off the shore are playing with our imaginations."

"Hmm. Regardless, the view is lovely. It'll be even more so on a sunny day, I'm sure."

Xan took it all in. The house was built at the top of a hill that sloped down to the dunes behind the house and then farther to the smooth expanse of private beach that gave way to the white-capped gray-green of the ocean.

It was a home designed for a powerful person, someone like the first Lofton to own it, who had been grandfather to Xan's pater, George. Flagler Lofton had presided over the town and controlled it with an iron fist, leaving his omega in charge of the estate, which they filled with children. Flagler Lofton had been the kind of alpha Xan's father had wanted in a son.

Too bad Xan couldn't imagine being that kind of person.

"It's so…white." Caleb whispered, as though still worried about ghosts.

"That's the first I've ever heard you imply something was too white."

Caleb smiled and fiddled with his silvery cowl again. "It's intimidating."

Xan knew what he meant. Even in their home in the city, there were signs of life. It was homey there, with warm fires roaring and rooms Caleb had decorated to his taste. This was a giant architectural echo of the once proud Lofton family and currently neither of them felt up to owning it.

"We'll plant winter flowers out front," Xan said briskly, hoping to reduce the house and all it represented down to something manageable in his mind. "Or hire some betas to do it, rather. Nice, bright colors that will enliven the place."

Caleb glanced around at the grounds as though trying to imagine it with winter flowers. "Does it ever snow, do you think?"

"I doubt it. The ocean currents come all the way from the tropics if I recall my science class correctly. Anyway, they're quite warm, from what I understand, even in winter. That brings with it a certain temperateness despite being farther north."

"Yes, I remember reading about that in school, too." Caleb gathered himself, tucked his long hair behind his ear, and smiled at Xan. "I'm happy with it. We'll make it beautiful, invite guests, and turn it into a real home. It's been empty too long, is all. We'll fill it with sound and noise and light."

"And children," Xan promised.

Caleb nodded. "At least one or two, yes. Strong children who'll one day run down that lovely hill to the ocean and swim like little fish."

"Romantic," Xan teased, slinging his arm around Caleb's shoulder.

"That's me. Mister romance."

Xan studied his omega's handsome face, curiosity welling in him. He knew their promise to always be family but he didn't understand Caleb's lack of interest in romantic feelings. "Don't you ever want to fall in love, Caleb?"

Caleb threw his arms around Xan's neck and rubbed his nose against Xan's cheek. "Darling, *this* is what I want. I tell you all the time! I love you more than I can ever say. My dream life is to be with you as the closest of friends and have your children." He smiled. "You worry too much. Let's go inside and find out how things stand. It's going to be a long afternoon and who knows if there's even any food in the kitchen."

"The beta servants came on ahead of us just for that reason. It should be stocked. I'm surprised Ren and the crew aren't out here to greet us."

"Ren can generally be trusted to think ahead, but the entire move was thrown together so quickly. He's probably in a panic trying to put everything in order before we arrive."

He and Caleb stepped toward the threshold of their new home together. Xan held Caleb back just before the door and said, "Take my hand."

Caleb did. His long fingers felt cool in Xan's warm clasp.

"The alpha and the omega," he whispered, unable to resist the pull of tradition.

"The beginning and end," Caleb answered, smiling warmly at him. "Now who's romantic?"

"Hey! It's traditional to recite the vow before entering a new home together for the first time."

"Traditional!" Caleb exclaimed, laughing and pulling Xan over the threshold by the hand. "We're anything but that, my dear."

As Xan followed him into the low lighting of the wide foyer— more of a great hall in the scheme of entry areas—he blinked to see better, clinging to Caleb's hand like a lifeline.

A large crystal chandelier wired for electric lights hung from the painted, domed ceiling, marble floors shone beneath their clacking heels, and a wide marble staircase, covered in what looked to be a moth-eaten red carpet, rose up and parted in the middle, taking two separate directions to the landing on the second floor.

"So this is what we've been exiled to," he murmured.

"It needs sprucing up, but it's got good bones." Caleb's eyes shone in the dimness.

"Ray said you'd be pleased with it."

"It's a bit rococo," he murmured, waving his hand toward the sculpted and gilded woodwork lining the ceiling, doors, and culminating in ornamental filigrees around the dome that made Xan's heart skip gleefully. But he knew such elements were the antithesis of Caleb's usual design choices.

"It's shiny," Xan enthused. "Or could be."

"Yes." Caleb nudged him with a smile. "It's a beautiful space."

Through the gloom, they saw where the drawing room and library branched off on opposite sides of the grand hall. Both appeared to be equally worn-looking rooms of fabulous, over-the-top design, complete with furnishings that looked usable if not entirely fashionable.

Near the back of the grand hall, walkways led to other rooms and, if the noises coming from the right were any indication, the kitchen and most likely the dining room as well. Visible through wide, arched, glass doors at the back of the hall was an overgrown open-air courtyard in the middle of the house.

"It's a good thing Ren is wonderful at hiring," Caleb said, nodding toward the greenery pressing against the glass. "Someone will need to tame it."

"Indeed. Should we go exploring?"

"Where are the servants?" Caleb asked, frowning. "They should be here getting things ready."

"I sent most of them to town," came a voice from the direction of the landing at the top of the right branch of the stairs.

"On whose authority?" Xan asked, peering into the darkness.

"Hello, cousin," the voice said. A blaze suddenly flamed from overhead, the chandelier bursting with light above them.

Xan squinted at the sudden brightness and then, stomach curdling, he caught sight of the source of the greeting. His cousin now stood in the middle of the staircase, one hand on the banister, the other lifted high in greeting.

"The light switches are in the most damnable places in this house," Janus said with a smirk. "The one for the chandelier is at the top of the stairs."

Dark hair curled gently around his smug face and smile, and his hazel eyes glittered in the now sharp light. Fit and tanned, he was dressed, as always, in tailored but sensual-looking clothes, showing off a sense of fashion and casual sexiness that Xan had always envied.

Next to him, Caleb went stiff and stifled a startled gasp.

"As I was saying, welcome to Virona, cousin," Janus said cheekily, sweeping his raised hand around. "I think you'll find things mostly in order for your arrival. You're welcome for that, by the way. Your servants are good, but someone had to make the hard choices these last few days. That person was me."

Xan gaped at him as Caleb drew closer to his side.

"And thank *you* for allowing me to be your houseguest for the next few months," Janus went on. "Though I doubt you had much to do with it. Truth be told, I'm rather looking forward to it."

"Houseguest?" Caleb asked, darting a glance Xan's way, his blue eyes wide and worried. "Did you know about this?"

Xan shook his head. No, he had certainly not. His smile was more of a snarl, but he managed to pull out the usual niceties all the same. "Thank you for greeting us after our journey, but I think it's my place to welcome you, cousin, since this is to be my home."

Janus only chuckled, and Xan clenched his jaw. He put his arm around Caleb's lower back. "Caleb, allow me to introduce you to Janus Heelies. My father's favorite spy. Janus, this is my omega, Caleb Riggs." Caleb's breath came in small, strange gasps.

Janus smirked. "Yes, I'd heard you'd contracted with the elusive beauty of the class of Wolf Path." He continued down the stairs now, his hand outstretched toward Caleb, who seemed to flinch away. "I've actually already had the honor. Haven't I, Caleb?"

Xan tightened his hold on Caleb's waist as his omega replied with a strange tension in his voice, "Indeed."

Xan asked, "You were in the same cohort, then?"

"We were," Janus agreed. "Many a Philia soirée did I spend watching our dear Caleb hiding in a corner, trying to douse his obvious light from attracting admirers. But no matter how he tried, he never lacked for those."

"So you were a spy even then?" Xan asked snidely.

"I've gotten better at it with age. As your father well knows."

Caleb narrowed his gaze at Janus. "I don't recall you hurting for admirers at those parties either and yet you're here alone."

"Alas, I never found one to suit."

Caleb hissed out a breath slowly.

"Caleb?" Xan asked, but his open-ended question was ignored.

Caleb lifted his chin high, stepped away from Xan's arm, and, with a distinct chill, put his hand out to Janus. He seemed to restrain a wince as Janus took it and placed a kiss on his knuckles. "You're a spy now, you say? Well, I'll endeavor to do something exciting for you to report back to the great Doxan Heelies."

Janus laughed and kissed Caleb's knuckles again. "You do that, pretty one. Because you? You've always been one I'm happy to watch."

Caleb snatched his hand back and turned on his heel. "When will Ren and the others be back? We have bags we need help with."

At that exact moment, Ren appeared from the hallway leading toward the kitchen with a handful of servants at his heels, including the new kitchen boy. Caleb set about ignoring Janus completely as he directed them on what to do with the luggage. As the servants scampered, he swept past Xan and Janus, stalking up the marble stairs with a coldness that Xan rarely experienced even on a snowy winter's day, and had never before seen in Caleb.

"What did I say?" Janus asked, genuinely puzzled by the looks of him, watching Caleb turn to the left and ascend to the landing. "I only wanted to flatter him."

"Caleb prefers to be respected. And so do I." Xan hardened his voice to growl. "Stay away from him. I know Father probably sent you here to keep tabs on me, and that's fine. Obviously, I can't kick you out immediately." He stepped into Janus's space, going up on his toes to be closer to the same height. "But if you upset him again, or I think for even a minute that you have, you can bet your last cent that I *will* throw you out on your ass, Father's spy or not. Assuming I don't actually take you apart first."

Janus raised his hands in surrender. "Never fear, cousin dear. I don't fancy him. For one thing, I like them a bit fleshier and with some hair on their chests."

"*They* are human beings and deserve to be talked about as more than a piece of meat." Xan gritted his teeth. His father couldn't seriously be considering Janus in his stead, could he? The man was a playboy and a half and had been caught in affairs with several contracted omegas. He had no respect for anyone at all, much less omegas, and clearly not for Caleb. "Why did Father send you here?"

"Because, like you said, I have spy work to do." Janus waggled his brows. "And maybe if I'm lucky, I'll find my *Érosgápe* here amongst the quaint villagers of Virona."

Xan shoved past him, following Caleb up the wide stairs. "I'll say it one more time: upset Caleb again and Father can't protect you."

Janus's eyes followed him, but to Xan's equal consternation and relief, he didn't bother with a reply.

Following the sound of Caleb's voice issuing orders to the servants, he stalked down the upstairs hallway, ignoring the view of the courtyard out the open windows. He passed by rooms both closed off and open to be aired out.

As he reached what must be the suite Caleb had chosen for himself, Xan muttered under his breath, "Welcome to Virona, my ass."

CHAPTER ELEVEN

URHO SAT BY the fire in his library, swirling a glass of bourbon and watching flames lick the grate. On the desk behind him, there was a vase of roses, delivered that evening with a note from Xan.

I promise, was all the note read, but that had been enough to get him hard.

The roses' scent drifted to him, a constant reminder of the man he missed already, though they'd had barely enough time together before he'd gone. Closing his eyes, he savored the taste of the liquor and let his mind go blessedly blank. The day had been yet another long one.

After saying goodbye to Xan and Caleb on the platform, he'd driven away confused by his own heart. His face, when he'd glimpsed it in the rearview mirror, was relatively the same, but his priorities seemed to have realigned entirely in the course of a week. The last normal day he could remember, when he'd last felt like the Urho that Riki had left behind, was the day before he'd been called to Jason and Vale's house to confirm what they both knew—that a babe was on the way.

Ever since that moment, he'd been thrown off course, and he barely recognized the thoughts that preoccupied him now, the commitments that he'd made, or the feelings that drove him.

"Sir," a quiet voice said from the door. "I'm sorry to disturb you, but may I have a word?"

Urho waved Mako forward. His longtime beta servant, chef,

and not-quite friend stood anxiously by the fire until Urho gestured for him to take a seat. He was looking good in middle-age, with only a little gray at his dark temples, and a few fine wrinkles by his eyes. He wore his usual chef's uniform over his pudgy stomach, and a kind smile.

"I don't want to offend, sir, but I wanted to ask if everything was all right. The other day, when your small alpha friend came by, there was…" Here he broke off, looking embarrassed and ashamed. "I believe the other servants misunderstood what took place. Because while rumors have long swirled about your friend's proclivities, you have always been far too law-abiding and fastidious in your person to have done anything improper. Right, sir?"

Urho swirled the bourbon again and waited for the rush of disgust and fear that should have filled him at having been discovered in his perversion and gossiped about by his own servants. It didn't come. Instead, a strange twitter of excitement filled his chest, and he had to hold back a sudden smile, for fear of frightening Mako.

"I apologize," Mako said, swallowing hard and rubbing his hands over his pants. "I shouldn't have said anything. I don't want you to believe that I had anything to do with this nasty gossip, sir. Or that I would spread it."

"Part of working in my home," Urho began carefully, "has always been the guarantee that you're working for an honorable man. I pay you on time. I give bonuses for the Autumn Nights holidays. I provide extra days off when needed."

"All of those are very honorable things," Mako agreed, leaning forward obsequiously. "I didn't mean to offend you, sir. I wanted only to—"

"But I am not a perfect man. There are times when the scriptures don't make sense to me. There are actions I have taken, both personally and as a doctor, that don't always fit into the…let us call them *expectations* of the world at large and the Holy Church of Wolf in particular."

Mako ducked his head.

"If you or any of the other servants have a problem working for me now that my imperfection is known, then I suppose I have no other choice than to offer a fair sum as a parting gift, seeing as the fault is mine, and look for servants who may not care so deeply about the personal failings of their employer."

"And who may not be so loyal," Mako was quick to put forth. "If, sir, this is your way of saying that there are to be more visits from the small alpha, and if this is your way of saying that we should be prepared to ignore or offer vague but believable replies to any questions about him, then let me assure you, I for one, and all the others working here will be willing to protect you."

"I see." A whisper of gratitude slipped through him.

"We're betas, sir. The rules don't make as much sense to us. I approached you as I did mainly because of a concern that you yourself would be offended and angered if you found out what the others here were thinking. If you're entertaining the, ah, well, the young alpha, then we'll go about our business as usual and see nothing, hear nothing, know nothing."

Urho sighed, taking another sip of his brandy. "I feel as though I should chastise you for your lack of concern regarding your employer's adherence to the law and the Holy Book of Wolf, but given my own position, that seems absurd."

"When we will see the young man again, sir? I can prepare something special for him. You could have a quiet night in together."

"You're trying a bit too hard now, Mako." Urho grimaced. "I'm not angry with you for asking. It's a good reminder that I won't always find easy acceptance should this continue, and I should be more careful." Though he had barely seen Xan at all. Being more careful than they had been already seemed impossible.

Mako spoke eagerly, "Or you should design a good reason to interact regularly and in private with him, sir. Something beyond a simple friendship, perhaps. A partnership that has to do with your clinic work, maybe."

"We don't have to worry about that for some time," Urho said with a hint of gloom. "He's gone away to Virona indefinitely."

Mako frowned. "I'm sorry to hear that, sir."

"I am, too."

"But given the complications of such an arrangement, maybe it's for the best."

"Perhaps."

"Though I'd hoped…"

"What?"

"That maybe you could be happy again, sir. If you came to care for him."

Urho grunted, an absurd gratitude for his beta servant's care welling in him.

Mako rose and nodded once in deference. "I'll be leaving you now, sir, if that's all right with you. Let me know if there's anything at all I can do to make things easier."

Urho nodded for Mako to go and considered picking up the phone to call Yosef for legal advice on how to best protect Xan and Caleb. Especially since he had no plans to stop indulging in his desire to know more of Xan's body and mind whatever chance he got.

He didn't call though.

With Xan hours away and their plans to meet half-formed, there was no need to rock that boat quite yet. He shifted his gaze from the fire up to the dark portrait above him, barely able to make out Riki's golden hair in the gloom. Xan didn't compare, not really.

And yet to Urho, he was breathtaking—beautiful in an entirely different way than Riki. For the first time in what felt like centuries, Urho was ready to risk a lot for what might turn out to be a little. Or perhaps Xan could turn out to be his whole world.

He finished his brandy and headed upstairs. He entered the room where he kept his memories of Riki and lit a stick of incense, saying a few prayers to wolf-god for his beloved.

Then he added on a prayer for Xan.

CHAPTER TWELVE

ORNING DAWNED, COLD and confusing, as Xan stared out at the ocean view he'd chosen with his bedroom. He stood gazing at the grey-green water, the undulation of it soothing his nerves. The unfamiliar creaking of the old house and restless thoughts of Urho had disturbed his sleep. He'd spared some tossing and turning for Janus, too, letting his mind run wild with the implications of his cousin's presence.

He sipped the still piping-hot coffee that someone had brought in while he slept. Carrying the mug in his hands, he opened the door that led to a private passage. It cut through to the room Caleb had chosen for himself. Caleb's doorway at his end was open, and Xan spotted Ren by the foot of Caleb's bed, laboring under a pile of baroque cushions as Caleb issued orders.

"This room is my worst nightmare." Caleb's voice drifted to Xan, pinched and tired. "There's so much *stuff* in here. Take it all. All of it. Out, out, out. Find some nice white linens and unpack my white things from the boxes I shipped ahead. I suppose there's nothing to be done about all this gilt ornamentation around the ceiling without destroying the history of the room, but call in painters to remove this stripy nonsense from the walls. I want them white, too."

"Of course," Ren said, swaying under the pile of red and gold decorative cushions he held in his arms.

Xan hit the first of two bathrooms within the hallway, the opposite side of the small corridor being made up of two large closets, and shut the door behind him. A piss, shower, and shave later, he felt like a new man, and he summoned a smile as he found Caleb in his room all pink and glowing from his own ablutions.

Caleb sat at the baroque vanity in his room, pinning a silver and gray barrette into his hair to keep the blond strands out of his face.

"Ren tells me that your cousin has already eaten and headed into town," Caleb bit out when he spotted Xan leaning against the doorjamb of his room. "Perhaps he'll stay gone."

"I'm sorry for his rudeness yesterday. I loathe him so much myself that I can't say much more than that."

Caleb shrugged.

"He said you'd already met. How?"

Caleb rolled his eyes. "I've met plenty of alphas in my time, Xan. It was at a Philia soirée."

"Oh, of course."

Caleb hated discussing the strain he'd been under at the Philia soirées before Xan came along, so Xan dropped the subject. "I heard you telling Ren how you'd like the room arranged."

Caleb dotted some silvery powder over his eyelids and smoothed the shimmer out. "Yes. I would have preferred to be at the end of the south end of the hall where wind blows hardest, but as we agreed last night, it's better for me to room beside you so Janus has fewer oddities to report home about."

"When he goes—" surely he *would* go! "—you can move into any room you like."

"Once I have this one the way I like it, I suppose I'll be content enough." Caleb smiled. "I'm sorry if I'm cranky this morning, darling. I had trouble sleeping with all this red and black everywhere." He waved a hand around at the canopy over his bed, the blood and coal striped wallpaper, and the still-lingering cushions. Xan couldn't imagine how many there must have been since he knew Ren had taken away an armful and a half already.

His own room was pleasantly masculine with heavy wood furniture and thick, warm blankets. The color scheme was beige, brown, and cream, with a hint of green to bring in the color of the sea from the windows. He was content with it as it was. But whoever had decorated the room Caleb had taken possessed very different tastes.

"We can switch rooms tonight," Xan ventured.

"No. I prefer the view out this one." He nodded toward the bed. "Lay down and see for yourself."

Xan plopped onto Caleb's bed, missing the soft nest of their old home, but awed by the scene out the window. With just a turn of his head, he could watch the giant ocean waves beat against the base of the cliff at the end of the beach on their property.

"Dramatic," he murmured.

"A real show." Caleb smiled and stood from the vanity. "Speaking of, we should get our show on the road. There's so much to still be done. And you should call Ray, don't you think? Find out what's expected of you and when you should start."

The servants they'd brought, as well as betas Ren or perhaps Janus had hired from the village, scurried all around the lower floor of the house, removing dust cloths, polishing wood, shining silver, moving furniture, and generally waking the house up after years of sleep.

Xan found his way to the library, positioned just off the great hall, and then into a small interior room that could serve as his office. It had a view of the north-eastern grounds, and out the window he saw some servants from wolf-god only knew where mulching and preparing flower beds within a small, twisting walk of a garden.

He supposed Ren had arranged for it in anticipation of his and Caleb's orders. The man was good at his job.

The small office contained a functional desk—less overwrought than the giant, sprawling one in the library—some filing cabinets, and a private phone on the desk. There was a comfortable-looking sofa pressed up against one wall and a small record player on a table by the doorway. Xan opened and closed the doors of the filing cabinets, making sure that Janus hadn't claimed this room for himself, and then, satisfied that it was sufficient for his needs, he shut and locked the door behind him.

His sat at the desk and picked up the receiver. His fingers itched over the dial, an urge to hear Urho's voice claiming him. He wanted to know how his lover—would he ever stop feeling the exclamation point after that word?—had liked the roses. Had wooing him like an omega worked? Or had Urho hated it?

Xan swallowed hard and put the receiver down again. He took slow breaths and watched the men outside his window carting wheelbarrowfuls of mulch and carrying slats of violet, gold, and yellow winter flowers. He decided to put off the call to Urho for last. The dessert could come after the vegetables.

Picking up the phone again, he put in a call to Ray, who asked, "How are things there?" His voice was warm and familiar in a way that uncoiled the knots from between Xan's shoulder blades.

He tucked the phone against his ear and twisted the long cord between his fingers. "Fine, except for the surprise guest we found already set up here upon our arrival."

Ray snorted lightly. "I'm guessing Janus was his usual charming self, then?"

"He immediately offended Caleb."

"Ah, well, he'd better watch that." Ray sounded a bit distracted, and Xan could hear papers rustling in the background. "Father wouldn't want your omega unhappy, especially with his heat coming up."

"Heaven forbid we do anything to upset an omega before his heat."

"I know you understand how important it is to keep Caleb

joyful and eager to conceive," Ray scolded. "Father wouldn't want Janus *or you* doing anything to offend him."

"But father doesn't mind if Janus offends *me*. Which he does just by being here."

Ray sighed. Xan heard the roll and scrape of his brother's chair against the floor of his office and knew Ray had risen to pace. "It's actually not all about you, Xan. Has it occurred to you that Father has his own reasons for sending Janus to Virona?"

Xan stood and pressed his forehead against the cool glass of the window, staring out at the men digging in the dirt. "Business reasons?"

"Personal ones, mostly, if you must know. But, yes, some business ones, too."

"Like what?" Xan wasn't sure if he was asking about the personal or the business, but Ray continued on like he knew, of course.

"Janus has experience setting up satellite offices, like he did when he was sent to Grundytown after his last big romantic scandal. And you, little brother, have none."

Xan pulled away from the window, leaving a smudge behind. He flopped backwards onto the sofa, the thick cushion catching his fall. It seemed unfair that Janus could stay in good standing with their father despite his many illicit affairs simply because they were all with omegas. But Xan had a few rumors flying around about his involvement with other alphas and he'd become the family pariah. "And how will I prove myself to Father if Janus is here to do all the work?"

Ray shuffled papers, a heavy sigh on his lips. Xan idly wondered how long his brother had already been in the office that morning. Caleb was right to point out that that Ray had no personal life.

Pages scraped and rustled, and the rumble of a drawer convinced Xan that, yes, even as they talked on the phone, his brother was toiling away. "First, get along with Janus. That would impress

Father a great deal since you haven't been able to accomplish that since you were toddlers together."

"I was a toddler. He was older than me and a bully."

Ray sighed again. "Second, don't just sit back and let Janus take over. Exert yourself and put yourself forward, give your opinion, make good deals, and use good judgment. Especially on when you should concede to his."

Xan rolled his eyes. "Why does Father respect him so much?"

"Respect isn't the word for what Father feels for Janus."

"Admiration then." Xan's throat went dry. "Adoration. Love. Whatever it is, he doesn't feel it for me."

Ray clicked his tongue. "You and Janus aren't so unalike."

Xan huffed. "If you're talking about his love affairs and scandals, we both know Father doesn't care about them because he has them with omegas."

Ray was silent for a moment, and Xan realized what he'd admitted. He sucked in a breath, the phone receiver sliding against his suddenly slick palm.

When Ray spoke, his voice was gentle with compassion. "Xan like I told you in my office, if it was only me, I wouldn't care who you love. But as Father's representative, I have to report that, yes, our board of directors and Father himself understand Janus's antics a great deal more than they could or would understand yours. But that doesn't mean Father thinks Janus hung wolf's moon."

"No, he saves that high opinion for Pater and you."

"He loves you, Xan, and he wants you to learn how to run the company." Xan could picture Ray rubbing between his brows in frustration and kicking back in his desk chair. "Let's not have this argument again. I hate having to defend him to you and then turn around and defend you to him."

Xan rose and crossed to the window again, watching the workers. "Being in the middle stinks, I know. I'm sorry, Ray."

As usual, his brother was willing to shrug off his own problems and focus on Xan's. "Make sure this next week gets off to a successful start. If Janus gets inappropriate with Caleb, let me know and I'll take care of it. It's almost like he can't help himself when a contracted omega is around. He has to test the boundaries of propriety."

"Caleb is special," Xan said fiercely. "I won't have him feeling harassed in his own home."

"All alphas think their omegas are special," Ray mused. "And I suppose they all are. But you're right. I don't want my brother-in-law feeling put out, either. We all like Caleb. But Father insists Janus stay with you for the time being."

"How much of his duties here consist of spying on me to make sure I'm behaving?"

"I suppose that depends on you." Ray sounded so tired. Xan wanted to tell him to go home and take a day for himself, but he knew Ray would ignore him. "Give Janus nothing to see or report, get the satellite office open as quickly as possible, and there will be less of a reason for him to stay on."

Xan remembered the papers he'd gone over on the train ride the day before, in between worrying about Urho, dreaming of his cock, and irritating Caleb with his insecurities. "According to the schedules and reports you sent me, the office won't be up and running for a couple of months at least."

Ray laughed. "I'm just impressed that you read what I sent. Already this Virona experiment is proving to have good results. Now I need to work, and you need to go into town to see whether or not the building is progressing as promised."

Xan swallowed hard. He'd already forgotten that Ray had asked him to do that by phone the day before. He should have been down there first thing this morning to meet with the contractors.

Ray didn't scold him though. "Behave yourself, little brother.

We'll talk again soon."

Xan hung up and stood in a hurry. He wanted to call Urho and hear his soothing voice, but he was already hours late to the very first assignment Ray had given. With his luck, that was where Janus had disappeared to this morning and why he wasn't there to bug Caleb at breakfast.

He hustled out of the library, past all the busy servants, and back up to his room to put on something more commanding in appearance. If he was going to show up late, the least he could do is look like he meant business.

THAT EVENING, THE roses perfumed the air of Urho's library with a taunting sweetness he couldn't escape. He stared up at the portrait of Riki while running his fingers over the smooth, cool bone of his phone receiver.

The day had passed much like any other before the madness with Xan started, and yet he'd felt wrong from the moment he'd rolled out of bed. The distance between them seemed vast, and some part of him kept seeking Xan's scent, like an alpha looking for his omega in a crowd. He never found it.

He'd even driven past Xan's house in the city like a lovesick alpha mooning over a reluctant omega, and he'd found himself breathing deeply, trying to find residual Xan-ness in the air.

Urho had half expected a phone call from Xan throughout the day, but none ever came, and he'd returned home after dropping by Jason and Vale's house to sit in solitude and brood on his feelings.

He was ridiculous. He knew that. But he couldn't seem to stop.

The cool receiver beneath his fingers beckoned to him. He considered something Vale had said once he'd mastered his glee at hearing that Urho had taken Xan as a lover, though Urho had refused to provide more details than that as he'd measured Vale's stomach that particular afternoon. "If you're not certain about this, now is the time to jump ship."

He could do that. Just swim away from temptation and pull himself up on the shores of wolf-god's rules and the country's regulations. He could watch that ship sail onto the horizon and then disappear. All it would take was…not making that phone call. Not answering if one came in. It would be so much safer. Saner. Smarter.

He swallowed hard and his gut knotted.

He lifted the receiver and placed the call.

When a servant answered on the other end of the line, he asked for Xan and waited with his eyes closed.

There was the sound of another extension connecting, and the first one disconnecting. And then Xan said, "Hello?" His voice was a blessing in Urho's ear, and he shivered.

"This is Urho. I wanted to make sure you arrived safely."

"Oh! It's you!" Xan's pleasure rolled through the line to him like the sweetness of an opiate being spooned into Urho's mouth. He swallowed it down, and it warmed him inside and out.

"It's me," Urho confirmed.

"I spent all day in endless meetings arguing with the contractors who are building the physical space for our satellite office and I assumed this call was going to be from my brother checking on the progress there. This is such a better surprise!"

As he rambled, Xan's voice grew a touch nervous. It made Urho want him close, to put his hands on him, and shove him down to his knees and stopper his mouth with his—

Wolf-god, he was depraved now.

"I wasn't sure when I'd hear from you. I'm glad it's now. Tonight, I mean. Did you get the roses? I wanted to surprise you with them, but maybe they're a little too much. I mean, you did get them? Right?"

"I got them. Thank you."

"Yes, of course. I'm glad. Okay, wow. I'm not sure what to say." Xan sounded out of breath and the sound of shoes clacking as the young man paced echoed through the receiver. "I should probably start with something simple, but I already blew that. I guess I'll try it now. Can't lose anything by trying, right? So, hi! How was your day?"

Urho chuckled and relaxed back into his chair. "Not as enjoyable as it would have been if I'd been able to see you."

Xan made a soft sound that woke Urho's cock. "Mine, either."

Urho pressed his hand over his crotch, feeling the rush of blood there. "Was the train comfortable?"

"It was. I hired a private compartment so I could sleep. Caleb read a book."

As Urho listened, Xan described the journey, the house—which sounded like a large project in and of itself—and his frustration at discovering that some cousin, a thorn in Xan's side, obviously, would be staying as a houseguest there at Xan's father's behest.

Xan's voice wove into Urho like a thread of sharp contentment, bordering on pleasure. Urho closed his eyes, letting that thread stab and pull through him again and again. He shivered.

"Caleb doesn't like him, either," Xan concluded irritably.

Urho stroked slow fingers over his thigh, sliding against his stiff cock. It'd filled as he'd followed the melodious ups and downs of Xan's animated descriptions.

"Why's that?" he rasped, teasing the fat head of his dick where it pressed against his trousers. He shifted his hips and imagined Xan at his feet, his head resting against his knee as he complained about his cousin. If Xan *were* at his feet, he'd stroke his hair, hear him out, and then fuck his mouth so roughly that—

He broke off his thoughts again, his nipples hardening beneath his shirt, and his balls drawing up tight.

"I'm not entirely sure," Xan said, answering his question about Caleb. "Something about the time when Caleb was first being sent to Philia soirées. I'm guessing it was the year before Janus got caught mid-coitus with a contracted omega and Father sent him away to 'start a new satellite office.'" Xan huffed. "Which is code in this family for letting the rumors die down, by the way."

Urho couldn't explain his reaction to Xan's voice. As far as he could tell Xan didn't share his longing right now, but he didn't need him to. He could enjoy this all on his own. He slowly teased himself, dragging out the pleasure, letting Xan's voice pierce him again and again.

"Speaking of, there's a ton to do for the satellite office. I was shocked at the state of the building site and the ineptitude of the contractors. When I seem to know more than they do about their work, it's a problem."

"What did the spy think?" Urho said.

"Janus? He wasn't there. I don't know where he'd gotten off to, but I had to deal with the contractors all on my own."

"Isn't that what you wanted?"

"Yes, but…there's a ton to do. An endless list, it seems. I guess I could have used the help." The sullenness in Xan's voice at the admission made Urho's dick throb. Wolf-god he wanted to hear that tone in person, directed at him, his alpha-shaped omega reluctantly admitting to some misdeed, and then Urho could bend him over his knee, like Xan had wanted, and—

"Urho?" Xan asked. "Are you all right? You're awfully quiet."

"Just thinking of how I wish I could be with you."

"Wolf-god, me, too." It was infused with such longing that Urho's cock released a wet burst of pre-come. He wished Xan was there to lick it up.

He tried to clear his thoughts and say something wise. "The

final product always seems impossible at the beginning of any new endeavor. But with your sharp brain I'm sure you'll have it up and running before your father expects you to."

"My sharp brain? Ha!" Xan's restless, clacking shoes started up again, beating a rhythm Urho followed by stroking over his trapped cock more rapidly. "I'm of average intelligence at best, and given some of my behavior of late, the argument could be made that 'average' is a generous assessment."

"You understand people and you have a brave heart." Urho tried very hard to keep his voice steady. His pulse rushed, and his cock ached. "I know you'll make good of this new assignment your father has placed in your hands."

"Do you?" Xan murmured, and Urho could just imagine his wide, blue eyes gazing at him with eager need for reassurance. His balls twitched. "I wish I wasn't trapped here. I want to see you again."

"I want to see you, too." He closed his eyes, tilted his head back, and was just getting ready to tell Xan that he was aroused for him when there was a knocking sound on the other end of the line.

Xan sighed. "Hold on a minute. Yes, Ren?"

Urho listened with mounting frustration to indistinct murmuring and then Xan was back, his voice crawling with disappointment. "I'm being summoned to discuss the plans for the house. Caleb has a lot to do to get it up to his standards and settled."

"Then I'll let you go. We'll talk again soon enough."

"When?"

"Tomorrow."

"Yes. Call me again tomorrow." Xan's enthusiasm quickened Urho's heart. "It'll be my reward for making it through another day without murdering Janus."

They ended the call without any declarations or further promises, but Urho leaned back in his seat, satisfied that an appointment had been set to speak again.

The ambiguity removed, he pulled his cock out and considered it, admiring his thick length with a nicely shaped, glistening head peeking out of his damp foreskin. Then he rested his head against the back of his chair and closed his eyes.

Imagining Xan kneeling between his legs, red mouth open, blue eyes hot and eager, he jerked himself off quickly and groaned when he came copiously into his palm.

There was no doubt of at least one thing when it came to Xan. The young man had fully woken his libido. It remained to be seen if he'd also woken his heart.

PART TWO

CHAPTER THIRTEEN

URHO FROWNED AS he pressed the stethoscope against Vale's chest. His heartbeat was a little rapid, but it could be due to nerves. He knew Vale's in-laws had been visiting often lately, and Vale was growing tense and weary of their attentions.

"Everything all right?" Jason asked with his arm around Vale's shoulder and his eyes glued to where the stethoscope pressed against Vale's skin. They were seated on the sofa in Vale's study with Urho kneeling in front of them.

"Shh, I'm listening." Urho moved the stethoscope down to press against Vale's belly.

Jason radiated impatience.

Urho's own patience had worn thin over the two-and-a-half months since Xan had moved to Virona. Sometimes the sex he'd had with his alpha-shaped omega seemed so distant as to be more like a dream, and other times, especially after a steamy phone call from Xan, or one of his deeply erotic letters, it seemed as though he'd die if he didn't touch Xan's skin again or hear the little noises he made when he came.

Jason huffed. "You've been listening a long time. Is there a problem?"

Urho shushed him. There was a problem, yes, indeed. And that problem was his mind wandered to Xan constantly.

But he forced himself to fully concentrate, and after counting the baby's heartbeats again, he lifted his head and nodded once. "The babe is getting along just fine, but Vale's blood pressure and heart rate are elevated. He's stressed."

"*He's* right here," Vale said testily, shifting on the sofa. His stomach bulged nicely, and the movements of the child inside could be detected by touch alone. The babe seemed to be exactly on track for the timeline Vale and Jason had provided regarding conception. "I don't like being talked about like I'm not present. I'm a grown man, for wolf-god's own fucking sake."

Jason clucked gently, stroking a soothing hand over Vale's arm. "Don't get upset. It's not good for the baby."

Vale glared at Jason with more force than Urho had ever seen.

Jason swallowed hard and looked down, whispering, "But, of course, we'll stop. Right away. I promise."

Vale groaned and rubbed his bulging, shifting stomach. "Is it normal for him to do that?" he asked, referring to the baby. "He head-butts my ribs and then pushes with his feet against the mouth of my womb."

"Perfectly normal."

"Well, I wish he'd stop!"

Jason rubbed Vale's shoulders and hushed him quietly.

"It's preparation for the life to come," Urho said. "Children rarely do what we wish they'd do. And, from what I've witnessed, their growth into adulthood is never without pain to the parent."

Vale sniffed and closed his eyes. "That's all fine and well, but I'm tired."

"I can prescribe something gentle to help you rest."

"Please do," Jason said, sounding desperate. "He was up walking last night. Nothing soothed him. Not even his usual bedtime tea— the one with the herbs that make him drowsy."

"Speaking of," Vale said, as he buttoned his shirt. "I want some tea. Daytime tea. Something strong and well steeped. Jason will you get it, please?"

Jason rose, obviously reluctant to leave Vale's side, but, like any alpha, he was also prepared to do whatever his pregnant omega demanded of him.

The doorbell rang.

Vale growled, almost pulling off the final button in his annoyance. "If that's your pater or father, I will murder them both. Do you hear me? *Murder. Them. Both.*"

Jason bent to run his fingers over Vale's dark beard, whispering, "If it's them, I'll tell them to leave. I promise."

Urho watched Jason rush off as the doorbell rang a second time, and then he began to gather his things. "I'll get out of your hair, too."

"You never come over anymore, except to examine me," Vale complained. His moss green eyes raked over Urho irritably.

"I come here every day." Urho buckled his bag and sat on the sofa next to Vale. "But I can stay awhile if you want."

Vale rose and began to pace. His stomach bulged, and Urho could see the baby rolling and kicking, even beneath Vale's loose shirt. "He moves around so much," Vale said, rubbing a hand over his stomach. "Is that normal?"

"Better than normal. It's a good sign."

"I can't stop eating. Sometimes I eat so much, I can't put any more in, but I'm still hungry."

"Another excellent sign."

"And everyone just pisses me the wolf-hell off."

"Normal enough," Urho said. "You're uncomfortable and the weight of the baby is putting a strain on the scar tissue now. That's enough to make anyone cranky."

With no segue, Vale said, "Jason is adorable."

Urho refrained from rolling his eyes. "I've heard that from you before, yes."

"But he's making me crazy!" Vale gestured wildly as he spoke. "Eat this. Drink that. Sleep more. Let me rub your feet. Don't tax yourself. Let's read together." Vale snorted. "Read together. *Read together!*"

"Did Jason not read before?" Urho raised a brow.

"No! He has a photographic memory and so he just skims books. No, he doesn't read. Unless I read to him."

"I see."

Vale seemed to interpret some kind of judgment in Urho's voice because he added defensively, "He tinkers. Out in the garden, mostly. Or with his microscope." He groaned. "But now he's glued to my side. Plus, he smells amazing to me. Like my alpha, yes, but I scent him even more strongly."

"This is normal."

"*This* leaves me aroused all the time. All the time, Urho!"

"I know but—"

"No but! Being aroused all the time is exhausting. Let me tell you this now. Are you listening?"

"Yes."

"I am getting *ridiculously* tired of being fisted every day."

Urho's lips quivered. Vale was lovely when he was angry—cheeks flushed above his beard, eyes bright, and his breath coming in quick bursts. Urho almost remembered why he'd been in love with him once. But he wasn't half as gorgeous as Xan in the throes of ecstasy. "I told him to do that."

"I know. Tell him to stop."

Urho sighed. "Love, it's important that you keep stretching that scar tissue. It's going to be a tough few months, but, in the end, you'll have a beautiful baby and it will be worth it."

"I know all that!" Vale exclaimed, his pacing stopped. He turned to Urho speculatively. "Wait, though. Should you still call me that?"

"What?"

"Love? Should you call me a pet name like that?" Vale tilted his head.

"If it bothers you, I can st—"

"No. I don't care, but does Xan mind, do you think?"

Urho frowned. "I've called you 'love' for years—"

"Not when Jason's around."

Urho scoffed. "Because I don't have a death wish."

"So what you have with Xan, it's not..." Vale rolled his hand.

"Nickname material?" Urho hazarded.

"No! Is it not serious, you fool? What you have isn't serious?"

"I have no idea *what* it is." Urho wiped a hand over his face. "I haven't seen him since he left for Virona. Between the twins, you, and this wretched flu season, I've barely had a moment, much less a day, away from the clinic or work. And he can't come here. He's 'banished' from the city, according to him. At least the work on his new office seems to satisfy him because otherwise I'd worry."

"Jason talks to him."

"I talk to him, too," Urho said defensively.

Vale's brows lifted, and his voice dropped conspiratorially. "How often?"

"Daily," Urho admitted. His cheeks felt warm.

"I see. So it's not serious, but you talk every day, and you miss him. I can tell."

"I didn't say it wasn't serious. I said it's complicated."

"You said you didn't know what it was."

"You're so exasperating today!" Urho started to stand, but Vale took hold of his shoulders and pressed him back down to the sofa.

"You have to tell me everything. Now."

"It's a long story, and it's been a long day."

Vale rolled his eyes. "I'm a miserably pregnant omega who is essentially trapped in this house by the flu epidemic and tortured daily by the attentions of my loving in-laws. *Please* talk to me."

Urho gave a quick half-smile and then eyed the liquor cabinet across the room. The truth would come out more smoothly with a bit of bourbon.

"I'll pour you a drink if you tell me how it all began." Vale crossed the room and lifted the bottle temptingly.

"I found out that he was involved…" Urho trailed off. That wasn't his information to share. "He was in a dangerous situation. So I offered to fuck him, like a surrogate for an omega."

Vale blinked rapidly and then choked on a laugh. After pouring a generous glass, he collapsed beside Urho on the sofa and passed the bourbon over with a grin spreading his lips. "I see."

Urho wet his throat with the bourbon before going on. "I didn't anticipate how that turned out."

"Oh, I imagine you didn't." Vale sounded utterly delighted.

Urho rolled his shoulders and took another drink. "I hadn't realized that it would become something so…"

"Different?"

"More."

Vale's grin sliced across his face again, and he leaned back on the sofa, his hand on his bulging stomach. "Ah, then you're still the idiot I've always known and loved."

Urho tried to explain it so that it made sense to them both. "I wanted to believe that what I was offering was no different than helping an omega in heat, but, in reality, it was nothing like that at all."

"It was forbidden," Vale supplied. "Which is definitely different."

"Yes, but—" He'd apparently developed feelings for the little brat somehow. What he wanted from Xan wasn't sex and sex alone, like with a typical surrogacy. He didn't want to fulfill his animal lusts and then walk away. He wanted to build something real.

"But?" Vale prompted.

"He reminds me of Riki."

"I thought Riki was a paragon of gentleness and obedience. Something Xan is decidedly not."

"Riki was. No, Xan isn't like him in that way at all." Urho scrubbed a hand over his head and tried to put the words into the right shape. "I meant the way I feel about him reminds me of Riki. The way I react to his scent and the way I want to…"

Vale sat up again. "Yes?"

"The way I want to own him."

"Oh, dear friend," Vale whispered, a hand on Urho's shoulder. "I suppose that must have shocked your old-fashioned, traditional soul nearly to death."

"I keep telling you. I'm not old-fashioned. If anything should prove it and put a nail in that coffin, I'd think it would be this situation." Urho smiled wryly. The illegal abortion he'd performed on Vale years before and the untraditional relationship they'd shared should have ended the rumors of his old-fashioned sensibilities well before. "I admit I did lose my mind at first."

"After you'd…" Vale made a lewd gesture.

"No. Before I made the offer to him. I was in a state—overwrought, afraid, and angry. I wanted to protect him and shake him. I wanted to…" Urho trailed off. "Once I settled on the idea of acting as a surrogate for him, everything seemed to click into place. I was able to make a peace with it."

"Well, you always did have a hero kink," Vale said, the knowing smile on his face almost annoying. "I think that was half your attraction for me."

"No." He'd cared about Vale for reasons that went beyond that.

"Oh, maybe our relationship eventually became more than heroism to you, but at first you were my surrogate during heats because you wanted to save me from ever being in a dangerous position again. And then we became lovers outside the heats…and, yes, I'll concede that was based more in friendship and fun than in heroism gone awry. But that was where it had started."

And based in a now-faded love.

But Urho wouldn't bring that up. Instead, he ventured toward the subject that had been pricking at him between bouts of dreaminess, longing, and intense phone calls with Xan. "It's wrong, though. Two alphas. It's against the Holy Book and the law." He took Vale's hand in his. "How do I reconcile that it feels so right?"

"I think you're smart enough to know the answer to that." Vale flicked him a harsh glance. "The laws and Holy Books are all about control. But hearts are wild things. They can't be controlled no matter how much those in power wish it."

"It's an obstacle," Urho mused. "We can never truly be together."

"Plus, there's Caleb."

Urho chuckled. "Yes, Caleb. Who is strangely accepting of all this."

Vale nodded. "Contracted relationships aren't like *Érosgápe*. I'm sure he has his reasons for being content with the arrangement."

Urho tilted his head. "You know."

"I know what?"

Urho said nothing, and Vale looked at him innocently. Clearly Xan had shared something with Jason—perhaps the failed heat—and Jason had shared that information with Vale. "Caleb is special."

"I think he's a wonderful man and Xan is lucky to have him," Vale said, shifting back uncomfortably and rubbing his stomach. "Good wolf-god above, this child! He never rests."

"When he's bigger, he'll have less room to move around. So he'll slow down."

Vale frowned at his stomach. "Then I'll panic and rejoice every time he makes himself known. I've heard as much from Miner."

Grateful for the change of topic, Urho asked, "Miner's driving you up a wall, is he?"

"They both are. They'd put me in a glass cage if they could and feed me only the freshest fruit and vegetables straight from golden tongs."

"Interesting image."

Vale sighed and rubbed his bulge again. "So with all that out on the table, indulge me some more. What's the plan now? How will you proceed with this relationship—is that even the term for what you have? And how are you coping with all of this time apart?"

Urho sighed. "I'm not sure. Making plans is difficult because his cousin, Janus, an alpha with a reputation for seducing contracted omegas, has been sent there to spy on Xan. Or so he believes."

"Oh, I can believe it." Vale rolled his eyes. "Xan's father is a controlling man from what I've seen and all I've heard."

"Yes. Well, Xan wishes he could get away from Virona to meet me halfway in Montrew, but he's so busy with his work. And I'm busy here, of course. Plus, his father has put the kibosh on Xan traveling anywhere near the city during this flu epidemic, and his cousin is there to enforce it."

"Jason didn't tell me about that. What if you went up to see him for a few days?"

"He says even if I did find a way to get up there, we wouldn't have any time alone. Not with his cousin keeping such a close eye on him."

Vale's face showed how ridiculous he found that argument. "You could be inconspicuous."

"Perhaps." Urho rubbed a hand over his forehead, thinking hard.

"Don't be such a coward," Vale said sharply.

"What?"

"Surely you could find someone to look after the omega who is pregnant with twins? And we could engage another doctor—just for a day or so. What's really stopping you?"

Urho's shoulders tightened. The idea of anyone else as Vale's doctor...no. He didn't want that. But the vibrating sensation in his body, the sense that he was a bell that'd been rung, was undeniable. Maybe he was too cowardly to see what he'd wrought, to test his mettle, and to keep his commitments to Xan and Caleb.

He cleared his throat. "This flu contagion is growing in proportions that frighten me. The omega expecting twins and his alpha have decided it's too risky to stay in town. They're heading west to Elinton for the rest of his pregnancy."

"Perfect. When they're gone, you should go up and stay with Xan."

"I could, but—"

Jason entered with a stack of mail and a tray of tea. "The door was only the postman. He was coughing up a storm. Ugly wracking coughs. I'm not sure he shouldn't be home." Jason nodded at the envelopes. "Out in this cold weather with a cough like that, he'll catch his death, as my father would say. And all for a stack of junk mail and fliers."

"Go wash your hands," Urho said, standing up. "And burn that mail."

Jason paled and stared down at the offending papers like he held a murder weapon in his hands. "The flu," he whispered.

"Do what I said," Urho commanded.

Jason fled the room, and Vale chewed on his bottom lip. "Do you think he'll get sick?"

"I hope not. For your sake. The real danger, though, is if *you* get sick."

Vale nodded. "I heard rumors that this flu is bad enough that some young people are dying from it. A boy just last week— younger than Jason, healthy and hale, and then he was gone."

"I think the omega with twins has the right idea." Urho sighed. If he fled the city with Vale and Jason, he'd be leaving his duty to the citizens behind, but keeping his promise to Jason to see Vale through to the end of the ordeal. "I can host you at my country home."

Another two hours south. Even farther from Xan. His heart ached.

Vale's eyes went wide, and he shook his head. "No, no."

Urho knew exactly why Vale didn't want to do that. Urho had handled many of Vale's heats at his country home, and it would be far too awkward for all of them to be there together. "What about the house at Seshwan-By-The-Sea? The one Jason's parents keep?"

"They're heading there for their anniversary in a few weeks, and, to be dramatic, I'd rather die than be caged in a house with the two of them right now. They're as bad as Jason, only I don't adore them. Miner's always trying to mother-hen me, while Yule is constantly shoving food into my mouth. Did you know he cooks extra every night and brings it over here? Then I have to eat it even though Jason's already fed me once."

"I don't know what to say."

"I know! I've been looking forward to them leaving town, just to get a break."

Urho said aloud, thinking to himself, "Virona is three hours north of here by train."

Vale raised a brow and stroked his stomach. "And?"

"And Xan is always saying that the house is empty and Caleb is lonely."

"I don't know if Jason will agree. He barely lets me leave the house to walk to the market or—"

"With this flu going around, I want you to stop that immediately."

"I haven't been in over a week. I'm going stir crazy here. The garden is dying, and the flowers are going, and I haven't written a decent poem since I got knocked up. Do babies suck out all your inspiration? Is there scientific evidence of that? Because I could contribute to the studies."

Jason came back into the room, looking shaken. "I burned the mail in the fireplace in the reception room and washed my hands in hot water. Do you think that's good enough? Should I shower?" He started to turn and leave again. "I can shower!"

"You're fine." Urho said, gesturing to the leather wing chair that used to be his favorite when he could snatch it from Vale. "Sit down. We need to discuss this flu epidemic and the risk to this pregnancy and Vale."

Jason sat immediately, eyes like saucers, intent on whatever Urho suggested. It felt good for a moment to have the boy's obedience because he hadn't always been willing to listen to Urho at all.

"I forgot to remake Vale's tea," he said quietly. "Can this wait until I get that for him?"

"Never mind, darling," Vale said softly. "I'm past wanting it now."

"He's very finicky lately. Is that normal?" Jason asked.

"Quite normal. Now, please listen. I was just telling Vale about the flu this season. It's ramping up, becoming an epidemic very quickly. Normally, I'd want to be here, in the thick of it, helping those who contract it, but I'm committed to Vale's health and dealing with whatever potentials come from this pregnancy. I won't put him in another doctor's hands."

Jason nodded gratefully.

"Which brings me to my suggestion: I think we should all three leave town."

"And go where?" Jason asked.

"Somewhere the flu hasn't reached yet. The sea, perhaps," Urho said, licking his lips. Did he sound too self-serving? Would they guess how desperately he wanted to see Xan and test himself against his own cowardice now that he'd recognized it? It shouldn't matter though. The suggestion was sound either way.

"My parents are already going to the cottage," Jason said, repeating Vale's comment from earlier. "Vale can barely stand their nightly visits. I don't think he'd want to be stuck with them in—"

"We can go to Xan's house in Virona," Vale interrupted. "He's invited us, hasn't he?"

"Well, yes, for the Autumn Nights feasts, but we declined of course."

"Don't you think the offer probably still stands?" Vale pushed. "Even though the feasts are past?"

"I'm sure it does," Jason agreed. "He's always complaining that the house is so big and yet his cousin seems to be everywhere at once."

"This cousin of his. Urho was telling me about him. You hadn't mentioned him before," Vale said to Jason curiously. "Why's that?"

"He's a little older than us, but I never liked him." Jason shrugged. "Aside from that, I've had my mind on other things." His brows drew down. "Seeing Janus would be a negative toward going, but if push came to shove, we could always rent our own little place in Virona if we need to get out of Xan's hair."

"I want to be with Caleb," Vale said suddenly, clutching Jason's hand. "When the time comes, it would be good to have him there."

"I didn't know you felt so strongly for Caleb." Jason kissed Vale's knuckles.

"Omega brooding instinct," Urho said softly. "They take solace in the presence of other omegas during their time. It's instinctual."

Vale gazed at Urho pointedly. "Or perhaps societal. And stop talking about me like I'm not here. Regardless, if Xan and Caleb will have us, then, yes, I'm willing to go."

"You're coming, too?" Jason asked Urho.

"I made a promise to you both that I'd deliver this baby and I will. So if Xan will have me—"

Jason laughed. "Oh, he'll have you. This way and that."

Heat rose up Urho's throat and made his ears burn. "Yes, well, then I'll be going, too."

"I think we just cinched our invite," Jason stage whispered in Vale's ear, eyes dancing.

Urho cleared his throat and looked at his hands. His heart beat rapidly. Soon he'd finally see Xan again. He clamped down on the squirmy feeling inside. He was terrified and yet he couldn't wait.

"CALEB!" XAN SHOUTED, racing over the dunes and down to the beach. His right ankle nearly twisted on the uneven ground, but he righted himself. The cold wind off the ocean stung his eyes and cheeks. "Caleb!"

Caleb stood by the water with an easel and canvas. He'd taken up painting while waiting for his printing materials to arrive from the city. Xan didn't know what was taking them so long, but apparently the printing mechanism itself was heavy and needed special equipment to move. Plus, the beta servants had trouble boxing it all up because there was so much of it.

Xan had offered to buy whatever Caleb needed in the meantime, but the proposal had been brushed aside in the hustle of redecorating the house, arranging for lonely, awkward Autumn Nights feasts with local business invitees, and keeping out of Janus's way.

"Caleb!" he cried again as he ran.

The blue slash of the sky on the canvas was brighter than the real blue above, but not half as bright as the blue of Caleb's eyes. He turned to Xan, paintbrush raised, and his red mouth open in surprise.

"What's wrong!" he shouted, tossing the paintbrush into the sand and rushing to Xan. "What's happened?"

Xan swept Caleb into his arms, squeezing him, breathless with joy. "They're coming!" His heart beat wildly, rattling his chest, and he felt like he might be able to jump into the air and fly away with Caleb crushed to him.

"Who?" Caleb gasped.

"Everyone!"

"Your family?"

"No! Thank wolf-god!" Xan laughed. "Urho! And Jason and Vale too! They're coming, Caleb! *He's* coming!"

They hugged tightly, the ocean waves pounding the shore and the gulls crying out above them. "I'm so glad, alpha mine," Caleb finally said. "I'm excited to see him, too. Your joy is my joy."

Xan kissed his cheek. "Thank you."

"If we're to have guests, then there's a lot to do. I'll need Ren and the others to get the guest rooms ready," Caleb said, obviously beginning a long list in his mind of what, who, when, and where. Caleb had been lonely since moving out of the city and away from his friends, and part of Xan's joy was for him as well.

Caleb started up toward the house, leaving the easel and canvas behind, as well as the paints and brushes. Xan thought of turning back for them, but changed his mind when Caleb called over his shoulder that he'd send someone down later. It was evident that Caleb's mind was on planning and parties now, and Xan was ready to go along for the ride.

An hour and a half later, beta servants were scampering around the upstairs of the house, opening windows and airing out rooms, putting fresh sheets on beds, and dusting where a dust cloth hadn't been in years. Caleb stood in the middle of the dining room, taking measure of the long table, his head cocked and his neck exposed.

Caleb patted his own cheek absently. "Now, what will we do

209

about seating? We need more chairs. I shouldn't have sent so many off to be reupholstered." He clucked his teeth. "And your alpha of course needs to be kept far away from your awful cousin."

"I love it when you talk dirty about me," Janus said from the doorway to the kitchen. He stepped out with a piece of pecan pie held in his hand like a hick farmer from Leitel, his lips glistening with the buttery filling. "Do it again."

Caleb's jaw clenched, but he said nothing in reply. Instead he simply turned and left the room.

"I've warned you," Xan said, pointing at Janus, who lifted his pecan pie up in a faux toast as he laughed.

"He's so sensitive. And whose alpha was he talking about just now?" Janus's tone was too casual.

Pulse racing, Xan kept the subject on Caleb. "You know as well as I do that he's off-limits to you. Plus, he's immune to your so-called 'charms' anyway."

"Is he? I wonder." Janus smirked.

"I don't think he could be more plain about it."

"Believe me, he wasn't always."

"Excuse me?"

"You heard me." Janus took another bite of his dessert. "There was a time when Caleb thought I was the sweetest cherry in the pie."

Xan stared at Janus, trying to parse what he was saying. "You knew each other? Outside the Philia parties?"

"We were intimate friends," Janus said with an air of satisfaction that Xan loathed. "He hasn't told you? In all these months we've been here together? Why keep it from you? Maybe he still harbors feelings for me after all this time."

"You lie."

"Ask him."

Xan's hands balled into fists, and he stepped closer to Janus, hot rage like a volcano in his gut.

"Duels are against the law," Janus said, half laughing. "But we could have fisticuffs here in the dining room. First blood or to the death?"

"Death," Xan muttered, his heart thudding fast. He drew close enough to smell the watered-down rose perfume Janus dabbed behind his ears. It gagged him. "Let's go."

Janus only stood there with his pecan pie, smiling like he had the upper hand.

"Stop!" Caleb's voice cut into the room again. "No fighting. No dueling, either. He's not worth it, Xan."

"Who says I wouldn't win?"

"Me," Janus said, laughing.

Caleb went white as a sheet and stalked to him, took the pie from his hand, and shoved it into his face, smearing the butter and syrup concoction all over his flushed cheeks and up into his hair.

Janus gasped, his eyes wide. "What—but, why—and—"

Caleb kicked Janus in the shin. Hard. Then he elbowed him in the back of the head, felling him to the floor.

"Never insult my alpha again," Caleb hissed. "Or I'll murder you in your sleep, you sorry, pompous, self-absorbed, lying, manipulative *prick*!"

Xan blinked in shock, staring as Caleb spun on his heel again and stomped from the room. Janus struggled up from the ground, his hands clutching his shin, his face smeared with pie. He sat back on his haunches, blinking dazedly after Caleb through the sticky goo. "Wow. Maybe he is immune to my charms after all."

"You think?"

"Tell him I'm sorry."

Xan almost commanded Janus to go tell Caleb himself, and on his knees at that, but he bit it back, not wanting Janus to upset Caleb any further.

Janus huffed and said with a surprising earnestness, "I didn't mean to upset him, Xan, I swear. I thought with our history, he'd take my comments in the vein I meant them, but I guess he still holds a grudge." He rose slowly to his feet and wiped his hand over his face, gathering some of the pie goo before sticking his fingers into his mouth. "Delicious."

"Get out of my sight."

Janus rolled his eyes, but then seemed to remember that he was talking to the irritated alpha of the omega who'd just taken him down several pegs. He bowed his head. "Don't mention this to your father, all right? Give me a chance to make it up to Caleb."

"Is that all you care about? My father?" Xan didn't know if his father would even believe him if he ratted out Janus. However, a call from Caleb would do the trick. He chewed on his cheek, trying to breathe through the urge to sock his cousin in the face.

"Of course, that's not all I care about." Janus's wide eyes made a good show of regret. "Truly, I'm sorry. For today, and for anything I said to hurt him since he arrived here." He hesitated before his eyes dropped to the carpet. "And, most especially, for what happened in the past. Tell him I said that, and I sincerely mean it, all right?"

Xan gritted his teeth and tried to imagine what his father would say if he called and told him, *I brained Janus with a candlestick in the middle of the dining room for flirting with Caleb.* He cleared his throat and pointed at Janus. "Let this be a lesson. Don't mess with Caleb again or give me any reason to come at you. Don't speak of whatever happened in the past. Never make him unhappy for even a second. Do you understand?"

"Yes."

"Good." Xan turned on his heel, his blood boiling, and an itchy, rageful desire to dispatch his cousin to the great wolf-den beyond still aching in him. Instead, he headed upstairs in search of

Caleb and answers.

Xan found Caleb in his room, his windows open, letting the frigid ocean air pour in. He stood facing out the sash, his shoulders trembling and his hands clenching the windowsill.

"I should have told you the first day," he said miserably.

Xan said nothing, his usually fast-running mouth fused shut. He sat on Caleb's now-voluminous bed, and the soft cushions and blankets cradled him. He tugged one blanket up over his shoulders to keep his shivering at bay.

He waited.

Out the window the clouds scattered across the sky, the setting sun shone on the water, and the rush and fall of the waves rose like a soothing whisper. The anger leeched out of him, and he waited some more, an inhuman patience settling over him. He'd wait as long as it took for Caleb to tell him.

Eventually, Caleb turned from the view.

"I loved him," Caleb said as he walked slowly toward Xan and took hold of his hand. "Philia love, of course. As always. Brotherly love. But not as profoundly as I love you."

"All right."

"But, at the time, I thought I might grow to care for him as deeply."

Xan tugged him onto the mattress and cuddled him close, both of them stretching out and getting under the blankets. Caleb shook against his body, chilled from the window and clearly rattled by old emotions.

"It was humiliating," Caleb whispered. "When he didn't bring it all up right away after we arrived, I decided to pretend it never happened. I thought he might be willing to play along. But then I realized he just wanted to needle me with it constantly and call the cruelties nothing more than flirtation."

Xan considered offering up Janus's apologies and assurances, but he held them back, a rare otherworldly certainty descending. He should give Caleb the space to share his story and feelings first.

"I didn't love him the way I love you," Caleb said again.

"All right," Xan repeated softly. The alpha in him wanted to cover Caleb completely and rub his scent all over, assert his dominance over him until slick began to slip from his hole. He also knew that would never happen. Caleb only produced slick during heat, and never in response to another person. He didn't experience attraction.

And Xan wasn't attracted to him, anyway. But whatever instincts he still had—even as an utter failure of an alpha—made him want to comfort Caleb in the way an alpha would. He almost laughed to himself; it would only make things so much worse. Besides, who was he to judge Caleb's past entanglements? After the horrors of his own?

"I knew he was your cousin when we contracted. I planned to tell you about it then, but he was never at any of the family dinners. I was grateful for that and let myself believe that your families weren't close. So when you started coming home from your father's office with complaints about Janus returning from some sort of exile to suck up to your father, I was horrified. And then..." Caleb's voice broke. "This is hard."

"I'm here."

"I'm so sorry, Xan."

"It's all right."

"It's not. Because when your father said we weren't to come to any family dinners anymore, I was relieved. I didn't want to see him again."

Shoving aside the prick of betrayal, Xan stayed on course. "Did he hurt you? Janus?"

"Not physically. And, to be fair, if I was hurt it was my own fault. He never pretended to be anything other than who and what he was, and apparently still is." Caleb sighed and snuggled in closer, scenting along Xan's neck for comfort.

Xan stroked a hand up and down his back. "You can tell me. I won't be angry." *With you.* As for Janus, well, he wouldn't promise that.

"I met him at a Philia soirée. He spotted me hiding in a corner, like he said. It was my second year out and my parents were set on finding an alpha for me. Janus didn't seem to care about my father's addiction or loss of fortune. He was funny and full of gossip. He pulled me in simply by coming around and refusing to leave."

"If I recall correctly, I used a similar tactic."

"You did. But unlike Janus, you had a good heart." Caleb kissed Xan's chest and then rubbed his cheek on his shirt. "I let him in. I laughed at his jokes. I allowed him to call on me at home. I took his phone calls. And while I didn't feel attraction for him—I never do—I felt warm and hopeful. I felt *something.* And that feeling allowed me to think I could tell him the truth."

Xan went cold. "He knows about you?"

"He hinted one day that he wanted to contract. It wasn't an actual proposal, but another inch in that direction. I went to my bed that night and tried to imagine letting him touch me, kiss me…. Fuck me."

Xan kissed Caleb's hair. His heart squeezed.

"I didn't want that. But I did want—remember I didn't know about you, that I would meet you and we could make a good life."

"It's all right," Xan reassured him. "You know I did things with others in the past. Felt things for other men and still do." He missed Urho so fiercely in that moment. He wished he could throw himself into Urho's arms and be comforted. But no, Caleb was his friend— his family—and Xan had to be strong.

"I imagined a future with him. A home, friends, and a life. I'd had one heat already at that point, so I knew I'd be willing when that time came. But the idea of being with him outside of heat was horrible to me." Caleb shuddered like he did every time he thought about having sex with someone else. "Still, I hoped."

"You hoped he loved you for you. Or could." Xan knew. He'd been there. Wolf-hell, he was there now with Urho. Could the man really love him? Or was their bond going to be purely physical? He shook the questions from his mind, returning his focus to Caleb.

"Yes. I was sure I'd be alone forever. I wanted to believe that all the things he told me—that I was everything he imagined in a contracted omega, that I was the most beautiful man he'd ever seen, and that he adored me—could be true. So when he came around again the next week, I took him out into my pater's garden, and I told him the truth." Caleb's voice hitched.

"He spurned you."

"He was kind enough in the moment. But, yes, he said that wasn't the kind of life he could stand to live. He never called me or came around again. It was humiliating. I saw him at Philia parties and he ignored me. He treated me like I was nothing. No one."

"I'm so sorry."

"Then he left the city for a long time and I thought that was the end of him. Until I met you. I knew he was your cousin, but he never came up in conversations and when I met your family, he wasn't discussed. I hoped he was someone I might see only once in a while at larger family functions, and hopefully after you and I had produced several beautiful children that I could parade in front of him. And I'd hoped he'd believe that with you at least I didn't suffer from this weird affliction."

"It's not an affliction. It's just who you are, Caleb. We aren't all the same."

"We both know that in this world, that's not true. We're both afflicted—you with taboo desires and me with an unacceptable lack of any desire at all."

Xan thought of his cousin, pie smeared all over his face, and his confused, stunned expression as Caleb had stalked out. "You should have seen him," he said, overcome with a giggle. "He looked so ridiculous. And he tried to play if off, but I could tell you'd put him in his place."

"I wasn't about to let him put a finger on you," Caleb said fiercely.

"I could have held my own."

Caleb made a noncommittal sound.

"You don't think I would have won?"

"I think you're brave. And like most alphas short sighted. He's got several years and many pounds on you. I can't remember the last time you pushed yourself physically beyond a game of ball with Jason now and again. How you remain so fit-looking is beyond me."

"I have training in fighting skills."

"Rusty skills left over from Mont Nessadare. Compare that to your cousin who runs on the beach every morning, lifts weights at the local gymnasium, and engages in wrestling matches on the weekends at the gentlemen's club. I had reason to be worried. But I also knew he'd never strike an omega, and that I had the advantage of surprise on my side."

"How do you know all this about him?"

"He brags about it, darling. Don't you listen?"

"I try to tune him out when we aren't at work." Xan didn't add that his mind was usually occupied with Urho and turning over whatever conversations they had most recently engaged in.

He could entertain himself for hours doing that—thinking of Urho's chuckle, or the small strain that would come into his voice when he was aroused, or the one time he'd felt sufficiently safe to jerk off with him over the phone, and Urho had grunted Xan's name when he came. That had been a particularly wonderful conversation, and he'd gotten a great deal of fantasy mileage out of it for nearly a week and a half.

"Over breakfast just this morning he suggested you go with him this weekend to the gentlemen's club to meet the more prominent alphas and their omegas. Something about there being a new member of the club and an upcoming match worth betting on."

Xan scoffed.

"Not that it doesn't pain me to credit anything your cousin suggests, but maybe you should consider going to the club with him. That's where you'll meet the sort of men your father admires and perhaps turn them into future clients for the business."

Xan wrinkled his nose. "Being near him is its own punishment, but soon Urho will be here, and leaving him to go with Janus to some ghastly gentlemen's club, especially when that will be the only time I can be sure Janus is out of the house and not spying for Father, seems too cruel."

Caleb lifted up onto an elbow, gazing down at Xan. "Urho will be here for some time, and there's no reason you can't take him with you. The club isn't far from the house and surely he's not going to be a prisoner here waiting for Vale and Jason's babe to be born."

Xan laughed. "I suppose you're right."

"And you don't have to go with Janus. You could just go when it suits your schedule. All I'm saying is that Janus is making connections in town while you're spending evenings here on the phone with Urho, or lounging in my room thinking about Urho, or walking on the beach dreaming of Urho, or—"

"All right, all right! I get it!" Xan chuckled. "You're right, of course. As usual."

"Now, about Janus..." Caleb pushed his hair behind his ears and chewed on his bottom lip.

"I will call Father and tell him that Janus can't stay here. That you have a history with him that's far too painful for you—"

"No. I don't want anyone to know. That must stay between us."

"Fair enough. But it will make it harder to explain to Father what it is about Janus that bothers you. I can say that he flirts with you, but then Father will wonder why I don't put an end to that myself. He'll bring up my failures as an alpha and we'll end up down some miserable path where I'm a horrible disappointment and he's a nightmare, and you're still stuck with Janus here reminding you of things you'd rather forget."

"I think the solution is for me to move past my bruised ego. If Janus wants to flirt with me why should I get upset about that? It means nothing in the scheme of our lives. It was years ago now that he shamed me and I'm happy with you now, planning a future, coming up on a heat that has every reason to be a successful one. I'm eager to start our family. Why should his barbs and teasing dig into my skin so deeply? I resolve to no longer let them."

"Perhaps you still care for him," Xan ventured carefully, both for Caleb's sake and to make sure his own possessive alpha response wouldn't destroy the potential for truth.

"No. He's handsome, and I used to find him funny years ago, but all that remains now is hurt. He saw me in a very vulnerable moment and whenever I look at him I want to show him that I'm strong now. That I'm not that boy he left crying in the garden."

"You're definitely a better man than he is. Handsome, strong, determined, loyal, and so much more. He missed out. And I got very lucky."

Caleb snuggled him again, kissing his chest and scenting his neck. "We both got lucky. You love me just the way I am, and I love you, too. More than you know. It doesn't have to be romantic love to be worthy. We're family, and it doesn't matter what anyone thinks. So, alpha mine, let's both resolve not to let Janus get to us anymore."

The rising moon shining through the windows caressed the room. For once, Xan let himself drift off to sleep in Caleb's bed, holding his omega close and taking comfort in his sweet presence.

CHAPTER FOURTEEN

URHO GLANCED OVER his shoulder at Jason and Vale in the back seat. The roads from the train station in Virona weren't paved, and the ruts had them all jolting all over the place. The old driver didn't seem to mind, obviously accustomed to it.

"We should have told him when we were arriving," Vale said. "He'll be annoyed when we simply show up."

"Xan won't care at all," Urho said. "He'll just be excited to see us." *Especially me. I hope.* As they got closer, ridiculous insecurities nagged at him.

"I didn't mean Xan. I meant Caleb. As omega, he oversees the house. He'll be embarrassed if they aren't ready for us when we arrive."

"They know it's sometime today," Jason soothed. "And we did try to reach them by phone, but the lines were busy."

Vale shifted in the seat, his stomach distorting the lines of his clothes. Urho smiled to see Jason reach out and touch his shifting belly, a happy lift to his lips. "Is he traveling all right?" Jason asked. "He's moving now, but it seems like he's been awfully quiet today."

"I think the motion of the train lulled him to sleep," Vale said, putting a fond hand over top of Jason's. "And now these potholes have woken him." He hissed and squirmed. "Don't stand on my bladder," he muttered darkly at his stomach. "You'd better be cute when you come out."

Jason laughed just as Zephyr screeched from the cat carrier at their feet. Vale had insisted on bringing her instead of sending her away to the cattery. Urho turned back to face the front, nodding at the beta driver, and remembering how Vale's green eyes had filled with tears. *"I can't leave her there for months!"* he'd wailed, and Jason had instantly caved, packing Zephyr into a travel case and suffering only half a dozen scratches and a single bite for his efforts.

"This here's the place," the beta driver said, entering the gates and going up the drive that led to a gorgeous, massive house at the top of the hill. The facade was faded, but newly planted winter flowers brightened the otherwise dismal-looking mansion.

"Lofton Estate," the man said as he came to a stop, spitting some tobacco into a cup he carried between his thighs for that purpose. "They got servants what will help with the bags. So if you want to pay up now..."

Urho found the correct amount in his wallet and offered it plus a generous tip. No harm in getting on the good side of some of the locals early on in his stay. "That's for avoiding the potholes when you could."

"Got an expecting omega aboard," the man said with a grin. "Can't let any harm come to that wee one."

Vale groaned as Jason helped him out of the car, and Urho hung back, staring up at the house and trying to place it into the puzzle of stories Xan had told him over the phone since arriving here. The dunes below in the back and the sea sweeping away from them in green-gray, white-capped waves, had played a role in many of Xan's babblings about walks with Caleb, or time alone, but the windows at the front of the house didn't offer up clues as to what lay beyond them.

The driver and Urho grabbed their luggage from the trunk and placed it beside the car. Urho shook the man's hand and then he was off just as the front door opened and a beta servant was pushed aside by Xan, who darted out with his dark curls combed neatly, and his fashionable, casual suit impeccably fit.

"You're here!" he cried, throwing himself into Urho's arms and hugging him like they were long-lost brothers. Urho ducked his head to take in Xan's unique scent. A warm, settled feeling passed over him, but then Xan pulled away and turned to Jason, embracing him as well, and—more cautiously—Vale. Urho had to fist his hands to keep from reaching out and hauling Xan back into his arms.

"You're huge!" Xan said to Vale, eyes wide. "There's only one in there, right?"

Vale narrowed his eyes, and Xan burst into laughter. "I'm kidding. You look amazing. Are you hungry? Caleb has a big lunch put aside for you, and a ton of other options, like fresh produce from the southern regions if you're not in the mood for something heavy."

He turned to the house, smiling in the direction of the door where Caleb stood barefoot and yet regal with his blond head held high and a welcoming smile on his face. He met Urho's gaze with a warmth that made every doubt and lingering guilt about Urho's relationship with Xan melt away.

Ren, the beta servant Xan had nearly bowled over, began taking their luggage inside, and a second beta came out to help him. Urho nodded absently when Ren said, "I'll take them up to your respective rooms, sir. If there's a mix-up of any kind, we can sort it out later. Your rooms will all be along the same hall."

Jason ruffled Xan's hair, and the two of them grappled playfully in the front yard, kicking up dust and laughing like pups. They'd nearly fallen to wrestling when Vale said, "Darling, I'm feeling tired." Instantly, Jason snapped back to attentiveness, and Xan, like any alpha dealing with a pregnant omega, was all solicitousness and help.

"Let's get you inside." Jason grabbed the cat carrier with Zephyr in it and Xan called out, "Caleb, Vale's tired."

Caleb wrapped his arm around Vale's shoulder as soon as they reached the door. "Oh, sweet thing. Let's get your feet up and a nice heating pad for your back. Do you want some fruit and cheese? Or would soup and a sandwich be better? We also have chicken, potatoes, and—"

"Soup and sandwich please." Vale touched his dark head to Caleb's blond one. "I'm so glad you're here."

"I feel exactly the same," Caleb said. "I know that we're going to become great friends."

Xan's hand tentatively touching his brought Urho's attention back to the boy beside him. Or young man. There was something in Xan's face that looked ever so slightly more mature than when they'd last met. He looked more settled, perhaps. Urho didn't know what it represented, but he slung an arm around Xan's shoulder and said, "How careful do we need to be? Is your cousin home?"

Xan smiled and sidled closer. "He's at his club right now. Ren and his people won't talk. We're safe enough."

Jason stooped to open the cat carrier at the doorway and Zephyr took off out of it like a shot. "The cat pan is there," Jason said to Ren, motioning to where it sat with the luggage. "Where should we put it? In our rooms?"

Ren called to a young beta boy. "Run to the village to find a few more cat pans and extra litter." Then he said to Jason, "The house is quite big, Mr. Sabel. It'll be best to offer the cat a few options."

"Thank you so much. We really appreciate it. She's a good cat, I promise."

"Just don't try to pet her," Urho called out.

Jason cringed. "Uh, yeah. Probably don't try to pet her."

Ren smiled at him, and Jason clapped some money into his hand for his extra trouble.

Urho kept his arm around Xan as they crossed the threshold. Once the others had disappeared into the drawing room, Xan tugged Urho into a library, and then deeper into a small office attached to it. He closed the door behind them.

"Hello," Xan said, a smile wreathing his face. "I can't believe you're really here."

Urho touched Xan's cheek, stroking the soft curve and the line where the razor left the skin smoother beneath his fingers. "I admit I'm not sure what to say. I've thought of almost nothing but getting to be with you again and now…"

Xan stepped closer. "You could kiss me."

Urho took hold of his chin and dragged him close, wrapping his arm firmly around his back and taking his mouth roughly. Xan melted against him, his body going pliant in his arms. "Oh," he whimpered when Urho released him, his blue eyes blinking dazedly. "Oh."

Urho's cock pressed against Xan's stomach, and he rubbed it there, watching Xan react to his hardness. The way his cheeks flushed, his eyes dilated, and his breath quickened was a beautiful thing to see, and the scent of his arousal saturating Urho's alpha senses was heavenly. Urho's mouth flooded with saliva, and an irresistible urge claimed him.

"Get on your knees," he muttered, helping Xan down when his legs buckled at the words. "That's right." Xan's hands came up to Urho's pants, but he batted them away. "Not yet. Look up at me."

Xan dropped his hands to his side and did as ordered. His pulse beat visibly in his throat, and he licked his red, open lips with such a hungry expression in his eyes that Urho's cock flexed. He ripped open his pants lest he mess up his underwear and exposed himself in the cool air of the small office.

Xan moaned softly and reached down to squeeze his own cock with shaking fingers. He leaned forward, mouth open, and tongue out.

"Not yet," Urho said again, pressing his length against Xan's cheek, smearing some pre-come on his skin. His heart felt full to bursting at seeing Xan on his knees. "Did you keep your promise?"

"Yes!"

"Your mouth, your hole…?"

"Yours."

Urho's balls drew up, and he stroked himself, contemplating the sheer beauty of Xan on his knees with his eyes wide and desperate. It made him feel like he could fly, soar, and take Xan with him.

"Please," Xan whispered. "I've waited so long. Let me."

"Kiss it," Urho said, gripping the base of his large, alpha cock and positioning the head in front of Xan's mouth. "Mouth shut. Soft lips."

Xan whimpered but pressed his mouth into a little pucker and leaned forward, kissing gently. When he pulled back, he licked the pre-come from his lips, and his eyes rolled back. He convulsed with pleasure.

"Like that?" Urho whispered, his balls throbbing.

"Yes."

"Again."

Xan kissed the sensitive head of his cock and then shuddered hard as he greedily licked the pre-come from his lips again.

"Good boy. That's my alpha-shaped omega."

Xan groaned and lunged forward, burying his head in Urho's crotch, scenting his musk in his pubes and rubbing his face along the crease where his leg met his groin. Then he slipped down to nuzzle his balls. Urho placed his hand in Xan's soft hair, gently fingering the curls, and held him steady as he wallowed in Urho's scent.

"That's it," he grunted. "I want you to smell like me for the rest of the day."

Xan shook, gripped with another spasm. He clenched the back of Urho's thighs to steady himself, never allowing his face to leave

Urho's crotch. His breath, ticklish and hot, rushed over Urho's balls, but he was a good boy and didn't do more than breathe him in.

Urho stroked himself, staring down at Xan on his knees. They were both wearing too many clothes—which was so wrong, but unavoidable at the moment. He loved the way his boy trembled, and he gulped in the sweet scent of Xan's dripping cock.

He gripped Xan's hair and pulled him away, gaining his gaze again. "Tongue out," he ordered.

Xan hastened to obey. His red tongue pressed forward for Urho to see.

He slid the tip of his cock over it and watched as the flavor hit Xan and his eyes rolled back in pleasure. Urho stroked his cock again, bringing another bubble of pre-come up, and rubbed it against Xan's tongue, enjoying the way Xan squirmed on the floor in front of him, holding himself back, working against his own instincts in order to obey his alpha.

Perfection.

"Open wide," Urho gritted out.

Xan stared up at him, swallowed once, and then showed Urho the full of his mouth. Staring at the white molars and beautiful tongue, Urho groaned and carefully took hold of Xan's jaw, holding it steady, as he aimed his cock and then fed it into Xan's hot, wet mouth.

Xan groaned. The vibration coursed up Urho's cock and into his balls. He shuddered and released his cock as it nudged the back of Xan's throat. He held steady, admiring Xan's ability to take him deep, and then took hold of his hair again.

Gripping jaw and hair both, he fucked into Xan's open mouth. The scent of Xan's arousal filled his nose and escalated the intoxication that riveted him thoroughly. He tried hard to keep his eyes glued to Xan's watering blue ones, but in the end, he tipped his head back and groaned at the ceiling. The wet, gasping sounds of Xan's throat wrapped around his dick made him feel wild, and his pulse throbbed in his body until he was only a sensitive, pounding heart—pumping with blood, and love, and life.

When Urho looked down at Xan again, he found him with his eyes rolled back and ecstasy on his face. His body had gone limp. Surrendering to Urho's command, Xan was held up by Urho's grip on his face and hair alone. Xan trembled all over, one hand gripping his cock through his pants, and the other twitching by his side.

Urho pulled out of Xan's throat and silenced his cry of disappointment by tugging him up into a brutal kiss. His tongue sought out the remnants of his own taste in Xan's mouth, and finding it there, mixed with Xan's saliva and breath, made his heart sing. He gripped Xan close, got his boy's pants open, and dropped to his knees.

Xan cried out as Urho engulfed his hard, thick alpha cock and took it inside. It brushed the back of Urho's mouth and he gagged slightly, unable to take it as deep as Xan had. Even so, Xan writhed and bucked in pleasure. He finally collapsed over Urho's head, supporting himself against Urho's back and groaning as he came in harsh, wild, flavorful bursts.

Urho gobbled the spunk down, licking it from his lips, and then rose for another brutal kiss. Xan huffed against his lips, breathless and shaking like a leaf. Unable to wait another moment, Urho pushed Xan back to his knees. He stared down at his wrecked boy, eyes glazed, mouth open and panting. He took aim, pumping his hand over his cock twice and shot onto Xan's tongue.

Xan closed his eyes, swallowing the load greedily, opening his mouth desperately for more as Urho shot another load, and another. The floor spattered with his come, and the scent of it exploded in the room. His muscles gripped, and he grunted hard as Xan's face and hair were striped by the proof of his pleasure.

Xan sagged against him with his face lifted up, eyes closed, and lashes sticky with Urho's seed. He rubbed at his cock exposed from his open pants, still twitching and dribbling.

Urho tangled his fingers into Xan's hair, swallowed around the thick taste of Xan's spunk lingering his mouth, and praised him softly. "That's my sweet omega. That's my boy."

Xan quivered as Urho swiped his fingers over Xan's eyes, cleaning the come off and then feeding it to him. As Xan sucked his digits clean, Urho's dick twitched, and he groaned. "I want you still. How do you make me so wild for you? Just the scent of you in the air and I want to do nothing but roll around in it until I die."

Xan moaned, speechless. Urho pulled a handkerchief from his pants pocket and wiped Xan's face clean.

"Let me help you," he said, pulling Xan up to standing. Xan's legs trembled so hard Urho feared he'd fall. Xan blinked in seeming shock as Urho touched his sticky cheek. "We need to wash up."

Xan nodded, and his knees buckled again, but he grabbed Urho to steady himself. "This way. Upstairs."

Beta servants were still taking luggage to the guest rooms, so Xan dragged Urho down a back hallway and up some back stairs. Zephyr streaked past them on their way with a yowl. They kept their heads down and a respectable distance between them, but Urho was under no illusions that the servants couldn't gossip if they wanted to do so. He hoped Xan's cousin Janus didn't have any of the betas in his pay. He'd need to talk to Xan about that later.

"This is your room," Xan said, motioning at an open door that led to a room with a view of the city below.

"Where's yours?"

Xan waved toward the open seating area at the end of the hallway. Several sofas and chairs were clustered there, across from a bay of windows that looked out into the courtyard. "That way. On the opposite wing."

A breeze floated in from the cracked windows all along the interior hallway wall overlooking the courtyard, ruffling their hair, and lending an ocean-scented freshness to the space.

"Show me." Urho would need to know how to find it in the dead of the night when everyone else was sleeping. He refused to even pretend otherwise to himself.

Xan bit into his bottom lip, a filthy smile threatening to burst forth. "All right."

Urho followed him past other guest rooms, only one of which was open and obviously intended for Jason and Vale, past the seating area, and across the east side of the house. The windows there looked out on gardens that had seen better days, but there were several beta servants down there even now putting in effort to bring it back to life. Jason would probably have some ideas on that front as well.

Then they took a right onto a wing that looked very similar to the one Urho's room was on, only with fewer rooms. The interior wall featured windows onto the courtyard below, and he took a glance out to see that it was well-tended. He had no doubt that it hadn't been when Xan and Caleb first arrived. Potted, green, winter-leafed trees and flowing fountains made for peaceful, almost private alcoves, so long as no one was watching from above.

Urho made note to himself not to seduce Xan out there.

Xan stopped outside the first closed door. "This is mine." He gestured to the next one down the hall. "That's Caleb's."

Urho nodded, catching the eye of a beta servant who bustled past and watched them with curious eyes.

"Ours are the only open bedrooms on this wing for now. There are several others that we hope to have occupants for one day. The room next to Caleb would make a good nursery. It's plenty big and a carer could stay in with the baby if necessary. Though I think Caleb will want to be the one to do all of that." Xan swallowed convulsively, ending his babbling stream of words. "Do you want to come in?"

Another beta servant passed with a stack of towels.

"I assume there's a bathroom on my wing?" Urho asked. They were attracting attention and no wonder! They both looked a mess. Good thing the betas couldn't smell them, though there'd been enough spunk, maybe they could!

"In your room, actually. There's one in your room and one in the guest room we've given to Vale and Jason. The other rooms on that side would share a bath on the hall." He took a long breath and darted a glance right and left. "I have a very large bathtub."

Urho quivered, temptation rooting in him like a strong vine, rising up and ready to choke out his logic. "As wonderful as that sounds, we should probably part ways here."

"Of course," Xan agreed softly, though his eyes took on a dark glint of hurt and disappointment.

"I expect you to show me that bathtub later. Tonight, perhaps, when the house is quiet."

Xan's eyes brightened again. "Janus's room is on the first floor. He chose it before we arrived. It's technically supposed to be the housekeeper's area, but Ren is content on the detached servant's wing behind the kitchens."

Urho smiled. "Why did he choose that, I wonder? If his job is to spy on you."

"He doesn't sleep well. He likes to walk the gardens at night and sometimes he heads down to the beach. Or so he says."

"Ah." That struck Urho as dangerous. "Will he notice if I…"

Xan shook his head. "I don't think so. If we're quiet and you leave before dawn."

Urho hoped Xan was right, but even if he wasn't, they'd deal with that when the time came. "I'll meet you downstairs," he said.

"Yes," Xan agreed.

Urho wanted to let Xan open the door to his room and show him what they could do in that large bathtub. But they'd already made a spectacle of themselves. If they didn't want to attract notice, then they needed to be more conscientious and less impulsive. Getting a handle on their libidos would be imperative.

Xan blinked up at him, his blue eyes so hopeful. Urho wanted to kiss the lids and then his mouth again. Instead, Urho said, "I'll see you soon."

"Yes. If you get turned around, one of the servants can show you the way."

Urho reached out and then let his hand fall as another servant came rushing down the hallway with a litter pan. He wished Caleb and Xan didn't employ so many. "Thank you for keeping your promise to me."

Xan's cheeks went dark red, and his smile went shy. "Always."

Then he ducked into his room and shut the door behind him. Urho fought the urge to open it and follow his lover inside.

Stalking down the hallway, he barely held back a groan of frustration. Keeping his hands off Xan Heelies was going to be harder than he'd ever imagined.

XAN WAS STILL running the bath water when the door opened and Caleb stepped in.

"Vale is in their rooms resting, and Jason is with him, of course. Urho is apparently showering," Caleb said sniffing delicately before rolling his eyes. "And I scent that it was sorely needed. You couldn't keep yourselves apart long enough for at least a semblance of propriety?"

Xan slid into the water and moaned as the scent of Urho's spunk washed away from his skin. He splashed his face, rubbing it with lavender and smoke-scented soap, washing away the remains of Urho there, too.

Caleb pulled up the chair from the vanity and sat beside the tub. "Here, let me." He took the soap and grabbed a cloth and a small wooden cup, and then proceeded to douse Xan's hair thoroughly, until the curls straightened and stuck to the side of his face.

Xan leaned back as Caleb took the soap to his hair. Caleb's hands were gentle and confident. Xan sighed. "Mmm, that's nice."

"So I take it he was worth the wait?"

"He's so commanding," Xan murmured. "He just tells me what to do and I do it."

Caleb hummed softly and used a washcloth on Xan's back.

Xan regretted that Urho's scent was being washed away, but it wasn't as if he could go down to dinner with Jason, Vale, and likely Janus, by that time, reeking of Urho and their combined sex fluids. It wasn't even right to subject Caleb to it, though he'd barged in on Xan's bath and taken on the task himself, so it wasn't Xan's fault exactly.

Caleb rinsed the soap away carefully, making sure to block Xan's eyes from the run-off. "Your hair is so silky," Caleb murmured. "I like how it curls around my fingers."

"You're so nice to me," Xan said, excitement and bliss bubbling wildly in his veins, like he was running on champagne and barely banked arousal. He could still smell Urho in the house, and he wanted to seek him out again, though he knew they had to be sensible.

Caleb assured him, "I'm happy to see you so well-satisfied by someone who doesn't hurt you." He chuckled. "Or doesn't hurt you more than you want."

Xan splashed the bathwater idly, a smile blossoming uncontrolled over his face. "I loved it. He's amazing. I admit I've been nervous. With all this time and distance, I thought maybe the intensity of the first time was a fluke, but no. It was just as good." He groaned, flopping back in the water and accidentally splashing Caleb's white shirt and pants. "I want him to fuck me."

"I have a feeling he plans to do just that," Caleb teased.

"I want him to fuck me forever," Xan said vehemently. "I want to be his omega for real and grow slick and hot when he looks at me. I want to open for him like an omega would. I want to go into heat and take his knot, and I want to have his babies grow inside of me."

Caleb sat back and pushed his blond hair behind his ear, gazing at him sympathetically. "I wish you could have all of that. If I could simply hand over my womb and everything that goes with it to you, I'd do that in a heartbeat, my love."

The sadness in Caleb's voice brought Xan out of his passionate reverie. He frowned. "I'm sorry. I'm being selfish."

"You're being in love, and I don't want you to feel badly about wanting what you want. I truly only wish I could solve the problem for you. For both of us." Caleb smiled softly and slipped his fingers down the side of Xan's cheek.

"What does a knot feel like?" Xan asked, after the moment had passed. He closed his eyes and tried to imagine it. Alpha cocks were already so large, and since his hole wasn't as robust as an omega's, and didn't make slick like an omega's, penetration could be painful for him. But glorious. The sensation of being stretched so wide, filled so very full, was unlike any other.

What would it feel like if something even larger pinned him in place? If he was held on his alpha's knot and forced to submit to it for long swaths of time. He shivered. It sounded delicious.

But, unfortunately, knots only came in the presence of the pheromones of an omega in heat, so it was unlikely he'd ever be able to experience it for himself, even if he was physically capable of enduring it.

"Do you really want to know?"

"I do. Please tell me." He wanted to be able to imagine it to the fullest whenever he finally had a chance to allow Urho to take him.

Caleb dipped his fingers into the warm tub and then brought them out, watching them drip onto the surface and make small ripples. "In the moment, while I'm being knotted, I adore it like nothing else," Caleb said, with a strange note in his voice. "It fills me until I can't think at all. I am nothing but sensation and pleasure. I feel…complete. I come. Over and over. It's pure, intense, physical satisfaction." His nose wrinkled, and he shuddered. "But when it's over, I hate it. And I resent it. I loathe that I turn into a rutting animal with no mind, and that I beg for something that I can't stand the thought of otherwise. Biology is a powerful thing."

Xan frowned, his burgeoning rush of arousal draining away in the face of Caleb's problems. "I never wanted you to feel that way about me."

"Oh!" Caleb shook himself. "I was thinking of before. With other men." He smiled, but his eyes still looked sad. "With you, the knot is made even better because I feel safe. And when it's over, I feel more peaceful than anything else. And, of course, I feel hopeful." His eyes took on a happy gleam. "I want so much for a babe to take root. I do very much look forward to my next heat for that reason, darling." He smiled, love and excitement glowing forth. "I want a family so much, Xan. I know you'll be a wonderful father, and I think—or hope—I'll be a good pater."

"You'll be a wonderful pater," Xan assured him. He sat up, taking hold of Caleb's hand and stroking the fingers tenderly. "I can't wait to see you with our babe in your arms, chestfeeding."

"I look forward to that, too." He smiled a bit wistfully. "I do envy how much you want all the rest, though. And while I pity you that you can't have it, I admit that at times I pity myself more for not wanting it at all." Caleb sighed. "So maybe I'm the selfish one."

"No. You're perfect."

Caleb grinned. "Oh, alpha mine. Of course, you think so. And Urho thinks you're perfect, too."

"I doubt that. I'm sure he wishes I could give him what his Riki could."

Caleb's brow went up. "Are you jealous of his lost omega?"

"No." Xan shrugged. He wasn't, not truly, anyway. "He's dead. Nothing can change that. I'm alive and that's real." He released Caleb's hand and took up the sponge, feeling stronger. "You don't have to baby me. I can finish up myself. I don't know what came over me."

"Exhaustion after the satisfaction of extreme lust?" Caleb asked, laughing. "I've never seen you like this—so weak with it. I can't imagine what you'll be like come tomorrow morning. Unable to leave the bed at all, I imagine."

Xan splashed water on his face again and laughed. "And sore as wolf's own hell, too."

"Yes. Quite sore." Caleb tossed the soap to Xan. "But promise me one thing. Do be sure to eventually take a break from fucking to get to know one another, all right? I think if there's any future in this, that's the direction it will lie."

He dropped a kiss on the top of Xan's head and left the bathroom. The steam from the water had fogged the mirror when Xan climbed out to dry off. He wiped it away and took a look at himself.

For the first time in a long time, he thought he could grow to like the person looking back at him.

CHAPTER FIFTEEN

D INNER WAS A quiet affair. The conversation revolved around Vale's pregnancy, Caleb and Xan's redecorating, and the plans for the next few days. Xan's heart leapt every time he looked across the table to see Urho staring back at him. The heat between them shimmered in the air until he could almost feel it on his skin. He wondered if the others could as well and were just too polite to mention it.

Jason monitored Vale's food intake like an obsessed man, and Vale looked on the verge of punching him for it more than once. "One cordial won't harm the baby, ask Urho," Vale huffed, sipping the dessert wine from a thimble-sized glass.

Urho tore his gaze away from Xan long enough to concur that such a small amount wouldn't bother the baby in the least, leaving Jason little choice but to be satisfied with his answer.

Caleb asked them all to withdraw to Xan's library for some quiet reading and music. He'd had the record player moved out of Xan's office, and he was having a wonderful time playing the records they'd found in the library and making up new dances.

He was in the middle of teaching them one when Janus returned from his evening out at the gentlemen's club. He came in looking freshly showered, wearing a fashionable suit, and smelling of peppermint. But that couldn't cover up the bruise blooming on his jaw or the scent of liquor also wafting off him. He must have stopped by the bar after losing one of his wrestling matches.

"What have we here?" Janus asked before Xan could ask about

his bruised face. "A party? With dancing? And I wasn't invited? You know how I love to dance, Caleb." He grinned flirtatiously.

Caleb pasted on a pretty smile and said, "Alas, we're short on partners here."

Janus smiled widely, something sloppy in it, like he was too drunk to control the muscles of his face properly. He motioned at Vale, who sat watching from the safety of the sofa. "I'd be happy to partner with this handsome omega. I don't believe we've met." He stepped forward, hand out and a wicked leer on his face, only to stop dead in his tracks when he spotted the obvious evidence of Vale's pregnancy.

Jason, who'd been dancing with Caleb, ostensibly so that Caleb could instruct him on the new moves, but really so that Xan and Urho had an excuse to dance together, released his hold on Caleb's waist. He came to stand between Janus and Vale.

"Janus," he said coldly. "It's been a long time. This is my *Érosgápe*, Vale Aman." He took Vale's hand and helped him to standing. "Vale, this is Janus Heelies, Xan's cousin."

"Jason, it's been a long time." Janus gulped and looked away from Vale toward where Caleb stood watching worriedly. "I'd heard you'd found your *Érosgápe*. Lucky man."

"To say the least," Jason said, but he sounded strained.

"Forgive me," Caleb said, darting over. "I should have done the introductions. I was out of breath from dancing."

"And hoping Janus would go away," Xan said, under his breath. His rudeness was ignored. He didn't know if he was grateful or disappointed by that.

"I see congratulations are in order," Janus said, sweeping a hand toward Vale's shifting, bulging stomach. All evidence of flirtation was gone from his tone and demeanor. No alpha was stupid enough to flirt with an omega who was with child, no matter how drunk he was. Especially between an *Érosgápe* couple—not unless he truly wanted to engage in violence with the omega's alpha. "When will the new babe come into the world?" His tongue sounded heavy, his words a bit slurred.

"Next month if all goes well," Jason said, still standing protectively at Vale's side. Xan noticed that no handshake had been exchanged.

Janus nodded. "Wolf's blessings on you both. And the babe, of course." Then he turned to Xan and Urho. His gaze swept between them, and his brow raised knowingly.

Xan immediately released Urho's waist, an embrace left over from where he'd been leading him through the motions of Caleb's new dance. He stepped away and smiled tightly at Janus. "Allow me to introduce Vale and Jason's friend, Dr. Urho Chase. He's here to deliver the baby when the time comes, and to make sure all goes well in the interim."

Janus's brow cocked up even higher, but he put out a hand to Urho with a sly, still-messy smile. "Welcome to Lofton. I'm sure Caleb's seen that you're comfortable here. He's making this house into quite a beautiful home."

Caleb stiffened, and Xan crossed to him, sliding an arm around his shoulder. "Caleb makes everything better," Xan said pointedly. Caleb lifted his chin.

Janus smirked. "The belief of all alphas! One day perhaps I'll find someone worthy of contracting with and get to experience such pure devotion for myself. Or, even better, perhaps I'll find my *Érosgápe*. I hear the sex is unbeatable."

Jason's jaw jumped as though he was gritting his teeth, and Vale's expression went strained.

Urho cleared his throat, a mildly scolding sound.

Janus, of course, gave no indication that he noticed the tension in the room, or, if he did, then he rather enjoyed it. "In the meantime," he slurred on. "I find I must shift for myself. Speaking of…" he crossed the room and poured himself a generous helping of bourbon from the liquor cabinet.

Caleb loosed a soft sound of irritation. Xan caught his eye and raised a brow, asking silently if he should stop his cousin from imbibing more. Caleb shook his head quickly once. His blue eyes shimmered with frustration.

Janus turned around and lifted the glass in a toast. "To friendship."

Everyone in the room merely stared at him as he drank. No echo of the toast touched anyone's lips.

It occurred to Xan that he didn't know if Janus had any friends. The man was always out socializing, but everyone knew there was a difference between someone to grab a drink with or talked business with, and a friend. Who would want to be friends with someone like Janus, anyway? Arrogant, smug, and self-important.

Janus swallowed the whole of his drink down, and then, rather grotesquely, wiped his mouth with his sleeve. "I've gotta surprise for you, cousin."

"Yeah?" Xan asked, dread slipping down his spine.

"I'll be out of your hair for a few weeks." He seemed to summon some clarity of mind from somewhere. His eyes were still drink-bleary, but he spoke more clearly. "I've been called back to the city."

Xan's heart did a strange leap and fall. Janus being gone was good, fantastic, *wonderful*. He could spend more time with Urho without fear of being tattled on. But Janus going back to the city meant he'd be back under Father's wing. And that meant Xan was still his father's second choice for heir.

Xan clenched his jaw. "Why?"

"A promotion for me. I'm being assigned a new project in another city. I believe the Capital was mentioned," Janus said with a drunken, smug smile. "Your father also wants to finalize the plans for the future of the office here in Virona."

"I should be part of that discussion."

"Do you really think so?" Janus cocked his head and sneered. "Your father doesn't. He said you should stay here." His eyes glinted meanly as he refilled his glass. "Which works out well, doesn't it? Since, as it turns out, you have *guests*." The emphasis on the word implied things that, while accurate, Xan had to reassure himself Janus had no way of truly knowing.

Urho's arm came around Xan's shoulder reassuringly, but he shrugged it off, not wanting to let on anything Janus might report to Father. "When will you be leaving?"

"In the morning. First thing. I admit I'm looking forward to my triumphant return to the city." His sloppy smile was back now, and he looked to Caleb as he said, "There's a certain, delicious omega there that I've been meaning to visit again. He just might be the one for me. If only he wasn't already spoken for."

Caleb shot him a hurt, angry look, and Janus smirked like Caleb's reaction pleased him in some way. He tipped his glass back to drain it.

Jason and Vale sat together, still as statues on the sofa, watching in uncomfortable silence as the scene unfolded in a mess around them. Urho lingered at Xan's back, offering reassurance with his presence, but the pleasure Xan took in that kindness didn't even begin to rival the embarrassment of his cousin's behavior.

"And with that, I'm off to bed." Janus's smile became ingratiating. "It's been lovely making your acquaintance, Vale." He turned to Jason. "Good to see you again, of course. We'll be working together in the future given our companies' contracts."

"Oh?" Jason said stiffly. "My father and I usually work with Xan or Ray directly."

"Xan won't be your go-to man for long," Janus said, wobbling a bit on his feet. "I will." Then he met Caleb's eye. "Looks like you chose the wrong Heelies. I'd have taken better care of you."

"At what price?" Caleb hissed and turned his back on Janus.

The room went silent and Xan heard his pulse pounding in his ears as his fists clenched and his vision blurred red.

"But wait," Janus added, an ugly expression twisting the handsome features of his face. "It was *me* who didn't want *you*, wasn't it? How could that be when you're so very perfect?" He snarled. "Luckily for us both, my memory on those details remains cloudy." His eyes grew inexplicably wet with unshed tears, and he spit out, "Too much liquor tonight, you see."

Only Urho's hand on Xan's shoulder prevented him from attacking Janus in his rage. He growled, "Get out of my house."

"Now, now. You know it's your father's house, and he wants me here."

"It's *my* house!" Xan lunged for him, but Urho held him back.

"Don't want to give your father any more reason to cut you out, do you?" Janus's laugh was as nasty as it was oddly broken. He paused in the doorway and shot Caleb's back a yearning look. "If you'd have just let me…"

Caleb's shoulders stiffened.

Janus shook his head hard and turned his attention back to Xan. "I'll give your pater your love, cousin. He misses you. Though he's the only one."

Then he waltzed out of the room on clumsy feet.

Xan started after him, but Jason and Urho didn't let him follow. "I'll murder him," Xan gritted out, struggling against Urho's strong grip and Jason's solid presence before him. "Let me go. I'm going to—"

"Stop!" Caleb said, his voice quavering. "Forget Janus. He's drunk and horrible, but not worth another moment's thought." His cheeks pinked as if he'd been slapped. He closed his eyes and shuddered. "He's loathsome. How did I ever think he was charming?"

Caleb stalked toward the sofa and sank down onto it beside Vale, who took his hand. Caleb smiled kindly but tugged his hand away, rubbing between his brows and trembling slightly. "Just calm down, Xan," Caleb whispered. "And don't make this worse."

Jason and Urho exchanged glances, and Xan moved to kneel beside Caleb, but stopped when Caleb shook his head. "Just give me some space. He sucks all the air from the room."

Said room trembled with awkward, emotional silence.

"Wow," Jason finally muttered. "It's like he walked in with dog shit on his shoe. The reek of him lingers."

"Is it very wrong to hope there's an accident, and he somehow falls on the tracks as the train approaches tomorrow?" Xan asked, stalking to the liquor cabinet and pouring a generous glass for himself. "He ruins everything just by existing."

Xan loathed the multitude of hateful needles Janus had pricked him, and worse, Caleb, with in just a very few awful minutes. He loathed even more that he hadn't taken his cousin out with a well-placed elbow to the throat. If Urho and Jason hadn't held him back...

He'd probably be in prison for murder tomorrow.

So it was undoubtedly for the best. But still he resented that Janus still breathed in his house. Even one more night of hospitality was too much after that little show.

"He's awful," Vale breathed. "I hadn't expected to like him, but that was...wolf-god."

Jason said, "I've always disliked him and thought he was arrogant. But what exactly *is* his problem, Xan? I don't remember him being cruel for the sake of it."

"He didn't used to be," Caleb murmured, his face half-covered by his elegant hand.

"So he's changed?" Vale asked.

Urho spit out, "It doesn't matter how he used to be if this is how he is now. What a jackass."

"Yes," Vale agreed. "But perhaps that jackass has a reason—"

"Excuses for hurtful behavior is for children and deathbeds," Urho said.

Vale rolled his eyes, and Jason looked like he might actually laugh. Xan didn't know how he felt about Urho's statement. He was too turned around after Janus's interruption to their beautiful evening. He wished his cousin had never arrived, and they'd continued to dance and be merry. But clearly the dancing portion of the evening was over.

"He always got under my skin," Xan muttered irritably. "Even when we were kids. But he definitely changed for the worse several years back. It doesn't matter. He's sleeping off his liquor and will be gone in the morning. I couldn't ask for more."

"That is good news." Jason glanced meaningfully between Urho and Xan. "That frees things up for everyone. There won't be quite the same need for subterfuge between the two of you."

"Exactly." Xan should be happy that Janus was going, but darkness shifted around in his belly with the liquor. He wanted to stalk down the hall, open Janus's door, and beat his ass. And he wanted to curl up in Urho's lap and cry, because he was tired, and hurt, and angry.

Because his father loved that nasty piece of work more, and would leave the company to him if given even half a chance.

Xan swallowed down his feelings with another big swig of liquor.

"At least there is a new project for him, somewhere far away," Caleb murmured. "He won't be here much longer."

"But *we* will," Xan said.

Caleb met his eye. He sighed, and his shoulders sagged. His handsome face fell. "I suppose you're right."

"It's not so bad here…" Jason ventured.

"Yes, you're making the place quite livable," Vale agreed.

Caleb whispered, "I do like Virona. But that's not what this is about."

Xan took another sip from his glass, closing his eyes on the burn. Urho's hand rested on his shoulder, squeezing lightly.

"It's a good house," Urho said carefully. "You could have a worthy life here, away from the interference of your family."

Xan caught Caleb's eye again, and they both sighed. "That's true. But like Caleb said, it's more complicated than that." He rubbed his temple. "I'm happy Janus is starting on a new project in a different city, but he said he'd also be handling the final details for this office in Virona."

"Which means Xan hasn't made the impression on his father he'd hoped to make," Caleb murmured. "Pass me a drink, darling. A strong one."

"I'll get it," Urho said, steering Xan to the chair next to the sofa, the one closest to Caleb. He then set about getting drinks for all of them. As the night ticked into the small hours, they sat together on the sofas and chairs in the library while Xan explained his situation: his father's threats, his pater's removal from his life, Ray's reassurances, and Janus's ambitions.

"I see," Urho said slowly as Xan finished up. "So this trip of Janus's could be quite damaging for you."

"He could paint Xan in all kinds of poor colors," Caleb said, swirling his drink and kicking off his shoes to expose his glittering toenails.

"He'll take all the credit for the success of the office in Virona," Xan muttered.

Never mind that Xan had done most of the work, supervising the day-to-day activities, solving problems and disputes between contractors, and more, while Janus had scampered off most days to "make connections" at the gentlemen's club, claiming that his aim was to "woo" the higher-ups in the community.

Virona wasn't as affluent as the city, or the Capital, but it wasn't without its aristocratic class. Xan hadn't protested because he was happy to have Janus out from under foot, and it made it so much easier to follow Ray's instructions to the letter, without having Janus there to question his every move.

Xan had imagined his father would *appreciate* his focus and diligence, see that he didn't get distracted, but actually stuck it out and got things done. But apparently only social connections were to be rewarded. "All that matters to my father is the company," Xan bit out. "Happiness, joy, love—all of those are ambitions for lesser types of men. The kind of man my father doesn't respect."

Jason murmured, "I wonder how his *Érosgápe* feels about that?"

"Pater is…" Xan trailed off, his throat tightening and his eyes burning. He squeezed them shut and rubbed them with his fingers.

"Xan's pater does whatever his father says," Caleb said gently. "It's his way."

"Yes, I remember," Jason said.

Murmurs of sympathy went all around, and Xan felt young and stupid in all the ways he hated most. But when he met Urho's gaze again, staring at him from the chair opposite, all he saw was a warm determination that gave him hope.

Urho kicked off one of his shoes to rub his foot. "Forgive me for questioning it, but are the servants loyal? If any of them are in your cousin's employ, they might report some unseemly behavior, and—"

"Ren would never allow it," Xan said. "He's been with me since I left Mont Nessadare, and he hires only servants he believes in and can trust."

"Still," Caleb said. "There is that new kitchen boy. He's been homesick and saving for a train ticket back to visit his pater. And while most betas are very open to any expression of sexuality, there are a few who are very strict adherents to the Holy Book of Wolf."

"In other words?" Xan said.

"I think I'll send that new kitchen boy home. If the cook needs more help, then we'll get someone from the village. Someone who can go home at night so there are fewer people in the house." Caleb smiled, but his eyes looked haunted. "It won't do to be lax, but in our home, you should feel safe. I won't have it any other way."

"That would be a good start," Urho said.

Caleb sighed, and his eyes went distant. "Perhaps I'll speak with Ren. Make sure that he's informed the others that anything that happens on the premises is to be kept absolutely to themselves, and not even shared with Janus."

"Luckily the servants' quarters are isolated," Jason pointed out. "So long as you act like gentlemen during the daylight hours, then no one will be the wiser."

"It's unfair and ridiculous to ask you to hide," Vale said, rubbing his stomach. Then he groaned. "My back is killing me. Urho, you've seen a lot of babies. Promise me he'll be cute."

"You'll think you've never seen one cuter," Urho said, clapping his hands against his thighs and standing up. "Let's leave this distressing topic behind for the night. Vale, I think you should let Jason take you to your room now."

"Yes, it's late." Caleb glanced toward the clock, sighing. "We should all go to bed. Tomorrow I'd planned for us to take a nice long walk on the beach, Vale, and you'll want plenty of strength for that."

Goodnights were exchanged all around and handshakes given.

After Vale and Jason left the room, Caleb kissed Urho's cheek and then Xan's, looking them both in the eye seriously. "Janus's room is far from you both, but I don't trust him. Try to keep the noise down tonight, no matter how lost you get in each other. If he even suggested to your father…"

Xan nodded and drew Caleb into an embrace. "We'll be careful. Thank you."

"I love you, Xan," Caleb whispered in his ear. "Enjoy yourself, but keep us safe."

Xan nodded, and Caleb tugged away. After another kiss on Urho's cheek, he left the room on his bare feet, carrying his shoes in his hands.

"Should you go to him? Does he need comforting?" Urho asked, his hand resting on Xan's shoulder. The heat tingled into the muscles of Xan's arm, and he leaned back into Urho's strong chest.

"He would have asked. Caleb isn't shy about what he needs from me."

Urho turned Xan around. "What's between him and your cousin? What was that all about?"

Xan let his head fall forward, resting it against Urho's chest, and he took slow breaths, enjoying Urho's strong, musky scent. "It's his story to tell. Suffice it to say, they were friends once, with the potential for more. It hurt Caleb when it was over, but he's moved on. Seeing Janus again, being treated that way, it opens old wounds, I think."

"Should we both go to him?"

Xan kissed the bottom of Urho's chin. "You're a good man. But no. He'll want to be alone. He's quiet like that."

"If you're sure."

"I am."

"Then I'll come to you in an hour," Urho said seriously. "Be ready for me."

Xan's throat clicked as he swallowed. "How?"

"Clean yourself. I won't want to wait."

Xan's balls tightened, and he found himself immediately hard. "Yes. I'll be ready."

Urho nodded and turned on his heel. No handshake, no kiss,

nothing but the scent of him still in the air after he'd walked away. Xan licked his lips, counted to twenty, and then followed, turning off the library lights on his way out.

"I'M NERVOUS," XAN said, laughing.

Urho stepped into Xan's richly decorated room and locked the door behind them. His breath came in stutteringly as he took in Xan wearing a red bathrobe that made him look positively indecent, exposing his pale chest and highlighting his red mouth.

"Why's that?" Urho asked, sounding as breathless as he felt. Though his stomach was flipping madly, too. He'd thought so much about fucking Xan over the last few months—wanting it, dreading it, questioning it, deciding he had to have more of him—that the nearness of the moment felt overwhelming.

"Why am I nervous?" Xan asked, his voice higher pitched than usual. "I guess because it's been so long since I've done this with someone who…" Xan trailed off. His pale chest grew rosy, and the color spread up his throat and into his cheeks. He tried again. "With someone who…"

Urho spoke softly. "Someone who didn't want to hurt you?"

"Yes. I suppose so." He sounded so uncertain that Urho's heart ached.

"We should talk about that before we do anything more," Urho said, though his cock was in vehement disagreement over that. He guided Xan to the wide, ornate bed with the covers already turned down. "What do you want tonight?"

"I want you to fuck me," Xan said firmly, though he took in a flighty breath afterward that sounded like a barely suppressed giggle. "I like it rough…I think."

"You think?"

"I don't know if I should talk about the things I've done in the past," Xan said, licking his lips anxiously. "Or the people I was with before."

"How many were there?"

"Just two. Jason and…the other."

"The monster."

"The so-called monster," Xan said, anxiety rippling in the air between them.

"There's nothing so-called about it. Don't forget I saw what he did to you. How he left you after…" Urho shuddered and touched Xan's cheek gently. "I don't ever want to see those kinds of bruises on you again. If you want me to hurt you like that—" He shook his head.

"I don't!" Xan gripped Urho's wrist, holding his hand against his cheek as though afraid Urho was going to pull away.

"Good." Urho whispered, "I can lose control, the way I have before with you, but I'll never be so rough that you're in real pain the next day. I don't treat my omegas like that."

Xan blushed and looked down.

"What? Talk to me," Urho urged.

"I like it when you call me an omega."

He nodded. He'd figured that much out already.

"And I think I'd like it if you called me some rough things, too."

Urho raised his brows in question.

Xan swallowed hard. "Like bitch or slut or…" Xan's ears were so red they looked painful. "Or worse things."

Urho touched Xan's chin. "Why? Do you not think you deserve to be cherished?"

Xan's eyes dropped to the carpet under their feet.

"Well? Answer me."

Xan sounded small and scared when he whispered, "I don't

know what that's like. With Jason, it was just games. Not..." He shuddered. "I've never had that. I didn't want to assume you'd give it to me. No one has ever wanted to give that to me before."

"What about Caleb?" Urho asked gently, his heart aching for his poor boy.

Xan explained shyly how during the heat with Caleb, the sex they'd accomplished had been desperate, terrifying, and frustrating. "There was no 'cherishing' between us. Just tears, and pain, and fear." He raised his eyes to Urho's, his voice trembling. "So I don't know if I'd like to be cherished in bed or not. I've never experienced that before."

Urho tugged him close and kissed his hair, his eyelids, and his hot ears, still red with shame and embarrassment. "Let's see if you like it. If you don't, then we can try something else."

"What if *you* don't like it?" Xan asked with a wobbly voice as Urho pressed him back against the bed and loomed over him, taking in his red cheeks, wide eyes, and flushed chest peeking out of his bathrobe. "Fucking me, I mean. What if you don't enjoy it? It won't feel like with an omega. The way I'm made is different, and—"

"I'm going to like it," Urho interrupted, sliding his hand into Xan's robe, stroking over the smooth, almost-hairless skin he found, and then pushing the garment off Xan's shoulders. "I've liked everything we've done so far. I don't know why this would be any different."

"I'm still nervous," Xan whispered as Urho untied the knot holding his robe closed. He spread the robe open, revealing Xan's smaller-than-average form, his thick alpha cock, and his pale skin flushing more and more with every breath.

"I'm nervous too," Urho admitted. "But I want you and we've made promises. Those might not be as good as contracts, not as formal, but I don't take them lightly."

"Me either."

And now he wanted so much more than just Xan's body. He wanted to carve his way into this man's life and heal his wounds, be his friend, his partner, and maybe, somehow, Caleb's, too, albeit in a different way. How this was all going to work, he had no clue, but it started here, in this bed, making Xan understand what it meant to feel love.

"Get comfortable. On your stomach for now."

"My stomach?" Xan asked, but he did as he was told, tugging a pillow down to cradle his face.

Urho straddled Xan's thighs and removed his own robe entirely, throwing it aside and letting his balls and hard dick slide over Xan's plump ass cheeks. Xan lifted up to gaze over his shoulder. "I wanted to see you…" His eyes were hungry as he took in what he could of Urho.

"You'll have plenty of time to see me when you turn over. Just relax. I want to check on how you've healed."

Xan released an odd half-sob and dropped his head to the pillow, his muscles trembling with emotion. Urho rubbed his hands soothingly up and down Xan's back, gently massaging his shoulders and squeezing down his arms.

"Just rest," Urho said. "Feel me here with you." He pushed his cock against Xan's buttocks, and then bent low to kiss his shoulder blades, one at a time. He then kissed his way down Xan's back, his knees digging into the soft mattress.

When he got to the place where Xan's lower back dipped in, he heard the soft sound of Xan's tears. "Are you all right?" he whispered against the last wet place his kisses had left on Xan's warm skin.

"I'm scared," Xan whispered back, his words almost obscured by the pillow he clutched.

"I won't hurt you."

"That's what I'm scared of," he said, a sob breaking free. "What if you don't hurt me and I love it? And then what if you never want to give it to me again?"

"Oh, sweet boy," Urho soothed, abandoning his quest to get a look at Xan's asshole to rise up and take Xan into his arms. He turned Xan and cradled him against his chest, kissing his hair and stroking his back and arms until Xan quieted. Their hard cocks slid against each other as Urho rocked them gently in a quiet rhythm. "Let me show you," he whispered. "I promise I'll never take it away from you."

"How can you know that?"

"Because I know my own heart."

"Do you?" Xan sounded amazed.

Urho held him close, squeezed his eyes shut, and felt the rightness of their bodies fitting together. He kissed Xan's head again. "I'm learning more of it every day. Let me show you."

"If I let you cherish me," Xan's voice broke again. "You'll never stop?"

It was a big ask, but Urho already knew the answer. "Not for as long as I live. I'll give you this and so much more."

"I don't believe you," Xan whispered, and Urho couldn't even be offended. Xan had been so hurt in his short life—physically, emotionally, and spiritually.

"Then I'll just have to prove it to you."

Urho kissed him then, slow and sweet, and Xan melted against him. He sobbed as Urho held and touched him. He finally calmed enough to turn onto his stomach again, lifting his hips onto a pillow so Urho could have a clear look at his asshole.

Urho's pulse pounded as he finally spread Xan open again. *There* was the intoxicating whorl of hair that surrounded that tender pucker of muscle. His heart sped up alarmingly, the scent of Xan's arousal and his own need layered over him like blankets of lust.

He leaned forward to kiss the place that had been so brutally used the last time he'd glimpsed it. Now it had healed up into a sweet, tight hole that cried out for the caress of his tongue and lips.

He closed his eyes and gave the loving touch Xan had always deserved.

"Please," Xan whimpered as Urho's tongue pierced him. "I can't take this. Please hurt me or call me names. Don't let me feel this good. *Please.*"

"Oh, no." Urho pulled away from the humid crack of Xan's ass long enough to reply. "This is how I'll cherish you."

Xan wept, and Urho kissed his asshole even more adoringly. He licked and loved him there until he'd worked his alpha-shaped omega into a sobbing frenzy of need—shame and fear seemingly abandoned in the pleasure. Xan rutted against the pillow under his hips, and then back against Urho's face, crying out as he dissolved in desire.

Urho wanted to fuck him now, but he wasn't ready for it to be over so soon. He gave Xan more of his mouth, using his fingers to work him open slowly. When he couldn't take it anymore, he flipped Xan over and shared his most intimate flavor in a kiss. Xan groaned and gripped Urho's hair, his body shaking so hard that Urho covered him completely, pressing him deeply into the bed to help give him solidity and comfort.

"Where's the oil?" he rasped, lips still brushing Xan's, breathing in the scent of his saliva and skin. Xan wouldn't make slick. Betas and alphas didn't. And Urho had been reminded of that as he'd eaten Xan's ass and not been flooded by the heavenly stuff omegas made naturally. But Xan's own taste was perfect on its own—heavy and solely his. Urho licked his lips again, loving the residual musk of Xan's most intimate place.

"In the drawer," Xan managed between his gasps of pleasure and half-sobs of overwrought emotion.

Urho didn't wait for him to clarify which drawer, simply guessing that it was the bottom one in the stand next to the bed. He was right, and he brought the bottle up to lube up his cock and pour some over Xan's saliva-wet anus.

"This is where you tell me if you want me to stop," he said, stroking his large alpha cock.

"Don't you dare," Xan hissed. He lifted his legs to give Urho access. His hard cock lay glistening with pre-come on his belly, over a small trail of hair from his navel down to his dark bush of pubic hair. His taint was pink and led to the dark hair that surrounded his anus, which beckoned to Urho, glistening with the oil and twitching with Xan's need.

"I want to make this good for you."

"Just fuck me," Xan ordered, his eyelashes wet with tears, but his voice firmer than it had been since Urho had come into the room. "*Now.* Don't make me wait anymore. Prove to me that you're going to do it. You promised."

Urho grabbed Xan's legs and began a slow thrust inside. Xan groaned and whined, arching and pushing, his body slow to open for Urho's thickness.

The pleasure of penetrating Xan was beyond Urho's expectations. One of Xan's legs rested on Urho's shoulder, the other Urho held wide by gripping his ankle. The view was incredible: Xan's lithe, sturdy form spread out under him, muscles jumping and trembling in anticipation and tension. A deeper ruddy flush crept up Xan's chest and into his neck, painting his cheeks and turning his mouth an even brighter red.

"Please," Xan whimpered. "Give me more."

Urho's thighs quivered, and his breath came in short gasps as he held back from shoving as deep as he could into Xan's body. The tight grip around his cock head and the thudding of Xan's pulse, the strain of Xan's muscles, told Urho that Xan was struggling to accommodate his size.

He reached down and rubbed the tight rim of Xan's flesh gripping his dick, holding himself firmly in check as Xan squirmed, trying to get Urho in deeper. "I want it all," Xan begged, sweat popping around his temples as he bore down and Urho sank farther in. "Give me your knot."

Urho groaned. He wished he could answer Xan's plea. Knotting only happened with an omega in heat, the pheromones of their pleasure and orgasm triggering it in the alpha breeding them. "You want me to breed you, little omega?"

Xan whined then, his head tossing back and forth and his hips twisting as he pressed himself onto Urho's thick cock. "That's right," Urho crooned. "You look so beautiful fucking yourself on my dick. Gorgeous."

Xan rolled his hips, taking Urho deeper and deeper with every twist and push, until he'd filled himself fully. Satisfaction crossed his face, and he stared up at Urho, his expression of challenge and surrender one that scoured Urho's heart and soul, scrubbing him down to raw nerves and emotion.

Urho's cock throbbed deep in the silken heat of Xan's ass. He was less robust and gripping than an omega on the inside, but tight and alive all the same. Interior muscles rippled around Urho, and Xan's body trembled at the effort of opening for him, of holding him inside. Urho moaned, slamming his hips forward to bring himself the final inch home.

"Yes. Fuck me," Xan demanded, his eyes alight and wild.

"You want me to make you come?" Urho grunted. One hand still clenching Xan's ankle, he brought his other up to lightly grasp his straining neck. "Just say yes, sweet omega, and I'll make you come."

"Yes!" Xan's eyes went wide, and then he collapsed entirely, surrendering. His cock spurt pre-come on his stomach. The scent of if made Urho's mouth water, and he squeezed Xan's neck a little more tightly.

"Oh, fuck yes," Xan moaned, his eyes rolling up in his head. *"Fuck. Yes."*

Urho held him in place with a grip on his throat, too light to choke, but hard enough to remind Xan of who was in control, who it was cherishing him tonight. Then he fucked into him with strong, long strokes, aiming to hit Xan's prostate.

He shuddered with pleasure as he worked, noting the differences—the absence of spongy, swollen omega glands and the constant spill of slick over his cock to smooth the way. But being in Xan, watching him fall apart with pleasure, watching him give in to his body and open for Urho's thickness was intensely satisfying in a way being with every omega since Riki had never been.

Xan's body convulsed with each slam home. His cock dribbled pre-come that smelled like slick, and when Urho swept some of it up into his fingers to add to the oiled place their bodies met, it acted like slick, too.

"My little omega," Urho muttered, shoving hard into Xan, rattling his teeth with the force of his thrust. "Gonna flood you with my seed and make you mine."

"Yours," Xan agreed, eyes dilated like he'd been drugged. Sweat slipped down the side of his flushed faced.

"Promise," Urho growled.

"Already promised."

Urho shuddered, his thrusts losing pace for a moment as his heart clenched. Yes, Xan had already promised his hole, but this was beyond that. *This* was intimacy and rough pleasure all rolled into one. He leaned down and kissed Xan hard, their teeth clacking before their lips moved together in a sensual give and take that echoed the thrust of Urho's dick into Xan's spasming body.

"Come for me." Urho squeezed Xan's throat firmly. "Shoot your hot load all over yourself while I fuck your sweet omega hole."

Xan seemed to have only been waiting for permission, because he hunched up, thighs flexing and asshole tightening almost painfully on Urho's cock.

Urho covered Xan's mouth as he screamed his pleasure and his cock erupted with come. Spurts of it went everywhere—the sheets, Xan's mess of dark curls, the headboard, and even some on the floor well beyond the bed itself.

Xan's head slammed against the mattress as he convulsed. His pink nipples were tight and begged for attention as his straining cock tensed and released again and again, the scent of spunk rising around them like steam.

"That's my good boy," Urho praised him. "Give it all up for me. Such a perfect omega."

"Please," Xan whimpered, shaking violently in the aftermath of his pleasure. "Give me more. *Take* more. Remake me, please."

Urho collapsed onto Xan's hot, sweaty body, releasing his ankle and wrapping his arms around him tightly. Xan's still-hard cock rammed against Urho's stomach again and again, and the muscles of his back and thighs twitched and quivered as Urho fucked him with intense, deep strokes.

"Yes, yes," Xan chanted. "Please, Urho. Call me your omega again."

"My omega," Urho muttered, the words slipping from his mouth easily. His heart echoed the sentiment irrationally and devotedly. "Mine."

"Yes, oh fuck yes." Xan's ass gripped and fluttered around Urho's cock. "I love that. I love it so much."

Urho shuddered, a hard sort of place inside him crumbling. He bent low to kiss Xan's neck, lick the come off his cheek, and then suckle his pointed nipples until Xan was frantic and moaning.

Xan's heels hammered the rhythm of their rut against Urho's plunging ass, and he crooned with pleasure. Urho buried his face, tension ramping up unbearably before shattering in pulsing, ecstatic release—a blinding, convulsing, consuming orgasm like a seizure grabbing him.

Ropes of alpha semen shot deep into Xan's body, so much that it gushed from his hole, lubricating the final aching perfection of their connection.

"Yes," Xan groaned, gripping him tightly.

Urho heaved and shuddered on top of his much-smaller body, sweaty and helpless in pleasure.

As the peak fell away and they were left in a tangle of wet, sweaty, come-covered limbs, they kissed, soft and intimate, for long, panting minutes.

Finally, Xan whispered, "I liked it. In case you were wondering. I liked being cherished."

Urho's heart ached, but with joy. "Then we'll do it that way every time. We'll do it like that until you get tired of it."

Xan clung to Urho, made like he fit him perfectly. "I don't think I will. I think when you leave again, I'm going to miss this—you—more than I've ever missed anything in my life."

"Then maybe I shouldn't leave."

The words fell between them like something solid into a heap of jelly. The mess was the awkward silence that followed. Urho pulled his cock from Xan's body and slid a hand down to press two fingers into Xan's twitching hole.

Xan relaxed against him, and they breathed in the sex-scented silence of the room.

"I wish you wouldn't. Leave, I mean," Xan said finally. "But I don't expect you to make promises you can't keep."

Urho nuzzled Xan's nape and closed his eyes. They drifted off together without discussing it any further.

They woke several times in the night to repeat the "cherishing" of Xan's body.

And when the sun came up, Urho was still buried deep in Xan's ass, enjoying the convulsions of Xan's latest orgasm around his cock and watching as his alpha-shaped omega's face broke open with trust and pleasure.

CHAPTER SIXTEEN

THE CLUB WAS built atop a cliff near the ocean. Its towers brushed the sky, and it dug deep into the earth below, with levels down the cliff face. Designed of red brick and grey stone, it boasted an Old World revival feel, as well as stunning views of the sea and the mountains north of Virona.

Climbing out of the new car Jason's father had had delivered to Xan and Caleb as a housewarming present, Xan admired Urho's tweed, khaki herringbone suit, and the pinstriped, brown and white button-up shirt beneath the high buttoning vest. The tie held the only pop of color, a touch of orange in the pattern, and the whole ensemble enhanced Urho's dark, russet brown skin, somehow making him look younger and more relaxed.

Or maybe he simply was more relaxed after the pleasurable week they'd had. Urho had bewitched Xan, body and soul. As far as he could tell, Urho felt the same. Always keeping within a certain distance of Xan and treating him with the respect he'd show an omega—and not just any omega, but one he was contracted to. As Caleb had commanded, they had "gotten to know one another."

And not just in the naked way.

They'd talked, and walked, and explored the grounds together. Xan had listened to stories of Urho's days at the university before he'd set up his new clinic and asked questions about Riki. It made Urho smile, and he found that he genuinely wanted to know more about the man Urho had loved and lost.

It hurt his heart to think of Urho's pain when Riki and their child died, and he could tell that pain eased when Xan asked about him, and that speaking of his lost *Érosgápe* made Urho happy. Xan wanted him to be happy. He wanted him to be so happy that he'd never leave.

The days had stretched into a beautiful, glossy, golden haze of hope—something Xan had never experienced before. Caleb seemed very pleased, treating Urho with such kindness that Xan felt almost delirious watching his omega interact with his lover.

The lines around Urho's eyes were lighter, and the tension he usually held in his shoulders—a habit of years, likely—was almost entirely gone. A puff of pride lifted Xan's chest. He'd done that. *He'd* left Urho sated and satisfied.

Janus had been gone a week and Caleb had encouraged Xan and Urho to go out on the town. Jason had also strongly suggested it since Xan and Urho's enthusiastic fucking was making poor Vale hornier than ever.

Urho reached out and adjusted Xan's fedora, made from a new gray wool and chinchilla felt mix with a darker gray silk band. He'd bought it locally to suck up to the tailor, and Caleb had declared it was as well made as any in the city.

"You look handsome," he said, brushing the shoulders of Xan's favorite suit, a gray-and-black checked wool-cotton blend with small, embroidered red hearts throughout. He'd embellished it with a black tie featuring lush roses. A romantic suit for a romantic night.

Xan stood taller, gazing up at his lover, heart in his throat and buzzing with excitement. He couldn't believe Urho was here with him in public, and they were together. No one else would know, of course, but it was enough that Xan did. Knowing the handsome, older man beside him was his and his alone made his possessive alpha instincts sing with joy.

"It's a nice night," Urho said, gazing up at the star-filled sky.

"But the wind off the ocean is chilly." He shivered slightly. They'd left their heavier coats behind in hopes that the warmer weather they'd enjoyed in the garden earlier in the day would hold.

"Let's head inside," Xan agreed, breathing in deeply and admiring the way Urho's skin scent mixed so well with the sea air. An aphrodisiac for the heart. It made Xan feel as though he floated into the five-story Virona Gentlemen's Club.

Admiring the interior décor and design, as well as the fashionable dress of all the other patrons, Xan held back a gasp. It was every bit as decadent as similar clubs in the city. "Janus comes here almost every night," he said, gazing around at the boldly patterned walls and hunting trophies.

Other members of the club milled about—mainly unattached alphas, but there were a few, quiet omegas in the mix as well, usually wearing the circle pin showing their contracted status. No betas aside from employees were allowed in, and Xan had to admit the inequality of the caste system they lived with daily blinked in and out of his privileged consciousness.

A smiling beta servant removed their suit coats—leaving them in just their vests and shirtsleeves, as was the current fashion at clubs—and offered up tickets to retrieve them later.

They made their way into a gaming room, where many men played games of chance and skill, like pool or cards. Others stood in groups, talking, and drinking. Xan relaxed as he noticed several admiring eyes on him and others on Urho. They did make a fine pair if he did say so himself.

"Can I get you drink?" Urho asked, nodding toward the bar along the back wall.

"Let's go together."

The bartender opened a tab for Xan as soon as proof of his new membership was displayed, and he poured generous drinks for them both. Xan hopped up on a barstool and took a long look around while sipping his drink. There were men of all ages here tonight. More wealth than he'd realized existed in Virona. He supposed this was what his father and Ray had been going on about. There were clients here and he should groom them.

"Janus has made a lot of connections at this club," Xan murmured, wondering which of these men his cousin had already bagged for the company and taken the credit for himself.

"Has he?" Urho asked, gazing about the room. The stately, polite play and the almost old-fashioned air of the place suited him. "It doesn't seem his speed."

Xan gave a nod to an alpha he recognized as Jol Martinez, the owner of the contracting firm they were using for the new office building. He got a smile and a lifted drink in return.

See? Connections were easy. He could make them, too. If he ever tried.

But tonight was about him and Urho spending time together away from the bed, so he smiled and then politely turned to Urho to let Jol know he was engaged elsewhere at the moment.

"Well, perhaps this area isn't his style, but Janus loves to socialize. I know he's become a big hit on the lower floors where the gym is housed and the wrestling matches take place."

"Wrestling?"

Xan rolled his eyes. "Yes. Apparently, he's quite the fighter."

Urho frowned but remained silent.

The drink was good, and Xan downed it more quickly than he should have, the pleasure of it sweeping through him and flushing him with heat. He wanted to touch Urho's chin, slip a hand around his neck, and tug him down for a kiss. He sighed and settled for a smile.

"I enjoyed a bit of boxing when I was young," Urho said, licking his lips and pulling his gaze up from Xan's mouth. Had he been having the same sorts of thoughts? "Riki found it thrilling, and I enjoyed thrilling him."

"You don't box now?" Urho looked like he could still take down a mountain if he chose. Muscled and strong, tall and well-made. He also moved with such steadiness and purpose that Xan could imagine him in a fight, landing solid punches like a machine.

"It's for young toughs. Like Janus, apparently."

"If the time he spends here is any indication, he's not just good at wrestling, but loves it, too. Though I suspect he also loves getting away from the house, almost as much as we enjoy having him gone." Xan smirked. "Especially since he and Caleb came to blows."

Urho's eyes went hard. "You're going to have to explain that a bit more. Particularly the part about how Janus is still breathing. He hurt Caleb?"

"No! Caleb hurt him!" Xan smiled with pride as he remembered the way Caleb had taken Janus down. "He kicked him in the shin and then elbowed him on the back of the head."

"Wolf-god."

Xan shrugged. "The idiot brought it on himself, of course."

"Caleb is fierce and beautiful. You're a lucky man to have him." Urho smiled fondly, admiration shining in his eyes.

"I am," Xan agreed. "He makes me as happy as any omega could."

"And *that* makes me happy," Urho said, nodding toward a tall, well-dressed, middle-aged beta approaching them. "That looks like the concierge you arranged to meet. Let's see what activities keep Janus so occupied."

The concierge of the club gave them a full tour even though it was night. He touted the club's golf course—glimpsed by the light of the moon from a balcony on the back of the building. He also pointed out their thirty-five-slip marina, and their outdoor and indoor swimming pools.

"Those are our most popular summer attractions," he said, with a slight lisp and a twinkle in his gray eyes.

They were on the stairwell headed down from the upper floors to the lower levels of the building within the cliff wall. The scent of sweat and musk drifted up from below.

"But in the winter, sirs, we offer indoor activities. Bowling, of course. And, as you saw, billiards, poker games—for the gambling types—and racquetball for the sporty men." His brow rose and his face took on a sly expression. Then he lowered his voice as though revealing something secret. "For those with a taste for something brutish, however, we also offer a more aggressive, *alpha*, form of indoor entertainment."

With that he opened the door at the bottom of the stairwell to a large interior gymnasium. It was almost rank with the scent of alpha pheromones and sweat. The smell stung Xan's nose, and he blinked as his eyes teared up from the intensity of it. Urho seemed to have a similar reaction, clearing his throat hard and wiping at his eyes.

The reek lit up Xan's nerves, his alpha instincts going on alert: danger, pain, suffering—and yes, sex—was to be had here. He could smell it. He gazed around at the vast room, divided into different sections and overrun with men.

This must be where all the alphas of Virona congregated at night. Between the upstairs and the down, how could there be any left at home with their omegas and their families?

Speaking of, there were no omegas in this room. Alphas only. That was evident at once and brought home by the sign across the back wall: *OMEGAS FORBIDDEN*. And in smaller letters: *due to the danger of alpha expression in their presence.*

"They'll fight—and not by the rules of competition, sir," the concierge said under his breath, noticing the direction of Xan's gaze. "No one wants to lose in front of their omega."

Urho nodded and loosened his tie.

The air was humid and thick. Half the room was dedicated to

boxing and wrestling rings, and the other half to punching bags and weights. There were seats set up in front of one ring, as though for an audience, but they remained empty at the moment.

Alphas prowled the room in tight shorts and shirts that exposed their ripped, muscled arms and sweaty shoulders. They punched and kicked sand-filled bags, and, in the rings, each other. Some wrestled on a mat in the corner, and another group of men were helping each other lift bars of heavy weights.

Xan's mouth went dry and his balls grew heavy. The scent of so many alphas in the room was thrilling and dangerous. He cleared his throat and looked up at Urho, who was watching him with an expression of amusement.

The concierge went on conspiratorially, "Of course, there is gambling to be had *here* as well, if that's your poison." He motioned at a large chalkboard with names and bets next to each one. Xan spotted Janus's name listed, though marked as absent for the evening's event. Other names were listed under the Virona Gentlemen's Club Wrestling team, and most were marked as present, and several had quite high odds next to their names. Another board for a visiting team was up as well, and a young man with strong arms was chalking in the names of the members in attendance.

"I take it there's going to be a series of bouts tonight?" Urho asked, nodding at the chalkboards.

"Yes, indeed. For future reference, there are gym clothes for rent here in the locker rooms, if you gentlemen would like to partake in any of the activities." He nodded toward doors on the left-hand side of the room marked with drawings of the male form.

Xan would rather die than come here amongst all these muscular alphas and take off his clothes. He was small and wiry enough, and definitely not ashamed of his body. He had no reason to be, given the way Urho seemed to want him, but he also didn't want to chance getting hard in public, or being teased for his size.

"However, the gym is going to be closing shortly for the main events," the concierge said apologetically. "So there's no time for that tonight. However, you really should stay and watch. It's quite a show."

Xan followed Urho's lead and undid his tie in the heat of the room and then met Urho's eyes. He seemed open to the idea. Xan swallowed hard, images of sweaty alphas grappling already filling his mind. "When does it begin?"

"Oh, you'll have plenty of time for dinner beforehand, just as you planned. The first pair will start in an hour."

"Is it quite violent?" Urho asked, his hand falling on Xan's shoulder and squeezing.

Xan leaned back into his palm and then had to steady himself when Urho suddenly removed it. It was wise, of course. They couldn't be seen as anything other than friends in public, and especially here. What would men like *these* do if they knew?

"Oh, quite violent, sir! But the tournaments are fun to observe from the safety of the seats around the ring," the concierge said, smiling. "I'm pleased to say our wrestling team is quite good. Though we are missing a very talented member tonight—Janus Heelies. Not only a fine businessman, from what I've overheard, but an excellent wrestler." The concierge leaned close and whispered, "He fights dirty, but you didn't hear it from me."

Urho chuckled and said, "You hear a lot, don't you," just as Xan muttered snidely, "Oh, I'd believe that."

The concierge ignored Urho's comment and turned to Xan. "You know the young man, then?"

"Too well."

"I see." The concierge smiled again, ingratiating and a little too smarmy for his own good. "Well, as I said, our team is quite talented. Tonight, we face off against the team from Blue Vein.

They come all the way from the *city*."

"Oh my," Urho said, and he managed to sound impressed instead of amused. But the twinkle in his eye gave it away.

"Indeed. They're our biggest rivals and I expect the room will be packed tonight. Why don't we go ahead and reserve two of the seats near the front for you?"

Urho and Xan agreed, and the concierge led them up the stairs again. "You have reservations for dinner in the Sea View dining room?"

"Yes," Xan confirmed.

"Excellent. It's the only mixed room in the club. We allow anyone from the community to dine with us, of course. So long as they can afford to pay."

Xan gestured for Urho to follow the concierge first into the dining room offering a wide view of the ocean. The tables were only half full. There were several tables of alphas, a few beta couples, and a good number of alpha and omega couples, including some *Érosgápe*—obvious from the way they were so absorbed in one another. However, compared to the activity in the games room and the gymnasium, it felt nearly empty. Obviously, the dining room was not the main draw of the club, despite its fantastic reputation for excellent cuisine.

"What a view," Urho murmured.

"We should invite Rosen and Yosef up," Xan said, once they were seated by the window, facing out to the sea. "After the baby is born, of course. And then we could all come out to dinner here and stay to watch a brawl."

"If Vale leaves that baby with a caretaker for more than five minutes during the first year, I'll be shocked," Urho said, laughing as he took a menu from the waiter who had come to serve them. "But otherwise, I think that's a fine plan."

They settled into their seats and chose a bottle of wine. After ordering their meals, Xan smiled and said, "Caleb thought we should take this opportunity to talk."

"About anything in particular?"

"I think about ourselves. He's worried we aren't getting to know each other."

Urho's smile was filthy as he whispered, "I'm getting to know you very well, in all kinds of interesting and intimate ways."

The waiter showed up again with the wine at that moment, and Xan was able to take a second to collect himself, hiding his arousal with his napkin. After the waiter left, Xan said, "Caleb says truly knowing someone comes from more than that."

"I've watched you for two years now, at parties, during our beach trips, over dinner at Vale and Jason's house, and now I see you here in your home. I've watched the way you treat your friends, your servants, and your omega. I've observed you put on a show to hide the tenderest parts of yourself from the casual eye. And now I've seen you in bed—your vulnerability, and your passion. How should I know you better?"

Xan grabbed his glass wine and took a large sip. He almost couldn't swallow around the gratitude welling up inside his chest. "I don't know," he finally murmured. "I feel the same. But Caleb says we should be friends first and foremost."

"That sounds like good advice. Aren't we friends?"

"Yes."

"And more than friends?"

"Yes," Xan said, his cock twitching dangerously beneath the napkin.

Urho leaned closer, his white teeth so compelling against his dark skin. "Is there something you feel like you need to know about me before you can trust in what we're building?"

The fact that they were building something was dizzying. And too good to be true. Aside from that though…

Xan thought carefully, sipping his wine and staring out at the dark, rough sea. "I've never seen you angry. Upset, yes. Maybe that day when you came to my house after...well, when I was hurt. You were stressed, confused—"

"Afraid. I was beyond afraid."

Xan swallowed hard. "For me?"

"Yes, I was afraid for you, obviously, but I was also terrified of what my reaction meant. What it said...about me." Urho's voice was calm now, a soothing, low tone that gave no indication of the man who'd been so bewildered.

"You don't seem afraid anymore."

"I should be," Urho said, glancing over his shoulder, clearly checking that, yes, the closest table to them was still several feet away. "But when I'm with you, I forget about all of that."

"That's dangerous."

"Only in public," Urho said, relaxing back into his seat with a shrug. "And we'll be smart. Keep our hands to ourselves."

"Of course."

It irked Xan, though, to look around the dining room. He saw omega and alpha couples canoodling in a corner, or beta couples holding hands at the table, and even one set of omegas hugging each other on the sofa near the far wall. How unfair that he would always be afraid to act naturally with Urho in public for fear of devastating repercussions.

"Virona is probably safer than the city," Urho said. "The culture of northern seaside towns is more relaxed, and people are accustomed to tourists coming through, bringing with them other ways and beliefs. But obviously we'll be as discreet as possible. We don't want to risk ourselves—or Caleb's safety."

Xan nodded and smiled tightly as the waiter returned with their meals. He found the flavor was a bit dull with the taste of regret fresh in his mouth. "If I'd been born an omega..." he started, but

Urho put a hand over his and squeezed briefly before letting go.

"There are things we can't change. Riki is gone. You're not an omega. The sky is blue. Water wet." He dropped his voice to a whisper. "It doesn't change my feelings for you; my lust or affection, either one. I want you just the way you are."

Xan couldn't help but want to turn the words "lust and affection" into *love*, but he knew that was a word that only came with time. Many *Érosgápe* didn't even use it for the first many months or even years of their relationship, despite quite obviously being in love. He still remembered the first time Vale said it to Jason, well after they'd contracted. Jason had been flying high for weeks after.

Yes, it was a good bit too early to think about declarations of love.

"I feel the same way," Xan said, smiling softly and taking a sip of his wine.

Urho turned back to his steak and lobster plate. "Is there anything you want to know about me? I'm happy to fill in blanks for you."

Xan tilted his head. "I know who you are—what kind of person, I mean. But I don't know a lot about your life before I met you. Why did you go into the military? Why didn't you just become a doctor immediately?"

"I wasn't born into wealth like you and Jason. I came into it via Riki when we contracted. Before that, I had to scrape and save. The military was the best option for me after I left school and before I met Riki. It trained me in the virtues of self-discipline, which I still sorely lack when it comes to you, and it paid for my physician's training. The war itself was horrific, and I'll spare you details, mainly for my own sake. There aren't a lot of memories there that I like to dredge up."

Xan nodded, eating his steak and fussing with the salad he'd ordered.

"I met Riki while I was still enlisted. It was a surprise, as all *Érosgápe* bonds tend to be, and I can't say his parents were impressed with me. In the end, his father didn't live to see Riki die, and his pater succumbed to cancer not long after."

"I'm sorry."

Urho frowned. "It was a dark time. I don't know how I survived it. Eventually, I learned to go on. But I didn't let go." He took a long swallow from his glass before meeting Xan's eyes. "But maybe it's time I consider how to do that."

"Letting go of Riki would be impossible, wouldn't it? He completed you as only one other person in the whole world could. I'm not going to replace him."

"You do understand," Urho said, squeezing Xan's hand again. "I don't want you to replace him. But holding on doesn't take me anywhere new, does it? You, though… With you, I could go somewhere different. A fresh journey to close out my life."

"You're not that old!"

"I'm a good deal older than you. It's better to accept that now so you can plan for it when you need to."

"Do you see us together that long?" Xan asked, his heart leaping with hope.

"I don't see why we wouldn't be, if we learn how to manage the taboo nature of our relationship and want to accept the risks of it indefinitely."

Xan swallowed hard, his hope a fluttering, twittering thing. "I do. I want that."

Urho smiled. "Right now, you do, but you're young. As I age, things may change. I might not be able to satisfy—"

"Stop. I've never had something like this in my life. Don't take it away from me before I even get a chance to enjoy it."

"Then let's enjoy this dinner instead."

Xan agreed with a smile. He was quite content with their friendship. Later he'd tell Caleb that he and Urho had more in common than perfect fucks—though, the sex was so good, Xan would have been entirely content to let that be the end all and be all of their relationship. It was beyond lucky that it didn't have to be.

Xan had never imagined he could be so truly happy.

Afterwards, they entered the gymnasium again, Urho saying, "When I was in the military, of course we held wrestling matches for entertainment, but it's been a long time since I saw one."

The chairs they'd reserved waited for them, despite the now-overflowing room. It seemed all the men from the upper floors had descended for the wrestling. The crowd paced the back of the space and the sides. Urho and Xan took their seats, eager for the matches to start.

"Interested in placing a bet?" Urho asked, nodding to the chalkboard which was now covered in numbers and names.

Xan shook his head. "Father would think even less of me if I took up gambling. I'll leave that to Janus. He's the golden one in the family and can seem to do no wrong in Father's eyes, even while doing plenty of wrong in the eyes of society. But never mind. I'll leave that aside for now. Let's just pretend that the only reason I'm not betting is that I have no idea who to put money on."

Urho grinned and shrugged. "Not much of a betting man, either. Riki used to bet on horses though."

"Did he win?"

Urho laughed heartily. "No, he lost like a fiend, but he loved it so much I didn't want to tell him to stop. He was always hopeful, and then so disappointed every time. Comforting him was worth whatever he lost. It was his money anyway."

"He sounds like a fun man."

"He was quiet, actually," Urho said, knocking Xan's shoulder. "Nothing like you. But his smile made my heart sing." Then he looked at Xan again. "So maybe a little like you after all."

Xan's own heart soared on the praise. To be compared in any way favorably to Urho's *Érosgápe* was the highest compliment he could imagine. He grinned up at Urho, pleasure suffusing him from head to toe.

"Yes," Urho murmured. "Exactly like that." He touched his chest and winked. "It's singing."

A whistle called the crowd's attention to the ring, and Xan laughed happily, his joy rushing louder than the announcement of the first two contenders. The Virona man wasn't familiar to Xan from his dealings setting up the new office, nor was the Blue Vein competitor from the city, but he took notice that the crowd cheered rousingly for both.

"This should be good," Urho said, leaning forward in his seat and gazing toward the ring with interest.

The match was quick. The Blue Vein competitor kicked the pants off the Virona man. Still, the moments between the bell and the call of victory had been thrilling. Man on man, grappling with effort, rolling around on the raised mat with hard panting breaths and flexing muscles.

Xan's cock had woken again. He couldn't help but imagine Urho pinning him like that as he struggled. How the ending might go differently between the two of them, especially if they were naked.

"Enjoy that?" Urho whispered in his ear, and Xan shivered happily.

"Yes."

"I thought so."

"The rug in my room is pretty big," Xan said softly, turning to Urho and pressing against his side recklessly. "We could try it for ourselves. You could teach me a thing or two."

"I could," Urho agreed. "And we could do some boxing in the garden, too. Less grappling. More tactical."

Xan nodded and sat back in his seat, breaking the sweet contact of their arms and torsos. That's when Xan saw him.

His heart stuttered and stopped for a long, wretched second and then thundered hard.

Standing by the ring, wearing the uniform of the Blue Vein Wrestling Club, and grinning right at Xan like a predator who'd spotted his prey, was Wilbet Monhundy. His muscled arms and powerful thighs were on display in the tight, Blue Vein wrestling uniform, and his cruel smile sent a horrible convulsion through Xan.

Monhundy looked at Urho significantly, raised a brow, and sneered at Xan, shaking his head in disgust. Xan went cold all over.

Urho leaned close again to explain some of the finer points of the next competitor's backgrounds as outlined in the pamphlet handed out at the door. Xan wanted to shove him away, keep him safe from Monhundy's knowing gaze, but he didn't want to react at all either. He held as still as possible, but an urge to stand and run, a strangled need to flee, made him squirm in his seat.

"Love, what's wrong?" Urho asked.

"Nothing," Xan gritted out. "This chair is uncomfortable."

Urho's eyes took on a concerned glimmer, and he whispered, "Are you sore? Have we been too rough? You should have said."

Xan swallowed hard, his focus on Monhundy, who was watching his interactions with Urho like a snake watched a mouse. "I'm fine. Don't worry. Everything's all right." He sounded as pale as he probably looked, and he squirmed convulsively again, pinned by the nastiness in Monhundy's gaze.

Urho's eyes followed Xan's stare to where Monhundy stood waiting his turn to wrestle. "Who's that man? Do you know him?"

Xan swallowed hard again and shook his head. "No." Then, reconsidering, he nodded once. "Yes. He's, uh, well, his family is in business with my father. The Monhundys."

Urho grimaced. "Ah yes. I remember that one—Wilbet, wasn't it?—from when I worked at the university. A nasty piece of work. A bully of the worst sort." Urho froze, the words sharp in the air between them. His eyes narrowed on Monhundy.

"Don't," Xan murmured.

Urho's fists clenched. "It's him. He hurt you. He's the one who—" He leapt up from his seat, pamphlet crushed in one hand and murder in his eyes.

Monhundy smirked and raised a challenging brow. Almost begging Urho to do something reckless.

Xan jumped up and tugged Urho down to sitting again. It was difficult, but he was determined, and he caught Urho off balance. "We can't make a scene," he hissed.

The announcer walked into the middle of the wrestling mat with a hand-held microphone. "Our next Blue Vein competitor is a hard man to beat!"

"I'll kill him," Urho whispered, gritting his teeth together and holding Monhundy's gaze. "I'll gut him. He raped you."

Xan squeezed his arm. "I went to him!"

Urho's cry of rage was covered by the excited yells of the crowd as the bell rang and the wrestling match began. The men grappled and rolled, broke apart and flew back together. It was brutal and violent, and the rules didn't seem to properly apply this time. The Virona opponent's nose began to bleed profusely, but no one called an end to the match.

Xan sat frozen, holding onto Urho's arm, watching the match with one eye on Monhundy in a haze of fear and barely banked rage. How dare Wilbet Monhundy show up here in Virona? How dare he show his face anywhere near Xan's recently almost-perfect life?

This time the Virona wrestler was declared champion, but Xan couldn't even enjoy Monhundy's team's defeat. Urho was on his feet again with determination on his face, and Xan leapt after him, managing to grab his arm and pull him out of the overcrowded and overheated room. Xan could feel Monhundy's gaze on their backs. Sweat slipped down the side of Xan's face as they fought their way toward the exit.

Urho was more than strong enough to break Xan's grasp, but thankfully he didn't. Once out of the gymnasium, though, it was Urho who yanked Xan up the stairs, down the hall, and toward the front door of the gentlemen's club without any care as to whether or not he was drawing any notice or stares.

Luckily, most everyone seemed to be in the gymnasium now watching the wrestling, except for beta employees. So there was no one to ask questions, or stop Urho, or ask if Xan was all right.

"What are you doing?" Xan finally gasped as Urho tugged him out into the cool evening air. The ocean pounded below, the roar of the waves rising up in a mist.

The valets stopped chatting and looked their way.

Urho motioned for them to bring the new car around, handing over the ticket, but saying nothing. His mouth was set in a straight line, his eyes hard, and a tension radiated from him that Xan hadn't seen since that day when Urho had stopped by his house to check on him and proceeded to put his finger up his ass during the following examination.

The wind stung through his shirtsleeves. "Our suit coats..." Xan said, looking back toward the foyer of the club. "This is my favorite one." The hearts he'd thought so darling earlier in the evening now seemed to be taunting him, pointing out how silly he'd been to think he'd get any kind of romantic night. That he deserved one.

Urho grimly stalked back into the club and returned with their suit coats. Xan shrugged his on, but Urho held his folded over one arm, panting as he stared out at the dark, churning water below the club. Xan wrapped his arms around himself, the chill from the night air soaking into him, a wet, damp misery.

Once the vehicle was brought around, Urho took the wheel, and Xan climbed into the passenger seat, even though it was his car. He tipped the valet and buckled his seat belt.

"Where are we going?"

Silence.

Xan tried to figure out where Urho was taking him by the turns they made, up and down twisted cliffside roads. But he didn't think Urho had a true destination in mind.

Eventually, they reached the bottom of the cliffs and drove alongside the beach for some time. Urho pulled off the road and parked the car by the dunes. He got out and marched toward the ocean, undoing his tie and throwing it into the wind. Xan followed after, his stomach churning and blood pumping hard.

Ahead of him, Urho tossed his shoes off into the dunes, and then his socks, before starting down toward the water.

"Urho?" Xan shouted after Urho's back as he struggled to un-knot his right shoe, before finally getting it. He kicked his shoes and socks into the weeds and ran hard after his lover, the cold sand shifting dangerously under his feet when he hit it at full speed.

Catching up to Urho, he grabbed his arm and forced him around, his thundering heart sinking at the dark, stony expression on Urho's face barely visible in the moonlight. "Talk to me!"

Urho squeezed his eyes shut and wrenched away, staring at the dark, roiling ocean. Clouds had rolled in, obscuring the stars, and the water was only visible as the tossing moon reflected on the waves. The sound of the ocean's fury was inescapable, though. Waves crashed on the beach, rushing up over their feet and soaking their hems, shockingly frigid.

"I didn't know he'd be there." Xan clutched Urho's arm again. "I haven't seen him since that night. I swear to wolf-god, Urho. I swear on everything I have and love. Please believe me!"

"I do believe you," Urho gritted out.

"Then why are you so angry with me?"

"I'm not angry with you," Urho barked, but he sounded angry as wolf-hell, so Xan didn't know what to believe.

"Look, I can't read minds!" he exclaimed desperately. "Talk to me. Please."

Urho stared at the black ocean. "You went to him. To get fucked."

Xan swallowed hard, and shame flooding him. "I did."

"And he hurt you."

"Yes."

"And you liked it." Urho sounded broken.

Xan ripped a hand through his hair, tugging hard. He sobbed, "I don't think I really did? I don't know!"

"You went back."

"I was messed up, Urho! I was angry. I hated myself. Please."

Urho turned to him then and grabbed him, tugging him into a tight embrace. He tucked his face in Xan's neck and scented him deeply, shaking all over. It was tough to breathe, squeezed by Urho's strength, but Xan didn't struggle or try to get free. Instead, he grabbed Urho back and held on for all he was worth, gasping shallowly as the world swirled around him.

Then Urho released him and sank down to the sand, his filthy bare feet pointing out to the ocean. The waves came up to wash over them and up to his calves. His suit was getting soaked, and he shivered.

"Urho." Xan squatted next to him. "I never cared for him. I told you that already. And if I have to, I'll tell you a million times."

"How long did you see him? How long did it last?"

"A year or so. I'll never see him again."

"I know you won't," Urho said, his voice raw and tight. "But I should have never let it happen."

"How could you have stopped it?" Xan asked, reaching out to

stroke Urho's cheek.

"That first time I truly met you—on the beach the summer after Vale and Jason contracted—I felt something for you, but I denied it."

Xan pushed windblown hair out his eyes and drew closer, trying to make sense of Urho's anger and cold rage. "I felt something for you too," he admitted.

"Fuck. It's true. It's my fault you were ever hurt." Urho's shoulders slumped, and he squeezed his eyes closed. "You could have been safe with me this whole time."

"That's ridiculous," Xan sputtered. "You barely knew me then."

"But I grew to know you. As much as I allowed myself to. I held you at a distance because something about you always got under my skin." He laughed bitterly. "You made me want things an alpha should never want."

Xan blinked at him, trying to make out his face in silver light of the moon. The club on the cliff above glowed. It hurt to see somehow. It was a reminder that up there, people were happy, laughing, gambling, and fighting—anything but having a conversation that cleaved open wounds with every word spoken.

"I let you down before we even began."

"Well, that's a fucking handy excuse!" Xan exclaimed, standing up to kick sand at Urho's feet. "Let me guess! You're going to end this now? Spare me any more suffering? What shit from wolf-god's own ass!"

Urho grabbed his hand and pulled him down to the sand, dragging Xan into his arms. "No. I'm never leaving you to the likes of that monster again," he bit out. "And I will see him *buried* before he ever lays a finger on you."

"Urho," Xan soothed, "he doesn't want me like that. If I don't go to him—and I won't—he'll never touch me."

"He'll still pay for what he did."

"Leave the past in the past." Xan's heart thumped. The surf

pounded at his back, racing up and wetting him all over. His favorite suit was now a wreck. "Anything you do to him will raise questions, and those questions will come back to us. Just let it go. I'm safe here with you now."

Urho gathered him closer, removed his tie, and scented along Xan's neck and collarbones. Opening Xan's shirt, Urho kissed his chest and sucked his nipples before coming up to claim his mouth.

Xan was shaking with cold and fear, so lust was a welcome hot distraction and comfort. The waves roared around them, crashing over their legs and wetting them, but Urho didn't let go, pushing Xan down, and shoving him into the sand. He kissed and rubbed against him until the sandy, gritty torture became too painful.

They pulled apart to walk, panting and shivering, hand-in-hand back to the car.

"Ren's going to be annoyed with me about this," Xan said, taking the driver's side this time and nodding as ocean water and sand muddied the interior of the car. "He'll flash me his angry eyes while outwardly smiling, and I'll have to wonder if my tea is poisoned for the rest of the week. I'll give him a bonus in his salary next pay period." His normal words sounded strange to his own ears after what had happened.

Urho remained quieter than usual, but the drive back to Lofton had lost the tension of the race to the sea after leaving the club. As Xan drove, Urho stared out the window at the ocean until they came around the curve that blocked it from view. Then he studied the town's houses and fields until they reached home.

"You can't blame yourself for my choices," Xan finally said, briefly reaching out for Urho's hand between changing gears.

"How did it start between you? The first time?" Urho asked.

Xan nearly swallowed his tongue. He couldn't bring himself to confess the reality of what had happened that first time with Monhundy. In part because the truth contradicted his statements that Monhundy only fucked him because Xan begged him to, and because it would show beyond a shadow of a doubt just how fucked up Xan was inside. How disturbed.

"I want the truth," Urho said, as though reading Xan's mind.

He chewed his lip and stared ahead, navigating the car through the gate leading up to the Lofton Estate. He was glad they were almost home. Maybe he could still get out of this.

"Was it alpha expression the first time? Did he rape you?"

Xan slowed the car to a halt and put on the brake halfway up the drive. He sat silently for a long moment until he thought he could speak without crying or hyperventilating. "I taunted him in a bar we were both visiting. He came at me, but his friends held him back. Said I was an unmanned shrimp and didn't deserve the trouble he'd get for starting something with me in a beta establishment."

Urho nodded.

"He waited outside the bar, though. It wasn't the first time we'd gotten into it. He'd bullied me at Mont Nessadare and we'd come to blows more than once. He always won." Xan gave a bitter smile. "It's true that I'm an unmanned shrimp."

Urho said nothing, but his fists clenched.

"You have to understand, what happened next... I didn't want it to go down the way it did. But when it was over, it was my choice to go back for more. To make him do it to me again, and again, and again."

"Stop now."

"He didn't rape me," Xan said softly, lancing the festering boil. "I wanted him to fuck me. No matter what form that came in—I wanted him however he'd give it to me. Brutal, cruel—it didn't matter. It was no worse than what I thought I deserved."

Urho choked beside him.

"So that's the truth of me. The worst thing I've ever been or done. I've never told anyone before. I'll understand if you hate me."

"I love you, dammit," Urho croaked.

Xan's heart clenched with a burst of joy amid the pain. *He loves me.*

"And that's what's killing me now. Because I love you and I hate myself. Why can't I turn back time and make it all go away? Make him go away. I want to hurt him like I've never wanted to hurt another man. I want to send him to a place he'll never come back from." The darkness in Urho's voice was something Xan had never heard, and it scared him. "I want him dead."

"Urho…"

"I want to see him spit-roasted and burned alive."

"Please…" Xan didn't know what to say. The darkness was terrifying. Especially because he couldn't say that some part of him didn't want the same thing. "Leave it behind. That kind of hate will just ruin whatever future we could have now. And we have to think of Caleb."

Urho jerked at that, his bright, dark eyes catching Xan's. "Yes, it's our responsibility to protect him."

"Mine, actually," Xan said. "He's my omega. I'll take care of him."

"And you're *my* omega," Urho whispered. "I'll take care of you."

Xan's eyes filled with tears, but he held them back. "We'll take care of each other."

"I'm sorry I let you down."

"You didn't." Xan unbuckled his seat belt to reach out and touch Urho's cheek again. "Neither of us could have known…" He trailed off, looking up at the lights on in the house. There was a beautiful warmth that came from knowing people waited for them, men who loved them both in various ways. "What we have now is too good to waste on what could have been. Forgive yourself. Please." A tear fell, and Urho touched it with the pad of his thumb, wiping it away. "Because if you can forgive yourself, then I can forgive myself, too."

"My sweet alpha-shaped omega…"

"We all have room for improvement in our lives. I'm working on being a better alpha to my omega and being a good lover to you. I want to be a better son to my father, and a better leader for Heelies Enterprises. So I figure you can work on this one thing to complete your perfection. Feel free to take your time."

"I'm not perfect." Urho placed his hand on the back of Xan's neck, rubbing his fingers back and forth possessively.

"I know. You're human." Xan smiled. "I love you. Flaws and all."

They kissed over the gear shift as the moon poured around the car. Their love overflowed in the sight of wolf's own eye, and it was pure.

THAT NIGHT, URHO held Xan for a long time before they made love. He kissed every place he remembered being bruised after the last time Xan had gone to Monhundy, and he kissed every place that might have *ever* been bruised by that demon's hands. His mind flashed to the smarmy, smug, handsome face of the man who'd hurt his beloved.

Urho wasn't going to let it go, no matter what Xan wanted. But he was going to let it rest. *For now.* Bide his time. Make good, strong choices for them all. Because that's what an alpha did when he was protecting his family.

Xan was his family now. He'd protect him with all his heart and soul, from damage past and future. And that meant protecting Caleb, too.

He'd protect them both always.

CHAPTER SEVENTEEN

I N THE DETACHED wing along the west side of the house, beneath the servant's quarters on the upper floor, Caleb had installed his printing machine. It'd been transported several weeks ago now from the city via a rented Sabel truck, along with boxes upon boxes of Caleb's artwork and supplies.

From what Urho could gather, the room had probably been intended as a servants' hall, but since Caleb and Xan had designated their out-of-the-way, and never-used ballroom and gaming rooms in the main house for their live-in beta servants' pleasure, the big room in the detached wing was left open for appropriation.

There'd been a vast number of square stones unloaded and carted into the new studio which Urho had found himself curious about. To Xan's surprise and obvious envy, Urho's questions to Caleb had earned him an exclusive invitation into the print studio to see how everything worked.

"When am I going to get an invitation to your studio?" Xan asked over breakfast. He was still flushed from that morning's exertions in the garden. Urho was teaching him to box. He never wanted his alpha-shaped omega in a position where he couldn't defend himself against a brute like Monhundy. And so boxing lessons had started the morning after their trip to the gentlemen's club. They were going well so far. Xan was strong and sturdy, despite being small.

This morning the three of them were eating alone because Vale and Jason had taken to rising later and later as the pregnancy progressed. All flushed and healthy, Xan looked exceptionally handsome in the suit he'd chosen to wear into the newly finished office. Though Urho found he could no longer trust his judgement in that regard because his opinion of Xan's looks grew more biased daily.

Several weeks had passed since the night at the gentlemen's club, and Xan looked healthier and more radiant by the hour. He positively glowed with beauty, and his scent made Urho's mouth water and his prick stiffen at even the most inappropriate times.

Maybe it was because Janus hadn't returned from the city yet. Maybe it was because his brother Ray was giving Xan a great deal of praise for the way things were playing out in Virona. Or maybe it was because he was in love. Urho didn't know. He didn't care.

He just wanted his boy to glow like that forever.

At Xan's question, Caleb barely looked up from the marmalade he was spreading. "When you show a genuine interest in the procedure, you may come. But if you just want to see what I make in there, then you can wait like everyone else."

"Wait for what?" Xan asked, cocking his head.

"For my show," Caleb said, like this wasn't news. His chest told another story, though, exposed as it was in his V-neck shirt. A pink stain started up into his neck.

"What show?" Xan's eyes brightened. "Do you *have* a show? And you haven't told me?"

Caleb shrugged. "Not yet. I think I'll put one on after my next heat. If I get pregnant, then I'll have a different theme to focus my art on in the future, I imagine."

"What's your theme now?" Urho asked.

Caleb winked, slathering more marmalade on his toast. "That's for me to know and you to find out."

Urho snorted. But he remembered that Vale was always private with his poems before they were published, so he understood

Caleb's sensitivities in these matters. He was grateful that he was even being allowed into the new studio space.

"But where would you put it on?" Xan asked.

"At the gentlemen's club, of course. They put on art shows in their upper rooms sometimes, I've heard. There's a large hallway on the top floor they call the galleria, even."

"Heard from whom?"

It was a fair question. For such a sweet, friendly, sociable guy, Caleb was definitely introverted as far as Urho could tell. He spent a lot of time in his room alone, or reading quietly in his drawing room, or in his studio with the prints. He seemed to enjoy their company when he was with them, but he withdrew for solitude quite happily.

"From Janus," Caleb replied with a grimace. "Just because the source was tainted doesn't mean the information is false. Anyway…" He flapped his hand, dismissing the ghost of Janus from the room. "People would come to my show of course, because they're curious about me. And about you, too. Not to mention, they'll be eager to please the heir to the family fortune. The man who can provide jobs and more to this town."

Urho smiled behind his napkin at Caleb's arrogance. It was charming in its own way. He almost wanted to bottle it and sprinkle it liberally over Xan when he was feeling insecure.

Caleb added, "I have no doubt the show will sell out. If only because of who I am. But I think we should invite people from the city, too, so the onus doesn't fall on Vironians alone to make my show a success."

Xan opened and closed his mouth a few times like he had more questions, but in the end, he simply stood from the table and announced that he was going to be late if he didn't get out the door. Then he kissed Caleb's forehead and nuzzled his neck before turning to Urho and kissing his lips.

After lunch, as directed, Urho walked down the path between the main house and the detached wing, passing a few beta servants who were on their way from their quarters on the second floor. The house itself was looking much better since the time he'd first arrived. The rooms were being cleaned and slowly redecorated, and the grounds were coming to life as the harder months of winter began to release their hold.

Not that the breeze up from the ocean wasn't a stiff one. He shivered against it as he walked alongside the wing, thinking that perhaps he should have worn a coat, and not counted on just his suit to keep him warm. He noted that the windows on the big room where Caleb worked were open.

The scent of chemicals and paint, familiar to him only as a residue on Caleb's skin and hair, accosted his nose. He twitched it lightly and wondered if the odor permeated the entire wing, and what the servants must think of that.

He paused at the end of the walk and saw that there were even more windows and a massive glass door on the ground floor facing out to the ocean. He could look right into the studio and yet he couldn't see much of anything. The interior was a maze of papers, stacks of stones, easels, and implements he didn't recognize. Filing cabinets overflowed already, and he wondered how often Caleb cleaned out his space. His rooms in the main house were spotless, but this...

He let himself in at the door, surprised to find the studio was freezing. Though he didn't know why he was shocked—after all, Xan said that Caleb preferred to be cold and liked to sleep with the windows open. But he wasn't prepared for the movement of air in the room, the vibrant odors mixing with the scent of the sea, churning in and out through all the open windows.

Three out of four sides of the room were made up almost entirely of windows. The back wall sported a massive fireplace, but obviously that was no longer in use, since the studio was otherwise a fire hazard. The cross breeze was stiff, but bracing, and it shuffled the papers around in the space so that there was a constant ruffling, rather like gentle mice or birds making a nest.

The abundance of light was perfect, and he saw the way it served Caleb as he walked deeper into the room crowded with tables, a large printing machine—a press, Caleb called it—slabs of rock, and various other accoutrements he didn't understand.

"You're here," Caleb called out from behind a table where he stood slathering some sort of stinky chemical over one of the slabs of rock. His hair was held back with bright, jeweled clips, and his pale skin was splotched here and there with blue and green ink. He smiled radiantly at Urho for a brief moment and then went back to his work. "This part's a bit touchy. No time to waste. The chemicals start their work once applied and I don't want the outcome to be uneven."

"No, of course not," Urho agreed, though he had no clue what Caleb was referencing. He studied the man at work. His pale skin glowed in the profusion of light from the windows, and his hair shone. His expression was peaceful but serious; concentration at its finest. His clothes were his usual—soft, white, and loose—but these were obviously reserved for his work, because they were covered with ink splotches in all colors of the rainbow. Though there was an abundance of black as well. He wore fine work gloves, thin enough to have some control over what he was doing with the stone block but protecting his skin from the corrosive elements.

He wasn't barefoot either, unlike his tendency to wander through the house with nothing covering his toes except glittery polish. Instead, he wore heavy work boots—much heavier than anything Urho had ever seen on him before—also ruined beyond the telling of it by ink splotches and what looked like chemical burns. The Caleb of the printing press was different from the Caleb of the house, and Urho felt suddenly sad that Xan hadn't had a chance to see him like this.

And he wondered why.

"I should have waited for you," Caleb said as he worked. "But I got impatient. I've wanted to print this piece for weeks. I couldn't hold back from beginning."

"I didn't realize I was late."

"You aren't. I should have invited you at an earlier time." Caleb glanced up from his work and motioned Urho closer. "Come here. You can't see anything from over there."

Urho slipped around the tables and cabinets, careful not to knock against anything. Every item in the room seemed potentially wet or fragile or both. He took his place by Caleb's side and watched him work.

Almost absently, Caleb explained what he was doing. He spoke calmly of the process of first etching the stone with chemicals, of the wax that repelled the water, which allowed the ink to remain on only the parts Caleb wanted the machine to print.

Eventually, Caleb was ready to load the stone onto the press, and he surprised Urho with his strength as he maneuvered the weight into place.

"If there's any imperfection in the stone, the intense pressure from the press will break it." Caleb placed a thick piece of fresh paper over the block.

"Does that happen often?" Urho asked.

"No. But when it does, it's a real bitch," Caleb said. Then he stood back, turned a crank, and the machine began to move. Pulling the crank again, Caleb asked, "When you worked in the labs at the university, did you ever think about how strange it is that some technologies survived the Holy Church's purge after the Great Death, like the printing press, but other arguably more important technologies, like how to manipulate genes, were lost entirely?"

As the machine bore down on the stone, Urho said, "I suppose the zealots thought printing technology wasn't as dangerous—and possibly more useful."

"But what could be more dangerous to us as a species than eradicating the knowledge that allowed the creation of omegas to begin with? And we were made so imperfectly at that! Every birth is a risk to our life."

"Now you're blaspheming." Urho watched as Caleb strained against the crank. He thought about offering to help but knew Caleb would turn him down.

"Ha!" Caleb smirked. "I suppose I am."

"But I have no problem with that."

Caleb smiled then, and it was his sparkly smile from his in-the-house Caleb self. It was good to see it. "I suppose you wouldn't."

"The zealots wanted power, and they got it by demanding complete devotion to wolf-god. They gave him credit for the appearance of omegas. Questioning that was punishable by death for a long time. The press no doubt furthered their ability to spread the word about what thoughts were allowed and what thoughts must be stamped out.

Caleb sighed, pausing in his work for a moment. "It was so short-sighted, though. I would have thought they'd want to further perfect the salvation of the human race. What could be more useful to them—to everyone—than omegas who could reproduce as easily as human women had before they were lost?"

"I can't disagree with you. All I know is that the desire to hold on to control and power all too often outweighs common sense."

Caleb nodded, twisting the crank again to move the weight away from the stone. He carefully lifted the paper and showed the outcome to Urho.

Urho gasped appreciatively. "It's perfect. It looks just like him."

"Do you think so?"

"Yes. That's his face. When he's worried."

Caleb contemplated the print. "It's based on a drawing I did." He studied Xan's face framed by a bird's nest growing from his dark curls. "I suppose you're right. I have to ask myself is that the right mood for this piece? I wonder if I shouldn't have aimed for something happier to round out my collection."

"I think it's beautiful, but if that wasn't the expression you were hoping to capture...well, I can't say. It's your work. You know better than I do what you were trying to accomplish."

"I started this piece a long time ago. The drawing it's based on, anyway." Caleb cocked his head, looking it over. "I still like the way his dark curls shine, and the bird's nest is perfect. But, this isn't who he is anymore. Not since you came." Caleb smiled and gazed up at Urho questioningly. "Do you plan to stay? Once Vale's baby comes and my heat is over...? Or will you go and leave him alone again?"

"I don't know how to answer that question." He didn't want to overstep. Xan was Caleb's alpha, and Lofton was his home.

"Honestly, if you can."

Urho swallowed hard. "I can't see a future without him in it. Going back to my house I shared with Riki...the place where the memories of his loss have held me for years? That doesn't feel right anymore." A burning ache grew in his belly. "But I understand if you don't want me to stay. It's your home and I'm a guest in it."

"You *shouldn't* be a guest," Caleb said firmly, turning his attention back to the print and examining it with narrowed eyes. He hummed under his breath with dissatisfaction and then tossed the paper over his shoulder, letting it flutter to the floor.

"I shouldn't?"

"No. You should make this your home, too."

Urho choked on his own saliva, surprise like a punch in the gut. "Why do you say that?"

"Because I don't want to do any more drawings or prints of Xan with this expression on his face. I want to capture the expression *you* give him: ease, trust, hope." He nodded thoughtfully, and then turned to another table, grabbing a pencil and a large sheet of paper. "I want to capture the change in him since you came, since you eased his pain and self-loathing."

Urho's throat grew tight. He glanced at where the paper had fallen to the floor. "But what about the stone you etched today?"

Caleb shrugged. "I'll give it to the gardeners. They'll find some use for it. They always do."

The hard work that had gone into the failed print left Urho with an empty feeling in his heart, but Caleb shrugged it off like it wasn't anything to spend time worrying about.

"And the print itself?" Urho asked, nodding to the abandoned piece on the floor.

"Trash," Caleb said.

"In that case, may I have it?"

"You want a reminder of how sad he used to be?" Caleb asked, surprised.

Urho picked the paper up from the floor, studying it carefully. It was still beautiful despite the smears and wrinkles from Caleb's careless treatment. "I want a reminder of what I have to lose."

Caleb nodded. "Take it. And stay here, Urho. Build a new life with him." Then Caleb looked up from where his pencil flew all around the fresh sheet. "A new life with *us.*"

Urho stepped closer. Peering down into Caleb's sincere face, he asked, "You'd want that? For yourself? For more than just Xan's happiness?"

"While my alpha's happiness is more than enough reason to want you here, the truth is, I like you. I trust you. I let you into my studio after all. Not even Xan has been in here." Caleb touched his arm and smiled up at him, a new kind of smile, a vulnerable and completely honest one. "So, yes, Urho, I'd like you to make Lofton your home."

"SO WHAT WAS it like in there?" Xan asked. He'd been curious all day and more than a little jealous.

His head rested on Urho's naked chest, and he trailed his fingers up and down Urho's forearm, feeling the small prickle of his dark arm hair beneath his fingertips.

"Messy," Urho said, his voice still tired after their long lovemaking session.

"Is he any good at it? Or am I just feeding into his delusions by buying him all those supplies?"

"He's excellent," Urho said, sitting up and jostling Xan from his comfortable resting place. "Here. Let me show you."

Rising from the bed, he crossed to the desk by the table. The view wasn't as good as in Xan's room, but they'd found the beta servants changing the sheets when they'd come up after Xan had arrived home, so they'd opted for Urho's room instead. Still, the town made for a beautiful scene, too, stretching away into the horizon, and the colorful buildings shone in the failing late-afternoon sun.

Urho returned with a rather large sheet of paper that he handed over to Xan. Staring up at him was his own face with an expression of such sadness that Xan felt overexposed. The likeness was good, though, he couldn't deny that. Except for his hair twisting into a bird's nest. He kept his hair very neat, thank you very much, Caleb.

"He did this?"

"He's talented," Urho said. "Rosen would probably claim it's far too representational. But he's a snob, so of course he would say that."

Xan continued to stare at the picture. "Caleb's a bit of snob, too."

"In his own way," Urho agreed. He tugged Xan close again, so they rested together naked and warm in Urho's soft bed. Xan snuggled up, breathing in Urho's scent and the mixture of them together.

They both stared at the paper. "Do you like it?" Urho asked.

"It's not what I expected." Xan tilted his head and frowned. "Is that how Caleb sees me, do you think? Sad with a bird's nest where my brain should be?"

"I think Caleb loves you," Urho said softly. "He told me he wasn't satisfied with this piece. He's going to do another one that will capture you better."

"Oh." Xan frowned. "What was wrong with this one?"

"You'd have to ask him," Urho said, but his tone gave away that he knew the reason. "Perhaps after making it, he missed your smile. I know that's my favorite of your features."

Xan sat the print aside on the small table by the bed before curling up on Urho's chest again. "Are you going to keep it?"

"I thought I'd frame it, yes." Urho's fingers slipped soothingly through Xan's hair. "Put it up somewhere as a reminder of how I don't want you to ever look again."

Xan squirmed and frowned.

Urho stilled his fingers. "What's wrong?"

"I don't know. Something about the picture, about my face in it, reminds me of my life before you made your offer."

"Before I loved you."

Xan's body twitched, half disbelieving and yet desperate for it to be true. He grabbed onto the words eagerly. "Yes, before you loved me. I don't want to go back to living like that. And I don't just mean Monhundy and all of that horrible abuse. I mean my day-to-day life. It was so much less without you in it." He sighed, rubbing his face against Urho's chest hair, wishing that the world were different. That *he* was different. "Still, you must be so bored here, waiting for Vale to give birth and spending your days reading, or whatever it is you do. What do you do, Urho, while I'm away?"

"I spend time with Vale, Jason, and Caleb. I walk on the beach and read in the garden if it isn't too cold. I spend time on the telephone consulting on cases in the city. I've walked into the village and explored the town. I haven't been bored."

"But it must only be a matter of time, don't you think? Before you do get bored?" Xan's eyes burned, but he wasn't going to let that show. He blinked back the tears. "And once Vale's baby comes, there won't be any real reason for you to remain here. Your clinic in the city must be suffering without you."

"Caleb brought up something similar to me today," Urho said hesitantly.

Xan let out a frustrated snort. He'd been working toward asking the scary questions he'd been avoiding for a while now. Of course, Caleb would beat him to the punch. "What's that?"

"He suggested that I stay on here after Vale's baby comes."

"For the heat, of course. But after that, if the babe's healthy, there won't really be any need, right? I mean, I suppose Jason and Vale will want to stay on until the flu risk has passed. But there won't be a need for you to be here with them."

"Well—"

"Or do you suspect the baby isn't well?" Xan asked, sitting up to peer into Urho's dark eyes. His heart hammered with sudden worry. He used to resent Vale, but now, with Urho in his life, he only saw his friend's good points and wanted only the best for him. "Vale's been complaining so much lately about pain. Do you think...is it damaged in some way?"

"Shh." Urho tugged Xan down against his chest again and kissed the top of his head. Xan closed his eyes, listening to the steady beat of Urho's heart, the susurration of his lungs, and let himself be soothed. "As far as I can tell, the pregnancy is going swimmingly. He could give birth quite soon and the babe would be all right. The lungs are the last to develop, though, and we need to hope that they are in good shape when the time comes. That's why I'm still delaying induction a bit longer. But I have no reason to believe there's a problem. The babe should be fine."

"Then what was Caleb going on about?" The irritation crept into him again. He wanted nothing more than for Urho to stay with him in Virona, but he wasn't a fool. Urho had a home to return to, a clinic, and a life. There was no reason for him to stay, no matter how much he claimed to care for Xan. And perhaps Caleb was tired of his alpha's lover living in his home. He'd have every right to be.

"Caleb told me earlier today that he'd like me to stay here. As my home."

Xan sat up again and stared at Urho unblinkingly. "Why? I mean—how would that work?"

"We didn't discuss the details, but the idea of returning to the city doesn't appeal to me much. I wanted to know your thoughts on it before I started to give it any real consideration." Urho brushed some sweaty curls out of Xan's eyes and then thumbed the small dent in his chin. "Would you be happy, Xan? If I stayed?"

Xan's heart fluttered, and he wrapped his arms around Urho's neck, crawling onto him and straddling his hips. He held him close, kissed his neck, and scented along his shoulders.

"How would that work?" Xan asked. "What would people think?"

"That's something we'd have to deal with, a risk we'd have to navigate," Urho murmured.

Xan swallowed hard. He knew it was more than he could ever hope to have, the blessing of his family or the rest of the world on what he felt for Urho, but some part of him wanted it. He felt bound by the ropes of law and religious regulations, by the likelihood of losing his family, his standing, his inheritance, and his place in the world if he agreed to something like what Caleb and

Urho were proposing.

Did Caleb even see the likelihood that they would be left with nothing? That Xan's inclinations, like Caleb's father's addiction, would lead them to financial and social ruin? Surely, he did. And yet this was Caleb's idea. How was that?

"Well?" Urho prompted. "Would you be happy if I stayed?"

Xan's throat went tight, and he sat back to look Urho in the eye. "I love you."

"Is that a yes? You'd be happy?"

"If you could stay here and make this your home, if you could live here with me as my lover forever, I don't even know the word for how happy I'd be," Xan said, his voice raw. "Ecstatic. Beyond ecstatic."

"But?"

"What will people think? My father will never understand. My place as heir is already uncertain. My pater... I haven't seen him in so long now."

Urho kissed his head. "There's a lot to consider. If I stayed, we'd have to decide how to carry on. I'd get my own place, perhaps. In town. Near the new clinic I could open."

Xan squirmed. He didn't want Urho in town. He wanted him here, in his bed, at the breakfast table, laughing with Caleb, making a family. He didn't want to live his life pretending that Urho was just a friend, or that he wasn't in love with the man entirely. He wanted everyone to know that the alpha with the big hands and even bigger heart was his, and his alone.

But did he dare such transparency? Could he risk his inheritance? Could he expect Caleb to? He shuddered and burrowed closer to Urho, his stomach twisting into knots and his fingers digging into Urho's biceps.

"Don't think about anything else right now," Urho murmured. "Just tell me if you want me to stay. The rest we can figure out later."

Xan kissed Urho's chest and whispered, "Please don't leave me."

Urho cradled him closer. "I can't promise that. Life has taught me there's no way to be sure on that count. But I promise I'll never go away on purpose, and if I do, I'll always come home to you."

Xan's eyes pricked with tears. He'd never imagined a declaration like that from an alpha like Urho. He didn't know what he'd done to earn or deserve it, but he vowed to be the kind of man who did.

He'd learn to be brave and certain. He'd be daring and firm. He would step up his game in all areas of life: as Caleb's alpha, as Jason's friend, as a citizen of Virona, and, if he didn't lose his inheritance entirely due to his choices, as the future head of his father's company.

His gaze drifted to the print Caleb had made, and he squeezed his eyes closed on the sight. Caleb was a smart man—smarter by far than Xan—and if he was the one to suggest cohabitation to Urho, then he knew the risks. Xan could only hope that he was willing to accept the potential fallout.

Because if Urho was willing to be his alpha for good, and Caleb wanted that, then Xan was determined to become the kind of man who deserved their courageous devotion.

Even if that meant losing everything Xan had always assumed was his by right. Like his family. His inheritance. His home.

"Shh," Urho breathed. "Rest. There's no need to decide anything now. We have time."

Xan relaxed in Urho's arms. They had time, yes. But how much? He wished he could see the future and know now that eventually everything turned out all right, but all he could know for certain was Urho loved him enough to change his life, to risk prison, to move to Virona. And Caleb loved him enough to want Urho to live here.

That was the present.

It was a massive responsibility—and a beautiful, wonderful, terrifying gift.

PART THREE

CHAPTER EIGHTEEN

"COUSIN, YOU LOOK like death!" Xan exclaimed, bolting up from the dinner table.

Janus had been gone well over a month, and Xan had heard he wasn't going to be returning to Virona at all, having been given a new assignment elsewhere. It was a shock on multiple levels to see him there in the dining room doorway, gray-faced and slick with sweat. Janus's eyes glowed with the radiance of sickness, and his frame trembled as if he was having a hard time supporting his own weight.

Silence ruled the table, a stunned expression twisting everyone's face. Vale and Jason recoiled, and Caleb sat still with an open mouth as Xan rushed to Janus's side. He took Janus's hands in his own and gasped at the heat radiating from them. "Wolf-god, you're hot as hell itself."

Janus coughed wetly before he collapsed into Xan's arms.

"Damn it all!" Urho exclaimed from behind them.

A confused and frightened looking Ren hustled in, panting with cheeks flushed. "Sir, your cousin only just arrived. I tried to convince him to go to his room, but he insisted on seeing you. I told him I'd get you, but—" Ren gestured helplessly, hanging back from the sweaty man in Xan's arms. "I'm sorry."

"Not your fault," Xan said, struggling under the weight of his bigger cousin. Janus's hot, clammy body rested heavily against him, and Xan grunted, trying to shore him up. "Run and grab some tea for him."

Urho was suddenly there, helping him with Janus's slack body, and Xan breathed a sigh of relief.

"Jason, take Vale upstairs through the kitchen," Urho commanded. "Keep him far away from Janus. Don't come back down until I say the coast is clear."

The shocked table came to life. Jason and Vale hastily left by the kitchen entrance, and Caleb hurried to Xan's side.

Together, they helped Janus into Urho's abandoned chair. His arm fell onto Urho's plate, dragging through the gravy and upsetting his glass of wine. His head lolled forward, and his eyes rolled back.

Urho slapped his cheek lightly. "Janus!" he shouted. Janus moaned, but didn't gain consciousness. "Both of you stay back! I need to get him to a bed."

"Yes. Somewhere away from the rest of the house," Xan said, his heart pounding and his palms sweaty.

"And away from the servants," Caleb added.

"For wolf-god's sake, where?" Urho asked as Janus's breathing grew labored.

"Not in the main house!" Xan said urgently. "He'll infect Vale!" He could never look Jason in the eye again if his child was lost because of their choices in this moment.

"To my room," Caleb said. "It's on the other side of the house from Vale and Jason."

"No," Urho said. "The detached wing."

Janus slumped even farther. Urho lifted him into an upright position, but he still leaned dangerously.

"Where the servants live?" Caleb shook his head. "No. We can't ask them to—"

"There are plenty of rooms upstairs," Xan said. "The servants can stay here with us in the main house. We can keep Janus separate. Just until we know if this is contagious or until it has passed."

Caleb nodded, and Urho heaved Janus up from the chair and

over his shoulder into a fireman's carry. Hustling through the great hall, ignoring the cries of the servants, they took Janus out of the main house and over the walkway to the detached wing.

"This way," Caleb said, leading them around the opposite way of his print studio. "There's an empty room downstairs. The servants all preferred the top story and the views there."

Urho settled Janus onto the dusty bed. Janus shuddered with his fever, and Caleb pressed his fingers against his forehead. Xan's stomach tightened.

"Don't get too close," Xan said. "You'll get sick."

"Someone has to care for him."

"Urho is a doctor."

"Urho is your lover. Do you want him to be the one to catch this?" Caleb snapped.

Panic gripped Xan. "Of course not!" The thought of anything befalling Urho was unbearable.

"Let's get Janus settled, for wolf-god's sake," Urho said. "Then we can argue about who is going to be exposed to this and how we're going to care for him without infecting Vale." He felt along Janus's throat and examined his eyes by lifting his fluttering lids.

"What's the matter with him?" Xan asked. "The flu?"

"I believe so," Urho said tightly. He pinched the bridge of his nose. "Damn it to wolf's own hell. This is exactly what we were trying to avoid by bringing Vale here."

"Well, I'm sure he didn't mean to compromise him," Caleb retorted, pushing past Urho to touch Janus's face again. "Janus, it's me, Caleb. Can you hear me?" He gasped when Janus blinked up at him in confusion.

"Caleb?"

"You're sick. We're going to get you well again."

"I have to tell Xan."

"He's right here," Caleb said, trailing his fingers down Janus's cheek.

Xan's stomach tightened uneasily, and he didn't know if it was from his omega's gentle touch on his cousin's face, or the ominous expression in Janus's eyes as he sought out Xan.

"Your pater…" Janus trailed off in a rattling cough.

"Yes?" Xan's heart skipped a beat.

"He's sick." Janus's feverish eyes burned into his. "And Ray. Both sick."

Xan swallowed hard, his pulse rushing in his ears. "Sick with the flu?"

Janus nodded. "Ray's bad. Might die."

"I need to go home." Xan's stomach flopped like a landed fish.

"No!" Janus exclaimed, reaching toward him. "Your father— You have to stay. Can't risk—" Janus coughed so hard the veins of his throat bulged. "Can't risk the heirs." Collapsing deeper into the bed, he cackled miserably, tears slipping from his eyes. "But it looks like one of us caught it, anyway."

"And now you're here coughing in the other heir's face," Urho barked, pushing Xan away from his cousin.

"Stop," Caleb said sharply. "He's feverish and not in his right mind. You're a doctor. You know that."

Janus rattled out another cough before his eyes rolled up, unconsciousness taking him.

"Damn it all." Urho turned to Xan. "Go. Leave here. Wash up. Change your clothes. And then have the cook send you ginger tea with lemon. Lots of lemon. Drink it all and then order more." He turned to Caleb. "You, too."

"I'm not leaving him until I know he's going to be well." Caleb tucked his hair behind his ear and looked up at Urho defiantly.

Urho caught Xan's eye, but Xan didn't know how to explain Caleb's determination with just his brows or his expression. So, he simply shrugged. "Urho, don't you need your medical bag?"

Urho glared at him. "I do. Be a love and get it for me."

"Why don't you go get it yourself? Caleb and I need a moment."

"And leave you both here? Exposed?"

"Like you said, we can argue about all of that once Janus is settled. Your bag's in your room, isn't it?"

Urho gritted his teeth, but one look at Caleb left him defeated. He stomped out of the room muttering under his breath about stubborn omegas.

Xan watched Caleb fuss over Janus for another few seconds, and then he took hold of Caleb's hand. "He's going to be all right."

"How do you know that?" Caleb jerked his hand away. "He looks like wolf-god's apprentice has come to snatch his soul."

"Urho's a good doctor and—"

"Urho's scared, can't you see that?" Caleb squeezed his eyes closed, and a tear slipped out. "Besides, he's got other priorities."

"What's that supposed to mean?" Xan asked, wiping Caleb's tear away.

"It means he cares more about you and Vale than he does about what happens to Janus."

Xan made a soft sound. "And you. He cares about you."

"I know. But…" Caleb shook his head.

"You're scared, too, and that's why you're saying all of this. Urho's a doctor. He cares for everyone who needs him."

Caleb's eyes burned into him. "Urho needs to stay well to deliver Vale's child. You know that. I know that. So I'll care for Janus."

"And what if you get sick?"

"Then I'll get sick." He shrugged. "I'm healthy. I'll survive it."

"Janus was healthy—and Ray. This flu is incredibly dangerous. I won't risk you." Xan squared his shoulders. "I'll be the one to care for him."

"You can't," Caleb shot back. "Your father needs an heir for his fortune and his business. Betas can't inherit. You know that. If you and Janus both get sick and if you both…" Caleb shuddered. "No. You can't."

"Like you said, I'm healthy. I'll be fine."

Urho must have run to his room and back because he came racing in, out of breath and sweating with the medicine bag in hand. "The servants are going to make the tea. They'll be bringing it and some fresh water out for him soon." He opened his bag and rummaged inside.

Xan caught Caleb's eye and saw that no further argument was going to change his mind. As Urho brought out his stethoscope and thermometer, Ren came in with a facemask strapped on and arms full of cloths. Similarly masked servants carrying bowls of water, boiling and cool, and the full stock of their medicine cabinets in the house followed him. "Perhaps some of this will be of use," Ren asked hopefully.

"Yes," Urho agreed. He popped the thermometer in Janus's mouth and they all watched anxiously as the mercury rose.

"Wolf-god," one of the betas whispered.

"Ice," Urho said. "We need ice and plenty of it to bring his fever down."

"Yes, sir. Is there anything else?" Ren asked, motioning with his hand and sending a beta scurrying to get the needed ice.

Xan's heart pounded so hard he felt like his chest couldn't hold it. He'd never seen a fever so high.

"Yes, Ren. Have the other servants gather their things from the rooms upstairs," Caleb said, taking a cloth from one of the betas and getting it damp. He pressed it to Janus's forehead as Urho did the same at his neck. "The servants will sleep in the extra rooms upstairs in the main wing until this danger is past us. Have them prepare those rooms for themselves."

Urho added, "Find out the name of the local doctor. Have him on call. Things could go sideways here very quickly, and we need to be prepared."

Ren left to carry out the orders, and as they waited for the ice to appear, Urho began to chant prayers to wolf-god—old fashioned prayers, the kind that Xan hadn't heard since he was a small child. It didn't soothe him.

Ending one prayer, Urho turned to Xan and implored, "Go

now. Do as I've asked. There's no way for you to help here."

Xan nodded, his eyes straying back to Janus's clammy, chalky face. "Come with me, Caleb."

"He needs me here," Caleb said, smoothing another cold, damp cloth over Janus's feverish forehead. "I can't leave him alone."

"Urho will be with him."

Caleb ignored him.

Xan kissed his omega's forehead and left him hovering over Janus with Urho. He couldn't help by hovering, too. He returned to the house and followed Urho's orders to a tee and then checked in on Jason and Vale in their rooms.

The rest of the night was a whirlwind of confusion. Liddy Bainson, a local doctor, agreed to be on call for either Vale or Janus, should Urho come down with the illness, or should Vale go into labor while Janus remained ill.

Jason and Vale were on edge, but after the beta servants cleaned all the surfaces in the dining room and entry hall, they relaxed enough to come down and have a snack to make up for their interrupted dinner.

Urho joined Xan in his bed that night after taking a shower and dousing himself in an antiseptic lotion, looking exhausted. He held Xan close and scented along his neck and shoulders. "You smell healthy," he said. "Stay that way."

"I'll try."

"Have you called your father?"

"I couldn't get through to anyone. There was no answer at the house at all." Xan tried not to let on how much that terrified him.

"You should go to the city. Tomorrow."

"Perhaps." Xan wanted to go, but he didn't want to make a mistake. With so much happening all at once, he didn't know the right thing to do. He hoped a good night's sleep would clarify that for him. "Where's Caleb?" He hadn't heard him go into his room or use the bathroom in their adjoining hallway.

"He's stubborn," Urho said.

"He is," Xan agreed, twining his fingers with Urho's. His heart ached, and his nerves sang anxiously. "I think he loves him."

"I think he might," Urho agreed, dropping a kiss on Xan's head. "Does that hurt you?"

"No."

"Do you fear he'll leave you for him?"

"I don't know."

Urho sighed. "Janus is a very sick man."

Xan tightened his grip on Urho's fingers. "I hope he doesn't die."

"Funny, the last time you saw him, you hoped he'd be hit by a train."

"Yes," Xan whispered, swallowing thickly. "But I didn't want him to *die*."

"I know," Urho said gently. "This thing with him and Caleb…"

"I don't know," Xan murmured. "We'll have to wait and see."

"Caleb loves you."

"Yes." Xan sighed and tucked in against Urho. "But we both know that love comes in different forms—philia, agapē, erōs. I don't know what form his love for Janus takes."

"Not eros."

"No." Xan sighed. "But there are levels to all those kinds of love. Take philia—brotherly love. I don't love my neighbor as I love my best friend. It might be that he loves Janus more deeply than he loves me."

Urho snuggled him close. "He loves *you*," Urho repeated again. "No matter how he's feeling now, Janus could be no competition for you."

Xan thought Urho's affection for him made him biased. But he didn't protest. He simply closed his eyes and let exhaustion wash them both out into an anxious, tossing sea of sleep.

CHAPTER NINETEEN

"WHAT DO WE know about the local hospital?" Vale asked the next morning over breakfast, cradling his stomach nervously. To Jason's pride and Urho's satisfaction, it had grown greatly over the last week or two. He was now obviously quite pregnant at even a glance.

"For you or for him?" Urho asked, rubbing his bleary eyes.

It'd been a long night. After Xan had fallen asleep, Urho had gotten out of bed, dressed, and left the main house to pace the hallway of the detached wing. He'd listened for Janus's cough, monitoring it lest it grew much worse, and tried very hard not to overhear the quiet words Caleb shared with him.

But he hadn't been able to miss everything.

Like one exchange that had troubled him all morning:

"Promise that you'll forgive me," Janus begged during a brief period of consciousness. "Promise, Caleb."

"I do forgive you, Janus. I promise. Now be quiet and rest."

"I love you. It's always been you."

Caleb released a choked sound.

"All the rest were..." Janus coughed violently.

"Shh. Rest. Sleep. Heal."

"They weren't you. None of them were you, Caleb."

"Janus..."

"Tell me you love me, too."

"I did care about you once—"

Janus cried, "Can't you even lie to a man on his deathbed?"

"You're not dying," Caleb whispered furiously. *"Now shut your mouth and sleep."*

Medicine had been delivered to the house from the pharmacy first thing in the morning, and Janus was resting more easily now. Well enough that Urho didn't mind leaving him to shower again, wipe down with the antiseptic lotion, and then eat breakfast with his very worried alpha-shaped omega and their nervous friends.

Caleb had refused to leave Janus. He'd declared that Ren would bring a plate for him when he brought the ginger broth Urho had prescribed for Janus. Urho had agreed to this only if Caleb promised to also drink the lemon, pepper, and ginger tea, and to wash up regularly, coating his hands with the antiseptic lotion.

Xan picked at his food, pushing it around the plate, his mind clearly elsewhere. Urho wondered if Xan had gotten through to his parents this morning. Xan had been holed up in his office until breakfast, as far as Urho knew, while he'd been so busy dealing with the patient and handling the hygiene orders for the servants.

"Are you listening?" Jason asked gently.

Urho blinked at him. "I'm sorry?"

"Never mind. You look exhausted." Jason went back to his breakfast, always able to pack away more food than Urho could manage in a full day.

Xan sat upright, tense, and radiating silent anxiety. Xan didn't meet his gaze, still focused on shoving around his eggs. Urho took a long swallow of his coffee, smiled at Jason, and said, "Forgive me. I'm tired. But please, ask the question again?"

"I'd wondered if you'd spoken with the local hospital and whether they had a place for Janus there. Obviously, we want you to deliver the baby, not a stranger at the hospital."

"Jason would lose his mind," Vale whispered, sipping his pre-scribed tea—the same that Urho was forcing down every gullet in the house—and looking quite pale with worry.

"Don't fret," Urho encouraged him. "It's all going to be fine."

Xan's fork banged against his plate, but he said nothing.

"So the hospital will take him?" Jason asked.

"No." Urho sighed. It would have been so much easier for him if they had, but he couldn't fault their reasoning. "They've asked us to keep him here. He's contagious, and the hospital is small. They'd endanger their already weak patients bringing him in. So, with him in the detached wing and all of you drinking strengthening tea and practicing good hygiene, we should get along just fine with him here." Urho hoped that was true.

"Especially since you're a doctor," Xan said with a heavy sigh. He shoved away from the table, flopping back in his chair miserably. He stared up at the ceiling with a pinched brow.

"What are you going to do about your family?" Urho asked gently.

Jason stopped eating, and Vale went very still, both of them wearing expressions of concern.

"I spoke to my father's assistant," Xan snarled, obviously stung that his father hadn't come to the phone to talk with him directly. But if his pater really was sick, then it was unlikely Doxan Heelies would leave his *Érosgápe* for any reason. Even to talk with his only alpha son. "He says Ray has taken a turn for the worse and Pater is…" His voice gave out on him, and he sat forward enough to take a sip of his water. Then he simply shook his head and said no more.

"You should go to them," Jason urged, his blue eyes wide and earnest. "You were always your pater's favorite. If he's that sick, you shouldn't risk remaining estranged."

Xan swallowed spasmodically, and his voice sounded tight. "Father ordered me to stay away."

"Your father is an asshole—and worse, he's wrong," Jason spat. "He's kept you from your pater this entire year and for what? Because he's always been jealous of you, that's why."

"No…" Xan flushed red, and Urho wanted to reach across the table to protect him from whatever he was about to confess. "It's because of the rumors."

"There have always been rumors," Jason said, waving it all aside. "He's jealous of how your pater adores you. *Érosgápe* can be unreasonably possessive even against their own children sometimes."

Vale rubbed his stomach thoughtfully again, a frown marring his forehead.

"Don't worry," Jason said, placing a hand on Vale's belly, too. "I won't be like that."

"I hope not."

Xan rolled his eyes and snapped, "Fine. Maybe my father is a jerk. Not everyone has perfect parents like yours, or a pater so accepting of perversions."

Jason's eyes gleamed smartly. "Your pater has never given a single wolf-goddamn about what you do in bed and you know it." He pointed at Xan with his fork. "He caught us that time when I was staying at your house while my parents went to the beach alone. He pretended he saw nothing."

Xan squirmed in his seat, his cheeks growing even redder. "Don't talk about that!"

"We all know about you and Jason," Vale said calmly. "You two don't have to pretend it never happened. Urho and I used to fuck, too. As everyone here is aware."

Urho shot Vale a silencing glance as Xan scrubbed at his face. Vale rolled his eyes.

"Yes, let's all stop pretending now," Jason agreed, his jaw set in that stubborn way Urho was all too familiar with from Jason's early days of courting Vale. "And let's stop pretending that the reason you didn't catch the first train this morning was because you want to respect your father's wishes. The truth is, you're scared to face him."

Xan's angry, hot eyes flashed at Jason as he clenched his fists. He opened and shut his mouth, like he was looking for the right retort, but his expression crumpled. He covered his face with his balled-up fists, hiding. "Maybe I am. How many times have you confronted the possibility of losing everything?"

"Xan..." Jason said tenderly. "I didn't mean... Look, you know what I'm saying is basically true."

Urho suspected it was *entirely* true. After all, Jason knew Xan's family well and interacted with his father and pater even more often than Xan did these days. He had every reason to have a good grip on the family dynamics.

Just then, Zephyr stalked into the dining room and sniffed the air delicately before turning around and marching right back out. Urho realized he hadn't seen her in days. Xan probably envied her ability to disappear whenever things got uncomfortable for her. No doubt he'd love to crawl into a hidey-hole somewhere right about now.

But Jason was right—at least about Xan needing to go see his pater and brother. Fantasies of escape must be pushed aside. The all-too-real world demanded he step up into it.

"Pater always said that if Father found out or suspected the truth about me, there'd be hell to pay for both of us," Xan whispered from behind his fists. "And he was right. He gave us both hell to pay by keeping us apart this year."

"So what? You're a grown alpha now," Jason said. The future father in him was easy to see in his determined face. "Take it from me—our parents think they know what's best for us long after they no longer actually do."

Xan stopped hiding. "What do you recommend then, oh Mighty One of Great Knowledge? Just show up on the doorstep and hope Joon lets me in?"

"Yes! Take charge of this situation and your life." Jason was getting fired up now, and he leaned forward over his food, his eyes bright and his voice ringing with certainty. "Show up on their doorstep and demand to be let in. You're Xan Heelies, Doxan's heir and only alpha son. You have rights. For wolf-god's sake, demand them!"

Xan swallowed again, but this time his chin came up. He met Urho's gaze, and Urho nodded at him. Jason was correct. Xan had rights.

"Go see your pater," Jason said more gently. "If he gets better, then no harm is done beyond enraging your father. Hey, you do that easily enough without even trying." Jason's voice went even softer, and yet the sobering possibility attached to his words surely dug into every heart at the table. "If your pater doesn't get better, then you didn't miss your chance."

Vale rubbed his stomach and frowned down at it. Urho was familiar with that look from his years of dealing with pregnant omegas. Vale was no doubt wondering who, exactly, was growing in his body, and what grief this child might cause him in the future. Urho hated to break it to him, but there was no way to tell. It was part of life's ever-evolving mystery.

His own father and pater, both religious and devout, would be horrified by what he did with and felt for Xan. He was no doubt far from the offspring they'd hoped for when he'd grown in his pater's stomach. That was the way of life.

"You make it sound so easy," Xan said, shoving his plate away. "I'd be risking Father's wrath, which isn't an easy thing to endure. Not only that, but I'd be risking losing my inheritance entirely. He's threatened already to give it over to Janus. Look, I've been banned from visiting the city and specifically banned from coming to see pater and Ray."

"Oh? Did he tell you himself today on the phone?" Vale asked quietly. "That you've been banned from these places and people?"

"No. He passed it through his assistant."

Vale's lips twitched into a devious smirk. "Obviously there's been a misunderstanding. All you heard from the assistant was that your pater and Ray were very sick. You thought you were wanted in the city *immediately*."

Xan's lips quirked up. "Maybe, but then his assistant would never hear the end of it. I'd think more highly of myself if I did it the way Jason advises. Chin up. Demanding my rights." Then he laughed bitterly. "But let's be honest. I'm Xan Heelies. Unmanned coward, so I'll probably do it Vale's way instead."

"You're brave," Urho said gruffly. "The bravest one at this table."

"I told you," Vale whispered to Urho, his dark brow raised.

"So you did," Urho conceded.

"Look," Jason said, sighing heavily. "I know that you're scared, but in the end your father isn't going to have you arrested for unnatural inclinations. He might find a way to disinherit you without taking it before the Church and courts, but I doubt it. Those laws are pretty tight. Even if he does go that far, without proof or witnesses you wouldn't be arrested."

"Just outcast," Xan said.

"Well, your life would be yours, won't it? I'm perfectly happy living in Vale's house on Oak Avenue, and we're going to bring our baby home there. I want to raise him in that house where Vale grew up."

Vale made a soft noise of surprise. "You do?"

Jason nodded. "That's important to me." He looked back to Xan. "You have this house in your own name, in the trust from your pater's father. You could live here. Or if you can't find a way to afford the upkeep, you could sell it and you and Caleb could live well enough on the proceeds. My father would give you a job. You've done such good work on the office here. You could help open a satellite facility for Sabel Industries, too."

"Your father would hire me? If I was known to be unmanned?"

"My father ignores rumors like that so long as the work gets done." Jason tilted his head earnestly. "All I'm saying is that you aren't without resources and friends. You could survive the loss of your family's money. And maybe you'd even be happier without it, Xan. If you could live honestly."

"And be true to who and how you love," Vale murmured, giving Urho a significant look.

Urho felt suddenly tongue-tied. "And... Well, obviously no matter what happens with your father, I'd never let you go without. Never."

Xan swallowed thickly. His eyes shone with love, and emotion swelled in Urho as well.

Urho cleared his throat. "That's it. End of discussion. Xan needs to go. Come on. You need to pack your bags and catch the next train."

Xan blinked at him in surprise. "You want me to leave?"

"No." He hated the idea of Xan being away from him for even a night, and even more hated the idea of him heading into a household of sickness, but Xan needed to do this. He needed to see his pater and Ray, and he needed to stand up for himself in the family. It was the only way he'd ever be free. "But you *need* to go."

Xan nodded and stood. His hands were still visibly shaking, and he licked his lips anxiously. "There's so much to do here, though. I need to call Edes and let him know I'll be gone. He'll need to take over at the office here in town in my absence."

"You can do that while I start packing for you," Urho said. Xan glanced around the room, worry creasing his face. "Don't fret about the house," Urho added. "I'll hold down the fort here. Me and Caleb."

"And we'll be happy to deal with any household issues that

don't involve direct contact with Janus," Jason said. "Or I will. Vale will probably just stare at his stomach and hum the entire time you're gone. But I can help keep the place going if Caleb is otherwise occupied."

Urho glanced to Vale, who nodded absently. He was indeed staring down at his stomach. Urho almost laughed. Yes, Vale's days would continue much the same until the babe arrived—a walk on the beach, a morning nap, a lunch on the veranda if the day was nice, another walk on the beach, another nap. Urho didn't resent it in the least. Every omega deserved to feel safe and pampered during pregnancy. He would want the same for Caleb when the time came. He couldn't wait to see the man round with Xan's child.

Wolf-god, Caleb...

Urho didn't know what to make of Xan's omega's devotion to Janus's health or the conversation he'd overheard. He'd suspected Caleb did still harbor feelings of some kind for Janus, but the evidence of it stung him considering how awful Janus had been to Xan, so it must sting Xan as well.

Certainly, Xan and Caleb weren't lovers like other alpha-omega pairs, but they were family, and Xan loved Caleb deeply. And while it would be petty to harbor jealousy when Caleb was so generous with Xan's feelings toward Urho, it was only natural that an alpha would feel proprietary urges toward his contracted omega.

Maybe if Urho had been given an opportunity to know Janus better, or Janus's behavior when they did meet had let him like him more—or if Janus had never hurt Caleb and Xan in the past—then Urho might feel the man deserved Xan's beautiful, kind omega's devotion. As it was, he resented any feeling Caleb carried for Janus. Perhaps even more than Xan himself did.

Still, he was determined to let the feelings go. After Janus was recovered, they could deal with the situation then. Should Caleb want to leave Xan and go to Janus for good... Well, Xan would have to face that fact, and Urho would be there for him during the fallout.

Until such a point, Urho wouldn't think on it further other than to feel proud that Caleb was such a loving, forgiving person, and so generous in his care of a sick man.

"I'll go make a few calls," Xan said. "Then I'll leave on the afternoon train."

With that settled, everyone went back to eating their breakfast. It wasn't a cheerful party with everyone's mind still obviously fixed on various worries and problems. When Jason's plate was clean, and Vale had been prodded into eating a few bites more, the two of them said they would retire to bed.

"You should take a nap as well before you go," Urho said. "I'll go check in on Janus. I'll come join you later if I can."

Xan nodded tiredly. "I'll go make those calls." He hesitated in the doorway, looking over his shoulder at them all. Urho's heart ached in his chest. "Thank you," Xan said softly. "For bullying me into the right thing."

"We're your friends. We want you to be happy," Vale murmured.

"Go make your calls," Urho said. "I'll meet you upstairs in your room."

XAN KEPT HIS shower short, too worried to enjoy lingering under the water for long. After he'd tugged on his silky, royal blue pajamas for the nap he'd promised Urho he'd take, he sat on his bed to brush his wet hair.

The sudden knock on the door made his pulse jump, and he called out for Urho to come in. But the head that popped through the door belonged to Caleb.

Dreadful. There was no other way to describe his appearance. He looked so pale in his white clothes. Gray smudges of worry darkened the fragile skin beneath his blue eyes. His chin-length blond hair was tousled and hung messily around his jawline.

"Hey," Xan said softly. "C'mere."

Caleb shut the door behind him and crept into the room as though ashamed and uncertain of his welcome.

When Xan stood and opened his arms wide, Caleb rushed into them with a soft sob. Xan kissed his hair and shushed him soothingly. They held each other for a long time before Caleb finally pulled free, wiping at his eyes. The dark smudges looked even darker.

"I'm sorry," he whispered.

"For what, love?" Xan asked, though of course he knew.

"For lying to you about my feelings for Janus," Caleb whispered, his chin wobbling. "I do love him. But not in the deep way I love you, and not in any romantic way. I never have. But I care for him more than I wanted to admit before. There was a time I would have contracted with him if he'd only wanted me enough. The real me."

"I know. You've already said."

"But I also said I didn't care for him any longer."

"No, if I recall correctly, you said you didn't want to be his omega." Xan's mouth went dry. "Was that a lie?"

Caleb shook his head as tears spilled down his cheeks. He looked at Xan imploringly. "No, I want to be *your* omega."

Xan led him to the bed, and they sat on the side of it together. "That works out well, then, because you are my omega."

"I want to have a family with *you*."

"You can. You will." Xan took his hands. "It's okay to care for more than one man. I do." He wasn't in love with Caleb and he could never be. Now he knew that for sure since he had fallen for Urho and loved him with his heart, soul, *and* body. But he and

Caleb still shared a deep bond.

"I know." Caleb pulled a hand free to wipe at his tears. "I didn't realize how much I still cared about that rat bastard until last night. Seeing him so sick… My heart broke again. And the last day could only have been more painful if it was *you* in quarantine, suffering like that. I can feel death in that room, Xan. I feel it."

"Urho says there's every chance he'll recover."

Caleb nodded. "I know. He told me the same. But my heart doesn't think he will, Xan. In my heart…" He shivered.

"Don't be superstitious."

Caleb's eyes flashed with hurt. "I'm being honest. Some part of me knows, deep down, he won't survive this."

"Janus is strong. Young, like us. He'll make it."

"I wish I was as certain as you."

Xan said nothing because Caleb *was* as certain as he was. He just didn't believe Janus would survive. "If he lives, what will you do?"

Caleb shook his head. "Nothing. This changes nothing."

"How can you say that? You care for the man."

"Not the way he wants me to care for him," Caleb said with a sad smile. "Or, rather *wanted* me to care for him a long time ago. I have no idea what he wants now."

Xan touched Caleb's wet cheek. "But you said your heart is broken by him."

"Friends can break your heart, too, Xan," Caleb whispered, tears welling again. "Just as badly, maybe sometimes worse than a lover. Because with a lover, from what I understand, you're aware that it might not work out from the beginning, aren't you? Unless you're *Érosgápe*. With a friend, though, you don't guard your heart."

Xan brushed Caleb's hair off his cheek. "He seems like he was more than a friend to you."

"He almost was. He was my first hope. And my first loss. My only heartbreak." Caleb shrugged. "Everyone suffers through it at least once. In some form or another. Just because my heartbreak isn't romantic, doesn't mean it's not real."

"Don't give up. He'll live and then you can find out if he cares for you, too."

Caleb sighed in a fast rush and shook his head, tears forming in his eyes again. "You aren't listening." He chewed his lip. "I don't feel attraction for him, or romantic love. I know it's hard for you to understand because you're so different from me in these ways. My heartbreak isn't because I want him."

"I know." Or he tried to know. Intellectually he understood, but some part of him could never fully grasp these truths when Caleb described them.

"I want you as my alpha, my best friend, my family."

"I know," Xan said again.

"So please don't say that about Janus again."

Xan nodded.

"I don't want him. But I don't want him to die." Then Caleb nuzzled Xan's neck and whispered, "Alpha mine, I love you. You're my future, the father of my children to come, and my choice."

Xan kissed Caleb's head again. "I love you, too. And it's all right to be sad that someone you cared for, a friend, an old hope, is so sick. I understand. Let me hold you."

Caleb rested in Xan's arms, breathing in his scent and letting Xan stroke his back. They cuddled together on the bed, taking comfort from the familiar scents and sounds of the other, the rise and fall of breath, their mutual steadfastness.

Eventually Xan murmured in Caleb's ear, "You need to rest. Take a break from looking in on Janus."

"Ren has taken over for the afternoon. I'll return to him tonight." Caleb nuzzled him again, scenting him for a long time. "No one makes me feel as safe as you do, Xan."

Tears pricked Xan's eyes, and he squeezed Caleb tight. "You're my omega. I'm your alpha. Of course, I make you feel safe."

Caleb made Xan feel safe, too. Their brand of love and friendship was just as Caleb had claimed—without boundaries.

Caleb turned to go, but he stopped with his pale hand on the doorknob. "Ren tells me you're leaving for the city this afternoon."

"I have to leave. Pater and Ray are very sick."

"Yes, you should go." Caleb nodded, looking a little lost.

"Urho will be here with you. But if you don't want me to leave while Janus is so ill, I can stay."

Caleb shook his head. "Go. I'll be all right here." He left solemnly.

Xan was still staring at the wood grain of the door when Urho opened it several minutes later. He pulled Xan up into his strong arms, and Xan sighed as he leaned into Urho's strength. It was Xan's duty to Caleb as his alpha and friend to be there for him, but the sensation of being held by his own alpha was comforting and *right* in a way Xan relished.

"I wish I could go with you," Urho said urgently. "I don't like the idea of you in the city by yourself, with your pater sick, and your father…" he trailed off. "Will you be all right?"

Xan unbuttoned Urho's shirt and rubbed his cheek against Urho's chest. "I don't know. I'm scared. I don't want to lose my pater or my brother. Or my cousin." He leaned back and looked into Urho's eyes. "How bad is Janus? Caleb said some pretty morbid things just now."

"He's right to be frightened for Janus. He doesn't seem to be responding to the prescriptions. Most of the time, the initial dose provides a great deal of relief within just a few hours. That hasn't been the case. He's deteriorated even more."

Xan chewed on his lower lip. "Caleb cares for him. He needs to live."

"Caleb has feelings for him? Sexual feelings?"

If Xan wasn't mistaken, he heard a strange thread of jealousy in Urho's voice. "Not sexual feelings, not attraction—no. Deep friendship feelings. Old ones that he thought long scarred over, but are now broken open again."

"Wolf-god's blessings on our Caleb," Urho murmured, wrapping his arms around Xan. "He has such a strong heart, and he doesn't deserve to suffer through this."

"So you agree with him?"

"Doctors have instincts." Urho kissed Xan's temple soothingly. "And, unfortunately, my instincts and Caleb's align. I'll do what I can for Janus, and the local hospital has agreed to continue to provide drips and medicines. Only time will tell."

"I hope you're both wrong."

"I do, too." Urho ran his fingers into Xan's damp, tumbled curls. "When you're in the city, promise me one thing."

Xan gazed up at him. "Anything."

"No matter what happens, don't go to him."

"Go to who?" Xan's mind scrambled in confusion. Pater? Ray? Father? He didn't know to whom Urho was referring with this strange request.

"That monster Monhundy."

Xan gasped in horror. "No. I'd never. Not now. Not since we…no." His throat clogged with unexpected tears. It hurt to think Urho believed he would betray him like that.

"I want to be sure you won't go to him."

"You think I would? After all you've shown me?"

Urho studied his face carefully. Whatever he saw there must have reassured him because he drew Xan even closer, kissing his eyelids and nose, kissing his mouth and his temples, before scenting along his neck and nuzzling him gently. "I'm sorry. Forgive me. I cherish you, and the thought of you in pain, of what he did to you before… It terrifies me."

"I don't want that anymore. I never will again. I want you. I want to be your omega. Even if…" Xan sighed.

Urho frowned. "What?"

"Even if that makes me weak. My father—"

"To wolf's own hell with your father and what he thinks. You're my omega, and that makes you strong."

Xan's mouth went dry. "Show me how strong I can be. Make me take it. Now." He licked his lips, staring at Urho's mouth. "Make me yours, Urho."

"Demanding little pup," Urho muttered. He quickly stripped Xan of his pajama top before shoving his hands into his silky pajama pants and clenching his buttocks firmly. "Get these off," he said, shoving them down.

Xan's cock filled fast, his asshole already gripping and releasing as he imagined the burning rush of penetration and the sweetness of a punishing fuck. "Make it rough. Make me feel it. On the train, I want to tighten my hole and still feel where you've been."

Urho growled, his exposed nipples peaking. "Finish what you started." He indicated his belt buckle and then removed his shirt, tossing it onto a nearby chair.

Xan got to work, his heart ramping up in excitement and his fingers going shaky. He slipped the tongue of Urho's belt through the buckle, shivering at the rasping slide through the loops as he tugged it off. He placed it carefully on the bed, an idea sparking inside his tumultuous mind. He turned back to Urho, getting his pants open and dropping to his knees as he tugged them down.

Urho kicked off his shoes and stepped out of his pants, indicating with a jerk of his chin that Xan should put them on the chair as well. Xan did so, never getting up off his knees. His cock pressed against his stomach, pre-come slipping down the sides already, his balls riding high and tight. He greedily pressed his face to Urho's groin, scenting his musk. Urho's dick was thick and engorged, rising up alongside Xan's cheek as he nuzzled the rough hair at the base.

Urho gripped Xan's hair and tugged his face away. He released Xan and sat on the bed, spreading his legs and ordering, "Get over here, omega. Mouth open. Tongue out."

Xan did as he was told, knee-walking between Urho's thighs, his mouth open and his thirsty tongue out, ready to catch the pearl of pre-come that swelled at Urho's slit.

"No sucking," Urho said. "Lick me." He gripped Xan's hair again and dragged him in. The sharp tug of pain went straight to Xan's cock, a zing of excitement that left him panting as he buried his face in Urho's crotch, licking greedily at his sac and taint, sliding his tongue up and down his shaft, greedy for the pre-come that slipped down the side in regular pulses.

Xan's cock begged for attention, and he put one hand on it, not moving it, as he worked. Urho rubbed his head, alternately soothing and tugging roughly on his hair, making him hiss.

"That's my sweet omega, eager to please."

Xan groaned. He loved being called an omega. It completed him like a hole being filled, almost as satisfying as his ass being plugged with Urho's cock. Still, he wanted more, something harder—something that would leave reminders to cherish in the city.

He pulled away, sitting on his heels and wiping his mouth with the back of his hand. He met Urho's eyes defiantly, a hint of challenge, and then reached for the belt he'd put on the bed. "I think you should remind your omega who's in charge," he whispered, letting the leather of the belt slip around his forearm, dragging cool and scary over his skin. "I might forget. In the city." His breath came in short gasps. "So many handsome alphas. So many temptations."

Urho's nostrils flared. "Who does your hole belong to?"

Xan groaned and handed the belt to Urho. "Remind me."

Urho gripped Xan's chin. "You want this?"

Xan nodded and gulped.

"If you say for me to stop, I'll stop."

Xan shivered. He wouldn't ask Urho to quit. He wanted this like air. Marks on his ass. Evidence of possession. Urho's marks. Urho's ownership of his body and soul. His father and inheritance be damned. This was his place—at Urho's feet, licking his balls and whining to be fucked.

"Get over here." Urho gripped the back of Xan's neck, dragging him close again.

Nestled between Urho's legs, with Urho's hard cock pressed against his cheek, he breathed in the scent of Urho's body. Urho bent low, kissed Xan's hair, murmured his love, and then pulled him roughly up into position. He wrapped one of his own legs over both of Xan's to hold him firmly in place and pushed Xan's body across his thigh, torso on the mattress, face in the sheets.

"Remember, if you say stop, I'll stop."

"Just do it!" Xan urged, sweat popping out as he struggled slightly against Urho's hold. "Maybe you're not sure who I belong to." He spoke with a bratty edge. "Maybe you don't know if I'm—" The sound of the belt in the air shut Xan up fast. He sucked in a breath and then grunted in pain, biting down on the sheets as a slash of heat sliced over his ass. "Fuck!" he cried when he could breathe again.

Urho wasn't joking around. He'd laid the belt down *hard*. Sweat popped out all over Xan's body as he panted. All thoughts of anything in the city, or anything outside of the moment were driven from his head.

"Who does your hole belong to?" Urho muttered.

Out of the corner of his eye, Xan saw Urho's arm raise again. He whimpered, the word "you" caught in his throat. He groaned,

"Show me."

Urho let the belt fly and Xan shuddered, his legs pushing against Urho's as the pain ripped through him, so harsh it rattled him inside and out. Another slap of the belt came, and then another. Xan was sweating and begging and not sure what he wanted now.

"Who does your hole belong to?" Urho asked again, his voice grim and firm.

Xan's voice shook as he rasped out, "Show me."

The pain was rough but laced with gold. Xan dropped into it, opening up to a glowing, empty place that seemed brighter than the sun and infinite. He burned in it happily, surrendering to the twitching, sharp thud of the belt falling on him again and again. He melted into a hot puddle of tears, sweat, and saliva as control evaporated and he breathed between the strokes.

"Who does your hole belong to?" The question pierced the brilliant, hot place where Xan sobbed and breathed in ragged, rushing gasps.

"You," Xan whimpered, his heart swelling with pride. "I belong to you. Your omega."

"*My* omega," Urho said, dropping the belt and rubbing both hands over Xan's trembling flanks and down over his flaming ass cheeks. "When you sit on this delicious ass of yours, you'll remember who you belong to—who you are. No matter what the world says, no matter what your father claims, you're not weak. You're strong. My omega is strong as wolf-god's love and braver than wolf-god's own apprentice."

Xan wept softly into the bed, his body aching through and through. He let Urho pamper his ass, rubbing lotion and other creams into it. And then he crawled up the bed to collapse on his stomach, spreading his legs and inviting Urho in. "Fuck me," Xan whimpered. "Use me. Make me your hole."

"*I'll* decide what to do with my omega's hole," Urho muttered, gently pushing Xan's burning cheeks apart and leaning in to kiss and lick his most intimate spot.

Xan groaned, his body shaking as Urho's tongue penetrated him. With each wet flick against the rim, followed by a deep press in, his legs trembled, and his cock twitched. He grew unbearably aware of the thudding in his cock, still stiff and growing stiffer, pounding with the beat of his heart.

Urho pulled back before returning with oiled up fingers, pressing two inside immediately. Xan hissed at the slight burn, but then got up onto his knees to push back for more. "Hurry," he whimpered. "I need it."

Urho moaned and tapped Xan's sore ass, making him clench and cry out. "Mouthy pup. Do you need to feel my hand?"

Xan groaned and nodded wildly. "Yes. Do it. Spank me."

Urho slapped his ass twice, fucking in and out with his fingers as he did, and Xan shuddered all over, pain and pleasure rocking him. He almost came when Urho smacked his ass again just as his fingers pushed against Xan's prostate.

Xan gripped his own nipples, pinching them firmly, trying to hold back and teetering on the edge. He didn't want to come without Urho's dick inside him.

"Please, Urho," he begged. "Please."

It was the magic word, just as he'd believed as a child, because Urho oiled up his cock and shoved the massive head into him, holding Xan's hips steady as he forced it inside.

"Fuck!" Xan shouted, head tipping back, lost in the pleasure-pain and shuddering all over. The pressure on his prostate grew as Urho pushed unrelentingly deeper, his cock head shoving over Xan's gland, and then the fat shaft rubbing it with each inch inside.

"Mmm," Urho murmured approvingly. "Open up. So tight around me. Look at your hole sucking me in. Such a good omega.

My omega."

Xan clenched the blankets and bore down, taking Urho as fully inside as possible until the scratchy crinkle of his pubic hair was pressed into Xan's sore ass cheeks.

"You're going to remember who you belong to," Urho said, sliding out and then shoving in roughly. Xan jerked and spurted pre-come onto the bed, his cock jolted by the shock of pleasure. "You're going to keep this hole just for me."

Xan whimpered. "Always."

"You're going to remember what's important, *who's* important."

"Yes."

"This is important, Xan. This. Us." He fucked him rough and steady, his hips pushing pain through Xan with every slap of body against body. "Fuck everything else," he grunted. "You're mine."

Xan reveled in the words, the possessive fuck, and the way Urho held him firm to take every single inch with each thrust. His legs twitched and kicked in spasms as he rode the delicious and rough thrusts, and his asshole convulsed in pleasure that echoed all over his body in waves of bliss so intense that it left him crying out. His cock pulsed and spurted pre-come, and his heart pounded faster and faster, until he braced himself against the swell and push of oncoming climax.

He reached for his cock, gripping it as Urho fucked into him roughly. His vision whited out, his nipples tingled, and his balls drew up tight. His orgasm ripped through him, copious jets of alpha come streaking the bed, splattering his thighs, and slicking his stomach.

Behind him, Urho shouted his joy. He pressed in deep, his cock swelling and firing off loads of come into Xan's aching ass. Urho kissed his shoulders madly, his whimpers of pleasure like little bits of soul that Xan could take in, swallow down. Urho's cock shuddered deep inside, and the sensation triggered an echo of Xan's climax, so that he quaked and came again, too.

"Let me see," Urho murmured when they had calmed down. He carefully withdrew from Xan's body, and then spread his cheeks wide, looking for the sweet evidence of his pleasure leaking from Xan's ass, as he always did these days. "That's my good omega." He swiped at the leaking come and rubbed it into the skin of Xan's sore buttocks. "Anti-inflammatory properties," he muttered. "It will help."

Xan whimpered and let Urho turn him over. "Wow," he whispered. "You know how to use that belt."

Urho smiled lovingly. "You have tender skin. I wasn't as rough as I could have been. I'd say that by tomorrow you won't even have bruises. Maybe a little sensitivity is all."

"It felt rough," Xan said, a bit of embarrassment flaring that he'd cried so hard over what, it turned out, were soft blows.

"I know." Urho kissed his mouth and settled in beside him, cuddling close. "And you're strong enough to take more, but I didn't want to leave you hurting on your trip. I don't ever want to hurt you, Xan. Not like…"

"It would never be like that." Xan turned to Urho urgently. "Because I love you. And…" He swallowed. He hadn't ever said these words aloud, even though Urho had admitted to the feeling, yet somehow it felt like a bigger thing to own. "And you love me."

"I do." Urho scented Xan's hair and neck. "You smell happy— like come and bliss. Like a little bit of pain enhances your pleasure."

"Yes," Xan gripped Urho's face. "It does."

"Because you're brave and strong and *mine*," Urho said, as if Xan's love of intense sensations and determination to experience them were something he could own.

"I won't forget." Xan clenched his anus, relieved to feel the twinge that he knew would at least follow him into the next day even if the spanking didn't.

"Nap now."

"Or I could ride you," Xan suggested, his cock jerking helplessly at the idea, but still not ready to return fully to life. Urho's was also soft again, and a part of Xan was saddened by that, but relieved too.

Urho tucked Xan in next to him, keeping an arm around him. "Sleep. The time will come to leave for the train and I'll have left you more worn out than ever."

"You leave me full of you." Xan squeezed his hole around the slip of come that still leaked out of him. "Full in my heart and my body. Strong in my soul."

Urho kissed his hair. "I love you, my strong, brave man. Now sleep."

CHAPTER TWENTY

THE HOUSE XAN was raised in loomed large. It was three stories and two wings of solid brick and full of mixed memories. He'd arrived too late the night before to dare go straight from the train station to his parents' house. So he'd spent the night in his own home, pulling the dust covers from his old bed and ignoring the drafty, creaking, lonesomeness of the entirely empty house. The residual soreness of his ass had provided a good distraction, though, and he'd rubbed it until he'd fallen asleep.

He'd called several times that morning and had finally spoken with the groundskeeper, a man named Berst who'd been working for the Heelies family since Xan was a child.

After confirming that Ray and his pater were both under quarantine in the house and not admitted to the local hospital—apparently for privacy reasons—he'd headed directly over, the morning sun shining pale on the unnaturally quiet city streets.

He'd managed not to think about it too much on the way over, but now, with the weight of worry, shame, and foreboding on his shoulders, he didn't know if he had the courage to ring the bell.

Time it was he had his own key and called this place his home. Then he'd contracted with Caleb and made a new home with him on the other side of town. But surely there was no home like the one that held all the memories of his youth. How he'd missed it! But once the rumors of Xan's perversions reached his father's ears, he'd been banned from visiting the Heelies house at all, or from meeting his pater outside of it.

He hadn't come all this way to stand outside the house and stare. He lifted his hand and rang the bell. It played the same chiming notes he remembered.

"Young Mr. Heelies!" Joon, the old, bald butler, glanced quickly over his shoulder after opening the door. Stepping onto the front stoop, he shut the door behind him. "Mr. Xan, you can't come inside."

"I want to see my pater and Ray."

Joon swallowed hard, clearly conflicted. "Your father expressly ordered that you're not allowed in the house. That's been true for months now, sir. And, well, the orders haven't changed."

"They're very sick," Xan said. It stood to reason that should change things.

"Yes." Joon's eyes cast down and his ruddy skin paled.

"I want to see them."

Joon wiped at his brow, his eyes blinking rapidly. "Your father is with your pater every moment of the day."

"I'm not afraid of my father." Xan's voice quavered, and Joon's skeptical expression let him know that he hadn't sounded convincing enough.

"I'd be fired, sir, if I let you in the house."

"So you won't let me see him? Or Ray?"

"Your brother's very poorly as well." Joon frowned. "But your father only visits him in the mornings." He scratched behind his ear nervously. "I could probably sneak you in to see Ray with no one the wiser. Though it's a dangerous mission, sir. The contagion is severe and your love for your brother won't necessarily protect you from catching it."

Xan studied Joon, taking in the familiar fond worry etched in the old beta servant's eyes, and nodded. "I'd like to see him, please." He'd make sure Ray was being cared for and then he'd see his pater, come hell or high water.

Following Joon through the marble-floored foyer and up the grand staircase, he noticed the sepulcher-like quiet of the mansion that was usually bustling with servants. "Where are the others?" he whispered.

Joon glanced back over his shoulder. "The ones not too sick to come in to work are needed at home caring for family members who've come down with this virulent, horrendous flu. There's only me and the cook left well enough to care for the house and your family."

"Aren't you worried that you'll get sick too?"

"I've never had the flu once in my life," Joon said, as though the insinuation that he might take ill was an insult. "And Cook, it seems, is immune to it as well. He's been helping feed all the sick families in the neighborhood, but he remains healthy as an ox."

"It's that bad here in the city then?"

"It's a wave of death, Mr. Heelies." Joon glanced at him curiously. "It hasn't reached Virona?"

"Only just. Janus brought it with him. We've been advised to keep him isolated, so it doesn't spread to the town."

"If they keep the trains running, it's only a matter of time before Virona is down with it, too. The doctors are run ragged here. They've brought some in from the countryside to help out, but this strain is too strong and moving too quickly for them to keep up."

Xan thought of Urho in Virona, and he could clearly imagine the mixed feelings this knowledge would bring up for him. He'd want to be here helping, but he would also want to ensure Vale and the baby's health first.

Once that was taken care of, though, there was no doubt in Xan's mind that Urho would put aside his sworn promises to stay in Virona with him and Caleb. He'd want to leave for the city immediately to do his duty as a doctor. And he should. But Xan hated the idea of Urho walking into the heart of this contagion like an armorless warrior into a lion's den.

But wasn't that exactly what he'd done himself? He wondered if Urho was worried about him. The thought gave him a warm glow. How strange to think he might be cared for even in his absence, and how sweet to feel certain that he was.

"Your brother was brought here last week by his omega friend who had found him passed out on his apartment floor. He'd already tried the hospitals, but they were full, and no doctor could be reached."

"What friend is this?"

"He didn't leave his name, sir." Joon cleared his throat awkwardly.

Xan suspected there was more to the story, but Joon put his finger to his lips as they passed the wing to his parents' rooms. Xan held his breath until they were behind the door of the "nursery wing," as they still called the hallway of rooms that had belonged to the Heelies children.

They stepped silently down the corridor past Xan's old room, then his long-dead brother Jordan's still-intact room, and stopped in front of Ray's room—usually only used during Autumn Nights feast weeks—at the end of the long length of blue carpet.

Joon nodded at the door. "He'll likely be asleep, sir. I'll leave you to it and don't linger too long. I'd hate for your presence to upset Mr. Heelies. He's already quite distraught over your pater and brother being so very sick."

"Thank you for letting me in, Joon."

The old man hugged Xan and patted his back, bringing a flood of fond memories of childhood. "You're a good boy. I'm sorry for all of this...this...." He shrugged, obviously not sure how to encompass all that he was sorry for in the lives of the Heelies family. Then he hustled on down the hall and closed the doors to the wing behind him.

Coughing came from Ray's bedroom, and Xan pushed the door open, stepping in carefully. It was gloomy and close inside, with the scent of sweat and sickness rising up all around him. It filled his nostrils, and he gagged slightly, holding in the horror at finding his brother so very ill. He wondered when his sheets had last been changed though he hated to doubt the dedication of Joon's care.

He crossed to the windows and opened the curtains slightly, letting fresh, morning light into the room. Ray stirred in the bed, coughing and moaning softly.

"Ray?" Xan asked, crossing to him.

Beneath layers of sheets and blankets, Ray shivered violently. Xan gasped. Ray was sweaty and sickly, with dark circles like stains beneath his eyes. His nose was red and sore-looking, and his lips dry and crusty. "Wolf-god," Xan swore under his breath.

Ray's cheeks blazed with fever, and his eyes as he blinked them open were glassy. "Xan?" He sounded so uncertain that Xan wondered if he'd been having hallucinations from his fever.

"It's me. I'm here. Let me help you drink some water." He turned to the pitcher and glass beside the bed.

"You can't—" Ray shook his head, coughing hard. "You can't be here. You have to leave."

"Father can't keep me away from you and Pater. Not when you need my help."

"Joon takes care of me," Ray said. His voice was a rasping version of its former warm, thick tenor. "The heirs need to stay well. This isn't a typical flu, Xan. People are dying."

"But not you," Xan said, touching his brother's cheek and almost hissing at the heat. "You're going to be just fine."

Ray shuddered and coughed again. Xan hustled into the bathroom and ran the tap. Once he had a cold, wet cloth, he hurried back to his brother. "What are they doing for the fever?"

"Elderflower tea and tablets."

"I'll get more for you."

Ray didn't protest, clearly too sick and weak to argue. Xan's heart ached, and his fingers shook as he stroked his brother's hair off his forehead with the cool cloth. "I'll be right back. We're going to get this fever down. No arguments."

Ray said nothing, his eyes so glassy and distant that it made Xan's insides quiver.

The house was still quiet as he took the back stairs down to the hall where his pater's study and the telephone resided. He paused outside the doorway, listening for any sound, but there was nothing. Unsurprising since his father was, according to Joon, with his pater every moment.

Standing next to the massive oak desk, he dialed the house in Virona. It rang five times before Ren picked up and Xan sent him for Urho.

While he waited, he gazed around the room, taking in the family portrait across the wall. His father stood tall and proud, his big hand resting on his seated pater's shoulder, while Xan and Ray stood off to the side. It had been made when Xan graduated from high school before his failures became too well-known for his father to ignore.

Xan stared at the painting. His father's dark, curly hair, so like Xan's, and his bright blue eyes were striking. He was bigger than Xan could ever hope to be, muscular and handsome, with a strong jaw and a masculine cruelty to his features. His pater, though, was nearly opposite in his looks: slight and short, with light brown hair and hazel eyes. Almost unremarkably bland in appearance. Handsome, yes, but in a dull, easily overlooked way. Of course, they were both older now, in their early sixties, but they were much the same.

Xan's eyes drifted next to the portrait of his pater when he was young, and the photograph of Jordan, an alpha, given a place of pride over the fireplace.

He wondered about Jordan sometimes. Xan had been so young when Jordan died that he didn't remember him. And his pater never spoke of him, not even when he made his yearly visits to the graveyard to leave flowers on the stone. His father, on the other hand, spoke fondly of his lost son—memories of swimming in the sea together in the Lofton house, and Ray teaching Jordan to ride a bicycle while Father ran uselessly behind saying, "Pedal! Pedal!"

Xan wondered if his father would speak so fondly of him if he were gone. He imagined not.

He was relieved to shove aside morbid thoughts when Urho's voice came on the line. "Xan, is all well?" Urho sounded troubled.

The rasp of his voice was enough to make Xan relax and breathe a sigh of relief. This was a man who loved him. This was an alpha who'd take his demise very much to heart. "No," Xan murmured, collapsing into his father's giant leather desk chair and rubbing his forehead. He was so damn glad to have Urho in his life. "My brother isn't being well-tended here. It's not the staff's fault. Everyone is gone except for old Joon and the cook. They're trying to hold the place together."

"Wolf-god. Do you need me to…" Urho trailed off, and Xan knew he'd bitten off an offer to come down to the city. His commitment to Vale and the baby prevented that. And as much as Xan wanted him here, to feel his steady presence and have his support—not to mention get his help in caring for Ray—he understood the promises Urho needed to keep.

"Ray's fever is very high," Xan went on. "They've given him elderflower tea and tablets, but there must be something else I can do to help him. I think he's been hallucinating from the fever."

"Isn't there a doctor who—"

"No. None. The epidemic here is beyond what we realized in Virona. Every doctor is occupied."

Urho was silent for a long minute but then he finally said in a no-nonsense tone that gave Xan strength, "Go to my house. Upstairs, in my bedroom, there is a cupboard with medicines inside. The tin with the willow-tree label has tablets normally reserved for doctors alone and given for only the worst fevers. Take the whole tin with you, but only dose Ray and your pater twice a day. There's also a bottle with black elderberry on it and a dark star on the brand's label. That's a prescription strength whole system booster. It also relieves congestion and over-production of mucus. Give it three times daily, with or without meals."

"Will your servants let me in?" Xan felt doubtful that the men he'd glimpsed in Urho's house would trust his word alone, and they shouldn't. No doubt they'd be protective of Urho's place with the city turned upside down with sickness.

"I'll call them." Then Urho added, a hint of worry in his voice, "Hopefully they're well."

"Surely they would have called you if they weren't?"

"I'd like to think so," Urho said, but he didn't sound convinced. "But you're safe?"

"So far," Xan replied with a snort. He didn't know how safe he'd be if his father discovered him in the house.

"Wash your hands in hot water, as hot as you can stand, after visiting the sick rooms and any time you can. Please, Xan, for the love of wolf-god, stay well."

"I'll try." His stomach fluttered, and a tender fondness that he wanted to roll up in like a blanket washed over him. "You too."

"I'm not worried about me."

Xan smiled. "I know. That's my job."

Urho huffed softly. "You should go. The sooner you get the medication into them, the faster the fever will drop."

Xan hesitated another moment and then confessed, "I'm not sure if I leave the house that I'll be granted access back inside. My father doesn't know I'm here. Our oldest beta servant snuck me in to see Ray."

"I believe in you. If you want back in that house, you'll find a way."

Xan pondered the problem once he hung up, not wanting to further involve Joon in his mission. He closed his eyes and considered. The answer presented itself almost immediately. Jason had always called him a wily thing and smarter than his grades suggested.

At the moment, Xan was willing to think he might have been right.

AT URHO'S HOUSE, the door swung open before he'd even rung the bell.

"Mr. Heelies, I'm Mako," the tall, casually dressed, middle-aged beta servant said, with a kind, welcoming smile. "I'm Dr. Chase's cook and, unfortunately," he clucked his teeth, "the only servant not ill."

Xan shook his head in amazement. The more he heard about this flu, the more he marveled at the intensity of it. Maybe he *should* be more frightened. "I'm so sorry to hear everyone has taken sick. Is there anything I can do?"

"No," Mako said, waving him inside. "I'm caring for the others and Dr. Chase has given me permission to use some of his medications. All in all, we've been lucky."

Xan scooted by him and into the posh foyer. He gazed up at the vaulted ceiling as he had the first time he'd come and let Mako take his coat. Once it was hung neatly in the foyer closet, Mako gestured at the staircase.

"His room is up there, at the back of the house. I'll let you find it on your own, sir. He's private and I don't normally go in there.

That's normally the housekeeper's job and since he's sick…" Mako shrugged helplessly. "I did go in earlier, though, and take the medication he said we could have."

"I'm sure that's fine. And, it's all right. I can find it myself."

"It's the last room, sir. Make yourself at home. Dr. Chase said to give you free rein of the house."

Xan smiled at Mako. "Thank you."

The banister was cool under his fingers. The entire house smelled like Urho's clothing usually did, or at least had before he came to Virona. It was warm, a little spicy, and somehow there was a hint of old pipe tobacco. Though, as far as Xan knew, Urho didn't smoke.

He followed the curve of the stairs up, and then around. The hallway was dark and cool, and he spotted the door near the end that must lead to Urho's bedroom.

Reaching it, he hesitated. Until that moment, he hadn't realized he'd hoped for something very different the first time he was granted access to Urho's bedroom—something more intimate, and sexier for sure. But this inner sanctuary, which even Mako admitted was special to Urho, seemed like such a revered place now that he had his hand on the door.

He wished Urho was here with him and that instead of fetching medicines for his brother and pater, his lover was bringing him to this room to share it with him.

Shaking off his disappointment, he opened the door and paused inside. The room was beautiful, but it looked nothing like Urho's tastes to him. On one wall there was a large painting of the ocean, full waves flooding over white sand and blue skies colliding with blue water.

Urho loved the ocean; that much was true. Xan had walked alongside it with him every day since Urho had arrived in Virona. But he didn't seem the kind of man to want the ocean in his bedroom, especially this cheerful, lively rendition of it.

The other wall was a mirror, reflecting the bed and the windows. Blue, gauzy curtains floated over the sparkling, clear panes of glass, light and airy. It was a gentle room, a youthful one, full of air and water, and a sense that laughter should ring tirelessly in the air around him. It was nothing like the staid, serious, intense man Xan had come to love.

For a moment, Xan wondered if he'd misjudged Urho so deeply, that this would be his bedroom. How was it that he understood so little of his lover that his most personal space would seem foreign and strange to him?

And then he realized.

The room had been decorated by Riki.

He sucked in a breath, shocked by the sharp pain he felt. No, he didn't want to have this reaction. It wasn't generous. It wasn't loving. It wasn't even kind.

He frowned, shook himself, and headed toward the medicine cupboard Urho had told him about. Ray and Pater were sick and there was really no time to lose in unwanted self-pity and silly jealousy. He opened the wooden chest carefully and looked inside for the tin with the willow-tree branding. He found it easily and pocketed it. Then he took the bottle with the black elderberry and the dark star.

As he turned back to the door, his eyes lingered on the bed and, against his will, his nose wrinkled. He couldn't imagine Urho taking him here, fucking him on this bed that was still so obviously Riki's. His heart knotted up, tangled between emotions, useless and strange.

His eyes landed on another door, half-open and, oddly, already lit from within by a lightly glowing electric lamp. He hesitated, something inside telling him that he'd only been granted permission to look in one cupboard.

And yet…

He had the door to the smaller room open before he'd fully made the decision to invade Urho's privacy in this way.

The painting above the desk of a pregnant Riki was, at first, all he could see. He couldn't tear his eyes away from the handsome, happy blond man, with his hand on his bulging belly. Pregnant with Urho's child—something Xan could never be. Bitterness filled his mouth.

Xan's hands shook slightly as he stepped deeper into the room and recognized it for what it was: a shrine. Urho's *Érosgápe* was forever worshiped here as his other half, as his soul mate, as the completion that Urho's very cells longed for day in and out forever.

The photos of them as young men burned into Xan's eyes. There were several of a baby-faced young Riki with a pipe in his mouth. He touched the picture with his index finger, smudging a subtle layer of dust.

"So that's where the lingering tobacco scent comes from," he muttered to himself.

Even all these years later? Did it truly linger so long, or was Riki's ghost present in the house, here for Urho in death as he'd been in life?

Xan shuddered. He didn't belong in this room. It wasn't his. This was a part of Urho that he didn't have permission to know about, and could never, ever fully share. He backed out of the chamber of grief—the shrine to two lives cut short, a joy that was never to be—and into Riki's bedroom again.

Xan couldn't think of it as Urho's bedroom at all.

He turned around, taking in the evidence that Urho had never moved on, and he girded himself against the rising tide of feelings. He didn't have time for them. He didn't want them. They were useless and ugly, and he wasn't going to give into them.

Hustling out of the room and down the stairs, he called to Mako over his shoulder as he grabbed his own coat from the closet. "Thank you, Mako. I have to go. I have what I need." Then, belatedly, "Please contact me at…" he didn't know where to say. "Please contact my house in Virona if you need anything. Urho will make sure you have it."

Mako stepped from the gloom behind the stairs and smiled at him. "Thank you, Mr. Heelies. You're always welcome here." Then he pressed a bag into his hand. "Food, sir. You look hungry."

"Thank you. I am."

"Anything for Dr. Chase's friends."

Xan smiled but didn't wait for Mako to open the front door for him. With the bag in hand, he dashed out, the frosty wind of lingering winter stinging his eyes, and he climbed into his father's silver new Sabel-made car. He quickly stuffed some of the sandwich Mako had given him into his mouth as he started the engine.

He drove back to his parents' home with the keys to the garage—and thus the house—hanging from the keychain. Whether his father liked it or not, Xan would not be denied.

CHAPTER TWENTY-ONE

Ray was asleep when Xan let himself carefully back into his brother's room. No one had seen him enter from the garage, and when he crept past his parents' wing, he'd heard only coughing and the light sounds of his pater's favorite music drifting down the hall. It'd touched him to imagine his father bringing the record player up and playing the soft, lyrical songs his *Érosgápe* loved best.

But as he stood by Ray's bedside, a glass of cold water in one hand and the pill from Urho's tin in the other, he frowned at the fear that kept him from simply stalking down the hall and demanding to see his pater immediately.

He took a deep breath, steeled himself, and determined that he was going to see his pater that night. It was only a matter of when and how bad it was all going to be. In the meantime, he had Ray to help.

"Ray," he whispered, trying not to startle his brother. "Wake up. I have medicine for you."

Ray stirred and stared at Xan, brow furrowed. Confusion marred his usually perceptive gaze. "I thought you were a dream."

"No. I just had to get a prescription filled for you." Filled from Urho's private stock, but that seemed too complicated to explain. "Some new medicine. For the fever."

Ray was too weak to sit up by himself, so Xan helped him. The pill went down easily, and Ray drank most of the water as Xan encouraged him. "That's it. You're doing so well."

"I miss Vince," Ray whispered when he was done, collapsing

back and staring at the ceiling.

"Who?" Xan asked.

Ray shook his head. "No one. Never mind."

Xan sat with his brother, cooling him with a bowl of cold water and cloth, dosing him again, and waiting through the morning and afternoon for the medicine to take effect. He knew the moment it really started to work because Ray's eyes grew less hazy, and he narrowed his focus on Xan curiously.

"Did Father let you come home, then? Is Pater...?" He swallowed hard and looked away, but then back again, searching Xan's face for the truth before he might speak it.

"Pater is very sick," Xan admitted. "But I haven't seen him yet. Joon told me Father is with him night and day, every second, though he comes to visit you in the mornings."

Ray looked toward the open curtains, taking in the setting sun. "Father doesn't know you're here."

"No," Xan said, standing up and taking the bowl of water and cloth into the bathroom. "But he will. Soon. I just needed to see you on the mend. This medication Urho..." He stopped himself just in time. "This medication my friend Dr. Chase sent seems to be doing the job."

Ray coughed as Xan returned to the room. "You're taking a risk. You might get sick and then everything will be left to Janus." His lips twisted half-heartedly into a sickly smile. "You don't want to leave me and the company to Janus's not-so-tender mercy, do you?"

Xan smiled, so relieved to hear Ray teasing him again. He left the topic of Janus aside, not wanting to say too much until he had more information on how his cousin was faring. "Let's get you in the shower. You smell disgusting and you'll feel a lot better."

"Well, so long as I smell nice enough not to offend you, little brother," Ray said with a wry smile.

But he was far too weak to get out of bed on his own. Xan

helped him into the bathroom and under the spray of the shower. He steadied him and washed him, his heart aching at finding the older brother he'd always admired as weak as a baby.

As he dried off Ray, his brother's eyes went distant again. "Xan, I need you to do something for me."

"Anything. Of course."

"I have a friend, an omega friend..." Ray frowned slightly, and then cleared his throat. "A lover. I know it's not as big a deal for uncontracted omegas to be involved with betas, but he's ashamed. We aren't..." Ray waved a thin hand around. "I care for him. But he..." He sighed and seemed to lose the thread before coming back to it. "I need to know if he's all right. He was with me when I got sick."

"This is Vince?"

Ray nodded. "Vince Ross. He lives in the Calitan district."

Xan's surprised expression must have reached Ray through his exhaustion and worry, because he said, "Yes, he's a prostitute."

"There are a lot of folks who live in Calitan that aren't prostitutes."

"Well, Vince is." Ray seemed drained as he let Xan lead him back to the bedroom.

Xan pressed him into a chair next to the open window. "I'm going to change the sheets and bedding."

"Joon does that."

"Today I'm doing it."

Xan left Ray coughing hard into his fist and found the linen closet right where he'd left it the last time he'd needed to change his own bed sheets after inappropriate dreams of Jason back before he'd moved out.

"Will you make sure Vince is all right?" Ray asked again when Xan returned.

Xan stripped the bed of the dirty sheets. "Do you know his

telephone number?"

Ray shook his head. "He doesn't have a phone. He doesn't live like we do."

"No, of course not." He pushed the pile of dirty bedclothes out the door and into the hall with his feet before coming back in to put on the fresh sheets.

"He works the corner by the Lincoln Deli. If he's healthy, he'll be there," Ray said, almost pleadingly. It was a tone Xan had never heard him use before. "Can you check on him?"

Xan finished up the pillowcases and fluffed the fresh duvet. "If he's not healthy, then what?"

"Ask around. The owner of the deli lets him sleep in the apartment over the shop sometimes if he doesn't have a client. He'll know if Vince isn't well…" Ray coughed violently and hacked up a large wad of mucous.

Xan shuddered but grabbed a handkerchief for him to spit it into. Then he gave him a dose of the black elderberry syrup Urho had said was for congestion and worked as a whole system booster.

"If he's not well, can you see that he gets some help?" Ray coughed again, but not so deeply. He wiped at his eyes and sighed. "I feel so much better since that pill. What was it?"

"I'm not sure. My friend Dr. Chase told me to give it to you. He said it was a new drug reserved for the worst fevers."

"Your *friend* Dr. Chase, huh?" Ray said softly, his tired eyes gone gray in the descending twilight coming in from the windows.

"Let's get you back in bed."

"But Vince—" Ray said, breaking off with a deeply earnest plea written on his face.

"I'll check on him soon."

"Lincoln Deli," Ray said again.

"Right. I'll remember."

The rest of the evening passed with Xan pacing by Ray's bed, fretting as his fever spiked and his coughing worsened. He administered Urho's drugs again as soon as he believed it was safe and was desperately relieved when Ray's fever broke. After a solid coughing fit, he fell into a deep sleep.

Once Ray was out, Xan held the tin in one hand and the bottle of black elderberry syrup in the other, like talismans against his own fear. When Joon had come earlier to check on Ray, Xan had given him tablets to slip to Pater. Xan didn't want Pater to wait for medicine that could help him while Xan gathered his so-called courage to walk down the hall and face Father.

He stood by Ray's window, looking out on the usually busy street below. Now it was silent, and not only because it was nighttime. The city was in the throes of this illness and it wasn't letting go. He'd noted it on both the ride to his own house from the station in the taxi and during the drive to Urho's place. The usually bustling city now looked like a resort town during the off-season.

He took off his suit jacket and draped it over the nearby chair, and then undid his tie, and rolled up his shirtsleeves. Going back to the window, he took a deep breath and let it out. He wasn't going to be kept from his pater any longer. Never mind the tumbling feeling in his gut when he thought of facing down his father—of staring into the man's cold, blue eyes and telling him the way things were going to be. Demanding it. Because he was the heir, and he had rights.

He wiped his hand over his upper lip, collecting the anxious sweat. He closed his eyes, determined to be strong. He took a slow, deep breath, and gazed out the window, searching the sky for the stars. They were the same ones that shone over Virona—that shone over the whole wolf-blessed world, after all—and he focused his thoughts on Urho, expecting to find comfort and strength there.

But instead Xan's brain served up images of the sanctuary in Urho's house devoted to his lost *Érosgápe*. Xan didn't know why he'd been surprised to find that Riki still dominated Urho's most private and intimate rooms, but he had been. In truth, he'd allowed himself to nearly forget over the last several weeks that he wasn't the most beloved man in Urho's world. That he never could be.

Ray sniffled, and Xan glanced over his shoulder at him, ensuring that he hadn't woken. Seeing his brother's eyes were still shut and his breath was coming in even, long strokes, he gazed back out at the night, wishing he could see the night sky without all the light pollution of the city. The way he could back home in Virona.

Home. In Virona.

How odd that he'd come to think of it as home, but he had. He missed the sound of the waves coming in the open windows, the chill of the winter air, the scent of the sea wafting through the house or buried in a fold of bedding or clothing, and most of all he missed the sound of Urho and Caleb's voices. The men that made him truly comprehend, for the first time in his adult life, the concept of home and family. He sighed.

Xan briefly let himself entertain the fantasy they could live together and never part. Urho had obviously entertained that fantasy, too, but it was absurd. As soon as Vale had delivered the baby, and once Urho knew the state of the sickness here in the city, he'd be on his way back.

And not just for duty.

Because, while he might love Xan, even care for him deeply, he'd never have room in his heart for Xan to be his home. Not in the way he was becoming Xan's home. Not truly. All that precious space was already completely taken up by Riki—the way it should be between *Érosgápe*.

Xan had been foolish to think he could be anywhere close to as precious to Urho as Urho was becoming to him, despite all they'd shared. Despite Urho's promises. If Urho was entertaining the fantasy of staying it was only to escape the pain of having lost his

Érosgápe, but in the end, Riki's memory would win out.

Wouldn't it?

Tired of that line of self-pitying thought, Xan turned to another. He wanted to see his pater so badly he ached, yet here he was in the same house and he was cowering. Enough was enough. He would see Pater, and he would see him now.

Before he could take a step, shouts from the hallway made him jump. Hesitating for a moment, pierced through with anxiety, he strained to hear words, but could only make out shouts.

Racing out of Ray's room and down the hall toward the staircase landing, he swallowed back his terror. The shouts grew louder as he ran down the other wing toward his parents' room.

When he burst into the familiar room, his heart pounding and his pulse rushing loudly enough to obscure the cries, he came to a halt beside his parents' raised, canopied bed. The room was blazing with lights, illuminating the striped maroon wallpaper and the disarray of a sick room.

Father was the source of the commotion. He sat on the bed by Pater in rumpled pants and shirt, shouting, crying, and begging. And Pater only lay there, skinnier than Xan had ever seen, clearly unconscious, paper white, and struggling to breathe. Father clutched Pater to his chest, and between wordless shouts he called for help and a doctor. His eyes went wide when he saw Xan, confusion and rage flashing briefly beneath his utter terror, but he only shouted at him to get help and to hurry about it.

Xan climbed onto the big bed and shoved in close to his pater. His father tried to push him off. "Get help!" he shouted.

But Xan held up the medicines. Father, eyes wild, balled up his fist and reared back as though to punch him. "I said get help!"

"I have help!" Xan yelled back, a hot rush flowing into him, rage pure and strong. "I have medicine for him! Get out of my way!"

He used all of his strength to shove his father aside, wrenching his pater's limp body from his father's arms. Then he propped his pater up on the pillows as his father struggled to get between them again. The last time Xan had seen Pater, he'd been a robust, happy man. But now he looked horribly thin and scarily sick.

He didn't have time to think about that though. He shoved his father back again, opened the bottle of elderberry syrup, and managed to get some of the reddish purple syrup between his pater's lips. Father tried to get between them, a growl in his chest.

But Xan was stronger now. He'd been taking boxing lessons from Urho, and he was over thirty years younger than the frightened, tired man who was frantic for his *Érosgápe*'s life. Xan massaged Pater's throat, working the liquid medicine down as Father begged Pater to breathe.

"Please George." His voice cracked. "Please breathe, baby. Breathe, my sweetheart, my one. Breathe. Breathe."

Xan poured more syrup into his pater's mouth and hoped it didn't choke him. He couldn't be sure how much was getting into his stomach.

"Get a doctor," Father said desperately. "What are you giving him? He needs a doctor!"

Joon appeared in the doorway then, wearing pajamas and a sleep-addled expression. He gasped as he came closer to the bed. "I'll call for a doctor, sir. I'll see if I can find one."

"Call for an ambulance if necessary," Xan said over his shoulder, wondering if there were any hospitals still accepting patients.

"No!" his father shouted. "The hospitals are full of sick people. We need to keep him here away from further exposure."

Xan ignored that, watching for another moment when he could slip a bit more of the black elderberry syrup between Pater's lips. Taking the opportunity when it finally came, he was relieved when Pater finally coughed and took a deep, rattling breath. Xan administered the syrup twice more, hopefully getting the amount of a full dose into his pater.

Then he sat back, watching and praying to wolf-god above to spare Pater's life. Father seemed to do the same. No words were spoken between them, but they both heaved a sigh when, after he'd coughed up a large amount of phlegm, Pater breathed more easily.

Joon appeared again, clearly wide-awake now. "I called all the doctors on our list, sir, but every last one of them is with other patients. I left word with three to come as soon as possible."

Father nodded, brushing soft, brown hair back from Pater's face where he'd regained some coloring. "We've turned the corner again, hopefully," he said, meeting Xan's eye. "Thanks to Xan."

Xan shook his head. "Thanks to this." He held up the bottle of medication.

"Black elderberry?" his father whispered. "That's been out of stock for over a week. Even hospitals are running out."

Xan turned to Joon and asking, "Were you able to give him the willow tablet?"

Joon shook his head, looking ashamed. "I couldn't find a time to introduce the idea. I'm sorry, Mr. Xan, I know I promised. But he was sleeping so well earlier. I hated to wake him, and your father said he thought Mr. Lofton was coming around on his own."

Xan pressed his hand to pater's forehead and then looked his father in the eye. "If you'll help me wake him, I have another medication for fever. I gave it to Ray, and he's doing much better now."

Father stared at him for a long moment before nodding. He lifted up Pater and patted his cheeks gently. "Darling, wake up. Can you hear me, George? I need you to wake up."

Pater's lashes fluttered, and with obvious effort he pried his lids apart. He sought out his alpha's face, and when he saw him, he smiled softly. "Doxan?"

"Shh. Don't try to talk right now. Xan's here."

Pater's eyes opened wider, a spark firing deep in them. He sought out Xan, and a weary smile spread over his face. Xan took hold of one of Pater's hands and squeezed.

"I'm here."

Pater licked his lips, but his mouth was too dry to talk.

"Get him some water," Father said. Joon was there instantly with a glass.

Father and Xan held Pater up so he could drink, and when he was done, he lay back on his pillow, exhausted but staring up at Xan with hungry eyes.

"You shouldn't be here," Pater finally rasped. "You'll get sick, too."

"I'm healthy as a horse. Don't worry about me."

Pater darted his eyes to Father. A worried expression flitted over his face, but he didn't give voice to it. Instead he turned his attention back to Xan and said, "I'm so happy to see you. I've missed you so much."

Xan's heart clenched hard, and his lips trembled. He leaned over and pressed a kiss to his pater's forehead. "I've missed you, too. I love you."

Father said nothing beside them.

Pater's eyes filled with tears. "I was afraid…"

"Shh. I'm here now."

Pater nodded slowly. "Thank wolf-god. My prayers were answered then."

Xan's heart ached. He'd missed his pater so deeply, and somehow it didn't make it hurt less to hear that his pater had felt the same. "Pater, I have medicine I need you to take," he finally said when his throat relaxed enough that he didn't think he'd burst into tears. "Right, Father?"

"Yes, George," Father whispered. "Take the pill. Xan has brought it just for you. It'll make you feel so much better, my one."

With effort, Pater sat up enough to take the small tablet with another sip of water. He smiled up at Xan as he lay back in the bed. "Your hair is different. And you look older."

Xan kissed his pater's forehead again. "Caleb's barber in Virona said this style would suit me."

"It makes you look like a man."

Father snorted, but otherwise remained quiet.

Xan squeezed Pater's hand.

"I've wanted to see you so badly," Pater whispered, his eyes filling with tears. "I thought I might never again."

Father loosed a short, hurt noise, but when Xan glanced his way, he was staring hard at the wallpaper across from the bed with a grim expression.

"You're going to get well now, and we'll see each other all the time," Xan murmured.

"I hope so."

Wanting to provide his pater with even more reason to recover, Xan said, "Caleb has a heat soon. You'll see your grandchild by next year's Autumn Feasts with any luck."

Pater's soft smile warmed Xan's heart, and they stared at each other, letting their devotion be felt. Xan curled up with his head against his pater's chest, listening to his heartbeat and feeling the soothing tug of his fingers in his hair until his father said, "He's asleep."

Sitting up, Xan saw that Pater's eyes had closed. Father touched his forehead and frowned. "Still feverish, but much better than before." He turned to where Joon stood by the door watching the events unfold. "Stay here with him. If his fever breaks, change his pajamas and the bedclothes. Xan and I have things to discuss in the library."

Joon swallowed hard and met Xan's gaze with an anxious eye, but only said, "Of course, sir. It'll be my pleasure to watch after Mr.

Lofton."

As Xan followed his father toward the staircase, his gut doing somersaults and his knees feeling like water, his father shot a glance toward the nursery wing and said, "Ray is doing better?"

"He's sleeping well. His fever has broken, and his cough seems to be under control with the elderberry syrup."

Father nodded curtly and took off down the steps at a rapid pace. Xan, shorter than his father by a good number of inches, had to work to keep up. The library was dark in the middle of the night, but it smelled exactly the same: a hint of old books and leather.

His father snapped on the light. The leather sofas positioned opposite each other next to the fireplace and the big wooden desk Xan had bent over on more than one occasion as a child to receive his father's belt for poor behavior were all illuminated with memories stretching back through his entire life.

The window with the potted palm next to it was the one he'd broken with a ball when he was seven and Ray was teaching him to hit. The child-sized chairs in the corner, clustered around a low table and surrounded by a mini-library of children's books, was where his pater had taught him to read.

Xan swallowed hard against a sudden influx of emotion, nostalgia hitting him like a weight on his chest.

"Sit," his father said, motioning toward the couches. He straightened the collar of his rumpled shirt. It looked as if he hadn't changed in days. He went to the liquor cabinet and poured only one drink.

Xan tensed at the lack of common courtesy, familiar with the disrespect inherent in it. His father never failed to offer a drink to Ray, or to Janus, or any other man he admired or, at the very least, respected. He stood defiantly.

"You shouldn't have come," Father said, turning back to Xan with a tight expression. He took a sip of his drink and crossed to the wall where the belts still hung—the ones used for punishment, the belts he used to make Xan choose between. He fingered them one-by-one and then sighed. "You're too old by far to take a belt to you now. It's a shame. It was the only way you ever behaved."

Xan grit his teeth together, a rush of fear and rage shooting through him. If he'd ever "misbehaved," it'd only been because he was a child with too much energy and no place to put it, and too many expectations on his shoulders from almost the very beginning.

His father turned to him again. "You're reckless and selfish and make decisions from your emotions. Pathetic. Useless. At this point, I'd be happy to leave the estate to Janus."

Xan's nostrils flared.

His father cocked his head and lifted a brow. "Do you know what Janus and I talked about when he was here?"

"No."

"He didn't tell you?"

Xan stared up at his father, the fear that had always underscored his interactions with him hardening into something more like loathing. He opened his mouth to tell him that Janus was sick and had brought the flu to Virona, but he clomped his lips shut again, holding that information for a later time.

"I'm surprised he didn't choose to gloat. Perhaps he's growing up after all."

Xan lifted a brow.

"We talked about a lot of things. But he regretted having to tell me about the quality of the work you're doing—or rather not doing—on the satellite office there."

Xan's soul hardened that much more. He knew it would do no good to argue that he was, in fact, the one doing the brunt of the work while Janus played around at the gentlemen's club, sucking up to people who may or may not ever become clients and wrestling other alphas for money.

Perhaps his father already knew all of that and considered *that* the greater work to be done. It didn't matter. Xan wasn't going to give his father the satisfaction of arguing with him. Not yet.

"We also talked about the arrival of Jason Sabel and his pregnant omega. I'd say that friendship is the only thing in your life you've ever done right."

Xan scoffed. If his father knew that Jason had once been his lover, he'd probably change his mind about that. Or maybe not. Perhaps the connections with the Sabel family and their estate was worth putting up with a little sexual deviance in his father's mind.

"But apparently, they weren't alone," his father said in clipped tones. "An alpha came with them. A doctor." He glared at Xan. "One Urho Chase, whom, no doubt, is the source of the medicine you gave your pater tonight."

How his father managed to make *that* sound aberrant, Xan didn't know. He took a deep breath, squared his shoulders, and lifted his chin in the face of it. He might not know anything, but he knew this: he couldn't live like this anymore. Not for one more minute.

"I'm not afraid of you," Xan said slowly. "I know that's what this 'talk' is all about. You want me to cower like I used to, promise to stay away from pater, or swear that I'll be a better son and heir to you. Well, I won't. I've taken worse hits than you ever gave me, and I did it by choice."

His father stared at him, lips flattening and a light of disgust shining in his eyes.

At least Xan's torture at Monhundy's hands was good for something. It'd shown him how much pain he could take and how little he cared for a life lived according to his father's rules. So little that he'd have let Monhundy kill him.

But no more.

Xan had something to live for now. A future promised to him

by Urho and Caleb. And he wasn't going to let anything—not his father, not his insecurities, not Urho's dead *Érosgápe*—stand in his way. He would have his home in Virona with Urho, the man he loved with all his heart. He would have his omega and friends, and he would have his children, and his pater, and his brother. And there was nothing his father could do to stop it.

He was the heir. He had rights. But so what? Perhaps he didn't even want them.

Xan stared his father down. "If you want Janus to inherit, give it all to him. But you know what you have to do in order to see to that. You'll have to proclaim the reasons in front of a judge and gain permission from the church. You'll have to say aloud, in front of everyone, what you've spent all these years pretending you don't know, pretending you can *fix*." Spittle flew from his mouth at the last word, and Xan wiped it away with the back of his hand. He stepped closer to his father. "So if you want to do that, declare me unmanned or otherwise incompetent in front of wolf-god and all your business partners and friends, go right ahead." He sneered. "I dare you to do it."

"I will," his father hissed. "You don't want to push me."

"Don't I? Don't I want to push you and push you and *push you*?" He took a step forward, arms outstretched, a nearly uncontrollable urge to shove his father held back by willpower alone.

His father jolted a step back, nearly tripping over the hearth.

"Because I'm not afraid of you, Father. Not in the least. If you disinherit me, who loses the most? You. You'll lose face and standing with everyone you know. And, worst of all, you'll lose Pater's respect." He raised a brow. "You heard Pater tonight. He loves me, even if you don't, and anything you do to harm me will hurt him. And then..." He shook his head and whispered, "Wolf-god help you."

His father sniffed and took another swallow of his liquor, but he looked a little rattled. He ran a hand into his salt-and-pepper hair. "You're disturbed," he said quietly.

"You know what I think?" Xan stepped close again. "I think you still want me to inherit. You just want me to be someone else entirely when I do it. You believe you can bully me in to being that person. And that's not going to happen."

His father stared at him.

"Janus is the sword you dangle over my head hoping that the threat of it falling will change my fundamental nature, make me more like Ray. Make me more like Jordan, the son you've made up in your mind because you can, because he's dead, and you'll never get to know what he was really like."

His father raised a hand to strike, but Xan ducked it and moved around to the other side of the sofa, as much to prevent himself from punching his father as to prevent his father from hitting him.

"You resent how Pater loves me. You're a selfish alpha who can't let his omega love even his own child. You see me as a threat to your relationship."

"Your pater is soft when it comes to you."

"He's just a good man who loves his child unconditionally." Xan sneered. "Something you don't understand."

"What have you done to earn my love?"

"That's just it. I shouldn't have to earn it. You should give it."

His father's nostrils quivered. "You're unmanned and you'll ruin us as a family."

"I'm unmanned," Xan agreed. "Nothing will change it. Not you hating me. Not you beating me with a belt. Not you keeping me from Pater. Not you disinheriting me and announcing my predilections to the world. Nothing will make me different than who I am." Xan took a deep breath, his heart pounding so hard it hurt. "If that's not something you can stomach, then go before the judge and the church. Speak the truth of me and get your estate out of my perverted hands. Leave it all to Janus. I'll survive. I'm a scrappy one and I'm tougher than I look."

His father's eyes blazed, and he tossed the rest of his liquor down before putting the glass on a nearby table with a clatter. He looked at Xan and smirked darkly. "Let's see about that."

And then he came at Xan with all the force of his powerful, tall body. He grappled Xan into a tight hold and clenched his hand around Xan's throat painfully. "Not so very tough!"

Xan elbowed him hard and swung around, bringing his hands up and guarding his face like Urho had taught him. "I don't want to hurt you, Father."

"I'm the one who's going to hurt you," his father hissed, coming at him again.

Punches landed, and Xan grunted, his breath coming in gasping bursts. The floodgates of aggression opened, and they hurtled at each other, fists and feet, even teeth came into play as they grappled.

In the end, he pushed his father to the carpet, foot to his throat. His chest heaved, but he'd done it. Gazing into his father's outraged blue eyes, he whispered, "Do what you have to do, Father. Because no matter what you choose, I'm still the son who bested you. The one who lived his truth. I'm unmanned and in love, and I'm proud of it. But I'm not proud of you."

He grabbed his father by the collar and dragged him up from the floor. It was awkward because Xan was much shorter, but his father had apparently gone slack in shock. "Make sure Pater and Ray get the rest of that medication."

Stumbling, his father ripped away from Xan and stared at him. "You're mad. Violent. Unreachable."

"I am," Xan agreed. "Do what you have to do, Father."

He turned his back and marched from the library toward the front door. He opened it and paused, hearing his father's steps behind him. He turned around, shocked to see the father he'd been so afraid of his whole life as a beaten, old, shell of a man.

"Thank you for the medicine. I'll make sure your pater and Ray get all they need of it," his father said gruffly. He limped slightly, and Xan felt a stab of regret that he'd hurt him. "As for you, don't come back. You're not welcome in this house. Your pater can come to you if he wants to spend time with his lunatic, unmanned son."

Xan gritted his teeth but said nothing.

"And don't think Joon won't face the music for allowing you in at all."

"It wasn't his doing. I broke in through the garage. But Joon can have a place with me. And you'll be left to care for Ray and Pater alone."

His father's haughty face seemed to crumple slightly as he gazed around him at the empty house echoing silently, too vast to even hold in the sounds of their argument.

"Goodbye, Father," Xan said. "Give Ray and Pater my love."

Then he slammed the door and stalked down the street, refusing to look back at the house he'd once called home. He had a new home now. And an alpha who was somehow in love with him. This, tonight with his father, was good. Hurtful. Horribly hurtful. But necessary and good.

Wiping at his damp eyes, he straightened his shoulders and started the walk to the Calitan district. His body ached where his father had gotten in a few solid thumps, but there was one more thing he needed to do for Ray before he could go back to his house in the city.

And then he'd go home to and beg Urho to stay. It might not be fair, and it might not be right, but he was going to ask him to walk away from the youthful blue ocean of his room with Riki and stay forever in Virona's gray-green ocean with Xan.

CHAPTER TWENTY-TWO

"ROSEN IS SICKER than I am," Yosef said to Urho, his tired voice somewhat sibilant with congestion over the phone. "So far neither of us are too bad off, though. And even though his fever is higher, I don't think he'll get much worse."

"Has a doctor been in to see him?" Urho asked, rubbing at his eyes and trying to figure out if there was a way for him to take a day trip down to the city to check on Rosen for himself.

"Yes, but only on the first day to confirm the flu diagnosis. He left us with some medication—not the elderberry you mentioned, but some yarrow syrup and a few other tablets."

"If he's fighting off the infection on his own, that should be good enough. Do you have plenty of fruit?"

"I haven't been able to make it out to the market."

"I'll send you something from here on the train. Fresh vegetables and some citrus fruit."

Yosef sounded exhausted as he allowed that he could use the provisions and listed the items he and Rosen could benefit from the most.

Urho didn't like the idea of not being able to do more, or of leaving his friends to fend for themselves, but he knew he couldn't break away. "I wish I could come check on Rosen myself, but we have one very sick with it here at the house. We have him in isolation and the village doctor comes up once a day, but I don't feel comfortable leaving Caleb alone right now with Xan gone into the city. He's in a vulnerable position at the moment. And then there's Vale. He could go into labor any day now."

"It's not a problem. I promise we are both going to get better. Keep Vale safe and let us know when he's delivered."

"Absolutely."

They wound up their phone conversation with good wishes for each other, and Urho muttered wolf-god's blessing for the sick before disconnecting. He leaned back at Xan's desk in the office he'd made for himself in Virona and took a long, slow breath. The air of the room was already losing the scent of Xan, and he wondered how many more days his lover would be gone.

The clock above the mantel gave an hour suitable for bed, but he was restless. He grabbed his coat and headed out to the ocean instead, finding the nighttime stroll along the beach less enjoyable without Xan there to sneak kisses and hold close as the cold water lapped at their feet.

The moon shone bright and uncaring. The winter in Virona was milder than the city, but chilly all the same. Urho wrapped his coat around tighter and stared up at the moon, the eye of wolf, and considered the wisdom of having let Xan go into the city with the contagion raging so strongly. He missed him viscerally, like a fist in his gut where ease should be.

He hadn't heard from Xan since he'd given the instructions for the medication, and he didn't know if that was good news or bad. He wasn't even sure how to get in touch with him, or if he'd be staying with his parents or in his own home. Their conversation had been short and to the point.

Urho strode down the beach, feeling hemmed in by the ocean in front of him and the house at his back. He resented feeling so hamstrung by his commitments. He wanted to follow the man who was, inch by steady inch, making an impossibly deep claim on his heart.

By the time he'd walked back up to the house, he'd resolved to call Xan's place if he hadn't heard from him by midnight and his parents' house if he hadn't heard from him by morning.

Just to be sure he was safe.

Because something in Urho's bones didn't feel right.

He didn't know how or why, but he was certain that Xan needed him. And that made him nervous. He'd come to know Xan better over the last few weeks, but there were still many things about the man that were a mystery.

Like what might prompt him to hurt himself with a visit to his monster.

And that thought alone made Urho sick to his stomach with worry and pain. Instead of heading up to bed, he went to Xan's office in the back of the library and sat by the phone, listlessly turning the pages of a book in his hand, waiting for a reason to believe his worry was unfounded.

XAN KEPT HIS eye out for a taxi, but the roads of the Calitan District were virtually empty. His hands stuffed into the pockets of his coat, he shivered in the darkness. It was a long walk home, but he didn't mind. It gave him time to think about all that had happened since he'd arrived from Virona.

Prostitutes lingered up and down the street outside the Lincoln Deli. He thought about branching off, but the other roads looked dim and seedy, and altogether vacant of human life. It seemed safer to stroll with the "'tutes", as Vince had called them, than to walk entirely alone.

Ray's lover hadn't been like any omega Xan had ever met. Big and beefy with a thick beard, he'd looked far more like a beta. He'd wept with joy when Xan had told him Ray lived, and had shared a bottle of brandy with Xan, refusing to take any money from him.

Xan's head swam now with too much alcohol as he walked. He had so many questions about his brother's relationship with Vince, but he supposed it was Ray's mess to figure out. Still, perhaps he'd let Xan help once he recovered from the flu. Because he would recover—there was no question.

Xan was near the shipping district now, and the prostitutes who'd been his companions thus far were thinning out. He glanced at the road that led toward more roads that eventually wound home. It was dark and eerily silent. He pulled up his coat collar and contemplated asking one of the streetwalkers where he could find a place to sleep for the night. Alone.

A new, top-of-the-line Sabel car pulled up alongside him, its engine purring in the quiet. He frowned, tightening his coat around him as the driver rolled the window down.

"Selling yourself now? That's a new low."

Xan stopped in his tracks, turning to stare at the handsome, sneering face framed by the darkness of the car's interior. The man inside wore an expensive but wrinkled suit, and an air of desperate cruelty. "Buying prostitutes now, Monhundy? What would your omega think of that?"

"My omega can rot is what I think," Monhundy barked, eyes catching fire with that old hate that Xan knew so well.

"Trouble in paradise?"

Monhundy laughed. "You'd know about that, wouldn't you? Unmanned alpha with his frigid omega."

Xan gritted his teeth.

"Get in," Monhundy said. "You're a long way from home."

Xan swallowed hard and fisted his hands in his pockets. "Why should I?"

"Because I told you to, and you're a good boy who does what I say, aren't you?"

"Not anymore."

"Get in the car, Xan," Monhundy said, rolling his eyes and gunning the engine. "Hurry up. I don't have all night."

At that moment, it began to rain. Xan stared up at the clouds in the sky, the wet, cold water pelting his face, and he laughed. Maybe it was Vince's brandy rushing in his blood, but the humor gripped him hard, rocking him with how incredibly terrible—how *perfect* it was—that in this dark place, on this fucked up night, after everything he'd said to his father, and what he'd learned about Ray's sad love affair, that Wilbet Mon-fucking-hundy would pull up next to him on a dark, abandoned street and demand he get in his car.

"I won't tell you again," Monhundy spit out.

In the rain, Xan's curls plastered against the side of his head. His chest ached. His feet hurt. He was still drunk enough that as he walked around the front of the car, opened the passenger side door, and climbed in that his tongue felt a little numb.

"You planning to fuck me, Monhundy?" Xan asked, slamming the car door behind him. He was soaked through, and still the rain came down. The windshield wipers waved desperately across the glass—like a warning, like they were begging Xan to get out of the car.

Monhundy looked at Xan, up and down, and then grinned an ugly, violent smile. "The betas complain when I hurt them. But you don't."

Xan's heart galloped hard. "You like how I take it, don't you?"

"I like when you cry."

"Take me home then. Make me cry."

Monhundy stared at him. "My omega's home."

Xan shrugged. "My place. Mine's not."

"You're sick, aren't you, Xan? And you need my cock."

Xan choked, but whispered, "Just make it hurt."

"Oh, I'll hurt you," Monhundy growled. "I'll hurt you so good." He put his hand on Xan's thigh, squeezing hard enough to bruise.

The car pulled away from the curb. The rain came down even harder.

By the time they reached Xan's dark and silent house, Monhundy was breathing heavily and his pants were distorted by his large erection.

Xan sat very still in the passenger seat, his blood pumping wildly and a kind of giddy terror flooding him. Was he really going to do this? Was he out of his mind?

It was the middle of the night. The rain hadn't eased, still the torrent that had burst over Xan's head in the Calitan District. The tapping of it on the roof and hood of the car rattled Xan's nerves, and he clenched his fists, trying to calm himself.

"Surprised to admit it, but I missed your tight ass," Monhundy bit out, like he loathed the words and himself for saying it. "Saw you that night in Virona. Shot right to my dick. I got hard as a rock."

"That was awkward for your opponent during your match, I'm sure," Xan said tightly, holding onto his sanity by a thread. He shook all over from the wet, cold rain and his adrenaline rush.

"Fuck you." Monhundy lifted his hand from where he still gripped Xan's thigh when he didn't need it to change gears. "Fuck. You." He pounded Xan's chest with his fist, knocking a gasp out of him and leaving a new, aching place on his body to match the ones he'd gathered from his father.

Nothing to lose. Not a damned thing to lose.

Except his life. And he had to admit he didn't want to lose that. Not anymore.

The car idled by the curb. Monhundy huffed and ripped open his pants. "Suck me."

Xan stared down at Monhundy's giant cock, the head wet with pre-come and his foreskin drawn back tightly beneath the exposed head. There was a time when he wouldn't have needed to be told twice. A time when he'd have sucked Monhundy down and been grateful for it.

"Inside," Xan said, shaking his head. "The neighbors will see."

Monhundy grimaced. "Let them." He cuffed Xan's cheek. "Mouth open, slut."

Xan shook his head. "Inside."

Monhundy snarled, grabbed Xan's curls, and pulled him toward his lap.

"Do you want me to bite it off?" Xan growled.

Monhundy let go of him, eyes going narrow and cruel. "Inside, you say? Fine. We'll go inside. Where you'll pay for that threat."

Xan nodded, and the two of them exited the car. Monhundy didn't bother zipping up his pants. His cock swung in the open air, and he stroked it at Xan menacingly on the empty, nighttime street in front of Xan's house.

Xan's knees shook so hard he was afraid he'd collapse, but he walked up the steps and tried to get his quivering hand to bring his keys from his pocket.

Monhundy was right behind him, shoving his cock against the back of Xan's pants. The neighborhood was asleep. The rain still came down, slipping down the side of Xan's face as he fumbled in his pocket, the key somehow evasive while his heart thundered and sweat broke over his wet skin.

"Open the door, or I'll fuck you right here," Monhundy whispered in Xan's ear, his voice sick with hatred and his big, hard cock rutting against Xan's backside, scrunching up the back of Xan's coat. "Want the neighbors to hear you squealing like a stuck pig? Want them to hear how you come for me, you unmanned piece of shit?"

Xan found the key. He stuck it in the lock. He turned it.

"Come *on*," Monhundy urged. "I'll make you cry. Hurt you

good. You're gonna love it. Get the wolf-damned door open."

Xan trembled all over. He closed his eyes, took a deep breath, and balled up his fists. He let his mind remember it all: every moment in Monhundy's grip, all the times he'd thought he was going to die, the horrible orgasms, and the bitter self-loathing that filled him each time. He thought of the knowing, nasty gleam in Monhundy's eyes when they met his across the meeting room tables in his father's office.

The threats. The pain. The humiliation.

Dredging up all of Urho's lessons, he rounded on Monhundy and punched him in the mouth, sending him reeling backwards. Pride swelled in his heart at the expression of shock on Monhundy's face as he touched his fingers to his bleeding lip. And then his heart caught as Monhundy's brows drew down, his bloody lip curled, and his fists came up.

Xan didn't back down. He lunged at him, shouting, "Rape! *Rape!*"

Monhundy tried to grab Xan's mouth to cover it, but Xan bit his hand and kicked his shins, fighting with every ounce of loathing he'd ever directed at himself. He spit, he punched, he bit, and he *screamed.*

Monhundy came at him, but each time he tried to grab Xan, he'd leap back to avoid teeth, or nails, or the sharp edges of Xan's elbows. This wasn't what Urho had taught him. There was nothing gentlemanly about the way Xan fought now. It was pure rage and pain, and he channeled it on Monhundy in the loudest, most shocking way he could.

"Never again!" he screamed. "You won't touch me again!"

Monhundy gasped as Xan bit his hand. Blood gushed into Xan's mouth and he spit the metallic wetness of it out onto the rain-wet ground.

Monhundy gripped his bitten hand with the other, his face a

mask of terror in the scant moonlight showing through the clouds. His hair was plastered on his head as the rain fell even harder, and Xan laughed. The slick, wet, wonder of rain washed away his last bit of fear.

"I'm unmanned, but I'm not your fuck toy to beat and abuse."

Monhundy backed away, his cock still flopping around, his eyes wide and dark.

Xan stepped toward him. "You're a coward. Fight me!"

Shivering, Monhundy shook his head. "You're a lunatic. Crazy."

"Crazy? No. I just have something to lose, Wilbet," Xan hissed, drawing even closer. "Something. Big. To. Lose." He had his life, and his love, and he wasn't going to give that up no matter what. Not for Wilbet Monhundy. Not for his father. Not for money. He wasn't a whore. He grinned, a mad sense of invincibility slashing through him like pain. "Try loving someone besides yourself sometime. It's freeing." He drew back his fist and took aim.

Monhundy ducked and shielded his face with his hands. "Stop," he whimpered.

"And you know what people do when they have something to lose?" Xan sneered. "They get fucking honest, Wilbet. Really fucking honest."

Monhundy blinked wildly. "Are you threatening me?"

"I don't know, am I threatening you?" Xan yelled, a crackling madness zipping up his spine. "Do your parents know you've been out in Calitan looking for a prostitute? Does Kerry? Does he know about how you've fucked me and beaten me? Does he know how brutal you are?"

The whites of Monhundy's eyes glowed in the moonlight, as the rain slapped the sidewalk around them. Lights flicked on in the houses across the street and next door. Windows opened. There came the sound of a door opening and shutting, and a neighbor yelling, "Hey, what's going on over there?"

Monhundy retreated further, his cock shriveled but still exposed. Rain spitting down on him like even wolf-god despised the monster of a man. No, not a monster. A scared, ugly bully. A disgusting, but human, piece of waste.

"Leave Kerry out of this," Monhundy snarled. "Or I'll kick your ass."

"Right, right," Xan said. "Because who would believe me, right? Somehow, I think Kerry would. There's that birthmark. Right at the base of your dick."

Monhundy licked his lips, the rain wet on his face. It looked like sweat.

Xan laughed, his mouth still tangy with the taste of Monhundy's blood, his body singing with pain and power. "Thought you were going to hurt me?" he shouted. "Make me cry?" He laughed again and raised his face to the rain.

Monhundy yelled, "You're crazy!"

"Come near me again and I'll make *you* cry. I'll make you *pay*."

Monhundy didn't wait any longer, looking around nervously, his body shaking. He ran to his car and started it. Xan laughed, raising his hands in the air, letting the rain fall over him. He walked into the middle of the street, ignoring the inquiries from his neighbors and the pain in his body from the punches he'd taken that night. He laughed and laughed. The water stung his face and exposed skin.

He laughed until he cried, and he cried until the rain washed him clean.

CHAPTER TWENTY-THREE

U RHO WAS STILL drowsing in bed, eyes closed against the morning sun, and dreaming lightly of Xan. He'd tried to call him the night before, but hadn't reached anyone at either house, and he wasn't sure where to try next. His gut had been in knots over it all night, and he was desperately trying to rest when a knock came at his bedroom door.

Before he could call for whoever it was to enter, Jason burst in.

"Urho, we have a problem." He was breathless and giving off a harsh, crackling scent.

Urho sat up. "Something's wrong with Vale?"

"No, something's wrong with Caleb." Jason paced back and forth, his expression grim. Another burst of the strange, harsh odor wafted off him.

"You reek," Urho muttered.

Jason stepped closer to Urho's bed. "I know. Because Caleb came past our room on his way to his own."

Confused, Urho rubbed at his forehead. "He's not with Janus?"

"*No.* And thank wolf-god for that."

"My thoughts exactly. He needs a break."

"You aren't getting it!" Jason raked a hand into his hair and huffed.

"He's sick?" Urho's heart skipped. He'd been making sure Caleb washed his hands in hot water as often as he could stand it, and he'd hoped he wouldn't catch the flu, despite his constant and dedicated care of Janus.

"No, but—" Jason drew even closer to Urho, radiating that agitating, strange scent, and whispered, "Caleb smells different."

"*You* smell different."

"Because of Caleb!"

Urho wiped his bleary eyes, relieved Caleb wasn't ill, but worried now about Jason, who was making absolutely no sense. He fluffed his pillow and lay down again, pressing his cheek against the cool side. "He's stressed out. It's changed his scent."

"No, dammit!" Jason shook Urho roughly. "He smells really different. *Heat* different."

Urho's eyes widened as he bolted up. He took a deep breath, sorting the scents in the air, pushing away Jason's new crackly odor and looking for the pheromones that spoke to all alphas. A rush of air came in through his open door, spilling in from the windows that opened onto the courtyard, carrying a hint of ocean as well as the scent of the rooms on the opposite side of the building.

The scent of Caleb's room. The scent of Caleb himself.

Fuck.

Urho's dick hardened. He glanced down at Jason's pants and saw the same reaction there.

"Vale better not see that," Urho muttered darkly.

"It's not my fault!" Jason covered his erection with his hands clasped in front. "It's instinctual around an omega going into heat. You know that. He needs to be isolated—for his own sake, and ours. And we need to get Xan home. Now."

"For fuck's sake," Urho muttered to himself. His limbs ached with exhaustion. He'd been getting so little sleep between worrying about Janus, and the new pains Vale was suffering from, and missing Xan, and fretting a little extra for Caleb, too. "The last thing we need right now is to have to deal with a heat!"

"Tell that to wolf-god, who, in all his glory, chose right now to set Caleb off." Jason shuddered. "He smells amazing."

"*Fuck*," Urho said aloud. "He does. They always do."

Jason huffed and shook his head as though to clear it. "Vale can smell it, too. It's making him cranky. And restless. He smells my reaction to it and that's...that's worse."

Urho groaned. He got out of bed and used the bathroom, dressing hastily.

Just as he finished buttoning his shirt, a cry of discomfort came from down the hallway. Jason jerked worriedly and clenched his fists. It was the same pained noise Vale had been making off and on for the last day. It didn't mean anything good.

"How much longer does Vale have to endure this?" Jason demanded. "He's in pain, Urho."

"I know that," Urho snapped back. "And I've been giving him the strongest muscle relaxer I have that won't hurt the baby." He searched his mind for another solution, aside from induction, coming up blank.

"He can't sleep. He aches all the time. The baby's shifted to a head-down position. This new thing with Caleb's scent changing has him in fits. How much longer do we have to wait until we can induce?"

"Jason, we've got a dangerous flu virus at large in the house. We've done our best to contain it, but the baby is safer in Vale's body than outside of it. At least until Janus either comes around or...doesn't."

Jason paced some more. "Vale could die if he doesn't give birth at the right time."

Urho took a calming breath, but jittery anxiety rode his nerves. "Stay calm. Vale is handling this pregnancy quite well."

"You don't listen to him cry at night!"

Urho shuddered, a shard of despair in his heart. The idea of Vale crying in pain gutted him. "It's that bad?"

"It's bad. And when I fist him now, he sobs. He doesn't want it.

The baby has grown big enough to make it hard to get my hand inside. I don't know if we can wait until Janus decides if he's going to stay on this earth or depart for wolf-god's waiting arms." Jason's eyes flashed. "I'm sorry if I sound callous, but Vale is my first priority."

"He's high on the list for me as well."

"Then help him!"

"I am, dammit!"

Another moan came from Vale and Jason's room.

"I'm going to him," Jason glared at Urho. "Do something about Caleb and that scent. I don't know how much time he has, but it can't be long. Send for Xan." Then Jason softened, shoved his hair out of his face and said, "Look, you need to get him somewhere safe. What if he runs off...?" He shook his head. "Xan is counting on us to take care of him. If you need help getting him into his quarters or summoning Xan, let me know. I'm happy to help, but right now I need to go check on Vale."

Urho scrubbed his face and waited until Jason had left the room before standing. Exhaustion and worry flooded him. He didn't know what to do. He hadn't been able to get through to Xan in the city, and here he was with a stubborn, frightened, grieving omega going into heat, another omega on the verge of going into labor, a sick and dying alpha, and another tense, worried alpha in fear for his *Erosgápe*'s life and the life of his unborn child.

He adjusted his heavy cock and went to close all the courtyard windows on their wing of the house. If nothing else, he'd try to prevent Jason from scenting Caleb's time coming, and that should keep him from radiating that scent that would put Vale, as his *Erosgapé*, on an irrationally jealous edge.

Then he called for Ren, issued some orders, and rustled up some alpha quell from his medicine bag. He took one and then slipped a handful of them into Jason's pocket as he went into Vale's room to check on him. "Take as needed," he whispered before he carefully approached a very aggravated Vale where he stood looking out the window to the town below.

Jason was right. The babe was head down, in the ready position, and Vale was more uncomfortable than Urho liked to see him. He was restless and pacing, moaning off and on. If he continued on this way, there was no doubt Urho would need to administer the pills that would start labor soon. Jason could barely take Vale's pain as it was, and the babe seemed determined.

Still, inducing now was no sure thing. The babe's lungs were hopefully developed, but there was a chance they might not be. And Urho hadn't been exaggerating the possible risk of contagion with Janus residing so near the house, especially with the servants who cared for him coming and going.

He considered isolating them in the detached wing, but then there was the problem of food and laundry. The only kitchen and laundry facilities were in the main house proper. Still, they scoured everything with boiling water. If they were careful, it was possible that he could go ahead and induce…

He chewed his lip as he headed towards Caleb's room, relieved to be out of the grip of his initial lust thanks to the calm, cool slip of alpha quell in his veins. Zephyr skirted past him with a mouse between her teeth. She leapt onto a table in the hallway, overturning a glass vase of winter flowers, and stared at him with dark, challenging eyes.

"Don't you cause problems, too," he groused at her as she proceeded to tear into her treat. He groaned, feeling sorry for Ren who was going to have to contend with the gruesome mess.

Caleb answered on the first knock. He was jumpy, scratching at his arms and chest in his white, short-sleeve V-necked shirt. He paced his room with the windows to the ocean flung wide. The air poured in, frigid enough to make Urho shudder with the chill, but

Caleb seemed untouched by it.

His cheeks were flushed, and the new, delicious aroma of heat joined the mélange of Caleb's usual odors in the room. But there was another new scent, a mouthwatering fragrance Urho had never had the opportunity to scent before—the musk of Caleb's slick.

He groaned. Caleb smelled ripe and ready, and Urho couldn't deny the throbbing reaction of his cock despite the alpha quell. Yes, he was quite aroused. His tongue swiped over his bottom lip as he stood in the doorway watching Caleb pace. A possessive urge struck him, familiar and hot. An alpha's need to corner an omega in heat, get him somewhere safe, somewhere he couldn't run off and...

He shook his head hard, trying to get his thoughts in order. He felt in his pocket for more alpha quell and took one.

"Caleb?"

Caleb stopped pacing and leaned against the opposite wall, his eyes sliding shut as he shuddered and shook. The scent of slick grew stronger, and his face twisted restlessly as he scratched at his arms. Urho knew the heat had to be pricking under his skin cruelly by the way he moved. It was coming on fast.

"Is it early?" Urho asked gruffly, crossing the room carefully so that he didn't frighten him.

"No," Caleb whispered, straining and rubbing against the wall. "It's right on time." Then he moaned and slipped to the floor. "It'll be here soon. I need... Oh no, I need an alpha to help me. Xan's not here." He gritted his teeth and met Urho's eyes with despair. "Can you...? You promised."

Urho moaned, his cock responding to the pheromones pouring off Caleb in abundance now that Urho had drawn close, the omega body's physiological attempt to seal the deal. "Darling, Xan's going to be here very soon. Try to wait for him."

Caleb snorted. "You know better than that," he said, quivering and digging his fingers into his skin. "There's no holding it back.

And he's not here. I need him, and he's gone."

"Shh," Urho said. "Let's get you in bed. You can nap and—"

"No!" Caleb wrenched away from him. "Xan should be here," he shouted. "But he's not, and you promised."

Urho groaned. Taking Caleb without Xan here with him, without even his permission over the phone would feel wrong. Like a violation of his commitment to Xan. At the same time, if he didn't take Caleb then he'd feel like he was violating his commitment to Xan in allowing his omega to suffer.

"There are other options. The village...there's probably an alpha—"

"You promised!" Caleb shouted, his body going rigid. "I hate this. I hate it. I hate it so much and I don't want a stranger touching me. I don't want it!" His body shook again as though in a small seizure. His eyes rolled up. He groaned and rolled away from Urho, slithering on the carpet, rubbing it against his pale skin. "Make it stop. Make it go away."

"Darling, I can't. You know I can't." Urho rubbed at his face. He needed help. He needed Xan. "Wolf-god! I need some assistance in here!" he shouted, hoping for a beta servant, hopefully Ren, to hear.

"You're going to lock me in," Caleb yelled, panic threading his voice. "You're going to leave me here." He started to sob, rubbing himself on the carpet. "No, no. I won't. I won't!"

"Caleb, please, listen to me."

"No, I need to get back to Janus. He'll wonder where I've gone. He needs me."

"Janus is unconscious, and your scent will only tax his system more. As an alpha, he'll respond to you even in his illness. He needs his strength to fight. Come on now. Let me get your clothes off, get you into bed. You'll be more comfortable."

"You're going to lock me in!" Caleb shouted again, struggling against Urho's grip when he reached down to try to haul him up. "Help me. Please help me. I don't want this at all—I don't want it. I don't want it with a stranger."

"Shh. I hear you, I understand. I promise, I won't get a stranger."

Caleb drooped against him. "Thank you, Urho. Thank you."

Urho rocked him, surprised at how thin Caleb felt, how fragile in comparison to Xan, who was more solid than he looked. He smoothed his hand through Caleb's hair and groaned when more slick released, perfuming the air around them and making his mouth water.

At that moment, Ren walked past Caleb's open door holding a wastebasket and wearing a grimace.

"Ren," Urho called out. Ren halted at the door and stared in, wide-eyed. Urho held his gaze firmly. "Call the city until you reach Xan. His home there, his office, his family's house. The residences of friends or family. His brother's place." Urho swallowed hard, but made himself add, "Call the house of Wilbet Monhundy, too, if you don't reach him anywhere else."

"Yes, of course, Dr. Chase. I'll do it at once." Ren's eyes went wide at the sight of Caleb's flushed skin and dilated eyes. "Flu?" he asked worriedly.

"Heat," Urho said, his cock twitching as even more slick slipped from Caleb's asshole. Caleb twitched restlessly in his arms, his cheeks flushed and his eyes glassy.

"Oh, wolf-god," Ren replied, panic registering on his face. "I'll call right away. At once." He rushed off, muttering, "Oh fucking wolf-hell below." The string of curses didn't stop, echoing as he raced down the hallway.

"Caleb? I need you to let go of me. I'm going to get the alpha dildo Xan keeps in his closet."

Caleb shuddered against him. "Knot me. I need it."

"Not yet, sweetheart. Let's give Xan a chance to get here." He squeezed his eyes shut, his throat dry. There was no way. Xan was a three-hour train ride away, and no one knew where he was in the city. The first big wave was going to hit Caleb soon. Very soon. Any second, really. And then...

He wondered where all the beta servants were now when he needed them. They'd been practically swarming the halls since Janus had been sick and the detached wing evacuated. But now, there was no one. He had more assignments to hand out, more messages to pass on, and he was trapped on Caleb's floor cradling his hot body, praying for a miracle.

Carefully, Urho unwound Caleb's arms and stood. "Wait here. I'll be right back."

Caleb moaned and commenced rubbing against the carpet again. Urho tried to smile reassuringly, but his gut ached as he headed down the connecting passage, past the bathrooms and closets, into Xan's room.

"I'm too old for all of this," he muttered to himself. "Riki, you and I should have been retired to the beach by now. Just look at me." He almost laughed then, but sobered when he realized it was the first time he'd spoken to Riki since he'd come to Virona.

He shoved those thoughts aside and ransacked Xan's closet, finally locating the alpha dildo. He'd seen it the first time one night after making love. Xan had the bright idea of having Urho restrain him with one of his ties for the next go-round, and the dildo had fallen out of the closet when he'd gone in search of a sartorial choice Xan approved of. Apparently, he couldn't be tied down by just any tie. He'd asked Xan about the dildo after the next set of orgasms, and he'd been told that, while it was a tempting toy, it was reserved for use during Caleb's heat.

Urho was relieved to have it now. Maybe he could stall for three or four hours until Xan had a chance to arrive. Hopefully Ren was having better luck finding him than Urho had had the night before.

"Sir! He's running, sir!" A beta servant Urho recognized as being one of the housekeepers burst into the room. "Ren told us to keep an eye on Mr. Riggs, and, *sir*, he's running."

"Fuck me sideways," Urho grunted, tossing the dildo to the servant. "Put that in his room." Then he took off down the corridor at top speed.

He caught up to Caleb in the great hall. He'd almost reached the front door.

"No, no, no," Caleb yelled as Urho wrapped his arms around his waist and hauled him up in the air. "I don't want this. I don't want it." He shivered and shook, his heart pounding fast as a rabbit's beneath Urho's hands.

"I know, darling, but there's no way to stop it now, and you won't be safe out there. Please, trust me. I want to take care of you."

Caleb started to sob, but he collapsed against Urho's chest. "You won't lock me in with a stranger?"

"No, I promise. I promise, sweetheart."

"I want Xan." Caleb whimpered, his tears dampening Urho's shirt.

"We're looking for him."

"I want him here with me."

"I know."

"He's my alpha."

"He'd want to be here, Caleb. He didn't know." More like he'd forgotten between Janus and his pater's illness.

Caleb nodded and snuffled. "I didn't remind him. I wanted to think it wouldn't come."

Urho sighed, carrying his lover's omega upstairs carefully, a terrible weight settling on his chest. This man was his responsibility now. He'd promised, and he had to carry it out.

Caleb relaxed in his arms. "I trust you," he whispered.

"Thank you," Urho said, and kissed the side of Caleb's head. "I'll try to make it enjoyable for you."

"I just want knots to make this agony stop. I don't care about the rest."

Urho squeezed him tighter.

As he took a right instead of a left at the top of the stairs, he thought he heard odd sounds coming from the guest room wing. Jason's voice raised in concern, and then a sharp cry from Vale. Caleb moaned against him. Sweat erupted on Urho's forehead and in the small of his back.

Another pained cry, different from the noises Vale had been making earlier, more urgent and scared, came as Urho fumbled getting Caleb's room open. He helped him toward the bathroom, his heart pumping hard.

"Listen to me," he said, as calmly as possible. "I want you to take a bath with the water as cold as you can stand to help keep the heat at bay." Another scream from the opposite side of the house. And a shout of worry from Jason. "There's something going on with Vale and the baby. But I'll be right back."

Caleb nodded, letting Urho put him on his feet on the tiled bathroom floor. He turned on the cold water, sweat running down the side of his face and giving off pheromones that Urho could barely stand to ignore, even with the alpha quell.

He turned to go, but Caleb grabbed his arm.

"The alpha dildo," Caleb grunted as he tore his clothes off like they were on fire. His pale skin gleamed in the sun rushing in the bathroom windows. It shone like some kind of cheerful devil in the face of the calamity Urho sensed coming.

"Of course." He raced back into Caleb's room to find the thick, wide dildo with a massive knot at the base placed in the middle of the bed, where the beta servant had left it. It was larger than Urho's own cock and knot, but it wouldn't be enough long term. Caleb would need to be knotted by an actual alpha.

The muffled urgency and cries of pain from Vale's room grew louder. Urho's heart pounded, and his mouth went dry as his mind raced urgently for a solution to the obvious crisis coming at him full-speed and straight ahead.

He returned to the bathroom. Caleb had slipped into the bath while waiting, and his pale skin was almost blue as his teeth chattered. Urho handed him the dildo.

"Use it if it will help," he said. "I have to check on Vale."

"I know. I hear him." Caleb shuddered in the cold water. His eyes were calmer and less glassy than before, and Urho breathed a sigh of relief that the cold water was helping.

Jason burst into the bathroom, a towel over his mouth and nose to protect him from Caleb's pheromones. Even so his pants were stiff with his erection. "Urho! There's something wrong. Vale's really hurting. I think the baby's coming!"

"I know," Urho barked. He held up the dildo. "Let me get Caleb situated and I'll come check on Vale right away. Get out."

Jason's eyes were wide as he hustled from the bathroom and back into the passage. He called over his shoulder, "Urho! Hurry! It's bad."

"I'm coming!" Urho shouted. He took a deep breath, trying to calm himself, to be the suitable, soothing alpha an omega needed during the start of their heat. "Use the dildo if you need it," he said as calmly as possible, but his voice trembled. "Hopefully, I won't be long."

At the word hopefully, all of Caleb's hard-won calm evaporated in a clear rush of panic. "Don't let me suffer," he begged suddenly, his eyes glassy and his voice shot through with anxiety. His teeth chattered from the cool water he'd poured into the tub. "Please. Don't leave me alone to hurt."

Urho groaned. The scent of Caleb's oncoming heat was maddening, and his cock strained against his pants. He took a slow, deep breath, determined to keep his wits about him. "I'll help you, Caleb. I promise. But I need to handle this crisis with Vale first. Use the dildo."

Caleb stared at the fat dildo still in his hand and shuddered violently. "I'm cold. But I'm too hot. I want out. I need to be in bed. I want to be in bed." He splashed the water around agitatedly, wetting the floor and Urho's pants.

Urho brushed a soothing hand into Caleb's soft hair. "Calm down," he said firmly, infusing his voice with dominance and all the certainty he didn't feel. "Do as you're commanded. Use the dildo."

A cry from Vale's room echoed down the corridors separating them, and Urho's heart thumped hard. He needed to go. He didn't want to leave Caleb to suffer, but what choice did he have? They needed another doctor as soon as possible. And there was Janus to consider, too.

"I'll be back." He dropped a reassuring kiss on Caleb's hair and rushed from the bathroom before he changed his mind.

Vale leaned his weight on the footboard of his bed and breathed shallowly. His eyes closed and his expression intense, everything about him was turned inward. He even ignored Urho and Jason's questions as he shifted from foot to foot, moaning and groaning.

It didn't take a full physical evaluation for Urho to become certain that inducing labor wasn't going to be necessary now—Vale was already in it and perhaps had been for several hours. The start to labor could be very sudden in omegas, and the pains he'd been experiencing might have been hidden contractions.

Urho berated himself silently for missing the signs. He'd been so intent on keeping the baby in that he hadn't given any thought to the baby's opinion on coming out.

"It's time, isn't it?" Jason said, his face pale and his eyes shocked. He stood beside Vale, one hand on his back, and his entire body shaking in fear.

"Yes. The babe's on his way."

"What do we do now?" Jason asked.

Urho rubbed a hand over his face and left the room. In the hallway again, he tore to the head of the stairs and yelled for help until two beta servants ran into the great hall, expressions of terror on their face.

"Call a doctor from the town," Urho said. "Tell him that he's needed here at once. We've got a very sick man succumbing to the flu, an omega in labor, and another omega going into heat."

The betas gasped. One broke free and ran off to follow his instructions.

"Has anyone heard from Mr. Heelies? Is he on his way?"

The servants shook their heads.

"I'm going to need hot water, towels, and alpha condoms. Does anyone know if there are alpha condoms on the premises?" He had three in his doctor's bag, but in the throes of heat, they wouldn't last very long.

The servants conferred between them. "We don't know, sir. We'll run to the village for some."

He nodded, trying to think of what else he needed. It felt unbearably wrong to take care of Caleb without Xan being here, and yet he couldn't leave him in agony. Neither Caleb nor Xan would forgive him for that. He tried to imagine knotting Caleb and then racing down the halls to deliver Vale's baby, but the absurdity was too much. Yes, calling the doctor was the right thing to do.

"Well, go!" he shouted at the remaining betas below. "Call the doctor! Boil the water! Buy condoms! We're going to need all of it immediately!"

The betas scampered, calling between themselves orders as to who was to fetch what. At that moment, Ren appeared in the great hall below, a worried expression on his face.

"You can't locate Xan," Urho guessed.

Ren shook his head. "He left his father's home yesterday late at night and no one has seen or heard from him since."

"Did you try Wilbet Monhundy's house?" he barked, gripping the bannister to hold his gorge down. The thought of Xan going to that man, of asking to be hurt again… He shook the thought free. He couldn't cope with that right now. Not with everything else going on.

"Yes, but there was no answer."

"Try again."

"Dr. Chase, it's worse. The epidemic in the city has progressed to the point that they've closed down train services in an attempt to contain the infection. Even if I reached Mr. Heelies, he'd have to drive here and that would take nearly six hours."

Urho cursed softly. "Keep calling anyway. After you organize those betas. I need hot water, condoms, and at least one doctor. Maybe two if you can get the village to spare a second."

"Two?"

"One for Janus and one for Vale. I'm going to have to deal with Caleb, so…"

"Mr. Aman is in labor?"

"Yes." Urho shook his head hard. He pressed his fingers to his eyes and tried to think of how to solve all the new crises, and how he could possibly be everywhere at once.

"Wolf-god," Ren said sharply. "What a mess."

That seemed an understatement of vast proportions.

"Speaking of Vale, I need to get back to him now." Cries of pain from both wings echoed through the house. Urho swiped a hand over his sweaty forehead. "Then I need to get back to Caleb."

He pinned Ren with his gaze. "I'm trusting you to do your level best to get at least one doctor up here immediately and *please* keep looking for Xan. Set one of the other servants to it if necessary. Call any place in the city you can think of—bars he might go to, friends' houses. Try Yosef and Rosen. Try the Monhundys again."

"Yes, Dr. Chase," Ren said, though he looked a bit green around the gills with terror. "I'll do whatever I can. But what about Mr. Riggs, sir? If we can't get a doctor up here in time, should I ask in town for an alpha surrogate?"

Urho gritted his teeth and clenched his fists. He'd promised Caleb not to lock him up with a stranger. And he wasn't going to break that promise. But, wolf-god help him if that meant Caleb ended up suffering.

"No. Mr. Riggs specifically asked that we not do that."

Ren paled but nodded. "I'll see to the rest."

Grateful for Ren's dependability, Urho fled back down the hall to his own room, where he grabbed his medical bag and sent up frantic prayers to wolf-god. He took deep breaths to banish any memories of Riki's birth. There would be no repeat of that trauma, not for Vale and Jason. Not for him. The babe would come healthy and strong, and Vale would come through it beautifully.

Calmer after his quick prayers, he walked back to Vale's room. He was glad to see that Vale was wearing nothing but a robe. That would make it easier to examine him. He was still standing, this time by the window, eyes closed and breathing hard through a contraction. Jason stood next to him, blue eyes wide with worry, but he kept a steady, firm hand on Vale's arm, making sure he didn't collapse.

"This is going faster than I expected," Jason said as Urho entered. "He's really hurting."

Urho nodded, opening his bag and pulling out a syringe. He filled it with a relaxant related to alpha quell and set it aside. It was for Jason, should anything go wrong. "The scar tissue isn't as flexible," Urho muttered. "The birth will likely be more painful than usual." And births were always plenty painful enough.

Jason paled, and Vale simply cursed before he gripped the windowsill even harder and whimpered. The contractions were coming in fast waves, apparently. Urho blinked in surprise. It was usually slower for a first birth.

"Are you going to be all right?" Urho whispered to Jason. "You need to stay steady for him."

"I'm fine," Jason lied. He was pale and obviously terrified, but he rubbed Vale's back. "I'm great. Besides, you'll be here with us. You'll help him."

Urho motioned toward the bed, ignoring the statement. "See if you can get him to lie down on his left side. I need to have a look at his passage to see how quickly his womb is opening." If it wasn't opening to match the speed of contractions, it could be a problem. The baby's head would be bashed against the mouth of the womb by the force of the contractions, and that could cause trauma, facial bruising, or worse.

Urho turned to the bathroom attached to the room and washed his hands in hot water as Jason tried to get Vale onto the bed.

"I don't want to," Vale said stubbornly. "I feel better standing up."

"But Urho needs to examine you, baby. Please. Just for a few minutes. I'll be right here with you the whole time."

Vale shot him a glare that brooked no argument. "I will *not*. I want to stand. I *will* stand."

Urho interrupted. "It's all right. There's a flashlight in my medical bag. I can check him while he's upright if you help him to lift his leg up onto this chair." It would be harder, but nothing about the day looked like it was going to be easy.

A pained scream came from across the house. Then a massive

crash, something large enough to rattle the entire upper floor. Vale hissed and then cried out, another contraction wracking him.

Vale and Caleb's voices rose in agonized harmony.

"Fuck!" Urho shouted. He shot Jason a desperate glance. "Get his leg up on this chair. I'll be right back." He took off down the hallway, leaving Vale's bedroom door open.

When he opened Caleb's room, he fell back as the pungent scent of heat and slick hit him in the face. He gasped, and his cock hardened in response, his cells roaring with suddenly renewed arousal. Urho spotted a tipped-over white marble-topped table by the door that led to the adjoining hallway. Caleb was stronger than he looked.

A naked Caleb darted from where he crouched by the bed, trying to make a run for the hallway. Still wet, he almost slipped through Urho's fingers.

"Sweetheart, you have to stay here," Urho said as soothingly as he could, but when Caleb tried to jerk free, his voice took on an alpha-firm edge. "I said you're staying here."

Caleb squeaked and started to cry. "I need help," he whimpered. "Help me. Please. It's too much. It's too much!"

Urho dragged him in close, pressing him into a full-bodied hug. His cock throbbed in his pants, pre-come pulsing from his slit and dampening his underwear. His hand drifted to Caleb's backside, and the copious amounts of slick sliding from between his cheeks made him groan.

Caleb wriggled against him. "Finger me. Fuck me. Do *something*."

"Oh, wolf-god," Urho grunted. "You're getting close."

"Need it," Caleb sobbed, wriggling in Urho's arms, rubbing himself against Urho's shirt and pants.

Urho glanced over his shoulder, desperately willing for some kind of help to arrive. He pushed Caleb backwards and down onto the bed.

Caleb didn't fight him, spreading his legs wide. His cock was deliciously hard and bright pink against his tight, pale stomach, and his breath came with heaving, sucking urgency. Fresh, fragrant slick shone all over his thighs and ass, and Urho's mouth watered, the desire to taste it gripping him.

He shook his head, trying to gain his composure. Another sharp, agonizing scream from Vale's side of the house brought him out of his stupor. He blinked down at Caleb and licked his lips at the sight of him on his back, open and offering, begging to be taken. He groaned. "Caleb, Vale's baby is coming. There's no other doctor here yet. I have to help him first right now. It's life or death."

Urho wasn't even sure Caleb understood, because just then Caleb shuddered all over, his eyes rolling up and his body convulsing as the heat wave gripped him fully. He screamed and arched, rolling onto his hands and knees, thrusting his ass into the air and taking on the beautiful, perfect lordosis position.

Urho's groin flared to life, his body burning to plug Caleb's trembling, wet hole. He had to close his eyes, grit his teeth, and concentrate on the wails of pain coming from Vale's side of the house to keep from simply ripping his pants open and plunging inside, just as their forefathers had wanted when they designed the biology of alphas and omegas.

Urho hurried back to Caleb's bathroom and grabbed the unused alpha dildo. Placing it in Caleb's hand, he commanded, "Use this." Then he smoothed the pale, sweaty hair back from Caleb's flushed, straining face, and kissed his forehead. It was all he could do to ignore Caleb's groans of pain. "I'll be back. I swear to you, I'll be back as soon as I can."

Caleb twisted and cried out, his body bucking under the consuming, tortuous need that defined heat. He rolled onto his back again, lifted his legs high, and stuffed his wet hole with four of his own fingers. Then he rolled onto his stomach and arched his back into the lordosis position again, fucking himself fervently. The alpha dildo lay forgotten on the bedspread.

The urge to mount Caleb and knot him filled Urho from head to toe. He stepped forward, his hand on his belt buckle. Vale's tortured scream from across the house stilled his hand. Shaking himself free before he could give in to overwhelming instinct and Caleb's agonized pleas, he left the room.

Grabbing a pacing servant in the hallway, he issued an order telling him to lock Caleb inside. "Lock Xan's door, too. And stay here. Don't let him out whatever he does or says."

"Yes, sir."

"Don't go anywhere. I mean it. I'll want back in his room soon."

The servant, a raw-boned teenager, stared at Urho with wide, scared eyes, but did as he was told, turning the key on Caleb's room with a shaking hand.

CHAPTER TWENTY-FOUR

"WELL?" JASON ASKED desperately when Urho made it back to Vale.

"Caleb's locked in. I don't know about the other doctors I've requested. Just let me look at Vale," Urho said, shaking with restraint and fear. He ripped open his medical bag again and retrieved the flashlight.

Jason had done his duty and had Vale exposed from the waist down with one leg propped on the chair so that Urho could examine his anus.

Dropping to his knees, Urho held the light between his teeth and spread Vale's slick-wet cheeks with both hands. The slick produced during childbirth was a similar consistency to that produced when an omega was aroused, or during heat, but it lacked the same powerful, exciting scent. The last thing an omega needed during labor was to deal with a horny alpha.

Unfortunately, Urho was beyond horny after being in Caleb's room. He took a deep breath, trying to clear his nose of Caleb's pheromones, and focused on his patient.

Jason paced restlessly beside them.

As Urho spread Vale's ass and then probed inside with his fingers, Jason growled next to him. "Back off," Urho ordered. "I'm checking him as a doctor, for wolf-god's sake."

Jason still crowded him as he finally worked his whole hand inside. Vale whined and shifted miserably, stuffed far too full with the babe and a large hand to be comfortable. Urho fingered the scar tissue, measuring its tension. When he pressed against it, there was more give than ever before. He felt the child move against his hand, and he checked the opening of the womb with his fingers. It was quite wide already.

"This is good," he said, nodding and withdrawing. "The tissue is pliable. His omega glands are—"

Another violent bang from Caleb's wing interrupted him, along with a suffering scream and a wail. Then another crash, another bang, cries of pain, and a desperate shout for help. Urho's heart was shredded.

Jason met Urho's eye, and he swallowed hard. "Where's the village doctor?"

"I don't know." Urho wiped his shaking hand on a towel and closed his eyes, trying to take a steadying breath. "Hopefully soon."

Jason stared at him, pale and scared.

"Vale's doing well," Urho assured him.

"But what about Caleb?" Jason whispered.

Urho groaned just as Vale screeched and hunched. His body tightened all over as he squirmed against some intense internal sensation. When the contraction had passed, Urho knelt again to check Vale's progress.

The beta servant he'd left in the hallway outside Caleb's room appeared in Vale's open doorway. "He's trying to get out! I think he's going to hurt himself!"

Urho considered the syringe he'd prepared for Jason. All evidence showed that the relaxer did little to stop the pain of heat, but it did calm a panicked omega enough for them to take an alpha cock or, at a higher dose, prevent them from running. Still the thought of drugging Caleb, of leaving him to suffer in helpless, stoned silence was abhorrent.

"Help me!" Caleb screamed, the words echoed around the massive house. "Help!"

Urho's heart rent even more at the pain in his lover's omega's voice.

"For wolf-god's sake, help him!" Vale shouted suddenly, nearly kicking Urho in the face where he knelt with his fingers in Vale's ass. He withdrew them quickly as Vale spun around, glaring at him. "He's hurting. He's *suffering*. Go in there and help him."

"No!" Jason exclaimed, grabbing Vale by the shoulders. His face was almost as flushed as Vale's was from straining. "We need him here. If something goes wro—" He bit off his words and added, "Vale, I can't deliver this baby. It's too risky. Urho stays with us until a doctor or our baby arrives."

"A doctor's coming," Urho said to Vale, standing up so as not to be kicked in the face again. He tried to sound as confident as he possibly could. "He should be here soon."

Vale looked like he was going to argue, but then he groaned and held his stomach. He strained, eyes bulging as another contraction gripped his body. His face grew purple with effort, and he clenched the back of the chair with white knuckles.

"That's it," Urho said. "Just breathe."

Vale sucked in a breath, and his body clenched. He screamed.

A matching, wrenching scream echoed through the halls and the still-open door. Caleb's cries grew louder and louder as Vale's labor intensified. Urho's mind spun. If he left now to help Caleb and something went wrong with the birth if the other doctor botched the job—assuming the other doctor even showed—he'd never forgive himself.

But if Caleb was left to suffer, he'd never forgive himself for that either. And neither would Xan, much less Caleb himself.

"Dr. Chase," Ren said from the doorway, a terror-filled expression not giving Urho hope for good news. Ren held a hand in front of his eyes as though to protect himself against the sight of Vale's nakedness.

Jason snarled protectively, but Urho put a hand on his chest and Jason calmed down, turning his attention back to Vale, who was rocking through another contraction.

Ren said, "I got a hold of Dr. Bainson in the village and he can't make it. He's actually delivering another omega right now. He suggested I call Dr. Snid, an alpha doctor on the outskirts of town, but according to his omega, he's gone into the city to help with the flu epidemic."

"Fuck," Urho muttered.

"Sir, Mr. Janus is seizing now. His fever has gone too high for his body to hold. The cook is trying to cool him with cold water, but he's not responding."

Urho tore into his medical bag, found a bottle of medication he kept on hand for such horrific situations, and passed it to Ren along with a syringe and another empty hypodermic needle. "One syringeful now. If he doesn't calm, then another in eight minutes." He shook his head. "I'm sorry. I know this isn't your job but—"

Another cry from Caleb's room rattled them all, and then Vale shouted as well, his body clenching as he bent over the chair he'd had his foot on. He groaned, gritting his teeth, and started to push. His asshole bulged, and Urho swore he saw the start of the babe's head.

"Wolf-god!" Ren exclaimed in horror. He grabbed the medicine from Urho's hand and rushed away to administer the medication to Janus.

Adrenaline flooded Urho's body, leaving him rushing with a giddy, razor-sharp focus as he knelt to the floor again to spread Vale's ass cheeks wider.

"Is the baby coming?" Jason asked, rubbing Vale's straining back and bending low to look. "Oh, wolf-god, is that his head?"

"Get out of the way." Urho shoved Jason aside.

Jason shoved him back with an angry growl. Vale whimpered

and then rasped, "I will murder you both if you get into a fight right now. There is a baby coming out of me and—aaahhhh!" He howled, hunching again, his entire body going tense as he pushed harder, flushing all over.

"Yes, that's the head," Urho said as slick rushed from Vale's asshole.

Another scream came from Caleb's wing, along with the sound of breaking wood. Then a violent thump. And another. Sweat slipped down Urho's forehead and back, his hands shaking and his heart pounding as he stared at Vale's asshole and waited.

"What *the fuck* is going on?" a voice snarled from the doorway.

Urho's head whipped around to see Xan standing outside Vale's open door, his blue eyes dangerously narrowed, his curly hair a mess, and a large bruise on his cheekbone and another on his jaw. A combination of confusion and rage warred on Xan's face. "What the fuck is happening here?"

Vale gripped the chair hard and pushed again. The screams from Caleb's room came even louder, and Urho turned to Jason. "Explain to him! I need to just..." He slipped a finger in beside the baby's head, and Vale shouted.

Jason kicked Urho in the thigh. "Hurt him again and I'll kill you."

"Stop!" Vale whimpered. "I can't... Let me... Oh wolf-god, *fuck!*" He grimaced and pushed again, his hole opening enough to reveal a large swath of the baby's brown-fuzzed head.

"Mr. Riggs is locked in, Mr. Heelies, sir," a beta servant from the hallway explained to Xan. "He's in heat."

"Well, don't just stand there—take me to him!" Xan barked.

Urho yearned to go to Xan and hold him, explain to him what was happening, but things with Vale's baby were moving too quickly. A rush of blood gushed down Vale's legs, Jason cried out in panic, and Urho shoved him away before he could get between

Urho and the prize.

The baby slipped out into Urho's hands. Perfect, whole, and covered with slick, mucous, and blood. The child let out a lusty scream. Vale collapsed onto the chair, blood still coursing from his asshole, but he was oblivious, reaching out for the baby. The umbilical cord pulsed between them.

Jason fell to his knees beside Vale, and Urho passed off their blood-covered, plump, and perfect child to them. They took the sweet thing into their arms, and Jason burst into tears. Vale kissed Jason's head, and then the baby's, and the three of them huddled close.

Urho took the opportunity of their distraction to pull Vale forward so his buttocks were off the chair and shove Vale's legs apart. He pressed his hand inside and felt for the stuck placenta—the source of all the blood. When he slipped a finger around the edge of it, he breathed a sigh of relief. As the placenta slipped from Vale's body, the rush of blood stopped, and Urho finally took the time to cut the cord.

Drained, Urho fell back on his ass, wet with blood and slick, covered in sweat from the strain and effort.

Vale and Jason glowed, beautiful and perfect, as they stared down at their screaming, flushed child. "I should feed him," Vale whispered. He tugged open his robe, placing the babe to his chest and cooing as the infant latched on and began to suckle.

Jason wiped tears from his eyes and kissed Vale's forehead. The moment was intimate and sweet, but Urho had some work to do on Vale's insides. The scar tissue had torn, and he needed to sew it up and paint it with iodine to prevent sepsis or infection.

It took only a little convincing to get Vale into the bed with Jason and their baby, and then Urho set about the work of making sure Vale would heal well. Jason and Vale snuggled their child and whispered names back and forth as Urho worked silently.

But between the babe, Vale when Urho's instruments pinched, and the sounds coming from Caleb's room, there was still plenty of screaming and shouting going on.

This crisis wasn't over yet.

AS SOON AS the door opened, Caleb burst out, but Xan grappled him back into his room, fingers slipping on sweat-damp, naked skin. The room was a disaster. Broken furniture was strewn everywhere. Xan's heart thundered.

"I'm here now, darling. I'm here." He held Caleb tight and pressed four fingers into Caleb's wet asshole. He kissed his sweaty hair and held him hard. "I'm sorry I'm so late."

Caleb burst into tears and clung to Xan as he shuddered and quaked in his arms. "I need help," he gritted out.

"I'm going to do such a good job helping you. I promise."

Caleb sobbed as Xan led him back to the bed. The intense wave seemed to have passed, but Caleb was clearly an aching wreck. An alpha dildo lay on the floor by the bed, apparently unused, and Xan picked it up, an idea flashing into his mind.

Caleb shuddered and squirmed, flushed all over and covered in scratch marks from where he'd tried to tear out the heat. Xan smoothed back Caleb's hair and kissed his forehead before helping him drink from a glass of water.

He then guided him from his ruined room to Xan's own, relieved to find it all in one piece still.

"You came," Caleb whispered as Xan soothed him, tucking him up into bed and curling in behind him.

"I got here as soon as I could." He didn't mention that he hadn't known about Caleb's heat until he'd arrived home.

Caleb nodded and shuddered. "He was going to help, but the

baby came."

"I know."

"I made him promise. No strangers."

Xan's throat went tight. "But you suffered."

Caleb's mouth worked, and he spit out words like gravel under a tire. "I'd rather suffer than take another stranger. I hate the way I feel after." He snuffled and held tighter to Xan. "I tried to run," he whispered, as though ashamed.

"It's instinct," Xan reassured him.

"I know, but I wasn't running to an alpha."

Xan rubbed Caleb's back and held him tight. Xan's clothes were dirty after driving half the night in an adrenaline-fueled daze, and he felt covered with filth and ripe with stress sweat, but all of that would have to wait. "You weren't?"

"It's stupid. I wanted to outrun *this*. The heat. I wanted to run away from it, away from me."

Xan squeezed his eyes closed and held tighter to Caleb. The scent of rising slick and the hint of a fresh wave on the way rose to his nostrils. He knew how his sweet omega had felt. He'd wanted to run away from himself, too. That's what he'd been doing every time he went to Monhundy. But he wasn't running anymore.

"We can't run from it, but we can face it together."

Xan shucked his clothes while whispering soothing words to Caleb, and then he took up the alpha dildo. Once he had it in hand, rifled through the bedside table drawer in search of the tablets Urho had given him all those weeks ago now. The pills for stamina.

He took two.

CHAPTER TWENTY-FIVE

S EVERAL HOURS LATER, with Caleb finally resting, Xan cleaned up and put on his robe. Thanks to the pills, he'd managed the knot and eased Caleb's suffering, and he couldn't help but feel proud. He'd forever wish he was an omega and could experience heat for himself, but he wasn't, and he couldn't. But at least he had satisfied Caleb and now he could find Urho and be his alpha-shaped omega.

But first he went to his office and called his parents' house. Joon answered, sounding tired, but evidently still employed. Xan got the information he needed to set aside some of his worries: Pater and Ray were both much improved and had continued to get better with the medication Xan had left behind.

"And my father?" he asked.

"Very angry."

"I'm sorry about that."

"Don't be," Joon said quietly. "Your pater is very angry, too, from what I've heard echoing in the hallways upstairs. I suspect your father will be on the phone to you with apologies before long."

Xan didn't bother to tell the old servant that he doubted that very much and doubted even more that he could ever deign to accept them. Instead, he asked Joon to keep him informed about Ray and his pater's health before saying goodbye.

In the kitchen, the cook seemed startled to see Xan in nothing but his robe and slippers. "Sir, you should be in bed with Mr. Riggs!"

Xan smiled tiredly. "The wave has passed, and he's hungry."

The part about Caleb's hunger wasn't true, but Xan was starving after his crazy night in the city, driving six hours in the small hours, eager to get home to the comforting arms of his lover, only to arrive to utter chaos. And *then* he'd held Caleb's heat at bay all on his own. He needed replenishment to carry on.

"How is the baby?" he asked. He'd noticed the door to Vale's room was closed when he'd passed through that hallway to offer his congratulations. He'd heard happy sounds from within, though only in Jason and Vale's tones, and he'd decided not to disturb them. As for Urho, he didn't know where he was, and he ached to see him.

"He's a howler! Strong lungs! Healthy!"

"Good news, then." Xan smiled.

He was about to ask the cook about Urho's whereabouts and the health of his cousin when Ren appeared from the door leading out to the detached wing where Janus was still staying. Carrying a tray with a full bowl of broth on it, Ren looked haggard and pale, but when he caught Xan's eye, he obviously tried to buck up.

"Sir, when I heard you'd arrived, I couldn't believe our luck. I'd started to despair."

"It *was* luck," Xan agreed. He almost began to explain that he had fled the city in the night, but then realized that would require explaining *why*, and the fight with his father and then Monhundy was absolutely not the servants' business. He finished lamely, "I'd have been here earlier if I'd known."

"Of course, you would have, sir. But you're here now. That's what matters."

"How's Janus?" Xan asked, pulling up a stool by the cook's prep counter. The cook frowned at him but didn't stop arranging a heaping plate of food for Caleb. Xan's belly rumbled, and the cook pulled out another plate and started to prepare it, too. "Is Urho with him now?"

"Dr. Bainson has been here for the last hour. Dr. Chase had to shower after the delivery, but he's consulting with the doctor now. Mr. Janus is…" Ren sighed, placed the tray in the sink to be washed, and dumped the contents of the bowl down the drain. "Not eating," he finished, though his slumped shoulders and miserable tone said so much more.

"He's doing worse then?"

"Mr. Heelies, he's a very sick man."

Xan swallowed hard and gazed past the cook out the kitchen window to vegetable gardens recently planted there. The afternoon sun—had he spent the whole day with Caleb? No wonder he was so tired!—shone on the fresh plants. He didn't know what to do with the news. And he knew so little about his cousin that he didn't know what he'd even *want*. Would he want a priest from the Holy Order of Wolf, or would he prefer to die unblessed? Was it even time to think about such things?

He snatched a carrot from the cook and chomped it thoughtfully. "I should go see him."

"Not now!" Ren exclaimed. "You can't risk carrying any sickness back to Mr. Riggs. You should wait until after the heat."

Xan opened his mouth to ask what the chances were that Janus would make it through the heat when he was interrupted.

"What happened to your face?" Urho's voice came sternly through the open kitchen door. Xan caught his breath as his lover walked into the kitchen, strong shoulders back, fresh suit, and his dark skin burnished by the rosy afternoon light from the kitchen windows. The salt-and-pepper of Urho's hair shimmered in the sun, and the smatter of wrinkles by his eyes crinkled reassuringly.

Xan's heart squeezed with joy. Urho looked like everything Xan needed to make it through the day—and everything he needed for the rest of his life. Here was the man Xan had probably thrown away his inheritance for, and Urho was worth every last cent.

Xan's stomach fluttered, and he glanced up from beneath his lashes. His reply caught on his tongue. He didn't know what had happened here at the house in his absence, and he didn't know how to explain what had happened in the city. Especially in the short amount of time afforded them before Caleb's next heat wave descended.

Urho stared at him intently. "You should be in bed."

"It's just a bruise. I'm fine."

"I meant you should be in bed with Caleb."

Xan flushed. He glanced toward the servants, and Ren excused himself from the room. The cook got busy finishing up the tray, making a show of humming under his breath.

"Caleb needed some food," Xan said, his stomach grinding with both hunger and now worry. He gestured toward the delicious-smelling fare the cook was piling up, knowing he'd be lucky to get Caleb to eat even two bites of it. However, he thought he could demolish both plates entirely himself.

"I see." Urho held himself tightly, his face carefully blank, and his eyes narrow.

Xan turned to the cook who was piling fruit salad into bowls for the tray, and said, "That's enough. Thank you."

When Xan made to take the tray, Urho stepped forward and grabbed it from the cook's hands. Following Urho out of the kitchen and into a private serving alcove just outside it, Xan's gut churned. He hadn't let himself think too much during his long drive about what he expected to find once he got home, but he'd definitely imagined his reunion with Urho quite a bit differently.

Urho placed the tray on the sideboard in the alcove and grabbed Xan roughly. His kiss was urgent, and Xan moaned into the shock of it. Urho's hands mapped his body, sliding beneath his robe and awakening his skin and his lust. Just the glide of his hands over

Xan's nipples filled him with more desire than the sex with Caleb had or ever could.

When Urho released him, he gripped Xan's face in both hands and stared into his eyes. "I'm sorry," he said, his voice gruff. "I needed to touch you. In the kitchen, I almost couldn't hold back."

"The servants don't care."

"Rumors don't care who start them either."

Xan didn't point out that they were currently only a doorway and a few steps from the cook, and that any of the other servants could come around the corner and spy them in each other's arms. Truth be told, he didn't care in the least.

Not anymore.

He didn't want to live his life hiding—not in his home, anyway. That was what he'd declared to his father, wasn't it? And to Wilbet Monhundy? And he intended to stand by those declarations.

"I'm sorry about locking Caleb in." Urho nuzzled Xan's temple, scenting his hair. "I did the best I could, but it hurt my soul to do it."

"I know. He knows, too."

"I don't think I can ever look him in the eye again."

"I hope you can, because he's requested that you join us in helping him through the rest of the heat. If Janus doesn't need you that is. Or Vale."

Urho kissed Xan's throat and then whispered, "Vale is doing better than I ever could have envisioned a few years ago. He's nursing the baby like a natural and making plenty of milk. His anus and channel are already responding to the post-birth hormones and are tightening well. He's—quite miraculously—safe."

"That's wonderful. And the baby? Is it an omega?"

"No. I believe he's an alpha based on his genitals."

"How perfect for them." Xan bit his lower lip, worry for his cousin still weighing on him. "And Janus? Does he need you?"

"The village doctor is staying with him now. He doesn't want the contagion getting down into Virona." Urho sighed and traced Xan's bruised jawline with his thumb. "As for me, well, Janus is past any help I could give. Whether or not he'll survive is up to his ability to fight. The servants are doing everything they can to make him comfortable and contain the sickness. We must keep the servants caring for him separate from any food or drink going to Vale's room. Ren knows this already. But now that Vale's delivered the baby, we have a small soul to consider as well."

"Ren will make sure every precaution is taken." Searching Urho's eyes for some hope, he asked, "Truly, though? Janus isn't likely to make it?"

Urho blinked a moment before dropping his hand from Xan's face and glancing down at his shoes. "Dr. Bainson thinks he still has a small chance, but it's touch and go." Urho met Xan's gaze again. "I tend to agree with him, though I've kept myself from direct contact for fear of catching the illness and taking it to Vale and the babe. If Janus makes it through the next few days, he might recover. Though his fever has raged so high, Dr. Bainson fears there might be ongoing problems. We can't know for sure."

"Oh, wolf-god," Xan sighed, rubbing at his eyes. He was so tired. The last twenty-four hours had been exhausting, and they still had Caleb's heat to get through before they could rest. He cleared his throat, his mind coming back to Janus. "I admit I never liked him and often resented him, but I didn't want this. Caleb will be devastated if Janus doesn't survive."

"There's a story there you haven't told me yet."

"Yes, and it's a long one."

"Xan?"

Xan looked up at Urho, taking in his kind, dark eyes, and the tender expression on his face. His stomach fluttered again. He loved this man, and maybe this man would never love him the way he'd loved his Riki, but Xan was going to take what he could get. And he'd take this man forever. Fight for him. Tell the world to fuck off for him. If only he wasn't so tired, he'd tell Urho all of that.

Urho touched the bruise on Xan's face, his fingers tracing it tenderly. "Did Caleb do this during the heat?"

"No." Xan quivered at Urho's touch.

"Then who?"

"My father," Xan said, and then added with a thick tongue, "Or maybe Monhundy."

"Your father or...?" Urho's eyes went dead, and his hand stilled in its caress. "Did you go to him?" Betrayal shone in his eyes.

"No. I would never. Please believe me. It's not what you're thinking."

Urho's expression cut Xan to the quick—the doubt and fear.

Xan's stomach curled in on itself. Stricken, he murmured, "I should be getting back to Caleb to make sure he eats."

Urho's eyes blazed, and he took hold of Xan possessively, cradling him in his arms. "I'll kill him."

Xan allowed Urho to hold him, aching with the joy of being so completely adored. He'd never experienced the kind of love Urho offered him. He struggled to reconcile it with the knowledge of Urho's room and shrine to Riki. He didn't want to be jealous of a dead man, but could he ever really compare? Wasn't he always going to be second-rate—not really an omega, and definitely not Urho's *Érosgápe*.

He shoved the thoughts aside, reveling in Urho's possessive embrace. It didn't matter. He refused to let it sidetrack him. This was his life, and his choice. Urho was his to love now.

"Monhundy's nothing to me," Xan said firmly. "Besides, I took care of it. He won't be touching me again."

"You're absolutely right he won't," Urho growled. "I'll kill him first."

Xan hastened to distract Urho from his anger. "What matters right now is Caleb, and Vale, his baby, and Janus. Monhundy is trash and his future is garbage, too." Xan rubbed Urho's arms soothingly. "I love you."

But Urho wasn't going to be distracted. "If you didn't go to him, he must have come to you."

"It doesn't matter. He's a miserable man with a miserable life." Plus Wilbet Monhundy was a coward. It gave Xan a thrill deep in his gut to remember the terror in Monhundy's eyes as he'd stared at Xan the night before. "Just leave it alone."

Urho gazed down at him, then touched the bruise again with gentle fingers. "You said this bruise could have been from your father. He hit you?"

"It's a long story. But my father and I…" Xan shook his head. "I think I might be poor before very long. Hopefully Caleb will forgive me."

Urho blinked at him. "Well, then. Lucky for you and Caleb, I have a lot of money."

"Let's discuss it later."

Urho touched the bruise again. Then he kissed it softly and moved to Xan's mouth. The kiss intensified, and Urho's hands slid beneath Xan's robe, rubbing his nipples, lighting him on fire.

"Caleb needs us," Urho whispered against Xan's lips. "Let's take the tray and see what we can get him to eat before the next wave hits."

Xan panted hard as Urho pulled away but followed him up the stairs. The wing toward Vale and Jason's room was quiet. No doubt the little family was taking a well-earned nap.

At the door to Caleb's room, Urho stopped him. "Are you sure he wants to see me?"

"He asked for you."

Urho nodded, but shame haunted his eyes. "I didn't want to

leave him like that."

"He's Caleb. He understands."

"Maybe he shouldn't." Urho huffed. "Doesn't Caleb deserve to be put first in someone's life? The way you're first in mine?"

Xan's eyes went wide, the tray he was holding suddenly heavy. "What do you mean?"

"I mean that I love you and when I think about the future, you're all that's important to me."

The rooms in Urho's house in the city seemed far away now. "I want to kiss you but—" he indicated the tray in his hands.

Urho leaned close and pressed a soft kiss to Xan's lips. "We can't share the way we love with Caleb, but we can share our devotion and friendship with him. Let's make Caleb our priority today. Let's focus on him."

Xan agreed, his heart full of respect and affection for Urho, and love for both his omega and his lover.

Caleb sat up in bed, a dazed, exhausted expression on his face, but his eyes lightened up when he spotted Urho with Xan. "That food smells dreadful," he murmured, his voice soft and wrecked. "But I'm glad to see the two of you." He smiled, relief and warm affection in his gaze.

"We brought marmalade," Urho said, dipping his head.

"And alpha condoms?" Caleb asked. "For you?"

Urho nodded, cleared his throat, and said, "I'm so sorry about—"

"Stop." Caleb held up a hand. "Just smear some marmalade on toast and feed it to me by hand as your penance. We'll call it all forgiven."

Urho chuckled, and Xan took off his robe.

"Oh, and get naked," Caleb said. "Because if this prickling is any indication, I'll be losing all this lovely clarity very, very soon."

URHO COULD BARELY remember the last time he'd been so relieved and simultaneously worried as he'd been the moment he saw Xan's mop of curls over his flushed cheeks in the kitchen. The bruises on his face had clenched Urho's gut, and Xan's tired, worn-out eyes hadn't helped matters. But the sheer joy of seeing him again—the lift in Urho's chest and the rush in his veins—couldn't be denied.

The news that the bruises came from two physical altercations with two different men who were much larger than Xan plagued Urho. No doubt he'd soon demand more information about both encounters, but for now, Xan was safe, and that was what mattered most. They had an omega in heat to deal with, and Caleb deserved every ounce of their attention, affection, and focus.

Once they were alone and naked in Caleb's room, the negotiations began. Urho was accustomed to servicing omegas in heat, but usually he simply went on instinct and the omegas were happy with that. Caleb, however, had rules.

"First," he said, munching on the orange piece that Xan had forced into his mouth. "I don't want this to be about 'making love.'"

Urho's eyebrows went up. "Come again?"

"Well, it can be about that for the two of you—in fact, that might be nice. But for me? No. I just want to be fucked and knotted to relieve the pain. I don't want a bunch of caressing and fondling, and I definitely don't want oral or even kissing. This isn't about that for me."

Urho nodded, vague confusion flitting around in his mind, but he didn't put voice to it. This was Caleb's heat and he should call the shots.

Xan asked, "Can I scent your shoulders, though? And your

neck?"

Caleb pondered. "Yes. You do that a lot, anyway. I've always liked it. So, yes."

"And can I kiss your forehead or run my fingers in your hair?" Urho asked.

Caleb nodded. "Anything you'd normally do with me, you can continue to do. Unless I say to stop, of course." He smiled at Urho, his blue eyes crinkling at the edges, and that look felt like forgiveness for having to lock him in before. Urho sighed in relief. Caleb added, "Both of those things sound nice to me. I don't want you to be cruel. That's not what I mean at all! But I prefer the sex be treated as perfunctory."

"I thought you didn't like to do this with strangers?" Urho asked, finally letting some of his confusion show.

"I don't," Caleb said. "But that doesn't mean I feel attracted to you, or particularly want this interaction to be about our 'relationship' to one another."

"I see." And he thought he did. Mostly.

"I've been lucky enough to only have to face a heat with a stranger twice in my life so far. Most of the time, the men my family hired were known to me, and they understood what I wanted. Or at least accepted it when I told them how I wanted to be treated."

"All right," Urho said.

"But you can make love with each other," Caleb said kindly, as though granting them a favor. "I wouldn't mind watching that, actually. It sounds nice even, to watch…" His cheeks went red. "I might even touch myself."

"Whatever you like," Urho said calmly, though everything about the requests were most unusual indeed.

"I can use the dildo on you, right? To help you?" Xan asked.

"Yes. You remember from the first heat what I like with that.

411

Once I get frenzied, though, I'd like you to fuck me. Hard."

"And Urho?" Xan asked.

"He should fuck *you*, most likely. But if you're having any trouble, then yes, he can fuck me. I do want to fall pregnant, though, Xan. So I'd rather it be you most of the time. Especially for knotting."

They nodded, and Xan reached for the pills on the bedside table. "I'll take a few of these."

Caleb smiled. "You were so wonderful earlier. Perfect, actually."

Xan grinned a little cockily. "I did do a good job, didn't I? I'm glad you think so, too."

Caleb laughed and let Urho feed him some marmalade on toast and another slice of orange. "I do like this pampering," he admitted a little shyly. "Afterward, you know? I like the cuddles during the knot, and even more once the knot is down. I like the attention. I feel very flattered by it."

"We can do that," Urho agreed. "I like to cuddle after knotting, too."

Xan smiled at Urho and then licked his lips. "This is a little awkward, isn't it?"

"That's how sex always seems to me," Caleb said, shrugging. "Awkward and uncomfortable, like I'm not sure where to begin."

"When the heat wave comes again, we'll help you through the awkwardness," Xan said reassuringly.

The scent of Caleb's heat pheromones and the delicious smell of his slick intensified as they continued to feed him and force him to drink. When Caleb pushed the food away firmly, they knew it was time to transition into something more. The wave was coming on harder now, and Caleb's chest flushed with the heat rising under his skin.

Urho waited for him to grow frantic again, to fight it the way he had before, but that never happened. Caleb was much calmer now that Xan was with him. Urho noticed immediately the way Caleb depended on Xan for reassurance that everything was all right, even as Caleb's body took control and spiraled him out into the delirious arousal of heat.

The trust he showed in Xan filled Urho's heart with affection, and his eyes grew damp more than once witnessing it so closely.

Xan held Caleb's hands, whispering soothing words as Urho slipped calming fingers through Caleb's hair. As the heat came on intensely, Xan fucked Caleb with the alpha dildo, helping him through several orgasms before Caleb began to beg to be fucked. Even in his delirium, Caleb knew what he wanted.

"I want to get pregnant," Caleb reminded them urgently. He gripped Urho's forearm as Xan moved in between Caleb's spread legs. "You fuck Xan, and that'll help Xan fuck me."

Urho briefly wondered if it was the right time for a pregnancy if Xan was about to be disinherited, but immediately dismissed his concern. If Caleb and Xan needed help, he'd give it to them. Any help—financial, physical, sexual—and happily so. Xan and Caleb would be just fine, no matter the situation with Xan's family. Urho would see to that. He'd pull every string, hire every attorney, tell every lie, and protect these men until his dying day.

He felt in his gut it was what he was meant to do. *This* was the reason he'd lived through the pain of losing Riki. This was his calling in life now, to protect and love Xan and his omega forever.

The sun had set long before Xan lowered himself carefully on top of Caleb, sighing as he penetrated him deeply. Caleb closed his eyes and hung onto Xan's back, accepting Xan scenting his neck and smiling a little when Xan began to move. "That's nice," Caleb murmured. "Thank you."

Xan scoffed. "No, thank *you*, Caleb, for being the best omega I could ever ask for."

"Mmm, you just think that because I'm yours." Caleb sighed,

arching up.

"Because you're perfect for me."

Caleb chuckled and then gasped. "A little harder now. And faster. Make me feel it."

Xan obeyed, the slap of his hips and balls against Caleb's body rising with the delicious, sweet scent of slick and pheromones. Urho's hard cock grew even harder, flexing and dribbling pre-come as he watched Xan and Caleb move together. The bruises on Xan's back and side worried him, but he soon forgot about them altogether, fascinated by the sensual scents, sounds, and visions before him.

He'd shared an omega in the past, especially when dealing with interminable heat, but this was different. Now he was sharing his alpha-shaped omega with Caleb and he couldn't stop the sense of proprietary pride that rose in him, the feeling that these men were his, and he was here to guide them.

He knelt behind Xan between his legs, sliding his hands down Xan's arching, hunching back as he fucked into Caleb, taking care not to press into his bruises. Then Caleb's eyes popped open, blue staring right into Urho's gaze, and he whispered, "Go on. Take him. Share him with me."

Urho didn't know how much of what he felt for Xan could be passed through to Caleb, or even how much of that Caleb would really want to experience, but he could help Xan fuck his omega and do his duty. That was something he and his achingly hard cock were absolutely ready and willing to do.

Xan thrust into Caleb's body, and he buried his face in Caleb's neck, his back flushed pink with effort. His ass crack flashed the swirl of hair that hid his beautiful hole. Urho scented along Xan's neck, taking in the odors of his sweat and excitement. Urho groaned, watching over Xan's shoulder as Caleb's eyes rolled back, relaxing into heat-driven arousal.

"That's good," he whispered into Xan's ear. "Fuck him harder. Make him come. You're doing such a good job—look how he's shaking now."

Xan moaned, his hips snapping forward, and he turned to kiss Urho. Their tongues slipped together, and Xan whimpered when Urho pulled back. "Focus," Urho said urgently. "Make him come again. You can do it."

Xan held Caleb's hips steady and fucked into him wildly.

"That's it," Urho encouraged, pressing his cock against Xan's thrusting buttocks. "Such a good boy. You're both so good."

Caleb's muscles went taut, his thighs and stomach clenching. He cried out, coming hard, his asshole convulsing around Xan's plunging cock and his dick exploding with delicious, wonderful omega come. Urho plunged his hands into it, gathering the white, slippery fluid and promptly rubbing it on his own cock.

"Perfect, my love," Urho muttered into Xan's ear. "Now hold still a moment. And then we'll make him come again. Together."

Xan grunted as Urho penetrated him, squirming as Urho's cock filled him up. "Fuck," he whispered, bowing his head. "Oh, wolf-god, this is...fuck."

"Feel good?" Urho asked, pumping gently, feeling the hot cling of Xan's body around him, reveling in the pounding of Xan's pulse against his cock, a living, loving beat that tied their lives together.

"Yes," Xan whispered, shuddering all over.

"Good. Now we'll make your omega come. We'll make him fly."

Caleb was far gone now, his body trembling as the heat wave took him, and Xan joined him in ecstasy as Urho plowed into him hard and fast, directing Xan's own thrusts into Caleb's gripping hole.

Urho knew the moment Caleb's womb finally dropped and opened, the moment Xan plunged into the heat of his womb. There was nothing like the pleasure of pushing into an omega's sweet womb—the way the mouth gripped the head of an alpha's cock, the way it seemed to kiss it and then open for it with every plunge inside.

"Fuck!" Xan cried, his head falling back. "Oh, wolf-god!"

"Yes," Urho grunted. "Come inside him. Fill him up. Give him a child."

Caleb rocked and shook, his asshole convulsing helplessly around Xan's big cock, lost in a long, brutal anal orgasm that left him drooling and incoherent. Xan continued to plow into his omega, his hips slapping against Caleb's ass and his head tossed back against Urho's shoulder.

The scent of Xan's pleasure, the rising tide of Caleb's heat pheromones, and the hot, slick, deliciousness of Xan's hole around Urho's cock aroused Urho completely. He bit down on Xan's shoulder, pumping in and out as hard and as fast as he could, and then he thrust deep, roaring with satisfaction. His body jerked hard, shoving Xan deeper into Caleb. Urho shuddered roughly as he came, spurting load after load deep into Xan's body.

Crying out in response to Urho's orgasm, Xan collapsed onto Caleb, and Urho followed him down. The wracking pleasure drew out, on and on. Urho gripped Xan's hips and shoved into him, grunting as another swell and jolt grabbed him.

"My omega," Urho whispered in Xan's ear. "Made for my cock."

Xan convulsed around Urho, shouting in lust as Urho bit his shoulder again and unloaded yet another soul-shaking spurt of come deep inside his gut.

As the violent pleasure finally passed, Urho shivered and tried to pull out, but his attempt at withdrawal was met with resistance and a cry of pain from Xan. Urho gasped, glancing to where he was plunged deep into Xan. He belatedly recognized the thick, fat feeling in the base of his cock, the tingling and pulsing as he swelled up, his knot growing hard inside Xan's body.

"Fuck," he whispered against Xan's sweat-damp skin. He licked Xan's neck and shoulder, pressing open-mouthed kisses to him. "Oh, sweet fucking wolf-god," he murmured. He gripped Xan, shoving in as deep as he could, feeling the rub of Xan's swollen prostate against the underside of his throbbing cock. He whispered, "I'm knotting you. Hang on. Breathe through it. Such a good boy. Such a good omega."

Xan froze in his arms, whimpering. As Urho's knot finished swelling, pressing hard against the walls of Xan's body and filling Xan's hole in a way it had never been filled before, Xan grabbed hold of Caleb, choked out a wordless cry, and convulsed on Urho's knot helplessly. The scent of Xan's come and the explosion of alpha mating pheromones burst in the air around them, making Urho roar and come again as Xan hunched in wildly and shot hard up into Caleb's womb, screaming in pleasure and knotting him, too.

Beneath them, Caleb groaned and convulsed. He was flushed all over, his eyes rolled back and his nipples hard as he took Xan's knot. His own cock spurted, and his body shook, riding out orgasms as the pressure against his omega glands and prostate overwhelmed him. Slick gushed out, allowing Xan to settle in even deeper, and everyone groaned, quaking, as every movement forced them all into ecstasy again.

Eventually, Urho came back from the freefall of pleasure long enough to maneuver them—with many cries of pain and pleasure—into a more comfortable position so they didn't crush Caleb with their combined weight. Carefully, and with the utmost gentleness and love pounding in his veins, Urho tipped them onto their sides. Urho pulled Xan flush against him, still buried deep inside, and Caleb hitched a leg up to sling over Xan and Urho's hips.

They clung to each other, letting the knots wring every scrap of pleasure from their bodies until they ached and moaned, and still came some more.

Xan and Caleb pressed their foreheads together, whimpering and whispering reassurances to each other. "That's good, Caleb," and "Yes, Xan, thank you," rose up between them. Urho nuzzled Xan's neck and breathed him in, holding tight to them both as they all trembled and shivered through aftershocks.

"I love you," Urho whispered in Xan's ear, while Xan twitched on his knot. "My own omega."

Xan reached back and threaded his fingers into Urho's hair, holding on as they blissed out together, flesh locked into flesh.

XAN QUIVERED, LOST in pleasure, knotted into Caleb at his front and knotted onto Urho at his back. His ass was stretched wider than he'd ever known possible, and his prostate was alight with pleasure. His cock was constantly milked by Caleb's ongoing orgasms, and the hot, sweet embrace of his lover holding them all together in his big, strong arms was heaven.

This joining went beyond his former understanding of love. It was blissful, erotic, and so full of tender, aching emotions that his whole body felt like an exposed heart, all shimmering nerve endings and pure adoration. This was his true home. They were the beginning and the end. For once, his inner alpha and omegas were both entirely satisfied.

Honest and perfect and complete.

CHAPTER TWENTY-SIX

DAYS SLIPPED BY in a haze of physical pleasure and emotional contentment the likes of which Xan had never known.

As they became accustomed to each other, the rules around their encounters relaxed—with renegotiations initiated only by Caleb during the rests between waves.

So long as neither Urho nor Xan behaved toward him in a way that was overly 'loverly,' Caleb grew more playful, giving himself up to enjoyment of his omega needs with a raw, focused abandon that Urho openly admired, praising him and using Caleb's pleasure to egg on Xan to greater heights.

And though the three of them eventually moved between most positions comfortably, it always ended with Xan knotted into Caleb and Urho knotted into Xan, and all of them delirious with bliss, just the way Xan liked it best.

As Caleb's heat ebbed away, though, Urho stopped fucking Xan and began tending to his asshole instead. Xan fussed about it, regretting the loss of the knot, knowing he wouldn't get to experience it again until the next time Caleb went into heat. And if Caleb fell pregnant, that could be more than a year!

But Urho was right to deny him. Not being an omega, Xan wasn't built for knots, or accustomed to taking them, and while he'd enjoyed it immensely, often begging for a knot as much as Caleb had, the reality was that he was swollen and bruised inside. Even a single finger inserted now hurt.

It wasn't particularly pleasant when Urho pressed ice and liniment into Xan between the final bouts of Caleb's heat, either. They alternately chilled and burned him, and the promise of reduced swelling didn't seem like enough to put up with the discomfort. Though Xan did love that Urho cuddled him close while the ice and medicine made Xan squirm and complain.

"Shh, don't argue," Urho murmured, kissing Xan's forehead. "You'll thank me when you've healed up and can take me again."

"Don't argue with your alpha," Caleb murmured sleepily, his face tucked against Xan's neck and his long body curled up, trembling with exhaustion. He was sticky and hot, but Xan wasn't ready to let go of him yet. "He knows what's best for you."

"You wouldn't say that if he'd put ice up your—"

Caleb clamped a hand over Xan's mouth. "Don't argue with your alpha."

Xan rolled his eyes but didn't protest again. And even though it didn't feel good at first, there was no doubt that as the last day wore on, his asshole became less swollen inside. He thought he'd be able to take Urho again before a week had passed with any luck.

Eventually, the heat was over, and Urho and Xan woke from a long, deep nap to the sound of the water running in Caleb's bathroom and Caleb gone from the bed. Xan yawned and stretched, Urho kissed his chest and stomach, and Xan chuckled as he dipped lower and mouthed Xan's cock.

"I'm broken," Xan muttered. "It's not going to get up again today."

Urho licked the head, smiling as a little dribble of pre-come bubbled up despite his flaccid state. He crawled up Xan's body to kiss his mouth. "I love you, alpha-shaped omega mine."

"I love you, too," Xan whispered against his lips. "Thank you for being here with us."

"It was an honor."

"You are both disgustingly in love," Caleb said from the doorway leading to the bathrooms and closets, wrapped in a robe and freshly showered. He smiled happily though. "But, I'm quite glad about that, because I think we managed something pretty wonderful together."

Xan sat up, his stomach flip-flopping. "Yeah?"

Caleb rubbed his flat belly. "I can't promise anything, and who knows if it will truly take, but I feel different. I think we did it." He broke into a grin. "I hope so. I've wanted a baby for so long. I hope he looks like you."

Xan laughed, and Urho kissed his shoulder, sending a shiver through him. "Well, I hope he looks like you. You're so beautiful."

Caleb rolled his eyes but looked pleased. "Let's just hope he doesn't look like Urho. Then we'd have some explaining to do."

They all laughed softly though it was impossible. Urho had only knotted Xan. There was a sudden quiet in the room as they all looked at each other and the future possibility hung in the air.

"Though perhaps one day..." Caleb said, shrugging. "Once an heir is secured. And once we've established that society and the rest of the world can simply go fuck off."

Urho scoffed softly at the idea, but his cheeks grew a bit darker, and a wetness appeared in his eyes. Xan wondered if a child was something Urho would want with the two of them. A biological child of his own. Or if that was something he'd only wanted with Riki.

"We'll start with this one," Caleb said, smiling widely again and going to the curtains to throw them wide. A fresh, bright sun was rising on a clear day, and Caleb glowed in it like an angel. "I think he will be a very good place to start."

Urho drew Xan into his arms, and the two of them admired Caleb, the hope of the future babe growing tangibly between them all, filling the room with promise.

"HE'S NOT YET fully recovered, Mr. Heelies," Ren said, his eyes drained and his skin gray with exhaustion. "But it appears your cousin will live. Though, if I may say so, he is much changed." Ren pressed his lips together and then whispered brokenly, "The fever has left some damage."

Xan, Caleb, and Urho sat in the library listening to Ren's report. Dr. Bainson had returned to the town the prior morning, leaving Ren to care for Janus for the rest of his recovery.

"What kind of damage?" Caleb asked, a hand resting protectively on his stomach the way it had all morning during breakfast with Jason, Vale, and the new babe, whom they'd chosen to name Virona Sabel.

Xan questioned the wisdom of the name wholeheartedly, finding it a bit too on the nose, and he questioned Vale's true poetic abilities if he didn't see it. But the pink, screaming thing wasn't his child to name, and in the end, they planned to call the babe Viro for short. That, in Xan's estimation, seemed much more reasonable.

"Has his mind been affected?" Urho asked when Ren paused for a long time after Caleb's question.

"In a way," Ren conceded. "He is lethargic and moody. I think he could use some encouragement. He seems to be profoundly full of regrets." He darted a glance at Caleb and then the floor.

"He's no longer contagious?" Urho asked, putting his hand on Caleb's knee, as though to stop him from rising and going to Janus immediately. Xan wondered how he'd known to do just that.

"He's not. The doctor said that once the sheets were burned, and the room scrubbed down, he was safe for any visitor. Mr. Sabel has gone to see him a few times since we followed those orders, but Mr. Janus doesn't talk with him. And he refuses to leave the detached wing. Frankly, sirs, the servants would like to move back, but none of them dare to with him there. He roams the place like a ghost."

"I see," Caleb said, pushing Urho's hand away and rising. "I'll go to him now."

Xan's heart clenched, and he rose to his feet, wanting to grab Caleb and hold him back from going to visit his first... Not *love*. That was wrong. His first hope. But he only hugged Caleb and murmured, "Come to me when you're done?"

"Of course," Caleb said, kissing his cheek as though sensing Xan's distress. "Don't worry. My heart is devoted to our life together. I only want to help him."

Xan nodded and watched with an anxiety he resented as Caleb followed Ren out the library door and into the great hall.

"He's going to come back to us," Urho said calmly. "Sit down. We'll wait for him here together."

"But what if he loves him?"

"He doesn't. But, if he did, he's carrying your child."

"Is he?"

"I scent a change in him, don't you? The spark of something different and new."

"Yes." Xan's heart thrilled. "That's our baby?"

"Yes." Urho tugged Xan close against his side, nuzzling his hair. "That's your baby."

"Ours," Xan insisted, and a beautiful smile creased Urho's face.

Xan tried to rest with Urho, but he couldn't stop imagining what was happening between Caleb and Janus. An hour passed, during which Urho read aloud to him from the small book he'd given Xan all those months ago. Urho had been pleased to find it in Xan's bedroom, packed in with other keepsakes he'd brought from the city. It was a comic collection featuring an alpha boy and his pet snail; silly, but typically entertaining enough. Not today, though.

The phone in Xan's office began to ring. He leapt up, eager for the excuse to move, but then his stomach knotted up hard. The only person who would call his library extension directly was Joon. Xan had left a message for him earlier in the day asking him to call and inform him of Ray and his pater's progress since he'd been so disconnected from the world after bolting himself into Caleb's room for the duration of the heat. He'd been waiting for a return call ever since.

"Lofton Estate in Virona, Xan Heelies speaking," he said breathlessly, dropping into the seat by his desk. His heart hammered, and he wiped a hand over his mouth. "Hello?"

"Darling, it's so good to hear your voice."

Tears filled Xan's eyes. "Pater?"

"I've called every day, and every day they told me that your omega was still in heat. Did it go well, love? Do you have hope?"

"Yes," Xan said, his throat tight.

Urho leaned against the doorjamb, watching him curiously.

"I'm so glad. And you're well?"

"I am. Are you?"

"Almost entirely."

"And Ray?"

"He's recovered beautifully. And all thanks to you and the medicine you brought for us. Your father has much to be grateful to you for."

"Pater…" Xan squeezed his eyes closed. He sighed as Urho drew close and slipped a reassuring hand into his hair. "Father and I…"

"I know, love. And your father is wrong, *was* wrong, and has been wrong for a long time. He's currently suffering the full weight of my displeasure. He's miserable."

Xan huffed a broken-sounding laugh and wiped at his wet cheeks. "I don't think this is something Father and I will be able to get past."

"Perhaps not." Pater sounded calm, as though he'd expected Xan to say exactly that, as though he didn't blame him. "I hope you and I will be able to move forward, though? I believe you promised me that this autumn I might meet a grandbaby?"

"Pater, you have to know—before you punish Father further—you need to know the truth about me."

His pater spoke calmly. "You're unmanned. I've known since you were a toddler with dimpled knees, darling. I've known since you turned to me with wide eyes and proclaimed Mr. Roling the most beautiful man you'd ever seen. Do you remember Mr. Roling, dear? A broad-chested, quite hairy, but kind-hearted alpha that used to direct the symphony?" Pater laughed softly. "We had him over for dinner once a month the entire year you were five."

"We did?"

"Oh, yes. Your father was trying to impress me with his deep abiding love of music, or some such nonsense. It's hard to remember. Your father is always trying to impress me with *something*."

"*Érosgápe*," Xan murmured.

"It's a delight and an absurdity, love. In some ways, I think you should be grateful you don't have one."

"I have a lover," Xan said softly.

"Do you? I'm glad. You deserve that, Xan. Does Caleb know?"

"He does. He likes him, too."

"That's lovely, darling. Truly."

"Pater, why…" Xan swallowed hard, his throat so tight he could barely breathe. "Why did you let him treat me so badly for so long? If this is how you feel? If you knew about me and you didn't care? I don't understand how you could just let him—"

Pater sighed heavily. "Your father is hard to live with, Xan. He's jealous and petty. He's always been afraid that I loved you more than him. Why you and not Ray, or even little Jordan, I don't know. But he focused all of that alpha possessiveness onto you. I thought if I followed his rules, if I let him handle things the way he wanted, then he might understand that I love him devotedly, as only *Érosgápe* can—and perhaps he'd leave you alone."

Xan scrubbed his face, tears slipping hotly down his cheeks.

"I was wrong. It never worked. He saw only what he feared to see. He heard only what he feared to hear." Pater grew quiet for a moment. "I'm sorry, Xan. I should have stood up for you before now. I love you. You're my dearest boy and I let you down horribly."

Xan couldn't tell Pater that he was wrong. He sat in silence, Urho's hands on his shoulders, listening to his pater breathe.

Finally, Pater asked humbly, "May I come meet my grandchild this autumn?"

"Yes," Xan whispered.

"I'll leave your father at home."

"Yes," Xan agreed again.

"Can I bring Ray?"

"Please do."

His pater sighed in relief. "Good. Let's talk again soon?"

"Yes." He felt like fool repeating the same answer, but the conversation felt too weighted and surreal for anything more.

"Oh, and, Xan? You will *not* be disinherited. Your father will do that over my dead body. Expect a call from Ray before long to discuss future assignments and plans with regards to the company. You are Xan Heelies, the rightful heir to Doxan Heelies, and my only living alpha son. You'll have what's yours." His pater's voice rang with determination.

"Thank you," Xan said.

When the phone rested in the cradle again, he buried his head in his arms and fought back tears. Urho rubbed his shoulders softly, and then, finally, drew him up into his arms, holding him while he cried.

URHO WATCHED AS Xan walked out to the beach where Caleb stood staring at the horizon. He hung back, not wanting to assume more than he should, or pressure Caleb in any way. He knew one worried alpha was enough for any omega to contend with, two would be unfair.

Yet when Caleb turned and saw Urho lingering by the dunes, he rolled his eyes and waved him over. "Join us. You should hear this," he called. Caleb grabbed Xan's arm and tugged him into a giant embrace.

When Urho reached them, Caleb was saying, "As if I would ever leave you! Why are you such an idiot, Xan Heelies?"

Xan hugged Caleb fiercely, and Caleb reached for Urho, too. The sea crashed behind them, waves pounding the sand as the sun slipped lower in the sky. It'd been a long first day after an intense heat, and they were all tired and emotional. Or that's what Urho told himself as his chest grew tight with feeling.

He held *so much* in his embrace—two wonderful men and a future that, for the first time since Riki's death, held real promise of joy. He hoped fiercely to keep it forever.

When they finally let go of each other, Caleb drew them down to the sand, where they sat letting the wind buffet their hair and beat at their clothes. Caleb finally spoke. "He says he's in love with me and he regrets his behavior before." He sounded tired— disappointed, perhaps, or something close to it. "When he rejected me after I told him that I was asexual."

"He should regret it," Xan said fiercely. "You're wonderful."

Caleb's smile was thin, but he nodded in agreement. "I am. And he should. But he also wants me to run away with him." He laughed at that, a belly laugh that lacked the bitterness Urho had expected. Then he shook his head and tried to shake the laugh off, growing somber again. "I told him no, of course. He cried. I held him. He's a spoiled child, truly. He's unaccustomed to not getting what he wants."

"And you're what he wants?" Xan asked anxiously. "Does he know…" he touched Caleb's stomach. "About this?"

"I didn't tell him. I don't know if he could scent it. I don't really care." Caleb waved a long, lovely hand in the air dismissively. "He doesn't want me, not truly. He thinks he does only because he's so lonely and so sad. The life he's made for himself—seducing married omegas and trying to take Xan's inheritance for his own—is pathetic. Never choosing something because he wants it, never trying for something that could actually be his, only wanting things because they belong to someone else. It's a child's game." Caleb sighed. "I hoped this illness would be a wake-up call for him. But I think he's still stuck in the same rut. He has no idea of what he wants for himself. Not truly."

"What if he truly does want you?"

Caleb snorted. "He doesn't. But so what? If he did, well, it's far too late." He turned to Xan, taking both hands. "Do you really doubt that I want to be your omega? After everything?" He pressed Xan's hand to his stomach. "After what we're making together? The three of us?"

Xan shook his head. "I don't doubt that you love me." He looked toward Urho, and Urho's heart skipped a beat. "That you love us."

"Then don't doubt that I want this life with you. I chose it. I chose *you*, remember? Not the other way around. We're going to build something unique and perfect for us. Our children will grow up knowing true love comes in all packages. That there are different kinds of love and friendship. We're going to quietly, gradually, begin to change the world."

"You're quite the optimist," Xan said, laughing, the wind from the ocean tossing his curls wildly. Urho's heart clenched with affection. He wanted to kiss each of Xan's curls.

"I suppose I am. Urho can be our pragmatist."

"Me? I'm the most ridiculous of us all," Urho muttered. "I'm the one who intends to walk away from a very staid, boring, and safe life to become a happy blasphemer living in the perversion of wolf-god's law."

"Oh, wolf-god," Caleb said lightly. "As if he cares whose dick goes where? Doesn't he have bigger things to worry about? Like how well we love each other?"

"If that's his biggest concern, then I think we're doing all right," Urho said.

Xan looked between them both. "I feel sorry for Janus. He's missing out on so much. Not the least of which is my inheritance."

"Oh?" Caleb asked, a smile spreading across his face. "Is that so?"

"According to my pater," Xan said. "I talked with him on the phone. He and Ray are safe. And he says so is my place as the heir."

"I knew he'd come around when it truly counted," Caleb said, nodding. "He loves you and, more than that, he knows what's right and what's wrong. Don't worry. He'll straighten your father out in no time. *Érosgápe* can do that."

Urho had guessed as much from what he'd overheard of Xan's conversation. But it was still a relief to know that Xan wasn't going to suffer the public humiliation of being disinherited, nor the potential legal ramifications of having his father declare before the Holy Church that Xan was unmanned.

"What do you think we should name him?" Caleb asked, turning his attention back to the sunset and putting his hand over his stomach again.

"It's a bit early for that, isn't it?" Urho said. "You have a lot of months to go."

"It's never too early to dream," Caleb said. "I'm thinking something bright. Something clean. Blanco, maybe. For white."

"Your favorite color," Urho said, nodding.

"Or lack of color," Caleb corrected.

"I like Riki," Xan blurted.

Urho's throat grew tight, but he remained silent.

Caleb's smile grew. "Oh, yes. Riki. That's a good name. Riki Heelies. I think that would be perfect."

"What do you think, Urho?" Xan asked cautiously, the light of sunset glowing in his eyes.

Urho grabbed them both and held on with all his might, his heart pounding terrifically and his eyes close to overflowing.

"I think he likes it, too," Xan said, laughing.

"I think he loves it," Urho gritted out. "Almost as much as I love you, Xan."

The three of them separated, and Urho took Xan's face in his hands, kissing him deeply.

"Ah," Caleb sighed, getting to his feet and wandering closer to the surf, his voice carrying on the wind as he left them to it. "A happy ending. I always love those."

Urho held the omega of his heart safely in his arms and had to agree.

EPILOGUE

R IKI HEELIES WAS born after a night of misery and screaming. He came kicking into the world feet first, scaring the pants off Xan and Urho, who'd delivered him. Hale and hardy, the baby unleashed a wail.

"What do I do?" Caleb asked, holding the screaming babe. "I can make a print, use a printing press, put on a show in the Virona art gallery with no problem, but already I'm failing at being a pater. I thought it was supposed to be natural?" His voice was high pitched and threaded with anxiety.

"Shh," Xan soothed. He wasn't accustomed to seeing his omega so flustered. Caleb was always collected, and even throughout the pregnancy he'd been calm. The labor, not so much, but that was painful and scary for all of them.

Urho sat on the bed next to them, took the baby in his big hands, and examined him. "He just needs a feed."

"That's all?" Caleb asked. "There's nothing wrong with him? What if there's something wrong with him?"

"He's healthy, omega mine, and so are you." Xan sat on Caleb's other side, watching as Urho carefully wiped the baby down, and then put on a little fold of cloth to cover his genitals. Then he wrapped Riki up again and handed him to Caleb.

"There," Urho whispered. "Hold him close. That's it."

Caleb gazed wonderingly as the babe latched onto his nipple, the wailing ceasing.

"How lucky am I?" Urho asked softly. "Sitting here with my

three beautiful omegas."

Caleb glanced up. "He's an omega?"

"Yes," Urho said. "Like his namesake. And his pater. And his father."

Xan laughed softly. "I'm not really an omega, you know."

"You're mine," Urho murmured. Xan's heart quickened, and he smiled helplessly.

Caleb kissed the baby's head. "I guess we'll have to make another one if we want an heir."

"Or we can say screw the rules," Xan said. "Continue our trend of giving the finger to the established way of doing things and leave it all to little Riki here."

"Or we can have more babies," Caleb repeated. "I do want at least one more, you know."

"You didn't think so a few hours ago!" Xan exclaimed, laughing. "You were very angry about it all!"

Caleb stared down at the baby in his arms. "He's worth it."

"He is," Urho agreed.

"Yes," Xan smiled and snuggled in close. "Welcome to the world, Riki Heelies. Your three parents already love you so much."

WITH CALEB AND the beautiful babe sleeping soundly, Xan and Urho walked along the shore, the warm surf swirling around their bare feet in the moonlight. They held hands and shared kisses.

Xan could hardly believe he was actually a father. He'd done it. It all seemed like a dream, and he squeezed Urho's hand, letting Urho's strong, steady presence ground him, as always.

The stress of the day ebbed away, and they began to talk of other things.

"How is the new clinic coming?" Xan asked, referring to the

office Urho was setting up in the village. Not only was it time he got back to his calling, but it also engendered good will in the village to cut down on the potential gossip. It would provide new jobs in both the creation of the clinic and in the running of it, plus the benefit of another skilled doctor in the area.

The flu epidemic of the prior year had just narrowly missed Virona and left thousands of casualties in the city. The sense that another episode like that might not leave the village unscathed also contributed to Urho's welcome in the area. An extra doctor made everyone feel safer.

So far, they'd dealt with any questions regarding Urho's choice to live at Lofton by saying that he'd spent many lonely years after the loss of his *Érosgápe* in his city home, and that he no longer had the stomach for such solitude. The mention of Riki did much to stop deeper questions, putting an end to most speculation. Everyone pitied an alpha that had suffered Urho's loss, and no one blamed him for soothing himself with the care and comfort of intimate friends.

"The contractors you recommended are doing great work. I think I can start interviewing for staff positions soon."

"That's good news." As Urho talked more about the clinic and what came next, Xan's mind went back to the interesting phone call he'd shared with his pater, announcing baby Riki's arrival.

After a few minutes, Xan interrupted Urho's discussion of new obstetric tools he intended to purchase by saying, "Pater was thrilled about Riki."

"I'm sure he was. Does he plan to visit soon?"

"Yes, though I convinced him to give Caleb a couple of weeks breathing room first."

"Good idea."

"He said that Janus is still playing the hermit in Montrew, and, even more surprisingly, behaving himself. No love affairs or poor behavior in months."

"Your father must be devastated by Janus's sudden loss of ambition."

"I think he's more baffled than anything. Pater also had some other interesting news." Xan bit his bottom lip. The next topic was always a tense one even though he'd shared all the gory details of his final run-in with Monhundy long ago. "Wilbet Monhundy was arrested last month."

Urho's fists clenched, and he was silent for a long moment before gritting out a single word. "Good."

"He was found guilty of raping prostitutes in the Calitan district."

Urho nodded curtly.

"It's not anticipated that he'll be released for a very long time. If ever."

"Excellent."

Xan cleared his throat. "Yes. I'm glad that he met such a poor end, but I do feel sorry for his omega. Kerry never had a brutal bone in his body."

"In all likelihood, he was abused, too." Urho cracked his knuckles. "Men like Monhundy enjoy giving pain."

"Yes."

They walked quietly for several more minutes, the moon sparkling over the water, and the water lapping at the shore, washing away the remains of the day.

"Anyway, I thought you'd like to know." Xan took Urho's clenched fingers and unfolded them. "That portion of my life is put away. For good."

Urho raised Xan's hand to his mouth and kissed the knuckles. "I love you and I'm glad you are safe from him. I'll feel better when you go into the city knowing that he's not there to accost you."

Xan nuzzled Urho's neck, and they held onto each other as the water swirled at their feet. Finally, Xan asked softly, "Speaking of, do you really have to go into the city tomorrow?"

"I need to see Yosef about making some legal preparations for you and Caleb should anything happen to me."

"Don't talk about that."

"It needs to be considered, love. And I need to see a real estate agent about the house. I promised Mako. It's time I decided what to do with the place."

"I don't want you to sell it," Xan blurted. "I want you to keep it. The house and, well, even the room. The one with all the mementos of your Riki."

Urho swallowed hard. "You know about that?"

"I saw then, when I…" Xan waved his hand. "It doesn't matter. What does matter is that it's important."

"That was the home I shared with Riki. It's no place to start a future with you, Caleb, and the baby."

"You're wrong. It's the perfect place. We can't forget Riki was here, or what you shared as *Érosgápe*, or…your son with him."

"We were going to name him Tarin."

"That's a good name."

Urho shrugged. "It was Riki's choice. I wanted the name of a friend of mine who'd died in the war. Evan."

"That's a good name, too." Xan held onto Urho's biceps. He needed to get this right. "If you sold the house, what would become of all that stuff? Or the bedroom you shared with him?"

"I can't just leave it there to molder." Urho frowned.

"We don't have to. I'll sell our place in the city. When we go in for business or family dinners, we'll stay at your home instead." He'd recently come to a cold but reasonable agreement with his father to attend family feast nights again for the sake of his pater. So long as Urho was invited as well. "We'll stay in one of the guest rooms."

"We can change the room," Urho said.

"Maybe. But if we do it this way, we can all learn about Riki and Tarin. Our new Riki should know about where we got his name. We should all know."

Urho gazed down at Xan. The moon shone in his eyes. "You're a good man."

"Am I?" Xan laughed. "I mean, I try to be, but—"

Urho took Xan's face in his hands and kissed him fiercely. "You are."

Desire sparked to life, and Xan begged against Urho's lips, "Show me."

They practically raced to their bedroom, all the emotions of the day coalescing into passion. They tore off their clothes, and Xan stretched out on his back on the mattress, Urho burying his face between his legs.

Xan groaned, "Oh, yes," spreading his legs wider and letting Urho's tongue get in his hole deeply. "That's right. There, *there*!" The sweet, slippery slide never failed to thrill Xan and bring every cell of his being into wild arousal.

Urho rose up above him, stroking his cock, and Xan's heart skittered in excitement. "What do you want?" Urho asked, his voice deep and scratchy with need.

"Fuck me," Xan said. "Hard."

"Are you going to come for me?"

"Yes."

"Are you going to milk my cock with your tight little hole?"

"Yes," Xan whimpered. He spread his legs wider. "Do it. Fuck me."

Urho grinned, a white slash in his dark face, and then he retrieved the lube from the side drawer by the bed. He worked it over his cock and bent Xan almost in half before driving deep inside with no more preparation.

"Yes!" Xan cried, arching up to meet him. "Hard."

"You sound like you're in heat," Urho grunted, fucking into him aggressively.

"Harder," Xan muttered, wanting to feel his lover tomorrow, wanting the anxiety and fear that had gripped him all day to be rattled out of his body with the force of Urho's thrusts.

"Like this?" Urho said, slamming into him. "Or like this?" He gently cradled Xan's throat in both hands, smirking down at him as he rammed him with his cock. There was no pressure, no threat, just pure ownership, and Xan collapsed into a rutting, wailing, wanting mess. His cock spurted pre-come, his body rocked with convulsions, and his ass worked Urho's cock with every plunge inside.

"That's right," Urho muttered. "That's my sweet omega."

Xan whined and reached down to take hold of his cock, but Urho shook his head. "That's not how omegas come," he taunted. "Show me how omegas come, Xan."

"Oh, fuck," Xan moaned, his eyes fluttering up and his hips hitching. "I don't know if I can." He was so high on adrenaline, so strung out. He needed the release of orgasm, but he wasn't sure he could reach it.

"You can. You will."

Urho's balls hit Xan's ass with each thrust, and Xan lifted his legs to try to rut his cock against Urho's stomach. "No, omega mine," Urho whispered. "Come on my cock. Milk my orgasm out of me."

Xan groaned. He closed his eyes, focusing on the pleasure of Urho's cock rubbing against his prostate, the sweet friction of him rushing in and out of his ass, the tightness of his hole around Urho's girth, and the burning, delicious stretch of taking him, again and again.

"That's right," Urho muttered. "Mmm-hmm, show me."

Climax hovered just outside Xan's reach, release elusive and yet so close. His balls ached, orgasm rising in him. And then it was on him, hard and explosive, bursting from his groin and rushing over his body in intense, throbbing pulses. He heard Urho's shout and felt his body grow tight, and when he opened his eyes, still aching all over with pleasure, he saw Urho's grimace as he came hard, shooting into Xan's convulsing hole.

The afterglow was sweet, the anxiety of the night and the intensity of their quickly-taken pleasure releasing them into a sweaty heap of intertwined limbs. Xan whimpered sadly when Urho eventually withdrew. "I wish you could stay inside me always."

The emptiness Urho left behind was always a little unsettling, but Xan knew it was only a matter of hours, days at most, before he'd feel him deeply again.

"I'm always inside you, remember?" Urho whispered, cuddling Xan close. "You're full of me—in your heart."

"In my soul."

"We're the beginning and the end."

"The alpha and the omega," Xan said with a violent, beautiful shiver. The words were sacred, a vow, an oath. "Forever."

Urho gazed into Xan's eyes. "Yes, my omega. Forever."

THE END

If you loved Urho, Xan, and Caleb, and if you'd like to read two bonus stories or cut scenes featuring them and/or other characters from Alpha Heat, sign up for my newsletter and receive immediate access!

Letter from Leta

Dear Reader,

Thank you so much for reading *Alpha Heat*, the second in the *Heat of Love* series! If you enjoyed this book, the universe expands with the third book, *Bitter Heat*. Also, in case you missed the first book, you can catch up with *Slow Heat*, and follow Jason and Vale on into their own side story in *Slow Birth*.

Extra stories for this and other book universes can be found at my Patreon.

Be sure to follow me on BookBub or Amazon to be notified of new releases in this series and others. And look for me on Facebook for snippets of the day-to-day writing life. To see some sources of my inspiration, follow my Pinterest boards. I'm also on Instagram, so add me there, too!

If you enjoyed the book, please take a moment to leave a review! Reviews not only help readers determine if a book is for them, but also help a book show up in searches.

Also, for the audiobook connoisseur, the first two books in the series, *Slow Heat* and *Alpha Heat*, are available at most retailers that sell audio, narrated by the talented Michael Ferraiuolo.

Thank you for being a reader!
Leta

Book 1 in the Heat of Love series

SLOW HEAT

by Leta Blake

A lustful young alpha meets his match in an older omega with a past.

Professor Vale Aman has crafted a good life for himself. An unbonded omega in his mid-thirties, he's long since given up hope that he'll meet a compatible alpha, let alone his destined mate. He's fulfilled by his career, his poetry, his cat, and his friends.

When Jason Sabel, a much younger alpha, imprints on Vale in a shocking and public way, longings are ignited that can't be ignored. Fighting their strong sexual urges, Jason and Vale must agree to contract with each other before they can consummate their passion.

But for Vale, being with Jason means giving up his independence and placing his future in the hands of an untested alpha—as well as facing the scars of his own tumultuous past. He isn't sure it's worth it. But Jason isn't giving up his destined mate without a fight.

Book 2.5 in the Heat of Love series

SLOW BIRTH

by Leta Blake

Jason and Vale are back in this side story set in the *Heat of Love* universe!

A romantic getaway turns dramatic when an unexpected heat descends on Vale, leaving Jason with no choice but to act. The resulting pregnancy is dangerous for Vale and terrifying for Jason, but with the help of friends and family, they choose to embrace their uncertain future. Together they find all the love, joy, and heat they need to guide them through!

While this story follows the characters from *Slow Heat*, it would be most enjoyable if read directly after *Alpha Heat*, as it takes place contemporaneously with that book.

Book 3 in the Heat of Love series

BITTER HEAT

by Leta Blake

A pregnant omega trapped in a desperate situation. An unattached alpha with a lot to prove. And an unexpected fall into love that could save them both.

Kerry Monkburn is contracted to a violent alpha in prison for brutal crimes. Now pregnant with the alpha's child, he lives high in the mountains, far above the city that once lured him in with promises of a better life. Enduring bitterness and fear, Kerry flirts with putting an end to his life of darkness, but fate intervenes.

Janus Heelies has made mistakes in the past. In an effort to redeem himself, integrity has become the watchword for his future. Training as a nurse under the only doctor willing to take him on, Janus is resolute in his intentions: he will live cleanly in the mountains and avoid all inappropriate affairs. But he doesn't anticipate the pull that Kerry exercises on his heart and mind.

As the question of Kerry's future health and safety comes to an explosive head, only the intervention of fate will see these desperate men through to a happy ending.

Winter's Heart

Winter-fox always brings Tristan the best gifts

Tristan wakes every winter holiday to find a present that delights him or teaches him an important lesson.

Learn more about the character of Tristan, *Bitter Heat*'s Kerry and Janus's son, in this short winter holiday-themed story. This small bonus book doesn't contain the heat level of the full-length novels in this series, but it has all the cozy, hopeful warmth for a sweet holiday read. While it ends on a romantic note, the story does **not** contain a romance arc.

This story is **not a standalone** and is best read as an addition to the *Heat of Love* series, preferably after reading *Bitter Heat*. But if you should happen to read it out of order, you can find the rest of the books on Amazon and in Kindle Unlimited. *Another Heat of Love bonus novella by Leta Blake.*

Winter's Truth

Winter-fox brings Viro some surprising truths for the holiday

Viro Sabel is eleven years old and still entirely innocent about life. This year winter-fox brings him some surprising truths that alter the way he sees the world and his place in it.

Learn more about the character of Viro, *Slow Heat*'s Vale and Jason's son, in this **winter holiday-themed novella**. This medium-sized bonus book **features spicy scenes** between Vale and Jason, family scenes, and emotional moments. While the novella's epilogue teases a relationship for an adult Viro, it ends with a mystery regarding this person's identity.

This story is ***not* a standalone** and is best read as an addition to the *Heat of Love* series, preferably after reading *Slow Heat, Alpha Heat,* and *Slow Birth*. But if you should happen to read it out of order, you can find the rest of the books in the series on Amazon and in Kindle Unlimited.

An Omegaverse by Leta Blake writing as Blake Moreno

HEAT FOR SALE

Heat can be sold but love is earned.

In a world where omegas sell their heats for profit, Adrien is a university student in need of funding. With no family to fall back on, he reluctantly allows the university's matcher to offer his virgin heat for auction online. Anxious, but aware this is the reality of life for all omegas, Adrien hopes whoever wins his heat will be kind.

Heath—a wealthy, older alpha—is rocked by the young man's resemblance to his dead lover, Nathan. When Heath discovers Adrien is Nathan's lost son from his first heat years before they met, he becomes obsessed with the idea of reclaiming a piece of Nathan.

Heath buys Adrien's heat with only one motivation: to impregnate Adrien, claim the child, and move on. But their undeniable passion shocks him. Adrien doesn't know what to make of the handsome, mysterious stranger he's pledged his body to, but he's soon swept away in the heat of the moment and surrenders to Heath entirely.

Once Adrien is pregnant, Heath secrets him away to his immense and secluded home. As the birth draws near, Heath grows to love Adrien for the man he is, not just for his connection to Nathan. Unaware of Heath's past with his omega parent and coming to depend on him heart and soul, Adrien begins to fall as well.

But as their love blossoms, Nathan's shadow looms. Can Heath keep his new love and the child they've made together once Adrien discovers his secrets?

Heat for Sale is a stand-alone m/m erotic romance by Leta Blake, writing as Blake Moreno. Infused with a du Maurier *Rebecca*-style secret, it features a well-realized omegaverse, an age-gap, dominance and submission, heats, knotting, and scorching hot scenes.

Gay Romance Newsletter

Leta's newsletter will keep you up to date on her latest releases and news from the world of M/M romance. Join the mailing list today and you're automatically entered into future giveaways.
letablake.com

Leta Blake on Patreon

Become part of Leta Blake's Patreon community in order to access exclusive content, deleted scenes, extras, bonus stories, rewards, prizes, interviews, and more.
www.patreon.com/letablake

Other Books by Leta Blake

Contemporary

Will & Patrick Wake Up Married
Will & Patrick's Endless Honeymoon
Cowboy Seeks Husband
The Difference Between
Bring on Forever
Stay Lucky

Sports

The River Leith

The Training Season Series
Training Season
Training Complex

Musicians

Smoky Mountain Dreams
Vespertine

New Adult

Punching the V-Card

Winter Holidays

The Home for the Holidays Series
Mr. Frosty Pants
Mr. Naughty List
Mr. Jingle Bells

Fantasy

Any Given Lifetime

Re-imagined Fairy Tales

Flight
Levity

Paranormal & Shifters

Angel Undone
Omega Mine

Horror

Raise Up Heart

Omegaverse

Heat of Love Series
Slow Heat
Alpha Heat
Slow Birth
Bitter Heat

For Sale Series
Heat for Sale

Coming of Age

'90s Coming of Age Series
Pictures of You
You Are Not Me

Audiobooks

Leta Blake at Audible

Discover more about the author online

Leta Blake
letablake.com

About the Author

Author of the bestselling book *Smoky Mountain Dreams* and the fan favorite Omegaverse series *Heat of Love*, Leta Blake's educational and professional background is in psychology and finance, respectively. However, her passion has always been for writing. She enjoys crafting romance stories and exploring the psyches of imaginary people. At home in the Southern U.S., Leta works hard at achieving balance between her writing and her family life.

Printed in Great Britain
by Amazon

17167540R10262